A
LOVE HATE
THING

A LOVE HATE THING

WHITNEY D. GRANDISON

ink
yard
press

ISBN-13: 978-1-335-01604-1

A Love Hate Thing

This edition published by arrangement with Harlequin Books S.A.

For questions and comments about the quality of this book, please contact us at CustomerService@Harlequin.com.

InkyardPress.com

Printed in U.S.A.

To the resilient, intellectual, beautiful, joyous, capable,
charismatic, undefeatable black boy.

The caterpillar is a prisoner to the streets that conceived it. Its only job is to eat or consume everything around it, in order to protect itself from this mad city.

—Kendrick Lamar, "Mortal Man"

1 | *TRICE*

Getting shot isn't the worst part. It's the aftermath that really fucks you up.

Six months ago, on a dark December night, I was lying in a pool of my own blood on the living room floor. Six months later, I was sitting in a car on the way to a new town to start fresh. In some ways, yeah, the wound had healed. In others, it never would. I didn't care, though. The last thing I'd cared about got me where I was.

"You'll like it there, Tyson. The Smiths have prepared a new home for you," Misty from social services was saying as she drove the long stretch of highway toward Pacific Hills. It was only an hour away from where I used to live in Lindenwood, California.

I didn't respond. *Home* was a meaningless word to me now.

Misty peeked at me. "Aren't you going to say anything?"

"I can leave as soon as I turn eighteen, right?" That was all that mattered. Fuck the rest. Five months, aka one hundred and sixty days, to go. On November twelfth, I'd be free.

Misty sighed. "Look, I know what you're going through—"

"Word? You've been shot too and all'at?" I glanced her way. This lady was going home to a million-thread-count sheet-and-pillowcase set, resting easy once I was off her hands.

Fuck outta here.

"Well, no, but—"

"Then shut up." I faced the road ahead, done talking.

Misty let out a breath, her light tan skin no doubt holding a blush upon her cheeks. "Do you kiss your—" She caught herself, as if realizing where she was about to go. "I—I'm sorry. You just shouldn't speak that way."

I felt an ache in my chest, but I let it go.

I didn't care.

Half a beat later Misty was rambling on about food. "Do you wanna stop and get something to eat, you must be starving."

"I told you I wasn't hungry."

"Oh, well, are you nervous?"

I hadn't thought about being nervous or the fact that I would never return home again and lead a normal life. Not like I'd ever led one to begin with.

"No."

"Well, good. Think of it as going to a sleepover at an old friend's house."

One thing was true, the Smiths were old friends, but this setup was for the next five months.

"It's been ten years since I last saw them," I spoke up. "This ain't no damn sleepover, and it's not about to be all kumbaya, neither."

At least they were black. Moving into the uppity setting of Pacific Hills was sure to be hell, but at least I would be with a black family. Even if I wouldn't exactly fit in.

I didn't look the same. I didn't act the same. I *wasn't* the same. And I didn't care.

"Tyson—"

"It's Trice." I had asked her to call me that from jump street. No one called me Tyson.

I didn't want to think about that. I didn't want to think about anything. I didn't care.

"Trice, please, try? I know it's been rough these past few months, but you have a chance at something fresh. The Smiths are good people, and Pacific Hills is a lovely town. I'm sure soon you'll be close to your old self."

Misty had no clue what she was talking about. My old self? She obviously hadn't paid attention to my file, or she would've been smart enough to leave it at *fresh* and not bring up my past.

Tyson Trice was dead.

He died on the floor in the living room that day, and he was never coming back.

When I didn't respond, Misty let up, probably getting that I didn't give a shit either way.

I didn't care.

2 | *Nandy*

I told myself I didn't care about the juvenile delinquent my parents were moving into our home. I told myself it was no big deal an ex-con would be sleeping right next door to me. I told myself that my parents hadn't made the worst decision in everdom.

It was just an everyday occurrence in the Smith household.

Still, it wasn't fair.

As I paced around the pool in my backyard and complained to my best friend, Erica Yee, over the phone, I expected her to be on my side and console me.

"This was supposed to be a great summer and they pull this?" I whined.

"You can still have a good summer," Erica responded. "This doesn't have to be the end."

But it *was* the end. My parents hadn't gone into detail about the boy's situation, just that he was in a "rough spot" and would be living with us for now. And that he was from Lindenwood, otherwise known as the ghetto.

I'd never gone there, but I'd heard enough stories to know to be cautious. When my parents watched the news, there was always a segment on some tragedy that had happened in Lindenwood. Some high-speed chase, or little kids killed during a drive-by, or a robbery gone wrong among the usual clutter of crime that kept the LPD busy. Lindenwood was notorious for its drugs, thefts, assaults, and murders.

I shivered.

It probably hadn't been the best idea to stay up lurking on the local news feeds right before the delinquent moved in.

Everything would be ruined.

"It *is* the end," I insisted. "I mean, they spent all this time whispering and having these hushed conversations behind closed doors, and they barely revealed last night that he's from Lindenwood!"

Maybe I was acting childishly, but I felt like a kid with the way my parents had shut me out on the biggest detail of all when it came to the boy coming to stay with us out of nowhere. For two weeks, they'd been scarce on the topic and evaded any and all questions. Now it felt like they'd dropped a bomb on me.

For all I knew, this kid was a total ex-gangbanger and my parents were intent on opening our home to wayward souls.

Dramatic? Sure.

Precautions? I was definitely taking them.

"Right now, you're probably pacing around your pool in

a Gucci bikini while your happily-in-love parents are inside preparing dinner together. God, Nan, your life is incredibly boring. You could use this delinquent to spice things up."

Well, it was a Sunday evening, and the sun was beginning to set. My parents always made dinner together on Sundays, because they were both off work and able to do so.

I stopped pacing and glanced down at my white Gucci bikini. "Yee, you try new hobbies to spice things up, not invite ex-cons to move in with you. Look, whatever, let's just get away for a few hours. The longer I put a halt on this, the better."

"When is he supposed to show up?"

"Sometime today. I just wanna blow it off. Maybe you, me, and Chad could grab a bite at the club or something."

My boyfriend's family had a reserved table at the local country club. Anything would be better than dinner with the delinquent. I wasn't 100 percent sure he *was* a criminal, but I wasn't taking any chances. When it came to Lindenwood, you couldn't be too sure.

"You in?" I asked.

"If we must." Erica pretended to sound exasperated. "Call me with the details in twenty, okay?"

"Deal." I hung up and sighed, tilting my head back toward the darkening sky and questioning what I had done to deserve this.

It was the first week of June, and school had ended last week. I intended to spend this summer before senior year going to beach bonfires and parties with my friends, lounging around, preparing for cotillion, and just staying as far away from home as possible.

With a plan in motion, I went around my pool and stepped into our family room through the patio doors.

"Shit!" I jumped back, dropping my phone and barely registering the sound of its rough *slap* against the hardwood floor.

My parents were standing in the room with an Asian woman who was dressed in a violet-red pantsuit. But it was the boy beside her that startled me. He towered over my father, with broad shoulders and a wide chest, and arms that let me know he worked out, even though he seemed drenched in black with his long-sleeved shirt and matching pants. He had deep, dark brown skin with a clean complexion. But what really stood out was his hair. The boy had cornrows braided to the back of his head—*well-aged* cornrows.

Ugh, he looked so unpolished.

Suddenly I remembered my fallen phone and looked down to discover the screen was cracked. *Because things aren't messed up enough already.*

"And you remember our daughter, Nandy." My mother played it cool, gesturing toward where I'd frozen near the patio doors.

Everyone faced me, looking just as uncomfortable as I felt.

Great, I was making my first impression completely inappropriate in a bikini.

Awkwardly, I waved and forced a smile onto my face, showing off the result of two years of braces.

"Nandy, this may be a little bit of a surprise, but you remember Tyson Trice, don't you?" my father asked, looking between the two of us.

At first, the name vaguely rang a bell, but then it hit me. *Tyson,* the boy I'd played with when I was younger. He used to come by in the summers when his grandfather would do lawn work around our subdivision. There'd been a few times during the school year when he'd come by too, but it was mostly a summer thing. Until he stopped coming altogether.

The revelation brought a sense of relief followed quickly by a foreign anger that I couldn't explain.

That was then; this is now.

Now Tyson Trice had hit a mega growth spurt and stood before me nearly a man, appearing not at all like the seventeen years young that we both were.

"Right." I nodded my head. "Tyson, hey."

Tyson didn't shift focus to my body. He stared straight into my eyes and bore no friendly expression or a tell of what he was thinking. He was far across the room, but I didn't need to be right up on him to know that he had the angriest eyes I'd ever seen. Dark, soulless abysses stared at me, making me shiver.

Right on, Dad. Thanks for inviting a possible murderer into our home.

"And this is our son, Jordy." My mother didn't miss a beat as she went on, downplaying how awkward everything was.

Jordy, my eleven-year-old little brother, was sitting against the ottoman, playing a video game on his handheld.

Tyson glanced at Jordy, and I felt protective, seeing curiosity briefly cross his face as he laid eyes on my Thai brother.

Jordy looked up from his game. "Hey."

Tyson lifted a brow and turned to face my parents in that familiar way most outsiders looked at my family once they realized a black family was raising a Thai son.

Jordy smirked, shaking his head. "They wish they could've spawned a kid as good-looking as me."

My father chuckled. "We spoke about adopting for years after having Nandy, and right around the time she was eight, we got approved and Jordy came into our lives."

"He was just two years old," my mother gushed. "He was so adorable, we fell in love with him instantly."

I came more into the room, wanting to shield my brother from Tyson. Someone had to think of the kids.

"Nandy, why don't you go put some clothes on." It wasn't a question. My mother was ordering me to cover up and look more presentable for our guests.

"I was actually on my way out to meet up with Erica, we've got this—"

"Right now?" she asked. "We've got company."

I glanced at Tyson, hating him again for spoiling my summer. I'd seen him, and I'd spoken to him. What more did she want?

"Yeah, but Erica and I had plans to go to the country club and talk about cotillion."

My mother pursed her lips. "Nandy—"

"You know what," my father stepped in, "that's a great idea. Nandy could take Tyson and the two could get reacquainted, and that'll give us time to talk to Ms. Tran here."

My eyes practically shot out of their sockets. There was no way in hell I'd share a car with Tyson.

After thinking it over, my mother seemed to agree. "That is a great idea. We can all sit down together later."

My jaw hit the ground.

I shook my head. "You know, never mind, suddenly I'm not as hungry as I thought. In fact, I feel sick to my stomach. I think I'll go lie down."

By the way my mother narrowed her eyes, I knew she'd be giving me hell later about my behavior. I didn't care. It wasn't fair to me to force some scary-looking guy into my hands to be babysat.

With one final look at the newest arrival to the Smith household, I picked up my phone from the floor and made my way up to my room.

Long after Ms. Tran had left and my mother had scolded me in our family office, I sat in my room, maneuvering with a broken phone as I texted my boyfriend. Going on a hunger strike didn't last long for me. After having refused to go down for dinner, I was starving.

My cell phone chirped as Chad texted me back.

Chad: Outside

Me: Thank God

My parents were probably still up, no doubt discussing either my punishment or how we were going to work Tyson into the family.

With their bedroom being in a different wing of our house, sneaking out was always an easy feat. Still, I made sure to keep extra quiet as I crept out of my room and slipped down the staircase.

Chad was waiting for me out front. He'd been pacing back and forth in front of our walk as he waited, and as I stepped outside I was elated to see him.

"I'm thinking sushi, you in?" I asked as I walked past him, heading for his car.

"Yeah, sure. What's going on?" Chad asked as he caught up to me and fell into step.

I peered up into his blue eyes. "You don't want to know."

Chad ran a hand through his auburn hair, appearing confused but conceding. "O-kay, let's go get some sushi."

At the feeling of being watched, I glanced back at my house. On the second floor, through one of the large bay windows, I caught sight of a silhouetted figure.

It was him.

Creep.

I turned back to Chad and reached out and caught his hand. "Yeah, let's get out of here."

This was *my* summer, and no one was getting in the way of that.

3 | *TRICE*

Even the birds sounded different here.

Monday morning, I found myself up, listening to them chirp merrily like they had no problem in the world. This wasn't Lindenwood. Where I was from, the street would be buzzing with chatter, the nearby construction or destruction of properties, or the perpetual sound of a siren going by.

The transfer to Pacific Hills had been a success, so not long into our introductions, Misty had left me to Parker and Maxine, or Max, as she preferred. Their family was an intimate four with their daughter, Nandy, and their son, Jordy. The young Asian boy hadn't been in the picture when I'd known the Smiths previously. The kid seemed nice, welcoming—unlike her.

Nandy.

It was hard to believe that once upon a time, we'd been friends. Clearly, we were no longer seven years old.

I'd been up when Parker went into work for the day, but I hadn't left my room except to go to the bathroom to freshen up. Not that staying in my room was a punishment; it was by far the nicest place I'd ever slept. My bedroom back home had been plain and basic. This room was alive with personality with its colorful walls. One, a navy blue, had a large painting hung on it. The painting captured an ocean wave, and the tiny splash of gold marbled within the image of teal, blue and white water was really nice. Another wall was a lighter blue and housed a window seat with big pillows set up for decoration: two gold, another fuzzy and light blue. The other two walls were seafoam green and royal blue.

My bed was queen-size and matched the color scheme with its navy blue comforter and light blue sheets and pillows.

As I stood in the center of the room, taking in all the furniture and fixtures, I appreciated that it was all very nice.

Soft knocking pulled me from my thoughts. It was half past eleven, and I wasn't too surprised someone was already checking in on me.

"Yeah?" I said as I went and pulled open my door.

Max was standing on the other side, smiling bright and chipper. There was a warmth about her that let me know she wasn't just taking me in to be nice; she genuinely wanted to, though I was still suspicious about why.

"Just seeing how you're settling in," she said, peeking her head in to look around. "How are you liking it?"

I took a step back, allowing her to enter my room—or *her* room, because it was her house. I was still wrapping my head around the idea of this being my new home and town.

"It's going to take a lot of getting used to," I told her.

Max wrapped her arms around herself, staring my way with affection. She meant well, but still I was uncomfortable.

Thankfully, Nandy breezed by in the hall, gaining her attention.

"Nandy," Max called out. "Come here."

With a heavy sigh, Nandy soon appeared in the doorway.

Max showed a hand to her daughter. "Nandy actually designed this room all by herself, with only a week's notice. It used to be painted all white with just a bed."

Nandy stood awkwardly with the spotlight on her. "Mom."

"Don't be shy. You did a wonderful job."

She had, especially because she'd started from scratch with the entire room in white. The Smith house was large, having five bedrooms total. It said something that they hadn't just stuck me in a spare room but had gone out of their way to decorate one to make it feel like home.

No matter how hard they tried, though, this would never *be* home.

Nandy offered a tight-lipped smile as she inched farther into the room. "They say blue is a soothing color, and I didn't know what shade to pick so I went with a few." She tucked a stray hair behind her ear, refusing to look at me too long. "Blue is cool, cozy, comforting, and I wanted this room to scream 'welcome,' you know? So, I hope you like it and you're not a Blood or whatever."

Max's mouth fell agape as she sucked in a gasp. "Nandy!"

I managed to stifle a laugh. This girl had spunk.

Nandy made a face, crossing her arms. "I'm joking, relax."

"It was cute," I said in her defense. "You did a nice job, thanks."

Nandy barely acknowledged my comment as her gaze drifted to the floor.

"Why don't you two spend the day becoming re-acquainted?" Max suggested.

Nandy frowned. "I've got plans with Chad. Everybody's going to this thing."

Max sighed. "Honestly, are Chad and his friends all you care about?"

"Yes, Mom, my *boyfriend* is important to me," Nandy said.

"Alyssa."

It was déjà vu. When we were younger, whenever Nandy would push Max's buttons, she'd be quick to scold Nandy with the use of her middle name. It was intriguing to see that not much had changed in that department.

I studied Nandy. She wore a small T-shirt that barely covered her svelte stomach, and a pair of shorts that accentuated how tall she was and the length of her legs.

Briefly, I remembered a moment when we were young, of Nandy taking a blanket and throwing it over our heads. To hide. To be safe. To be *cozy, warm,* and *enveloped.*

Noticing my stare, Nandy stepped back toward the hall. "We've got all summer, and I don't want to keep Chad waiting."

Max rolled her eyes. "Fine. I'm off for the day, what do you think about pasta for dinner?"

Nandy hugged her middle. "No thanks, I'm only eating fruit and vegetables until cotillion. I want to look good in my dress." A ringtone sounded from Nandy's hand, where she was clutching her cell phone. By the lovey-dovey lyrics and melody, I assumed it was her boyfriend. "Gotta go, I'll be back later."

She was out of the room and down the hall before Max could protest.

Max turned back to me with a helpless shrug. "Don't have kids."

I sincerely wasn't planning on it. "Noted."

Max angled her head, appearing thoughtful. "What's your middle name?"

"Jeremy," I let her know. Curious, I went on to ask, "What's cotillion?"

Max leaned against the wall and rolled her eyes heavenward. "An annual event where the young ladies of this town make their formal debut into Pacific Hills society. Being that Nandy is practically the star, it's been a royal pain in the making."

"Star?"

Max seemed almost proud. "Nandy's popular around here. The committee practically begged her to help out. So mark your calendar. Friday, July fifteenth, is Nandy's big day."

I wasn't so sure I was interested. "Can I sit it out?"

Max chuckled. "'Fraid not, we've been down that road with Jordy. It's important to this family. I mean, sure, the whole thing is really about a bunch of spoiled divas getting a spotlight for the day, but Nandy and her friends actually deserve it."

"Spoiled divas?"

"The hardest many of these kids have ever worked is maybe a week's worth of chores to get a shiny new car or phone. Nandy and her friends are like the poster children around here for extracurricular activities."

I couldn't relate. I hadn't grown up poor, but I definitely hadn't grown up like this, either. My life before was simple middle class; this was the lap of luxury. "Priorities, right?"

Max chuckled. "We try to instill strong values in our kids, but we do our share of spoiling."

"You from here?" I wanted to know.

"Born and raised right here," Max said. "My parents moved to Atlanta a while ago. They visit every now and then, so look forward to getting a goody bag. Parker's parents are in Jersey, and we hear from them every now and then, too. Sometimes I forget there's a whole world out there, but at the same time, this is home, and I can't imagine living somewhere else, no matter how neurotic and myopic these people can be."

"And Jordy?"

She softened at the mention of her youngest. "I don't like to think of him as adopted. He's my baby. I wiped his nose, cleaned his bottom, and potty trained him. He's as natural to me as Nandy."

Her heart was big. She was more selfless than anyone I'd ever known.

Max spoke fondly of Pacific Hills despite the drawbacks of entitled brats and showy events. Her life and her family were simple.

Where did I fit in?

"Why'd you say yes?" I asked.

Max blinked. "What do you mean?"

My grandfather, Pops, was dead, and for some reason, instead of leaving me to the system, he'd reached out to the Smiths, a family he'd worked for several years ago before he got too sick and had to retire. When the cancer was taking the last of Pops, he'd surprised me with the idea of living with them.

At the time, I'd said no, but Pops hadn't listened, and here we were.

The Smiths had agreed to become my legal guardians in

the event of Pops's passing, and once they'd agreed, he'd taken his cue and peacefully left this earth.

I'd met these people when I was five years old and Pops was the neighborhood landscaper. From the time I was five until I was seven, I'd played with Nandy whenever Pops had brought me along on his jobs.

That was ten years ago.

"Why did you agree to take me in? You don't know me," I said.

Max relaxed. "Well, it's hard to turn down a dying man. Phillip was a good man, and from what I remember, you were a sweet little boy. When I heard the details of what happened to you, my heart broke, and Parker's, too. You watched three people who were dear to you die. I believe this is what's best for you."

"Two," I corrected.

"Excuse me?"

"I watched *two* people who were dear to me die."

Realization hit Max and she quickly recovered. "Oh, Trice, I'm sorry. You're right, *two* people. I said yes because I'm human and I care. And for the record, Parker and I thought long and hard about what to say to the kids, and we decided your story is yours—we haven't told them what happened to you. This all came together so fast, and my main concern was making you feel comfortable and welcome and not like a lab rat being fussed over."

I could tell she meant well. She had this honest air about her.

Trouble was, I wasn't used to experiencing good things.

Life had a way of taking from me, and I wasn't about to get attached, no matter how sincere and genuine Max came off.

There was no good left in the world, and even if there had been, one thing was certain—I didn't deserve it.

4 | *Nandy*

I couldn't get out of the house fast enough. Even though that meant walking straight into the lion's den as I drove across town to Oliver Stein's beach house.

Chad had sent me a text prompting me to link up as everyone was hanging out at Oliver's family's vacation property to kick-start summer. I wasn't fond of Oliver, who was entirely too obnoxious, but he was one of Chad's best friends, so I buried my discomfort as I got ready to show my face.

In this town, appearances were everything.

Pacific Hills was an exclusive community, where greatness was the only acceptable thing. In school we were competitive, gearing up for affluent and prominent futures. There was no way a kid from Lindenwood would fit in. What were my parents thinking?

By the time I pulled up to the beach house, it was eight cars deep with vehicles in the driveway. I managed to park my little BMW down the block—all the better for making a clean getaway.

Loud rap music filtered through the air as I made my way to the front door. With my hand on the knob, I debated going home and dealing with Tyson instead. It wouldn't be the first time I'd ditched one of Oliver's parties.

I'd already stopped by the Apple store after leaving home and gotten my phone screen fixed; I couldn't stall any longer. Chad had been all over my case the night before about why I was so antsy. I hadn't wanted to talk about it—I *still* didn't want to talk about it, but I knew eventually I'd have to.

Knowing that Chad would freak out and blow up my cell if I ditched him, I took a deep breath and slipped inside.

It was nearly one in the afternoon, but the party was well underway. Mimosas were everywhere, and the smoky stench of weed filled the air.

"Aw yeah, Nandy's in the house!" Dickie Carter shouted, putting his hands by his mouth to project his voice. His dark hair was a mess and his button-down was hanging loosely on his body as he stood in the kitchen mixing drinks in his swimming trunks and flip-flops.

Dickie was obviously high, on what I wasn't sure. I hated being around him when he was on something.

Some kids weren't shy about using coke or pills, or smoking up. That was not me, though. No amount of peer pressure could get me to use.

I found Chad in the living room, crowded by some of his close friends and their girlfriends.

For just a moment, as I often did, I paused and took in my boyfriend.

Chad Bradley.

It was a total heartthrob name, and I loved the sound of it. It was the type of name associated with a really cute guy who was a young star either in acting or singing, one whose gorgeous face was plastered all over posters and pinups ripped from teen magazine pages.

And Chad *was* gorgeous—super tall, swoon-worthy ocean-blue eyes, flawless coppery-auburn hair, and the perfect athletic build from all his years on the lacrosse team.

Chad was always the man of the hour. He was a big deal for Pacific Hills; his dad was a major businessman and a big donor for events and new projects, and his mom was someone all the women wanted to rub elbows with. If Mrs. Bradley didn't like you, then you were a nobody, and no one wanted to be a nobody, not in this town. In a way, Mr. and Mrs. Bradley were the gatekeepers of Pacific Hills—at least, Mrs. Bradley seemed that way.

I took a deep breath and greeted Chad, going and wrapping my arms around him. "Hey!"

"Aww, there she is!" Chad said enthusiastically. He faced a friend and slapped his chest. "Get Nan a drink, will ya?"

"It's a little early," I spoke up.

Chad tossed me a goofy grin. "It's never too early."

Shouting drew our attention to the kitchen, where Dickie was attempting to do shots off some girl as she lay across the counter.

I wrinkled my nose at the scene. "What's Dickie on?"

Chad blew it off. "He probably cut a few lines or something. You know Dick."

I reeled back to get a good look at my boyfriend. "And you?"

"You know I don't touch that stuff," Chad assured. "Dickie means no harm."

Chad never did hard-core drugs that I knew of; he'd drink a few beers at the occasional party. But with his friends so openly using, sometimes I wondered.

"Okay," I let out.

"I'm glad you came. What's a little fun without the greatest girl in the world by my side?" Chad came close and kissed my cheek, his lips lingering against my skin with the promise of more. I should've been into it, but with the newest arrival to the Smith household, I was off my game.

Tyson Trice.

I'd never known his full name, but of course he had one, and it even fit him.

Randomly, I wondered if anyone ever called him TT.

Probably not.

Tyson was a strong, masculine name, perfectly fitting for the man he had grown into.

He must work out regularly to maintain that build.

Chad snuggled me close, sending butterflies to my belly. With him, I always felt safe.

Relaxing, I reached out and cupped his jaw. "Thanks for the sushi run."

At first he nodded, but then he became quizzical. "What was up last night?"

"Oh, that? It's just a major, minor, inconvenience."

Chad grinned. "Well, which is it, major or minor?"

I didn't want to explain Tyson to him. "It's complicated. Let's just focus on today."

Chad shrugged it off. "That reminds me, I need a *huge* favor."

"What?"

He left my side and went to the kitchen, then dug below the island, in the cabinet, before coming up with a bouquet of flowers.

My heart lifted as I began to smile. I loved that Chad wasn't afraid to be sweet in front of his friends. Some guys thought that was lame or corny, but not my guy.

My boyfriend came over and bestowed upon me the colorful arrangement of carnations and lilies as the most adorable expression covered his face. "Say yes."

I giggled as I accepted the flowers. "Is this your way of buttering me up?"

Chad shook his head. "Nah, I just realized I hadn't gotten you flowers in a while. I've been slacking."

He hadn't been, but I admired the effort. "Okay, what's the favor?"

He clasped his hands together as if in prayer. "My mom's friend, Charlotte Ray, is throwing an event next weekend, and she's showing off some pieces she designed…and my mom promised she'd get some girls to model for her."

I took a step back as my stomach instantly knotted up at the mention of his mother *and* Charlotte Ray. The music was a little loud. Maybe I hadn't heard him. "What?"

He frowned. "Come on, Nan, you heard me."

I'd known Mrs. Ray all my life in passing. Unfortunately. "Since when is she into fashion?"

"Since she recently got divorced and is a few mil richer and bored, babe."

"Ugh, previously on *The Real Housewives of Pacific Hills*," I groaned.

"You know how my mom gets," Chad responded, holding me close. "She personally suggested you due to all that shit you do for school, and you know my mom always gets her way. She's going to be a pain come time for cotillion."

Mrs. Bradley was on the cotillion committee—she kind of *was* the cotillion committee—which meant I had to play nice if I wanted things to run smoothly.

I pouted. "I hate schmoozing."

"Yeah, I know, but I'll make it up to you. Anything you want." A flash of that handsome smile had me loosening up. He had come through for me the night before, as he always did whenever I needed him.

"Fine, let me talk to the girls and we'll figure this out," I told him.

"Awesome." He came down for a quick peck, and my lips felt stiff against his.

Really, I was off my game.

"Oh my God, Nan, you two are such goals," Sophie Morris gushed as Chad took me under his arm.

"You're way too good to your girl, man," Oliver commented. "Keep that up and we're all going to have to start treating ours nice."

Pig.

Sophie only playfully nudged Oliver for his remark.

I left Chad's side to go grab a bottle of water and bumped into Edi Gómez along the way.

Edi was one of my closest friends, and seeing her amongst the crowd made the party all the better. She lived two houses down from me, and had I known she was coming, we could've carpooled, each of us being the other's reason to go at any time.

"Nandy!" she squealed from where she stood, nursing a

frozen blue drink. The bright color almost made me want one, but it *was* early.

A look around the small beach house showed me that no one cared about the time of day. More than a few of my peers were actively drinking or acting goofy due to being under the influence. Chad's crowd came with this atmosphere; my close friends tended to keep things much more chill.

"Who supplied the party favors this time?" I asked as I studied the scene.

"Jared's mom just got her hip done, and she's got all the pills," Edi informed me. "And you know these kids can't function without poppin' a few. I declined."

Edi's dad was a cop, so she was saying no for more reasons than one.

"Tell me about it. I don't know how long I'm staying," I said.

"Ten minutes with Captain Ginger is long enough for me." Edi pretended to gag as she gestured toward Chad and his boys.

"If you hate Chad and his friends, why are you here?" I teased as I nudged her.

Edi shrugged as she took a sip of her drink. "Girl, it was either come out or stay in and watch Hector and Mani, and I ain't spending my summer babysitting."

The Gómezes were the parents of two sets of twins. Edi and her brother Warhol, and their eleven-year-old younger siblings, Hector and Manuela. On many occasions Edi had gotten stuck babysitting instead of coming out with the girls and me.

Speaking of her twin, I couldn't spot him in the vicinity. "Where is Warhol?"

Edi waved me off. "Probably still asleep at home. I told

him he better get his act together if he's going to pass summer school."

It was already a pain getting up early every morning for regular school; it had to be hell doing it in the summer. "That's gotta suck."

"That's what he gets for slacking off. All these boys do around here is eat, sleep, and shit football and lacrosse."

And Chad was the captain of the lacrosse team. Even if Edi wasn't fond of my boyfriend, he was as much a part of her world as her brother was, whether she liked it or not. Warhol played football and Edi was a cheerleader; coexisting with Chad came with the territory, because both sports crowds usually hung together.

People had expected me to be a cheerleader, but I was too busy running other things around school to put on a uniform and jump around with glee. Student council, student government, and a few academic clubs, not to mention community service. Even at the end of summer, I'd be back at Cross High helping with new student orientation.

Part of my commitments were solely for my résumé, and part were because I enjoyed organizing things and helping new kids transition to our school. Being a leader was natural for me. When I'd hit my teens and started dating Chad, I'd become "queen of Pacific Hills" to a lot of my peers—I didn't take myself *that* seriously. In some ways, I viewed cotillion as my reward for all the hard work I'd done over the years. My debut would be my crowning achievement.

"I'm glad you're here," I said, walking with her toward the patio doors. Fresh air sounded nice. "You know how I feel about Chad's friends."

"Strike three, huh?" Edi quipped.

I sighed. "Edi."

"Let's not pretend the signs aren't there, Nan," Edi said. "I mean, the guy lives in the biggest house on Narcissus Avenue. It's like the universe is laughing at the irony."

Chad did actually live on a street called Narcissus Avenue, a few blocks from me. But he wasn't as terrible as Edi tried to paint him to be.

My defense of Chad was half-hearted, though. Edi's usual spiel against my boyfriend was no match for where my thoughts kept drifting.

Tyson's arrival played constantly in my brain. Even though it had been ten years, I hadn't forgotten him. But things were different. I was different. He was different. We were from two different worlds.

Who knew how much had changed? As much as part of me wanted to welcome him in, another was intent on freezing him out—for more reasons than one.

It had been only one day, and Tyson was already ruining my summer.

5 | *TRICE*

One hundred and fifty-eight days to go.

I wrote it down on the calendar that hung on the wall in my bedroom as soon as I got up Tuesday morning. Two nights down, over a hundred more to go.

There was no official plan for what would happen once I was eighteen and free to go, but I knew I'd be leaving. More than likely back to Lindenwood. Nandy had made it clear by her continued icy glare that she wasn't up for renewing our former friendship.

I didn't care for the Smiths' charity anyway.

When I came out of the bathroom after washing up, Jordy was in the hall. From the way he was staring at me, I knew my scar was showing, as it often did when I wore a tank top. The mark wasn't grotesque, but it was definitely a sign that shit got real outside of the Hills.

"It's crazy out there in these streets, huh?" Jordy yawned and walked by me into the bathroom, then closed the door.

I touched the lesion, the scar, the memory of six months prior. The shots echoed in my head, harsh and loud—so loud that I felt the need to hold my hands to my ears to make the noise stop. The wound burned just as it had when I'd first been shot and fallen to the floor. My stomach twisted, my mouth ran dry, and I felt dizzy.

Like a chant, I told myself I didn't care and pushed forward.

It was seven fifteen in the morning and I had to register for summer school. I'd missed a lot of school, resulting in my needing to take classes in math and English to get into the twelfth grade. The Smiths had set up a meeting for me to register for the classes I needed and to talk to the school's counselor, I'd learned this Sunday evening when we'd talked with Misty.

I didn't care about finishing school, but I knew that, realistically, I wouldn't get anywhere without at least a high school diploma. Even though I wanted to leave as soon as I turned eighteen, I planned on using my summer wisely and getting my credits up to become a senior. Maybe after I was free, I'd go and finish high school back in the 'Wood.

I made my way downstairs and followed voices along with the sweet smell of cinnamon to the kitchen. From my two nights with the Smiths, I was still getting used to their home and all its glory. *Nice* wasn't the word to describe their crib and its setup. *Expensive* was more like it. Half of the things they owned left me feeling anxious and not wanting to touch anything, just in case I slipped up and broke something. Most of their stuff probably cost a car payment or two, like the wine bottles in their private wine room, or the fancy imported dishes in their dining room along with their glass table and plush cream-colored chairs. Max had us put away the display dishes into their china cabinet before we'd eaten at the table both Sunday and Monday night.

Their kitchen was simple, yet impressive. It was a bright room thanks to a fancy light fixture hanging above their island. Unlike my bedroom, where Nandy had gone out of her way to add a pop of color, the kitchen was a gentle and subtle gray, ranging from dark to light. The stainless-steel appliances—they had two ovens, one above the other—added on to their pricey image. With how neat and organized everything was, I questioned how often they really took the time to cook in such an immaculate space.

The dining room was a room over, and as I hung back in the doorway, I noted that only Nandy and Max were up in the kitchen. Nandy was at the long and wide island while Max leaned back against the kitchen counter nursing a mug of coffee. She was dressed professionally for work. Parker was MIA.

Nandy looked upset, and Max looked annoyed.

"The last time I was around him, I didn't have breasts, Mom!" Nandy was whining. They both were oblivious to my stance in the doorway. "He's been to juvie—who knows what he's learned about taking advantage of girls like me!"

Girls who sounded like whiny rich white girls and who wouldn't shut the fuck up until they got their way?

And *juvie*? That was ironic. Had I gone to juvie, I'd be dead. Just like I was supposed to be dead instead of standing in the Smiths' kitchen.

I took in Nandy's brown skin, her blemish-free face, and the long, dark hair that she'd pulled up in a ponytail. She'd always been pretty, but she had definitely changed. For one, she was eating a bowl of fruit. When we were kids, you couldn't blink without catching her munching on a bag of potato chips.

I wondered if that white boy she'd snuck out with had anything to do with the new Nandy.

Max sighed. "For God's sake, quit acting like he's some stranger from the street."

Nandy poked at her mango. "Might as well be."

"Tyson—*Trice* is a friend to this family, and now he lives here. He might as well be a new family member." Max sipped her coffee and appeared to think over her words. Nandy wasn't paying attention, but I watched as Max smiled, as if she liked the idea.

There was something honest about Max that I'd always liked, that and the fact that when I mentioned my preferring to be called *Trice* rather than *Tyson*, Max immediately took to my new name while Misty kept forgetting.

Max's gaze flickered to me. "Trice! You're up."

Nandy turned and instantly scowled, then stood up from the island. "Excuse me, I've gotta get dressed for the day."

She slipped past as I stepped into the room. Across the island was a small array of breakfast foods. From hot: eggs, bacon, and cinnamon rolls, to cold: fruit, boxes of cereal, and what looked like bottles of smoothies.

Max waved a hand toward the island. "Help yourself. We went shopping and bought a bunch of stuff. Do you like pulp in your orange juice or none?"

I took a seat at the end of the island farthest from the chair Nandy had abandoned along with her unfinished breakfast. "Pulp."

Max was amused. "Nandy's the same way."

"It tastes more natural."

"That's what Nandy says. I see you two will get along again."

Had she met her daughter? That girl hadn't seemed that willing to sit with me, let alone forge a bond. She'd practically glared at me for stepping foot in the house. That, and her repeated absence from dinner the past two nights, revealed the truth.

Kumbaya my ass.

I poured a glass of orange juice. The island had a lot of food on it and, as much as I wanted nothing to do with the Smiths, I appreciated Max's efforts. The smell of the eggs and bacon reminded me of home, waking up on a Saturday to breakfast… Lead seemed to fill my stomach at the memory, and the thought of eating the hot foods turned me off. Honestly, I didn't want to eat just then, but being wasteful was rude.

"What's your favorite cereal?" Max asked as she came over to the island.

"Fruity Pebbles," I answered as I gestured to the box. "But I should probably pitch in. I like to eat them in a big mixing bowl."

A smile touched Max's lips. "Don't worry, money's not a problem here. Eat to your heart's content."

I grabbed the fruit-flavored cereal and poured myself a bowl.

The room fell silent, but I felt Max's gaze on me.

I looked at her, finding her unashamed in all her staring. "What?"

She shook her head, reaching up to wipe her eyes. "Oh, nothing. I was thinking of when you and Nandy were kids, and how I always wondered what happened to you. I'm just grateful you're alive. Thank God."

Her words taunted me, stirring up something I couldn't

swallow as she juxtaposed the past and present in such a way that I almost lost interest in my cereal.

Max was a good woman, she didn't know any better, yet still I asked, "You believe in God?"

She shrugged. "I like to think there's more to how we got here than this big bang mumbo jumbo. You?"

"Sometimes I do, and sometimes I think it's all bullshit. If God's real, then what good is He for letting all the bad shit happen in the world? Cancer, robberies, rape…murder." I looked down at the tabletop. "I don't know about you, but I'd rather believe in the big bang mumbo jumbo than have faith in a guy who's not there when you really need him, who leaves you hanging in the balance."

Max came and squeezed my shoulder. "If that's true, then why didn't you die on the floor that day?"

Maybe He was just evening the score. "Maybe He gets a kick out of watching us suffer."

"I'm not the most religious person, Trice, but I'd like to think God is out there and He has a plan for us, that everything happens for a reason."

I shook my head, squeezing my fists shut. "There's no fuckin' reason for what happened. There's no good out of that. I may be alive, but for what? To serve some greater purpose? Bullshit. I should've just died alongside them."

"Trice—"

"I'm supposed to believe that God 'got another angel' or 'needed someone in heaven' or some shit? When babies die, people say that to make themselves feel better, but it's complete bullshit. What would God need with a baby? Either I lost faith, or there's never really been a God, and now I've got lucid clarity."

Max frowned. I sensed she wanted to say something but

was at a loss for words. She squeezed my shoulder again and went back to the counter. "There's no swearing in this home, Trice. We don't want Jordy to get the wrong idea."

"But *shit*'s okay to say when you're meeting people?" I challenged, remembering Nandy's slip as she'd been coming into the house from the pool Sunday.

Max laughed. "Glad to see you have a sense of humor."

Nandy came back into the kitchen and took her place at the other end of the island. When she looked up and caught sight of me, she grabbed a box of cereal and stuck it in front of her, as if that would block my view. I was six foot three; I had no problem seeing Nandy over a tiny-ass box of cornflakes.

"So, Nandy, what do you have planned for today?" Max asked.

Nandy shrugged. "I was thinking of hitting the beach with Erica and Shayne."

"Well, you be sure to come home for dinner." Max turned to me. "We'll let Trice pick what he wants for takeout. We eat that a lot around here. With me busy at the office and Parker always at work as well, it gets pretty hard trying to cook a meal at the end of the workday."

"They manage to do it Sundays, though," Nandy spoke up. "Always."

"We mostly eat Chinese—"

"My best friend Erica's family owns this restaurant, it's more loyalty than anything."

"—but whatever you want tonight is fine by us," Max concluded.

Takeout was good, but nothing beat a homemade meal.

"Mind if I cook?" I offered.

Max and Nandy faced each other, eyebrows raised.

"Yeah?" Max asked.

I nodded. "I could see what you got in the fridge and put something together."

"Oh, you don't—"

"I just spent six months eating nothing but food that came in plastic containers. No offense, but I wouldn't mind whipping something up."

Max was impressed. "Okay by me. We've got plenty of food." She eyed her wristwatch. "I've gotta get to work, but Nandy will take you to school. It's not too far from here. Until we figure out a vehicle situation, we'll have her take you."

"Every morning?" Nandy's whine had returned tenfold.

Max lifted a brow, and Nandy said nothing else.

"Well, I'll see you tonight, Trice. I look forward to dinner." She left the room with a skip in her step. Maybe she meant her words.

Nandy's algid stare was hard to miss. She stood from her end of the island and marched over to mine, leaning into my face, trying to intimidate me or something. "Listen up. I will *not* be your bitch and chauffeur you around all summer. You are not going to ruin my good time."

I reeled away. "At least you're half right."

"What's that supposed to mean?"

"It means you're good on the bitch part, but you should start working on the chauffeur part and go start up the car."

She caught her breath, as if she hadn't expected me to bite back. Fuck that. Nandy wasn't about to get on my nerves all summer with her pissy-ass attitude. I'd be *damned*.

Her phone rang, and I took that as my cue to walk my bowl to the sink.

Nandy answered the call as she retreated from the room. "Oh my G, Erica, you will not believe what just happened."

Oh my G? I wondered if the white boy had anything to do with Nandy's vocabulary as well.

I went outside and headed down the front walkway. At the end, I stood and observed my surroundings.

The Smiths lived on a street called Holiday Road, and with a name like that, there was no way anyone could not feel like they were in paradise. Large house after large house lay before me, and the Smiths' palatial estate was no different. Some properties were larger than the next, stretching across acres of land with fancy gates at the ends of their driveways. None of the houses were styled the same. The house next door was more Mediterranean compared to the contemporary structure that was the Smiths' house, and a house across the street was almost entirely composed of glass and metal. Back home, in some neighborhoods, we had nice cribs, but not like this—I couldn't get used to *this*.

The area was quiet. The only signs of life were a lone jogger across the street, running by with her dog, and a couple of gardeners out attending to colorful flowers or watering green lawns. A car or two passed as I looked up and down the block, noting that everyone had to feel safe and secure in Pacific Hills.

Some guy on a longboard was coasting down the street. When he spotted me, he stopped in front of our walk and eyed me from head to toe.

"Fresh meat," he muttered. One of his eyes was blue and the other was hazel, and his jet-black hair was a little wet from the perspiration he'd acquired out in the hot morning sun. Even the tank top he was wearing was beginning to stick to him.

He grinned at me. "Who might you be?"

Without answering, I stared, wanting him to get on with his longboarding.

My silence didn't deter him. He smiled more, gesturing to himself. "Travis Catalano."

Behind me, the front door shut and someone marched down the path.

Travis gazed behind me, and a salacious look passed through his weird-colored eyes. "Nandy, hey, I see you have another victim."

When I glanced at Nandy, she was smirking at Travis. Good to know she was generally a bitch to everyone. "Come on, Tyson, let's go."

"Later." Travis set down his longboard and glided down the street, angling his body as he steered and balanced on the board.

I got into Nandy's car. For a girl who'd taken her time in designing my room, I found it odd that she drove what looked to be a brand-new *white* BMW. Even if she had a sour disposition, something about Nandy screamed color. The tie-dye scrunchie looped around her gear shift along with the pink dream catcher hanging from her rearview mirror added some spark of personality that seemed all Nandy.

"Stay away from Travis Catalano," she warned. "He's trouble. Behind him is nothing but a trail of used condoms, broken hearts, and tickets from the law."

That was exactly the mental image I needed to prepare for summer school.

She started the car, and we were immersed in some sad-sounding song by some white woman singing in a whispery voice.

I waited for Nandy to change the station, but she pulled out of the driveway and started driving.

"This is Lana Del Rey, Tyson—"

"It's Trice," I corrected as I pulled my attention away from scowling at her stereo.

"—and in my car, I listen to what I enjoy. Don't like it, get your own car."

I sat back in my seat and stared ahead, knowing full well that I was going to kill her by the end of the summer. I had two months to decide what to do with the body.

Less than ten minutes later, Nandy parked in front of the entrance to Cross High School. She barely turned to acknowledge me, and I knew that was my cue to get out of the car and give her space.

"Look, I don't know how long you're going to be, but I'm sure you can walk back. I mean, it's not like it's that far from here," she said.

She had to be kidding. A six-foot black guy walking around the posh streets of Pacific Hills, trying to find his way home? I'd be arrested by local security in five minutes for looking like I was casing the place.

But fuck it, I wasn't about to play that game with Nandy.

Outside, I could see that only a few other vehicles were in the parking lot. A sign nearby illustrated that this parking area was for staff only. I faced the main entrance. In the distance, above the doors, was a mural reading HOME OF THE KNIGHTS along with the image of a knight posing with a shield and sword.

Ready or not.

I got out of the car and wasn't even fazed when Nandy drove off without a goodbye after I'd shut the door.

There was a fountain a few yards to my right, and the sound of gushing water was tranquil, alleviating the small bit of tension remaining from my continued strife with Nandy.

Taking a deep breath, I eased up and made my way inside.

Some woman in a polo top and shorts was going somewhere with a stack of papers, and I made it my business to follow her in hopes that she was heading for the main office. It was just my luck that she was.

Along the way, I noticed photo upon photo of Nandy. One of her at some field game for some cause, another at a bake sale, and a few more at various school events. Max hadn't been kidding; Nandy was a big deal at this school, and I had no doubt that she was highly admired in Pacific Hills. Stuck-up or not, her reputation was impressive. At least she wasn't a credit-card-carrying socialite with no real attributes, like some cliché.

Maybe, beneath her bitchy facade, she was actually a decent person.

Maybe.

At the main office, the secretary gave me instructions to head up to the second floor, where the junior office was located. Once there, I found a few students waiting as well and took a seat near some kid who was kicked back with his arms crossed over his wide chest, his thick, dark hair poking out from under a trucker hat.

As I filled the seat next to him, the boy sat up. He stared at me without shame, his dark eyes assessing me boldly.

"You new?" he asked.

I sat back and nodded.

"Where you from?"

"Lindenwood."

The boy whistled. "Shit."

This was going to be the typical reaction from everyone I met.

"Hey, man, I've got some family in the 'Wood, trust me,

I know it ain't no joke. But at least you made it. Can't say the same for some of my cousins." He held out a tan hand. "Warhol, Warhol Gómez."

"Like the artist?" I wondered.

"Yeah, my parents were big fans. My twin sister's name is Edi," he continued.

"Tyson Trice, but most people call me Trice."

"Pleasure serving time with you, Trice." Warhol smiled, exposing pearly white teeth. "Let me tell you, if it was boring as hell the first time learning it, it's sure as shit worse the second time. This is my second summer in this place. Sometimes I'm sure I'll die in these halls."

"I'm here for math and English."

"Lucky you. I've got chem to make up for, *no bueno.*"

The door to the office opened, and in walked a black guy who was as tall as I was and a couple shades lighter. He greeted Warhol with a fist bump. "I knew I'd see your dumb ass in here again this summer."

Warhol smirked. "What's that say about you, though?"

The boy chuckled and turned to me. He held out his fist. "Ashley."

His parents had named him that on purpose? I knocked my fist against his anyway. At least I wasn't the only black guy in town. "Trice."

Ashley took the seat on Warhol's right, and they started talking while I continued to wait on my meeting with my new guidance counselor.

When the office door opened again, a scrawny kid walked into the room carrying papers. He was tall, lanky, and by the way he carried himself, someone who stayed in the shadows.

"What's Frogger doing here?" Ashley asked loudly, catching the boy's attention.

He turned around from where he was talking to the secretary, whipping shaggy hair out of his eyes. "Did you say something?"

"I know *you're* not in summer school," Warhol spoke up.

The boy shook his head. "No, I'm volunteering as a student aide."

Warhol rolled his eyes. "Of course." He sat up. "There's this party tonight—do you think you'd be able to pull yourself away from *Star Wars* and shit and come out? It's at the beach."

The boy gave a tight-lipped smile. "Since that invitation was only mildly insulting, I'll consider it."

"We miss you on the football team, Kyle. You oughta come back next year," Ashley said.

Kyle shrugged and headed for the door. "We'll see."

"Best damn water boy Cross's ever had."

Kyle left the office, and Warhol and Ashley began to snicker. Obviously they weren't really friends with Kyle.

"So, man, what's ya hustle?" Ashley asked after sizing me up.

Hustle? What did any trust fund baby know about hustling?

"Right now," I told him, "this."

Ashley bobbed his head. "If you ever looking for fun, I'm your man. My girl is the hottest DJ in town and I throw the livest parties. You ever wanna get down, hit me up."

Warhol tapped my arm. "Actually, there really is a party tonight. You should come."

I didn't care about some party. I wasn't in the mood to hear loud music and laughter, and answer the inevitable questions about who I was and where I was from.

I just wanted silence and peace.

"We'll see," was all I said.

The boys went back to talking, and I kept waiting.

A door opened across from me and a woman stepped out of a room. "Tyson Trice?"

I stood.

She held out her hand. "Lydia Gonzalez, but you can call me Lydia."

I shook her hand and entered her office.

Lydia closed the door and took a seat behind her desk. "So, Tyson, the Smiths tell me you're from Lindenwood and will be joining us now—after you complete summer school, of course."

I shrugged. "That's their plan."

Lydia squinted. "And what's your plan, Tyson?"

I sat back in the hard plastic chair. "To be called Trice."

Lydia folded her hands. "Okay, *Trice*, what are your plans?"

"To turn eighteen and leave."

"You're running away?"

"You a therapist?" She was getting deep when I was only supposed to be registering for my classes.

Lydia seemed to suppress a smirk. "That's what my degree allows. Beyond academics, I'm here to help in any way I can."

I didn't want help. "I'm not running. I just want space from…everything."

"Okay. And after you leave, what's next?"

"There's no official plan, but it's a start."

Lydia leaned back and stared at me, gears seeming to turn in her head. "Do you want to talk about what happened?"

I blocked out all thoughts of *there*. "I don't care."

"Ah yes, it says in your file that that seems to be your catchphrase."

"I don't care."

"Tyson—Trice, I've been near where you are. When I was your age, I went through something traumatic with someone

I cared about, and they let me down. At the time, I blocked it out, decided I didn't care. But I gotta be honest with you—not caring doesn't make it go away. Not caring doesn't stop the pain, it only prolongs an inevitable breakdown. And trust me, it's not pretty."

"So, what, you're here to tell me it gets better?" I hated when people said that shit. There was no "better" from here.

"It will get better, I promise."

"Did it feel that way when you were my age?"

"When I was your age, I was sure nothing could make the pain or the scars go away, but in time, they did."

"Time and space."

Lydia met my gaze and held it. "The pain *will* fade, Trice."

"I don't feel anything."

She nodded, but I could see the doubt in her brown eyes. "Do you sleep much?"

No. "Some nights."

"Have any dreams about it?"

Just the look on her face. "Some nights."

"I don't wanna push you. I want you to know that when the time comes and you want to talk, I'm here," said Lydia. "This place, Pacific Hills, it's not so bad. Cross High, it's not so bad. This summer, you're one of us—you're officially a Knight. Well, more of a *summer* Knight, but while you're here, we're going to get you back on your academic track."

At least she wasn't pushy. The people before her, the other doctors and shrinks, they all wanted in my head, wanted to know how I felt, how close I was to cracking. At least Lydia respected me enough to throw the ball in my court.

"Thanks," I said.

Lydia smiled. "Summer school starts June thirteenth, next Monday. For now, let's relax and talk about your classes."

According to the courts and the Smiths, I was stuck here in Pacific Hills no matter what. I might as well make the most of it. I faced the challenge of summer school head-on, meeting Lydia's eyes and nodding. "Okay."

6 | *Nandy*

Summer activities in Pacific Hills were endless. Most of us opted for the simple things: the beach, pools, movies, shopping, and brunch.

Bland for some, but hell, it beat school and cramming for some exam.

The beach wasn't too crowded. It was mostly full of morning joggers and surfers catching some waves, along with a few other girls out to soak up the sun.

My other best friend, Shayne Mancini, was late. Before leaving my house, I'd texted her that Erica and I were going to the beach, and she'd agreed to show up. But as Erica and I lay out enjoying our summer freedom, Shayne had yet to show.

"So what's he like?" Erica asked.

I leaned over and grabbed my Fiji Water, then took a long, quenching sip as I ruminated on my answer.

The Tyson Trice I'd known had been a scrawny boy with sad eyes, but he'd always had the biggest smile on his face. We'd played both indoors and out. When we were inside, we'd eat junk food and watch TV, sometimes *The Proud Family*, and sometimes he'd make me watch *Static Shock* too, because "boy shows are just as good." The old Tyson Trice was a sweet boy.

I didn't know this new Tyson. This new Tyson who wanted to be called *Trice*. This new Tyson who was big and scary-looking. The anger in his eyes was intense from afar, but up close it was terrifying. He didn't even believe in God, I'd overhead him say, something that made him seem even more cutthroat.

Maybe there wasn't a God in Lindenwood.

"Different," I settled on saying.

"Oh yeah? Does he like hip-hop? Maybe we'll invite him to one of my shows."

Erica was half black and half Chinese. Black from her mother and Chinese from her father. Her parents came from two different worlds but somehow fell in love. Mrs. Yee was into neo-soul while Mr. Yee liked any and everything. Erica was crazy into hip-hop, some rap, and a lot of the old stuff from the '80s all the way up to the early 2000s. She was a DJ and an aspiring radio personality. She often got paid to do gigs at parties and clubs, where her sets always had people on their feet dancing. With her easygoing personality and cheerful voice, she was made for the radio.

I was more of an indie and alternative girl, but Erica was my best friend, so I supported her regardless.

"I'm not trying to be buddy-buddy with him."

Erica glanced at me. "Why not? He's going to need friends, Nan."

"And it has to be me?"

My best friend shook her head and said nothing.

I failed to tell Erica that Tyson wasn't a legit stranger to my family.

A frown soon marred my face. He'd called me a bitch. That morning, Tyson had looked me straight in the eyes and said I was a bitch. He'd had no expression on his face when he said it. He was cold—from the moment I'd met him in my family room, he'd been stone-cold. How could I not judge him?

Shayne appeared and grabbed the chair beside me, then set her things down with a sigh. "Sorry I'm late—my stepmonster totally tried to bleach all my dad's clothes. Again."

A cold air of silence washed over us and Shayne made a show of kicking off her flip-flops, her trembling scowl letting us know she wasn't joking.

Erica and I shared the same frown. "Oh my God, Shayne."

She waved me off. "Ugh, I know. She acts like he doesn't wear the same three outfits when he's off anyway."

Typical Shayne.

Her stepmother had been unhappy for so long, but Shayne swore everything she did was for attention due to Sheen's— Shayne's father's—busy work schedule.

Shayne lathered herself with sun tanning lotion before settling down and breathing in the sun.

The heat rained down on us as we lay side by side, soaking it all in. It should've been nice and peaceful, with the sound of the nearby waves soothing my senses, but I couldn't escape my anxiety. My brain was going a million miles a minute, and I didn't know how to feel. A good hour passed and all I could think about was—

Shayne lifted her head, facing Erica and me. "So, what's new?"

Erica nudged me. "Nandy's got a new housemate."

I shoved Erica. "We don't have to talk about that."

"Why not?" Shayne asked. "What's she like?"

I groaned. "*She's* a he, and I don't want to talk about it."

"Tough shit." Shayne raised her oversize sunglasses and gawked at me. "Well? Is he hot or what?"

I cringed. "He's from Lindenwood."

Shayne frowned. "Ugh, never mind."

Erica threw her hands up. "Why are we judging him? We barely know this guy."

"What's to know?" Shayne tapped her chin. "On second thought, I say if he's cute, go for it."

I scoffed. "Seriously, Shay?"

She shrugged as she sat up and eyed some surfer. "What? He's gotta be better than Chad. I mean, Chad's cute and all, but he doesn't exactly strike me as the fun and kinky type."

He wasn't. But that wasn't a problem for me. I liked how slow and romantic he was when we were together—unless he was in a rush and had to see some shitty game on TV and barely cared if I got my happy ending.

Chad was safe, though, safe and normal and from Pacific Hills—not that that was saying much, since Pacific Hills had its faults. A lot of women were surgically enhanced gossip queens, and a lot of men were absent due to work or affairs. We might have been safer, but we knew how to cook up some pretty steamy drama as well.

Shayne was no stranger to drama. When her parents had

gone through their messy divorce, she became Shayne 2.0, lost and sad most of the time due to their constant fighting. And then there was the custody battle that left her completely drained. Taylor, her mother, was heavily medicated or liquored up most of the time, so Sheen, her father, had won.

That all happened before high school. The present Shayne wasn't one to do personal drama and let people in on her private affairs, but she sure loved getting the scoop on others. I didn't want to feed her appetite for entertainment, and if it killed me, I would keep the Tyson situation under control.

"I love Chad, Shayne, I'm not going to cheat on him with some creep," I replied.

Shayne shrugged. "Suit yourself. Mind if I give it a go?"

Erica sat up and removed her sunglasses and began packing her bag. "No way, Shayne, we're not going there."

"Why not? Nandy doesn't want him."

"You haven't even met him! And didn't the last guy you messed with go stalker on you?"

Shayne sat back and thought about it. "Hmm, maybe you're right, but still."

Shayne Mancini was a beautiful Sicilian girl. She had curly dark brown hair that never got frizzy or out of place, big chocolate-brown eyes, and a perfect tan. She liked boys, and boys *loved* her. Only Erica and I knew that she was more of a romantic and super picky when it came to guys.

I was with Erica—Shayne messing with Tyson seemed like a bad idea.

"Looks like I've gotta warn him away from you, too," I said as I stood and gathered my things.

"What?" Shayne wanted to know.

"He's already met Travis, and trust me, I won't let that duo start."

Shayne scowled. "Travis Catalano is vagina kryptonite. I swear, you look into those eyes of his and see that smile, and the next thing you know, you're horizontal in some changing room at the mall wondering if the sales tag is going to leave a mark as it's digging into your back."

Seeing the confused looks from both Erica and me, Shayne smiled. "Or so I've heard."

"Didn't that happen to Kayla Nichol?" Erica questioned as she stood as well.

Shayne grabbed her things and stood up, too. "You didn't hear it from me, but she left the state for a month to get over him."

"And now Carina Botwin is obsessed with him." I sighed, thinking of the bubbly blonde who talked about Travis every chance she got.

Shayne took the lead to the parking lot as we followed behind. "Be careful, girls, we don't want either of you becoming one of Travis Catalano's victims."

I'd known Travis since he and his family had moved in next door when I was eleven. I'd thought he was the cutest thing for all of two seconds, before he kissed Valerie Ortega and Jenna Fox and the two fought over him. He thought it was a big joke and wanted neither girl in the end. Some said rich boys didn't have hearts. Travis Catalano proved they were right.

"Done," I said as we made it to my car, where Shayne was parked beside me. "We're going to the club, right? And then back to my place to surf Netflix?"

"I can do lunch, but I gotta jet after. The stepmonster needs a ride to go shopping to cope with her latest attempt, and *I'm* her chauffeur since her Audi's in the shop."

My shoulders sagged and I went forth to hug her. "Sorry, Shayne."

"Don't worry, tonight I'll meet you guys at the party."

Dickie was throwing a party at the beach, and I had to think of a way to go without being forced to take Tyson along.

"Can't wait," I said, putting on a convincing smile.

After lunch Erica and I went back to my place to watch some TV and relax. Or I would've been able to do so had it not been for the sight that greeted us as we got out of my car and made our way to the front door. Tyson sat out on our front step getting his hair braided by some girl who was listening to rap music that was playing on her phone, and neither of them seemed ashamed of what they were doing out in broad daylight for all to see.

Erica wasn't fazed as she bobbed her head to the beat of the song. "Gotta love K-Dot."

I didn't know who that was, nor did I care. I was too busy being embarrassed.

What would our neighbors think?

I would not let Tyson and his antics ruin my debut—or ruin me.

"Go inside, E," I said as I glared at Tyson.

Erica rolled her eyes, facing Tyson and the girl and offering a wave. "Hey, I'm Erica."

The girl lifted her chin in greeting while Tyson spoke up. "Trice."

"Atasha, but my friends call me Tasha," the girl responded with a friendly smile. "And you right about Kendrick."

With pleasantries made, Erica went in without me, and I stood where I was, keeping a safe distance between myself and the two teens in front of me.

Tyson looked at me impassively.

"This ain't the hood, Tyson. We do not braid hair on the front step," I said.

Tasha stopped what she was doing and cocked her head, seeming offended.

Without turning around, Tyson simply raised his hand, and Tasha went back to his hair.

Instead of saying anything, Tyson returned to reading the book I suddenly realized was in his hands. To make matters more messed up, Tasha wasn't braiding his hair, I realized, but undoing his braids. Beside her sat some clippers. He was getting a haircut. On the front step!

Further embarrassed, I stomped by them and headed inside.

In the kitchen, I found a bag of groceries on the counter and pans taken out. He was seriously going to cook us dinner, and he'd even gone out of his way to get food. My stomach felt fuzzy at the thought of him preparing a meal for us.

Jordy came into the kitchen and grabbed a bottle of water from the fridge. "Hey."

"Hey," I said softly, still staring at the things on the counter, unable to believe what was before my eyes.

"I'm going to play soccer with Hector, okay? I'll be back later. Trice said he'd play me on Xbox."

My head snapped in my younger brother's direction. "What?"

Jordy fiddled with the soccer ball in his hands. "Well, he's new here and he has no friends. I figured it wouldn't hurt to make him feel like he belongs, you know?"

I couldn't tell my brother to mistreat someone he didn't know. I couldn't teach him that it was wrong to make new people feel like they belonged. I couldn't say anything.

"Yeah, that's nice, I'll see you later." I went up to my room and sat with Erica, watching TV and thinking of anything that didn't revolve around the newest arrival to the Smith household.

7 | *TRICE*

Dinner was served. Lemon-and-herb-seasoned chicken breasts over brown rice with a side of broccoli and asparagus. Max had gotten out wine for Parker and herself, while Nandy, Jordy, and I settled between water, iced tea, and Diet Coke. I'd made a salad as well, since Nandy was preparing for some debut and might be picky about what she ate.

We all sat in the Smiths' luxury dining room, under the crystal chandelier, with Parker and Max on each end of the table, Jordy beside me and Nandy on the other side of the long table, nearest Parker.

"This is very good, Trice," Max spoke up, interrupting the sounds of forks and knives hitting plates. "I don't think Parker and I have ever done so well."

She was being modest. The dinners she'd made Sunday and Monday had been good, far better than the takeout I'd been forced to eat for months.

"Thank you," I said anyway.

"I think with the amount of money we spend each year on takeout, we'd be able to fund a few college tuitions around here," Parker joked.

"This *is* really good," Jordy said. "I'm glad we didn't get takeout."

The Smiths collectively agreed, except Nandy, who continued eating quietly.

"I like what you did with your hair. I think you look very handsome," Max noted.

Parker eyed my haircut and nodded. "Who lined you up? They did a pretty good job."

"My friend Tasha from back home." Tasha had been raised in a house full of boys, and her father had bailed when they were all young. With her being the second oldest, and looking up to her older brother, she was more of a tomboy than anything. She'd learned to cut and braid hair and give advice. She'd been cutting my hair since we were kids, and at first some of my friends thought it was lame that I was going to a girl instead of one of the neighborhood barbers, but when they saw how skilled she was with a set of clippers, they shut up.

I'd needed a ride after my meeting at the school, and Tasha was one of the only civil-headed people I knew from Lindenwood whom I trusted to come and help me out. She thought Pacific Hills was strange, too uppity and nosy. When we'd gone shopping, we'd gotten stared at. Me probably for being over six foot, dark-skinned with braids, and wearing black clothing, and her for wearing baggy basketball shorts, a black tank top, and having her hair up in a ponytail. It was obvious we didn't belong, but unlike some of my friends, Tasha didn't act up due to the rude stares and whispers, she just kept telling me about the neighborhood and I pretended no one was paying us any attention.

"She did a great job. Maybe we can get Jordy in her chair," Parker joked, causing Jordy to make a face.

"Or her step," Nandy mumbled.

"How was the meeting?" Parker asked.

Nandy looked up from her plate, her eyes alarmed, as if she were nervous I'd snitch on her.

"It was okay."

I thought back to the meeting. Lydia was one of those people who believed in everybody, no matter where they came from. Something about her left me feeling comfortable, and maybe a little optimistic, too. After we'd finished talking about things someday getting better, she'd opened my file and made a face that let me know I was in for a lecture.

She'd shaken her head and set the file aside, then stared at me, appearing unimpressed. "Trice, you're ironic, you know that?"

"How so?"

"Truancy upon truancy, and yet your test scores are immaculate."

I hadn't ditched school because it was hard. I'd ditched to be with my friends. But even when I had ditched, I'd managed to study at the end of the day.

"I'm not seeing the issue," I replied.

Lydia smirked. "No more truancy, okay? Now, your papers in English are another thing."

"What's wrong with them?"

"It's what's not wrong with them. You've got an amazing voice. Have you ever thought about being a writer?"

From there I shot her down. I just wanted to pass the classes I'd failed. I wasn't up for career advice, even if she did think I had a story to tell that boys from all notorious cities could relate to. A story of survival and resilience.

I didn't care about all that.

It wasn't like I'd gotten an elated feeling out of living through it anyway.

"They're making you read?" Jordy asked, drawing my attention back to the current conversation. "I saw you reading earlier."

"School starts next week, and Lydia said I've gotta write a paper on a book of my choosing for English."

"Oh yeah? What are you reading?" Max asked.

"Roots," I answered as I glanced her way. "I've read it before, and it's one of my favorites."

"Mine, too. I feel like every black child should read it and watch the film."

Nandy clicked her tongue. "That book is so thick."

Her words irritated me. "It goes all the way back to Africa—it tells everything."

"Doesn't make it any less of a long read. I did like the original series, though."

"The book gives more detail. It's our history. Everyone should read about where they come from."

Max gave me an apologetic smile. "She doesn't even like her name."

I bet she didn't.

Nandy cringed. "It's a weird name. I prefer *Nan.*"

People like Nandy annoyed the hell out of me. I bet if she had a choice, she'd read about Marie Antoinette or some shit.

"I bet you wish your name was Jessica or Rebecca, huh?"

I doubt she caught my annoyance by the way she perked up at the suggestion.

"Anything's better than Nandy," she said.

"If you knew your history, you'd know that Nandi was an African queen, mother of Shaka, one of the most influential leaders in African culture. It is not a weird name, it's an honor." I stopped, feeling way too connected to the story of Shaka and Nandi.

Nandy appeared surprised at the revelation.

"We actually named Nandy after Queen Nandi. Perhaps we'll all watch *Shaka Zulu* together one day," said Max. "It's a great film."

Parker nodded, raising his glass of wine to agree with his wife. "That sounds like an excellent idea, Max."

Nandy actually seemed on board by the small smile on her face, almost like the idea didn't bother her. Maybe she'd grow to appreciate her name if she saw the film.

"Hey, do you guys remember when you were kids and Nandy had you square dancing in the street?" Max brought up.

I looked at Nandy, and she looked at me, her eyes softening. She remembered, just as I did. She'd demanded that we go outside and dance right after we'd kissed in the closet. She was always bossy like that, so of course Max found us five minutes later out in the street dancing away, linked by our elbows.

Nandy focused back on her plate for just a moment before pulling out her cell phone and standing up. "Dinner was amazing, Tyson, thanks." She studied her parents. "I sorta made plans to go to this party with my friends, can I go now?"

Parker peered at Max, who was already looking his way.

"Sure, and why don't you bring Trice along? I'm sure he could stand to make a few new friends," Parker suggested.

Nandy frowned. "I don't think *Trice* would want to miss out on reading."

"As he said, he's already read the book." Parker went on, "Either Trice goes, or you don't." He stared at his daughter, clearly meaning business. "Now, which will it be?"

Nandy didn't bother hiding her scowl as she faced me. "It's at the beach, suit up."

I waited on the front step for Nandy to get ready. Parker and Max had gone into the family room to talk, and I didn't want to overhear how much of a mess my coming to stay was. Nandy didn't want me in Pacific Hills any more than I wanted to be in Pacific Hills.

Just one hundred and fifty-eight more days to go, I reminded myself.

"Trice?" Jordy came out and sat beside me. He was still wearing some soccer jersey from earlier and a pair of shorts with no shoes on. Back home, hardly anyone walked around barefoot; you had to be ready to go at all times.

"What's up?" I asked.

"About what you said in there, to Nandy," Jordy began, sounding shy. "It got me thinking." He looked down at the concrete. "Mom and Dad say next summer we're all going to Thailand to learn about where I come from." Jordy peered up at me. "And if you can keep a secret, I wasn't thrilled about it."

"Why not?"

"Because *this* is where I come from, this is my home," Jordy said. "Mom, Dad, and Nandy are all I know." He went back to staring down at the concrete. "But hearing what you said— you're right, I gotta learn about my homeland, because I was born in Thailand, and that's where I come from." He gave me a small smile. "Maybe next summer you'll come with us and learn, too?"

The kid sounded genuine and nice. He didn't look at me like I was some thug or murderer. He saw me as some new person attached to his family.

I didn't have the heart to tell him I was planning to ditch the Smiths as soon as I was legal. Instead, I just told him, "It would be nice to see someplace new."

Nandy came out wearing a see-through tunic over a white bikini. Her hair was up in a bun and, even though it was late and the sun was gone, she wore oversize sunglasses on her head.

"Come on, Tyson. 'Bye, Jordy." She flew past us to her car and got in.

I frowned, hoping I wasn't about to endure more Lana Del Rey.

I had to, and I spent the entire ride to the beach planning to invest in downloading more songs on my phone to keep myself busy while receiving rides from Nandy. Her taste in music was terrible, and I'd die before the summer was over if I had to spend every car ride listening to it.

Nandy parked, and we walked in silence up some street, passing by Mercedes, Range Rovers, and other expensive vehicles to get some small beach house before going toward the backyard, where all the mayhem was taking place. Lights were strung from poles to add a luminescent glow to the scene as music from the nearby back porch played loudly. Some kids danced offbeat in the distance, while others were up and around talking or going for the water.

Nandy gazed back at me, taking me in from head to toe. "Don't start any shit, okay?"

There were only so many times I was going to let her get

away with the way she was painting me. I wasn't some hoodlum, and she needed to get off my back.

"Sure thing, *Nan*," I let her know.

We descended from the back patio to the beach itself, but not without bumping into her neighbor, Travis Catalano.

"What's up, girl?" Travis appraised her with obvious approval. "Your beach is better."

Nandy rolled her eyes and walked off toward her friends.

Travis grinned, watching her go to one of the many bonfires. "I bet it's wetter, too."

As salty as Nandy acted, I bet her beach was more of a desert.

Travis turned back to me, the same weird smile he'd given me that morning crossing his face. "And we meet again." He brought his gaze to my attire and smirked. "Black T-shirt and black jeans, because that's not conspicuous at all."

I had a feeling the kid had a knack for saying whatever the fuck came to his mind. There was no filter. By his muscular stature, I hoped for his sake he was able to back up all that mouth.

He focused on my face. "So, what sport do you play?"

"I'm not a sports guy."

His eyebrows drew down and his gaze ran over my torso once more. "No? So you just juice up for the fuck of it, huh?"

He definitely didn't give a shit about what came out of his mouth.

Travis chuckled. "I'm just fuckin' with you man." He held out his hand. "We cool?"

When I didn't shake his hand, he brought it back to his side.

Travis appeared amused. "Listen, we—" he gestured from himself to me "—sorta got off on the wrong foot here."

"Fresh meat?"

That smirk increased. "That was an ill joke, my bad. You don't look like you belong here. Don't worry, neither do I. Only the real can relate."

Real. What did any kid from Pacific Hills know about real? Hell, half their people were made of synthetics.

Travis's gaze moved in Nandy's direction, and mine followed to where she was sitting with her boyfriend and some other people. "So I'm assuming Nandy informed you about me. Gave you all the dirty deets about my extracurricular activities?"

I kept staring, wanting him to get to his point.

He nodded, not seeming offended in the least. "I think it's only fair that I warn you about Nandy." He waved toward her friends. "Beyond the glitz and glamour, the oh-so-cool popular crowd is bullshit. They're nothing but plastic smiles and silicone friendships. They'll do anything to make themselves look *and* feel superior. You always gotta watch your back."

There was no way to hide my grimace. Fuck, I could find less drama where I was from. Real did recognize real back in Lindenwood. If you didn't fuck with someone, you didn't fuck with them, period. All that hanging out and pretending shit wasn't our style.

"Nandy's cool, though, sometimes," Travis quipped.

"And let me guess, she misjudged you?" I asked.

Travis grinned, moving closer and leaning over to speak in my ear. "I never said she was wrong about me." He stood back and observed our surroundings. "I like to have fun and live my life. If that bothers anyone, that's their problem. Why give a fuck when I don't have to?"

"At least you're honest."

"Only way to live, Tyson."

"It's Trice."

"Nandy said—"

"I prefer my last name."

Travis didn't argue. He threw an arm over my shoulders and steered me in the direction of the party. He pointed past me at two guys holding Solo cups and standing away from everyone else. "That's my best friend, Matt, and his boyfriend, Ben. They're sports and adrenaline junkies. I can get down with some adrenaline, but I don't care much for organized sports."

That was ironic. The way Nandy painted him, you'd think he'd be captain of some shitty cliché. "No? Then what do you do?"

Travis opened his arms, smiling with pride. "I'm on the drumline. I bring the flavor the marching band's been missing."

This was no cliché. While standing in the midst of Pacific Hills' local teens, I got the feeling that I was about to be living in something straight out of a white teen drama, appropriately named *Pretty Filthy Rich Kids*, but if Travis was as devious as Nandy said and he was in marching band, then things were far from ordinary. Hell, Nandy probably wasn't some cheerleader either, although with her sour mood, I could see why she wouldn't be.

"You play the drum for the school marching band?" I just had to clarify.

"Fuck yeah, you'd think that'd be lame, but the girls love the way I work my sticks, man." Travis finished gazing at some girl who was bent over grabbing a beer from a cooler. He whistled. "Warhol's gonna kill me someday."

The pretty Latina came over and punched Travis's arm. "Hey, Trav." She glanced at me, lifting a brow. "New guy."

Travis pulled the girl under his arm. "Edi Gómez, Trice. Trice, Edi Gómez."

"I've met your brother," I said, finding no resemblance between the twins.

Edi smiled. "Warhol said he met some new kid from the 'Wood today."

Travis studied me and squinted. "You're from Lindenwood?"

I nodded.

"I guess things just got interesting." He peered down at Edi. "I was just telling him how fake your friends can be."

Edi rolled her eyes and said something in Spanish as she moved from beneath his arm.

"I love it when you speak that telenovela shit, Edi." He winked, and she blushed. I had to admit, Travis had charisma. That was evident as Edi stood staring at him.

"Back off my sister, Catalano." Warhol came over and pushed Travis away. "Jeez, she's not about to become one of your *skonkas*."

Travis held his hands up, proclaiming innocence. "I was just saying hi."

Warhol snorted and noticed me. "Trice, what's up?" He reached out and slapped my hand, then pulled me in for a brief hug. "I'm glad you made it. Welcome to the neighborhood."

"He's with Nandy," Travis spoke up.

Warhol made a face and observed Nandy and her friends. "Careful."

Even I had to look at Nandy. The Smiths seemed like nice, wholesome people, but if every guy I met warned me about Nandy, then perhaps she wasn't so innocent after all.

"Yeah?" I asked.

Edi rolled her eyes and shoved her brother. "He's just holding a grudge because they used to date."

"Before Chad came through and pulled a robbery," Travis added.

Warhol gave me an annoyed look, as if what his sister and Travis were saying was exaggerated. "I don't hold grudges, but I'm just saying be careful. Those girls are sneaky."

"It wasn't even that serious between you two," Edi said.

"We hit second base!" Warhol whined.

Edi pulled Warhol away, and the two went bickering over to where Nandy was sitting. Warhol obviously didn't have a major issue, because he sat with Nandy as if it weren't a big deal that they used to date.

Matt and Ben came over and introduced themselves to me, having less of a dramatic introduction than Travis or Warhol and his sister.

"You look like you play ball, do you?" Matt asked as he sized me up.

I shook my head. "I don't do sports."

Ben seemed slightly disappointed. "I have a feeling you'd kill on the lacrosse team."

I wasn't planning on staying long enough to join any teams or make any real connections. I shrugged, as if I found the thought interesting but wasn't willing to commit.

Matt and Ben were holding hands, and Travis scowled once he noticed. "It's barely been an hour."

"Ben's leaving in the morning, cut me some slack," Matt said as he led his boyfriend away.

"Wear a condom!" Travis shouted in their direction.

Matt and Ben seemed like decent guys, and then there was Travis. He was trouble, or at least his mouth was. But even if that was true, I had a feeling there'd be no bullshit with him.

"I'm gonna go have some debauched fun and do my best to live up to my reputation. You kick back. The Hills get real interesting at night." Travis patted my arm and walked off to where a group of people was standing around a keg.

"Well, well, well, look what the stork dropped off." Behind me stood a girl who wasn't hiding the fact that she was checking me out. With her tan skin, dark curly hair, big brown eyes, and obvious beauty, this girl made me think that Travis had walked away far too early. She tilted her head. "So, you're who Nandy's been fussing about."

At the mention of Nandy, I looked over and caught her glaring my way.

"Something like that," I said as I focused back on the girl in the black bikini.

"Shayne Mancini." She held her hand out daintily, as if she expected me to kiss it.

I lifted a brow and did nothing. "Nice to meet you."

She took her hand back but kept smiling. It was like she was playing a game and she didn't mind playing harder. "I hear you're from Lindenwood."

Again, I looked at Nandy, giving her my own glare for the shit she'd probably been talking. I wondered how many robberies she'd told Shayne I'd been a part of. "Yep."

"Fascinating. Is it true what they say?" Shayne took a step closer.

"What do they say?" I dared to ask.

Shayne opened her mouth, staring at my arms and admiring my muscles. "Well—"

"Shayne!" Kyle materialized beside her and held out a Solo cup. "I... I n-noticed you were empty-handed, s-so I grabbed you this."

Shayne peered at the scrawny boy and took the cup from him. She studied the contents and scowled, then handed it back. "What's that?"

Kyle moved some hair out of his eyes. "Sprite."

"And what color is it?"

"Cah-lear," he said, announcing each syllable with confusion.

"I only drink pink drinks, Froggie, everyone knows that."

"It's Frogge, actually," Kyle said. "I'll, uh, go get you another."

"Yeah, do that, please." Shayne returned to me and rolled her eyes.

If I were keeping score on the bizarre, twisted teen drama I'd fallen into, I had to take a guess and say I'd just met the extrabitchy best friend to Nandy's main mean-girl character.

Shayne grabbed my hand and led me to her group of friends. She pointed at everyone and said their names—names I didn't care to memorize—but Nandy's boyfriend, Chad, stuck out.

They were talking about their summer plans, and I couldn't relate to any of it. My family had never had the type of money where my parents could take me on trips to other countries. If my height and intimidating look weren't enough to count me out of belonging in Pacific Hills, my background was the ticket I needed to get sent back home.

"I'm trying to get Nandy's parents to let her come with my parents and me when we take our yacht for the first sail of the summer. It'll be so much fun," Chad was saying as he sat with Nandy under his arm.

Shayne was beautiful, and so was Nandy's other friend, Erica, but it was obvious, as I looked around the bonfire at the other girls and the other guys, that Nandy was the most attractive girl in the inner circle, and if she and Chad ever broke up, she'd have a ton of admirers at her door. It was becoming more and more noticeable as each guy looked at Nandy every time her name was mentioned.

A few girls swooned, as if Chad's statement were the most romantic thing in the world, and Nandy gave a shy smile.

"Then you can get laid while you sail the high seas," some kid sitting on Chad's right said, making a bunch of the guys laugh.

Chad slapped the boy's hand, causing Nandy to sit up and scowl. Chad was quick to backtrack. "Aw, baby, come on, it'll be fun."

"There would be no time for that if your parents are on board," she said.

Shayne chuckled. "What's a good time for you, then, Nan?"

"Besides when his parents aren't around, anytime when Chad decides to turn off the TV instead of muting it."

The guys teased Chad while the girls glowered at him.

"What?" he asked. "I like to make sure my teams are scoring, too."

Nandy rolled her eyes. "He's quite the romantic."

More like a redheaded fuck boy.

Tired of hearing about their shitty plans and ill attempts at romance, I stood up and walked off.

Music was blasting, and it was actually decent. Nandy's friend Erica was controlling the music up on the patio, and she put on some Drake before coming down and meeting up with me.

"Having a good time?" A loud laugh carried to us from the bonfire, and Erica looked over and scrunched up her nose. "Don't mind Chad and his friends, they're assholes."

"I gathered."

Erica tossed me a smile. "But if you show them no bullshit, they'll show you the same. You just gotta stand strong. They're kinda like dogs—they smell fear and weakness, and once they do, they'll walk all over you."

In the distance, I caught sight of Kyle giving Shayne a new drink and her quickly shooing him away instead of offering him my empty seat.

They smell fear and weakness.

"So you deejay?" I asked, coming back to Erica. "What got you into that?"

"My cousin Geordan and a few of my other cousins like to dance to hip-hop. Once when I was twelve and over at their house, he asked me to control the music, and I just fell in love with it, I guess. When they're not working at the restaurant they're usually working on dance moves, and I get to work on some mixes," Erica explained. "My boyfriend actually gets paid to host club events, and I get to deejay since we're a package deal now. I almost feel legit."

She sounded big-time, almost. "What do you go by?"

She appeared confused. *"Erica?"*

I chuckled for the first time in almost six months. "No offense, but that's a bland DJ name."

Erica rolled her eyes. "Geordan says I should go by DJ Yee, but then people think I'm some Chinese guy."

Erica was beyond cute. Nandy had mentioned that she was half black, half Chinese and with one look at her I found that she was a strong combination of both with her sepia skin tone, defined cheekbones, and full lips. She had long silky onyx hair and pretty eyes that lit up whenever she smiled.

"Yeah, but you're still gonna wanna work on that name," I let her know.

Erica waved me off. "What do you like listening to?"

"Kendrick, some 'Pac, but a lot of Pusha T lately."

Erica's lips made a perfect O shape. "Ooh, good shit. Pusha's debut is one of my favorite albums. The beats were insane and the lyrics were out of there." She glanced back at the patio and frowned as Ashley went and stood at her laptop. "I love that boy to death, but he can't do my job." She gazed back at me. "I'm going to play you something."

She headed back up to the patio with the wind blowing in her long curly hair. She shoved Ashley away from her laptop, and soon "Nosetalgia" came through the speakers. I gave her a thumbs-up before distancing myself from the party and walking closer to the ocean, watching the waves crash as they hit the shore.

Nostalgia.

Her words echoed in my head. *You deserve a good life, baby.*

My words came next as I had disagreed with her remark. *No*, we *do*.

Looking around, I wondered if our good life could've been lived in a place like Pacific Hills.

A place full of ease, comfort, and sunny days.

Not too far into my reverie, the shots and screams from that day sounded in my head, and I knew without a doubt that it couldn't have.

8 | *Nandy*

The party was over and everyone was packing up and going home. Usually I would ride with Erica, Edi, or Shayne and rehash the night or gossip about things we couldn't say in front of the group. We'd make smoothies and stay up late talking or watching movies.

But I had to take Tyson home.

"Warhol's such a flirt." Shayne was giggling as she walked back to the street with Erica and me.

Erica's and my faces shared the same expression. *Pot, kettle, much?*

"Sure," Erica responded.

Shayne made a face. Everyone flirted with Shayne; she was beautiful, and much like Edi, she was available. Erica was in-

fatuated with Ashley, and I had Chad. Shayne loved the attention regardless.

"Why didn't you tell us your new housemate was a total
hot fudge sundae?" Shayne asked, batting her eyelashes.

I wasn't sure what bothered me more, her referring to Tyson
as a dessert, or her flirting with him. The way he was so gung
ho about Africa, I doubted he'd give Shayne a chance.

She wasn't the only girl who'd noticed Tyson. A couple
others had stared at him off and on all night. I guess if you
got past the cold exterior, he was handsome—*very*.

I gave my best friend a big fake smile. "Oh, I don't know,
it must've slipped my mind."

Shayne marched out in front of us, walking backward as
she held her hand in the air. "I call first dibs."

Erica scoffed. "He doesn't need your drama."

Ahead of us I spotted Tyson leaning against my car, arms
crossed as he stared down at his shoes. I could hear Shayne
sigh, but all I could wonder was why he'd worn such heavy
clothes to the beach.

Shayne walked to Edi's car and hopped in, and Erica stood
with me, staring at Tyson.

"Be nice, Nandy," Erica told me.

I was lugging him around whether I liked it or not. What
more could I do? "This is me being nice."

My best friend blatantly scowled at me. "First off, we're
privileged and maybe he's not—that doesn't give any of us
the right to judge him."

"Erica—"

"I'm for real—you and Shayne were sounding like those
snooty old white people who are stuck in their ways. I know
it's scary because he's from Lindenwood, and he's big and
intense-looking, but I *know* you, and *you* know you. This

stuck-up, judgmental girl is not the Nandy Smith we all know. Get over yourself and welcome him like you'd welcome anyone else into our school and town." Erica gave me a little shove. "You're the friendliest girl I know, and if you keep acting like this I'ma catch a case."

Her words incited the internal battle I felt at the idea of breaking down my prejudices and showing Tyson around willingly versus steering clear of him. There was a part of me that wanted to be nice, wanted to be myself, but then there was a deeper part of me that didn't. That felt angry at the sight of him, that remembered every summer after age seven spent by the window waiting, and waiting, only for him not to return.

I waved and headed to Tyson, or I would've, if it hadn't been for my suddenly being airborne and swung in a circle as, I was assuming, Chad had engulfed me in his arms.

"You weren't going to say goodbye?" he asked.

He set me down and was quick to pull me into a kiss, deep and aggressive, right in the middle of the street for all to see.

I felt embarrassed, especially when from the corner of my eye I caught Tyson rolling his eyes and Erica doing the same as she went to her car.

Pressing both hands to Chad's chest, I pushed him back a little, giggling. "What was that about? I'm just going home, silly."

Chad smiled. "Still, I'm going to miss my girl. Can't you sneak out?"

"So we can have sex while ESPN plays in the background?" I teased.

"I'll mute it, I swear!"

Were all boys like this? Forever obsessed with some dumb

sport? Even Jordy was falling in love with soccer, which he played with his best friend, Hector Gómez.

"I can't."

Chad frowned, pouting. "Why not?"

"I probably have to get up early to take Tyson somewhere."

Chad looked past me at Tyson, his face impassive, but his eyes showing his annoyance. "That kid's gonna ruin your summer if you have to shuttle him around."

"Believe me, I know." Thinking of Erica's words, I back-tracked. "But I'm working on it. Maybe he just needs his license or something. I can teach him to drive and—"

"Doesn't he have his own family for that?"

I'd never known much about Tyson's family. I always assumed they were decent people. He used to wear the nicest little outfits when he'd come over to play with me. The only thing odd about it all was the sadness in his eyes. Now that sadness had been replaced by a burning anger, and I didn't know why.

"According to my parents, we're his family now." I looked into my boyfriend's blue eyes and gave a sad smile. "I will make time for you, I promise, okay?"

"Okay." With another sigh, he kissed me and let me go.

Tyson walked around to the passenger door and waited for me to unlock the car for him.

Erica knew me well, and she knew I wasn't the type to judge or ice people out, but Tyson was a different case. Even so, I decided to take my best friend's advice and *try*.

I almost wanted to give Tyson my customary greeting when it came to newbies. *Where are you from, and what do you like?* But instead, I fumbled and asked, "Music?"

Tyson blinked, staring at me funny. "Sure."

Instead of listening to my preferred music, I turned the

radio to a rap station. Each time we'd ridden in my car, he'd scowled at Lana's singing.

While I wasn't the most educated in hip-hop or rap, I recognized the Notorious B.I.G.'s voice as I settled on a song. He was rapping about who shot someone, and even though I found the topic gritty, I let the song play.

Seconds hadn't passed since I'd settled on the song when Tyson suddenly reached out and punched a button, turning the station to some Adele song.

Guess he's not a Biggie fan.

Adele was one of my favorite singers anyway, so I let Tyson and his weirdness go as I continued home.

He was quiet the whole way there, and as we entered the door, I tried one more time to be the nice Nandy Erica knew me to be.

"Tyson," I said, catching his attention as he shut the door behind us.

He took a deep breath as he faced me, his eyes hardening.

"I just wanted to warn you to stay away from Shayne. Trust me." She might be one of my best friends, but I was doing her and Tyson a favor by sparing them the drama.

He rolled his eyes, walking by me. "Gee, anyone else I should stay away from?"

My nostrils flared at the tone of his voice and his attitude.

"Maybe you can stay away from my family and go back to yours," I mumbled as I set my car keys in the dish that sat on the table in the hall.

Tyson stopped walking, his body tensing. Before I knew what was happening, he was coming at me, fast, blocking me against the wall. He stared me in the eyes with a look that caused me to tremble. With a glance, he eyed my body up and down and sneered.

"Go back to my family?" he asked. "I don't have a fucking family, Nandy. And you wanna know why?" He got closer to my face, not letting me look away. "Because that motherfucker shot me. He shot my mom and killed her, he shot me, and then himself, and he died. All that's left *is* me." He slammed his hand against the wall, causing pictures to rattle and me to let out a small, scared *squeak.* "So fuck you!"

The anger from his eyes had traveled to his face and magnified, making him look lethal. He backed away from me and stalked out the front door, slamming it shut behind himself.

Time froze as my heart dropped to the pit of my stomach and breath evaded me. I couldn't form a complete thought as I felt myself slide down against the wall into a sitting position.

Covering my mouth to stop the sobs from escaping, I felt my vision blur as tears soaked my eyes.

Shot.

He'd been shot.

How?

Why?

It was like there were two Tysons—the Tyson from when we were kids, and this new guarded and cold Tyson. No longer did I have to question the reason, because here it was— he'd been shot.

Not only that, he'd lost everything. He'd watched his own mother die. I couldn't begin to imagine going through that, what it must've been like.

Tyson was right. I'd been a total bitch, self-involved to the point where I hadn't questioned the whereabouts of his parents or even his grandfather, who'd been the one who brought him to Pacific Hills.

No, all it took was the word *Lindenwood* for me to expect the worst of the stranger moving in with my family.

But he wasn't a stranger.

He was Tyson, a boy I'd once known. To think that, when he'd disappeared from my life, he'd been swallowed by the dark sea that was Lindenwood was heartbreaking. When I was seven, I never cared about the reason Tyson stopped coming around. I'd hated him for abandoning me without so much as a goodbye.

Now all I wanted to do was talk to him and ask him what had happened. If he'd talk to me again. Or more important, if he ever came back.

9 | TRICE

Welcome to Lindenwood.

It was home. Or it used to be, right until my father killed my mother and shot me before killing himself.

I wanted to ruin Nandy's world for her bringing me back to that vivid memory of that night. I wanted to pound my fists into the wall until they were stumps and I couldn't feel anymore. Though the last rational part of me knew it was better to just leave altogether before doing damage and becoming the monster she thought I was.

An hour after storming out of the Smiths' house, I found myself back where it all began. Standing in front of my childhood home, now all boarded up, I felt numb and hard at the same time. The voices in my head were louder than they'd ever been, and I fought to block them out.

It was to no avail.

"You think you can leave me, bitch?"

The scene unfolded as if a projector were plugged in to my memory, taunting me with what I didn't want to remember, let alone think about.

She screamed as he dragged her through the house by her hair before throwing her on the floor in the living room. I watched a version of myself from six months prior trying to go to her and stop him. But just like before, he pulled out a gun and aimed at me. I kept going. It was only when she held up a hand, tears streaming down her cheeks as she begged me to stay away, that I stopped.

"Ty, baby, go upstairs. Don't be here for this."

I couldn't move. Couldn't let him do it anymore. I couldn't let him hurt her.

He looked at me and back to her, becoming visibly angrier. *"You thought you was just going to leave? You thought you was going to take him and go?"*

She begged him to calm down, and I inched closer, willing to do more than take a bullet for her.

"You belong to me, bitch!"

The next few seconds were forever engraved in my mind. Everything was silent, and I could hear my heartbeat in my ears as he pulled the trigger and she fell farther down, letting out a cry I would never forget for as long as I lived.

My own voice sounded foreign to me as I screamed for her and moved forward.

He turned and faced me, still angry, still vicious.

"We're a family, dammit. No one leaves."

He didn't hesitate before aiming at me and pulling the trigger once more.

I could barely recall the impact or the pain. I was too busy feeling shocked and worrying about my mother. It wasn't until I was on the floor, too weak to move my right arm, that I realized how much it hurt. Even then, I didn't care about myself. I wanted to get to her, to help her.

Another shot sounded, and I saw him collapse, dead before his body bounced onto the ground.

Looking over, I could see her weakening, her blood pooling beneath her, staining the white carpeted floor he'd spent years demanding she keep clean.

I watched her die reaching out for me as I reached out for her. I watched her take her last breath and stare at me. I watched her drift away right in front of me as I lay there, too paralyzed to do anything.

In seconds, all went dark.

The projector stopped, and the scene faded away. My fists were shaking, and I fought to gain control of my breathing.

Fuck Nandy.

It was late, but there was one place I could go where I knew the residents would still be up. Ten minutes later, I knocked on the wrought iron door of a house where I'd spent many days growing up. Seeing the familiar setup of an old wooden chair and a turned-over milk crate on the concrete porch felt like home. It *was* my second home, and the reason I kept with the tradition of knocking instead of just going inside like some people I knew often did was simply respect.

The door opened and a familiar figure stepped outside and walked past me, and then did a double take.

"Trice? Is that you?" Gerald asked as he squinted, trying

to see me in the dim porchlight. He looked dressed for the night shift at his job.

"What's up, G?" I asked, reaching out and giving him a hug. It wasn't brief; he held on for a moment longer than he might have in the past.

"I thought you was dead, boy." He held me at arm's length, examining me with shock in his old eyes. "I heard it all on the news, and then you was gone."

I hadn't been home in six months. My grandfather had lived forty-five minutes away.

"It all happened so fast. I was recovering with Pops," I said.

"How he doin'?"

"Cancer got him."

Gerald frowned with pity. "At least it's that that got him other than this."

"This *is* cancer, G."

Gerald didn't disagree. "Ain't that the truth." He lifted his chin at me. "You here to see Proph?"

"Yeah, it's been a minute."

"They all down in the basement playin' cards. Go an' see 'em, and tell 'em not to smoke up all that shit. I'ma get me some after I get off."

Gerald headed to his rusty van and got in, and I went inside.

I'd spent most of my youth at this house practically being raised by Gerald, Alma, and her son, Prophet. I'd learned so much from all three that, after the shit Nandy had pulled back in Pacific Hills, I'd wanted to come here.

I stepped down into the basement, not surprised by all the commotion I could hear before I even reached the bottom step.

The boys were huddled around a card table. There was weed

on it, some cash, and plenty of smoke in the air along with shit talk. While the other guys played, Read was stretched across the couch watching TV, some book of his lying on the coffee table within his reach.

Prophet noticed me first. "Trice," he said as he greeted me, standing with an elated smile on his face. "What's been happenin'?"

I went and gave him a hug and a pat on the back and mirrored the same to Khalil, Pretty, and Money.

"Nothing much, y'all?"

Money passed Pretty the blunt and blew out smoke. "Nothin', chillin', tryna stay alive."

Pretty eyed me. "For the record, had your father survived, we would've got 'em." He set his Beretta on the table, and I eyed the .9mm and its cold silver frame, knowing how one of its bullets felt. "We would've got him, man, on the dead homies. He would've got straight chipped."

I nearly allowed myself to feel, to connect to that night and that moment all over again, but I blocked it out.

"I appreciate it," I replied, "but I would've handled it."

"I never liked Tyson Sr., man," Money went on, shaking his head. "I would've smoked him a long time ago had I known he was gon' pull this shit." He appraised me, eyes hard. "You straight, man?"

I didn't care.

I took a seat at the table and shrugged. "It's whatever. Pops passed, and now I'm down in Pacific Hills. It is what it is."

"I'm sorry about your grandfather, man, he was good people. How they treatin' you in the Hills, young brother?" Prophet asked, looking my way with concern.

"Typical," I answered. "Reason why I'm here. I'm about to go crazy if I stay there too long."

"They shittin' on you?" Money asked. "Just say the word and we will dump on 'em."

And then Nandy would die being right about me. "Unless you're going to go against a girl, it ain't worth it."

Pretty sucked his teeth. "Shit, a bitch can catch it just as quick as a dude. Ain't no one exempt, especially if she treatin' you some type of way."

"I can handle her."

Pretty eyed his gun with a mischievous grin. "Maybe she just needs a good scare, is all. Shit, we can teach her—"

Prophet cleared his throat. "Who is she?"

"Just some girl I live with. I'm staying with some old friends, and they got a daughter and a son."

"She think you're a thug?"

"Yeah."

Pretty tried to pass me the blunt, but as usual I passed. Everyone knew I didn't smoke or drink, yet on occasions when they were getting high, Pretty or Money would always try to pass me whatever it was that they were smoking.

Khalil clicked his tongue. "Y'all dudes know Trice don't smoke. Pass that right here."

Khalil and I were the same age, but total opposites. Read was eighteen; Money and Pretty were older at nineteen and twenty. In ways, they'd both lived more than the three of us had yet to.

Money got his name because that was all he cared about. He didn't care what he had to do to get it—he'd rob an old lady, steal from kids who weren't a part of our territory, and if he had to kill, he more than likely would.

Pretty was just as cutthroat as Money, willing to do anything to get money or pleasure, and he just straight didn't give a fuck. We called him Pretty because of his lighter skin tone and the way he wore his hair—that, and he was quick to make sure he was groomed to perfection. It didn't help that a lot of the girls we grew up with were always sweating him, too.

Read got his name because he always had his head in some book and was quick to avoid drama. He was quiet unless spoken to, but he'd been down since day one.

Khalil and I might have been the same age, but he felt younger; he did what he was told and drank and got high just to go along.

Prophet was a different story. He was the oldest at twenty-three and somewhat our leader. He was smart—not just street-smart, but booksmart too, though he'd never finished school. He was always there to guide us, ever since we were kids. He'd taught us how to hold a gun and how to pull the trigger. He'd taught us how to run the streets and make money and to stay in line. He taught us how to survive Lindenwood.

Prophet wasn't his real name—I couldn't even remember his real name after so much time, but he lived up to his moniker through and through. He was sure that he wouldn't live to see twenty-five; he was sure most of his friends wouldn't either, but when it came to me, for some reason, he had faith. Next to my mother, Alma, and Gerald, Prophet was probably the only person who believed in me.

He shook his head. "That's a shame. She obviously doesn't know you."

What kind of hurt, when I thought about it, was the fact that Nandy did know me. At least, at one time she had.

"Fuck her," I said. "She just some uppity white girl wannabe with a fuck boy for a boyfriend."

Pretty picked up his gun and stared at her beauty. "Say the word, T, we can handle this easy."

As far as I knew, the boys hadn't ever killed anyone, but

that didn't mean they wouldn't. Back when we were kids, there used to be this old lady who lived across the street from me. She was always yelling at us to turn down our music and to keep off her lawn. She was mean and annoying, and all of us couldn't stand her. Money and Pretty used to do shit on purpose just to set her off. One night, there were shots, and an hour later my parents and I found out she'd been robbed and killed. I used to wonder if it had been one of the boys, but then I let it go.

Money shook his head and slammed his hand down, declaring he'd won.

I watched as he pulled all the money his way, his eyes lit up with greed.

"She's nothing to worry about," I declared.

"Don't let her get to you." Prophet held up one finger. "She's wrong about you. You're gonna make it, Trice. You ain't gon' die in these streets. You weren't built for that."

I was tired of talking about it. "Do you mind if I crash here?"

"*Mi casa es tu casa.*" Prophet patted my back. "How'd you get here?"

"I caught a bus and walked most of the way."

"Need a car?"

"I can't ride dirty, Proph."

"You got five hundred?"

"Yeah."

"I'll get you one legit, a nice one." Prophet had connections in everything, it felt like. "Tomorrow I'll get it here for you. You ain't ridin' no bus home."

"Thanks."

Pretty slapped my arm. "Yo, go get me another beer?"

I stood from the table and headed up the steps to the

kitchen. Prophet's younger sister, Cherish, was in the room, holding Rain on her hip. He was wearing only a T-shirt and a diaper, his thumb in his mouth.

"Trice!" Cherish squealed as she came over and hugged me, adjusting her son so that he wasn't being smushed. "I haven't seen you in forever!"

"What's good with you?" I asked, rubbing Rain's head and enjoying the little smile he gave me.

"Nothing. Where've you been?" She punched my arm. "I heard what happened, and then you went straight ghost. Tasha said she seen you, but *we* ain't."

"I had to stay with Pops. He got sick and sent me to live with some old friends in Pacific Hills."

Cherish's eyes bugged out. "Word?"

I bobbed my head as I went to the fridge and grabbed a bottle of beer for Pretty. "It's just until I'm eighteen."

"Dang, they gon' kick you out?"

"Nah, I just can't stay there. It's not where I belong." I had no clue where I was supposed to be, but Pacific Hills wasn't it. Nandy had all but proved that from the moment I'd stepped into her house.

Cherish gave me a lopsided frown. "Stay here."

I looked around the house I'd hung out in since I was a kid. "Here?"

"Yeah, we got room."

"No. I can't put you out like that."

Cherish swatted at me. "Boy, you know you're family, stop playing. Momma would love to have you."

You ask the media and the uppity, Lindenwood was a war zone capable only of ending lives and tragedy. But it wasn't all bad; there was heart and good health and wealth where it could be found. What I lacked in a family at home outside of my mom and Pops, I found here amongst my friends, and especially Prophet and his mother and uncle. With Pacific Hills rejecting me, I had no place to go upon leaving the Smiths. "For real?"

"Yeah, just help out a little, that's all."

"I've got money."

"Then you're set. I'll talk to Momma, and she'll be happy to have you here." Cherish stared into my eyes. She was only fifteen but had been through a lot. Her father was killed when she was little, and Prophet had all but lost his mind when that had happened. It was one of the reasons he knew he wouldn't live long. Not many in our neighborhood did. It wasn't until his uncle Gerald moved in that things had settled down a bit for him. "Prophet missed you. I did, too. I'm glad you're okay, and I'm happy Tyson's dead. He's probably burning in hell as we speak."

"There is no hell or God, Cherish," I let her know. "Don't be believin' in that nonsense, okay?"

She appeared appalled, covering Rain's ears. "How can you say that?"

I smirked. "Look around you. Do you think He's real?"

Cherish frowned. "He is, Trice, or else you wouldn't be here. He looked out for you."

"Why not my mom, then?"

"Maybe He only had room for you."

"That's some bullshit."

"Maybe she needed to be set free. Don't go talkin' like that, okay? Or else you'll turn into Money and Pretty. You and Read are the only ones with some sense around here, and I can't have you being like them. God is real and He saved your life—don't you go actin' like it was otherwise, you hear me?"

She was pleading with me, sounding almost like Max. I

had a soft spot for Cherish, otherwise I wouldn't have been willing to go agnostic for her. "A'ight."

Footsteps on the basement steps told us that the boys were coming upstairs. Pretty accepted the beer from me before going and messing with Rain's head. He looked to me. "Let's step outside for a bit and catch up."

We left Cherish in the kitchen and posted up outside as we always used to do before.

"So you livin' down in the big time now, huh?" Money said before taking a sip of his beer.

I shrugged. "I guess. Just a bunch of spoiled kids really."

Money faced Pretty, who looked to Khalil, who just went with it. "Probably a great place to start some work, huh?"

I knew what he was talking about and I didn't want to go there with him.

"Money—"

"You in the land of honey, Trice, you can't tell me you ain't been thinkin' about how much we could pull off," Pretty stepped in.

Prophet came and stood between me and the boys. "Didn't y'all hear him in there? They think he's like that, why set him up to prove them right? Trice can't do that there, and he shouldn't be here, either." He turned to me. "You got a second chance, my brother. Not a lot of us get those. You shouldn't be here."

I used to hate how he and my mother thought I'd amount to so much more than this neighborhood, this city, this place.

"Man, fuck that, this is the perfect setup for all of us. We can all get out of here after a few runs." Money stood up and got close to Prophet.

Prophet wasn't intimidated. "Stand down, Money. He ain't

doing it. We'll do on our own like we've been doing. We've been all right. We've been eatin'."

Money sucked his teeth. "This could take care of us for a while." He pointed to me. "Why does he get to leave and have a good life? What? We ain't shit?"

"You wanna tell him what you did to Lester?" Read spoke up from where he sat in the chair with his book.

Lester was a bum, and even if Money had done something heinous, who knew if Lester hadn't asked for it?

"What?" I asked.

Prophet faced me. "He pistol-whipped him and took out his front teeth and broke his nose."

I winced.

"All because he owed you some money," said Read.

Money smirked. "He was at the pool hall bragging about all the shit he just bought his girl. I just asked if he had my money, and he started actin' up. He told me to suck his dick, and I don't take that shit too kindly."

"You would've shot him!" Prophet snapped. "Look at you, you're an animal. Trice is nothing like you, like me, or like any of us. He deserves this second chance."

Growing up, it had seemed like Money was itching to kill, itching to prove himself, especially because his dad had died in front of him and his older brother had gotten stabbed and killed during a robbery.

"Let's just drop it," I said.

The boys backed off each other and settled down.

"We oughta call Asiah up, let her know you home," Pretty said with a sneaky grin. "Tash said you was lookin' good."

Asiah was…something else. She was mean and as tough as Money and Pretty, but on a rare occasion she'd give me a peek into her soft side. We'd been on and off, but I wasn't in-

terested anymore. She'd ask questions, and if I told her about
Nandy, she'd probably hop the first bus all the way down to
Pacific Hills and scar Nandy's face and beat her up. Asiah
wasn't slow to tell anyone she always carried a razor on her,
and for Nandy's sake, I wasn't about to deal with Asiah catching another case.

I shook my head. "Nah, I'm tired, it's late. I think I'm
about to crash."

Prophet patted my shoulder. "I'll get on the car thing
ASAP, okay?"

I nodded and headed inside.

This was home. Prophet thought I deserved more. Funny
thing was, *more* didn't accept me like home did. Maybe my
mother and Prophet were wrong; maybe the streets of Lindenwood were my destiny, and my ending would be as tragic as
my family's.

Welcome to Lindenwood.

10 | *Nandy*

It was nine in the morning, and there was no sign of Tyson anywhere. I'd told my father before he left that Tyson had had an errand to run and hadn't wanted to wake him or my mother. My father had believed me, and so had my mother, which gave Tyson enough room to fume before coming home—*if* he came home.

I was pretending to take interest in something on my phone as I hung around the foyer, hoping and waiting, when my mother came down the staircase just as the front door opened and Tyson miraculously stepped inside.

"Hey, Trice," my mother greeted him. "Did you finish your errands? I saw from the window upstairs a new car in the driveway, is it yours?"

As if we'd constructed the lie together, Tyson nodded without hesitating. "Yes. A friend back home helped me get it. I'm sorry I didn't tell you first."

My mother shrugged. "I'm glad you have your own car. Next time just leave a note to let us know where you're going." She patted his arm and walked on out the door, leaving us alone.

Tyson faced me, his eyes burning into mine.

After his confession, I had no angst against him.

I hadn't had a right to begin with. I slowly advanced closer to him. "Can we talk, please?"

He snorted. "Back off, Nandy."

"No."

He leaned into my face. "I spared you last night. I'm not in the mood to do it twice."

I stared him down, letting him know I wasn't intimidated. "Then don't."

Like I expected, he just stared at me.

Grabbing his arm, I steered him toward the door...or I tried to. He was hard as stone and didn't budge. The hot, silky feel of his skin gave me goose bumps.

"Come on, Tyson, we have to talk," I insisted.

"Don't touch me!"

He was still angry, and rightfully so, but I wanted to make it better. If he'd let me. "Tyson, please—"

"You keep calling me *Tyson* and that's not my name!"

I frowned, unsure what to say and what to do. "I... I—"

"Stop it!" Jordy's voice broke the tension, and his little hand on Tyson's massive bicep caught both of our attention.

Jordy studied Tyson and me. "Don't yell at her like that."

I could tell by the way Tyson looked at my brother that he liked him. Just as he liked my mom.

Tyson calmed down and rubbed the back of his neck. "I'm sorry, Jordy."

Jordy came to me next. "And you stop being so mean to him! He's been through enough. If you weren't being such a brat and avoiding him, you would know that he hasn't had it easy. You're always so nice to all those annoying friends of yours, but the moment a person who really needs help comes along, you shut them out?" Jordy shook his head. "Mom and Dad taught you better than that, Nan."

It was like he was the adult, scolding both Tyson and me.

I regarded Tyson, practically pleading. "We *have* to talk."

As if he were trying to be peaceful, Tyson tipped his head toward Jordy before heaving a sigh and stepping outside.

Jordy still looked frustrated with me. "This is your fault."

"I know. I'm going to fix it, okay?"

I went past Jordy outside, and found a new car in our driveway. A black Yukon Denali. Tyson was heading toward it. It had to be at least a decade old, not at all like the latest model Oliver Stein drove, but by its well-kept exterior I could guess that it was in good running shape. As much as I wanted to question where the SUV had come from, I didn't, not wanting to upset Tyson more.

"Let me drive," I spoke up. "I know where we can go."

Tyson turned and stared at me as if I were crazy.

"We're taking my car."

"If it wasn't for Jordy, I wouldn't be doing this," Tyson told me.

"I know." I left it at that and got in my car and waited for Tyson to join me before starting it up.

I turned off the radio and decided to keep up with my own personal cold front as I pulled out of the driveway and took off.

"First off," I began, glancing at Tyson, "it's been ten years, okay? You don't know shit about me and I don't know shit about you. I was wrong for judging you, but you've clearly been doing some judging of me on your own, so don't act all innocent."

Tyson smirked. "Call this an apology?"

"I'm getting there," I snapped. "When you left I had no one. The kids at school weren't like you—"

"They didn't fall for your looks and do everything you said? Tough shit," Tyson mocked.

I paused. *He'd found me pretty?*

"No," I said, getting back on track. "I had to learn to be like them and fit in. I hated you for abandoning me. For not coming back. The girls didn't wanna go on adventures or climb trees, and the boys didn't want to do that stuff with a girl. It was hell."

Tyson ran his hand down his face and let out a breath. "Spare me the sob story, because I don't give a fuck."

Ugh, did he have to be such an asshole?

We arrived at our destination, and I pulled the car into the driveway and parked.

"Well, tough shit, you're going to give a fuck." I glared at him before I got out of the car and started for the front door.

My mother worked in real estate development at this successful conglomerate known as the Pacific Hills Agency, or the PHA. One of their nearest projects was this beautiful model home in the Malibu Pointe subdivisions my mother had showed me when I was thirteen. It was complete with electricity, furnished impeccably for showings, and was in a quiet neighborhood. The home had never sold, and I had a feeling it was long forgotten. It was my hideaway from home and drama, and I'd been coming to it ever since my first visit.

It wasn't too far from our own development, a good twenty-minute walk or a ten-minute bike ride away.

I hadn't even told Chad or the girls about the place, but bringing Tyson here felt right. When we were kids, he liked building forts out of the cushions from the couches in the living room and using sheets to cover us. He used to tell me we were safe as long as we had our own spot together. It used to make me curious. What did he have to feel unsafe about? Why were his eyes so sad?

The boy standing in the model home with me was no longer sad, but angry. I wanted to know why, and if it involved yelling or cussing, then so be it.

"Your family has two houses?" Tyson asked as he stood in the foyer, staring up at the crystal chandelier hanging from the high ceiling.

"My mom works in real estate—this is one of her company's model homes," I explained as I led the way to the kitchen. I grabbed two bottles of water from the fridge and handed Tyson one. "I think they forgot about it. It hasn't been visited in years. I think of it as my own personal hideaway. I haven't even shown my friends."

"So why me?" Tyson didn't accept my water and crossed his arms, leaning against the post of the doorway from the kitchen to the next room.

"Because I think you'll appreciate it." I walked past the dining room to the spacious living room and settled down on the sofa. "I love this place. I think in life, we all need our own model homes. Our own spots to breathe and be at peace. Our own sanctuaries. I've decorated some of this house on my own. I think this is what I wanna do—decorate spaces of tranquility."

Tyson sat across from me on the leather chair by the fireplace. He looked around and kept quiet for a moment.

"I'm sorry for what I said. It was wrong. I've never known anything about your family, and I should've assumed that they were the reason behind your sadness."

"I'm not sad," Tyson said.

"Not now, but when you were a little boy, I noticed how sad your eyes were."

He made a face. "I was never sad when I was with you."

His words made me smile. "True, but the happiness never quite reached your eyes." I shook my head, frowning. "I should've remembered that. When my parents told me you were coming to stay with us, they didn't say it was my friend Ty—" I omitted saying his full name and left off there. "They just said a boy from Lindenwood, and I freaked out."

"You're right," Tyson said. "About all of it. Everything you thought about me is right. I'm a criminal and a thug, and I don't belong here."

"It's not true. You're not like that."

Tyson snorted. "I've done things that could have me locked up."

He was just trying to scare me. He was mocking the way I'd judged him. "Did you steal that car?"

For a moment Tyson stared at me from his spot across the room. "If I'd stolen that car, Nandy, trust me, it would not be sitting in your driveway right now."

His words were vague, making me curious, but I was too afraid to ask for an explanation. "You're not like that."

"And why am I suddenly this pure guy to you?"

"Because I've seen you with Jordy, with my mom, with Erica. You're *not* that guy, and I was wrong to assume you were."

"Like I said, I don't belong here. I know how to survive Lindenwood. I'm going back."

"To die?" I asked.

Tyson covered his face with his hands, his shoulders rising and falling as he sighed. "Maybe that's my fate."

"Stop it!" I snapped. This wasn't a stranger or a thug; this was my childhood friend. Someone I'd cared about greatly. The Tyson from back then was gentle, quiet, and harmless. I refused to believe that, during the decade we'd been apart, he'd become a monster like the reputation of his town and home hinted. "You are not a bad person."

"Maybe I am!" he yelled, startling me. "Maybe you are all wrong about me. I'm sick of you all trying to make me out to be this good kid. Prophet, Lydia, Pops—*her*." His voice broke at the last mention. "I'm just like *them*."

"No you're not." I didn't know who exactly he was talking about, but from what I'd seen of him in my home, around my friends, he *was* a good kid.

"I've done things, Nandy. Things she never knew. Things that got her killed." He was shaking, and I forced myself to stay in my position, sensing he wasn't the type that reacted well to affection. "You wanna know why I was so sad all the time? I didn't have a dad like Parker. Mine was overworked and never satisfied. He beat the shit out of my mom and I never did anything to stop it. Sometimes he'd hit me, and I'd have to wear long sleeves to school.

"That was when I started going away with Pops while he cleaned lawns in Pacific Hills. That's when we met. Pops told me to keep quiet. He knew how angry Tyson could get, and he knew how he was no match. Tyson once beat him up, too."

It all fell into place. *Tyson* was his father, his adversary, and the reason he denounced his given name.

"I can barely remember a time when she was happy with him." Tyson cleared his throat and found a moment to think before speaking again. "I hated him, for so long I fucking hated him. I hated myself, because I wasn't good enough to protect her. She liked that I was going away with Pops during the day, and she liked the way I described you."

He'd told his mother about me?

"She did?" I asked.

"She would tease me about my crush, and I would act all hard, as if you had the cooties." He offered a quick smile before getting back to his story. "For a while, it was like things were okay. I would go with Pops, and she would stay home and try to make Tyson happy. But then one day I came home and she had a black eye. The next time Pops came around trying to take me with him, I refused. I couldn't be too far away from my mother, especially when I wasn't sure if any moment was going to be her last.

"I started hanging out with the boys in my neighborhood. Prophet was a teenager, but he basically taught us everything he knew about how to survive. I did some things to make money—things that would've disappointed my mother."

"Selling drugs?"

Tyson shook his head. "Something else." He stared down at the Persian rug, face impassive. "I wanted to save up enough to take her away or send her away. She used to tell me all the time that I deserved a good life."

"You do."

Tyson brought his attention to me, appearing irritated. "I hated when she said that shit. Why did *I* deserve a good life above her? I was becoming just like the boys she didn't want me hanging with, and she was just this good person."

"You were doing what you had to do to get out of there," I reasoned.

"It's what killed her!" he shouted, appearing hopeless. He stood from the chair and started pacing. "One day we stayed up talking about going away and never coming back. She said she was sick of living in fear, and she didn't want me to waste away. I told her I had money, and she didn't question where it came from. Prophet gave me a gun in case Tyson tried something. I kept it in my drawer."

He stared at nothing in the distance as the rest of the story was left hanging in the air.

"One night I came home from Prophet's house, and I heard her crying. He was beating her and dragging her through the house. He'd heard us talking, and he was confronting her. I tried to stop him, but he pulled out a gun—*my* gun." Tyson bowed his head. "He shot her. He shot me. He shot himself, and I watched her die."

Despite my attempts, tears leaked from my eyes, and I had to wipe them away more than once.

"I killed my mother, Nandy. If it wasn't for me—"

"No." I sniffled, realizing the facts, as ugly as they were. He had severe survivor's guilt. "It's not your fault. You had no idea that would happen. And you tried to save her, but your father got the better of you."

"If I hadn't put the idea in her head—"

"She needed a reason to leave, and you helped her. None of it is your fault." I stood and crossed the room to stand in front of him. "There was nothing you could do. Your father almost got you, but he didn't. Going back and becoming a real criminal would be letting him win and letting your mother down. You got a second chance, and that's what matters."

"Why not her?" he demanded. "Why me and not her?"

"Life is unfair, and blaming yourself and hating God is not going to bring her back. It's not your fault, and it's not on God—it was your father."

Tyson wasn't convinced. "She was all that I had. He took her from me. What do I have now? This fucking town? You didn't even want me here until I threw this at you. I have to go back, because at least they accept me and understand."

"Dying isn't the way," I said. "I messed up. I'm sorry for stereotyping you from the beginning. I feel like such a dickhead for it. I was wrong. You were my best friend, and I'm sorry. Don't go." I wiped away tears as I pleaded with him. "Going back isn't going to solve anything. Your mother was right—you deserve a good life. Let it be here. Okay, yeah, you're going to have to get used to some overly surgically enhanced Pacific wives whispering about you, and a lot of drunk girls throwing themselves at you, but it's not so bad."

My words managed to get a laugh out of Tyson as he calmed down. "Fuck, that sounds terrible."

"It is, and I hate every bit of the drama and gossip, but you know what, there's heart here, there's character here. Not all of us are so bad."

Tyson softened up just a little. "You really mean it?"

I wanted to touch him, to hug and hold him, but I was afraid he'd push me away. "Yeah, I do. I'm not that girl who judges people. The way I've been acting toward you isn't me, and I'm sorry. I got paranoid and stuck-up. I promise you, if you stay, you'll see the real, nice Nandy that I am."

Tyson sighed, walked to the fireplace and rested against the mantel. "I don't know, Nandy. I think about it all the time. I don't sleep without seeing her face. You can say it's not my fault, but I have to live with the fact that my scheme got my mom killed. I have to think about how she died by my gun. It ain't easy."

After all that he'd gone through, that was an understatement. On the outside, Tyson seemed so strong and intimidating, but on the inside, he was broken, hurting deeply. My heart ached for him, and I feared being in a new place wasn't enough. "I know it's been rough, but maybe you should see a therapist, to help you cope."

"Now you sound like Misty." Tyson waved me off. "Been there, done that."

"You just went through hell, and if you think you can manage the trauma on your own, you're so wrong. Shayne saw a therapist after her parents got divorced, and she hated it at first, but she said the best part about it was having someone willing to listen. What happened won't go away, but it'll be easier to live your life if you talk to someone."

Tyson slowly nodded. "Lydia wants me to write about it, to release the energy and transform it onto paper."

"You're in summer school anyway. Why not, right?"

He shrugged and sat back down in the leather chair. "This isn't going to be easy. Six months is a long time to fester in guilt and memories."

"You're not alone. You have my family, and you have me."

Tyson folded his hands and became quiet, seeming to ruminate on my words.

My cell phone vibrated and I dug it out of my pocket to find a text from Chad. I chewed my lip, feeling like it so wasn't the time to talk to my boyfriend.

Chad: You free?

Me: No, w/ Ty

Chad: Tonite then?

Me: We'll see

Chad: My parents are gone ;)

I looked up and found Tyson studying me.

"So, despite the decade, you remember me and our childhood?" he asked.

"Of course I do. As crazy as it sounds...I missed you." I wouldn't allow myself to be completely vulnerable, but that I would admit.

Tyson smiled just a little. "I missed you, too."

Emotion singed in my chest and I blinked to conceal this fact. "You don't have to say it because I did."

"I know that. I say what I mean. I was dealing with a lot of shit back then, and coming here, being with you, it was my escape. The one good thing I had besides my mom. I never forgot that. You were my Neverland."

Tears pooled in my eyes and I had to look away. For a second, I was seven years old again and my heart was clenching at his words. At one time, Tyson was my everything, and now he'd come back.

"You were my first kiss." And crush. And heartache when he'd disappeared.

"And now you've had plenty more."

I felt myself blush. "You must've heard about me and Warhol."

Tyson didn't deny it.

"That was a middle school thing. Once I got to high school it was all about Chad."

This caused Tyson to snort. "Yes, and how are things with the redheaded fuck boy?"

I scowled, disliking the nickname. "Chad's amazing. I love him. We've been together since freshman year."

"Oh yeah, I got that feeling last night, hearing all about your relationship." His sarcasm was palpable.

"Sometimes he's an ass, but he's not entirely bad."

"Hmmph, I guess he's worth the shit, then, huh?"

It felt like I could tell him about all the good things Chad had done for me, and Tyson would still look unimpressed. It didn't matter, though. I got what Chad and I had. It didn't matter if anyone else did. Erica thought Chad had too many asshole moments, Shayne didn't think we had enough spice, and Edi just thought Chad was *tedioso*. All of them were admittedly no experts on love or relationships. My parents liked Chad just fine, and his parents loved me. We were fine.

"Whatever," I said, getting past it. "Bottom line, I'm sorry for coming off like a whiny rich girl."

Tyson lifted a brow as if to challenge my statement. *"Like?"*

"Okay, that's well deserved. But, are you good? Will you stay?"

Tyson shoved his hands into his pockets, tilting his head to the side. "On one condition."

"Name it."

"You've gotta give me a list of who I can't hang out with."

After we got back from the model home, I went up to my room and lay out on my balcony, enjoying the warm sun against the bare skin of my back. Chad hated the idea of my sunbathing topless out in the open, but I loved the feel of the sun on my skin and the smell of my mother's roses from down below by our back patio.

For Chad's sake, I lay on my stomach as I texted back and forth with Shayne, setting up a beach date.

Knocking caught my attention and I looked over, discovering the sound coming from inside my room on my bedroom door.

"Come in," I said loudly.

The door opened and Tyson entered carrying a book. He joined me on the balcony, briefly looking out at our backyard before kneeling down to my level and handing me the book.

"It's one of my mother's favorites. It talks about Africa, and it's not as thick as *Roots*. Maybe you'll like it," he said.

Taking the book in my hand, I read its title. *The Color Purple*. If his mother loved it, then I would read it. "Great, I'll start it right now. Thanks."

Tyson stood up. "I'll let you get back to what you were doing."

He rose to go, and I fiddled with the book, feeling the urge to let him know once more. "Tyson."

He turned back to me.

"Ty," I restated, "I know you don't believe in God because of what happened. But maybe living here with us and being here this summer will help you start to believe in something."

Tyson peered out at the sky, watching nothing in particular. "Maybe."

11 | TRICE

It was noon and I was starving. Going down to the kitchen, I discovered Nandy at the island, chopping a cucumber with a big knife. She was doing it all wrong, making her slices too thick.

"Hey," she greeted me. "I'm heading to the beach with Shayne, figured I'd pack a salad."

I went behind her and took her hand to show her the proper way to get the slices just right.

"Okay, we get it, you're such a good cook, Master Chef." Nandy pretended to sound exasperated.

"Cucumbers taste better as hints," I told her.

"Where'd you learn to cook, your mom?"

"Yeah, she didn't want me being the type of guy who expected his girl to cook all the time." Not that Asiah had ever wanted to cook anyway. Her mother had really been the best in the kitchen.

"That sounds perfect. The only hot thing I can cook is toast. Thank God for takeout. Even Chad's family has a personal chef."

Life in Pacific Hills would take a lot of getting used to. Country clubs, chefs, and model homes. This wasn't my world.

Footsteps sounded in the hall, and I recognized Shayne's voice.

"Ugh, Nandy, Bryce is so becoming a problem for me. I get that we're neighbors, but it's just not going to happen. I mean, he has a beard, and I *so* do not do beards. I just keep imagining how weird it'd feel between my legs." Shayne came into the room as she finished talking. Once she noticed me, she bore a look of surprise but not a hint of embarrassment.

"Hey, Tricey," she said with a flirtatious smile.

O-kay, it was time to go.

"Hey, Shayne," said Nandy. "I see Bryce hasn't given up, or shaved, for that matter."

Shayne barely acknowledged Nandy's comment as she was busy staring at me. "You know, this is kinda cute. You two almost look like a couple." She gave Nandy a smile. "Hard to believe you're dating Captain Douchebag." She gave me a once-over. "And you're all alone."

"Hey," Nandy snapped. "Chad's not a douchebag. He's the sweetest guy I know."

I stepped from behind Nandy, agreeing to disagree on the status of her boyfriend.

Nandy peered at the clock on the wall before placing a lid on her Tupperware. "Let's get going, Shayne. I want to find a good spot before it's too crowded."

Shayne pouted. "Can we just wait a sec? Travis is out there with Matt."

"He bothering you?" I asked.

For a second I thought they were a perfect match. Travis had a knack for saying whatever the hell came to his mind, and Shayne was right behind him.

"She's afraid she's going to end up in his bed," Nandy informed me with a tired expression on her face.

"What?" Shayne frowned. "You know his reputation. The old guidance counselor totally slept with him and went insane."

"That's a rumor."

"Then why did she get divorced after she started giving Travis private sessions?"

Nandy opened her mouth but quickly shut it. "I don't know, but I'm sure it's a coincidence."

These kids were all fucking nuts.

I headed outside anyway, wondering if Travis had been bothering Shayne. At the party the previous evening, he'd been buzzing around and making good with everyone. No one seemed to have an issue with Travis. From the smile on his face and the way he greeted everyone, it was clear he was highly liked—that, and he was a floater.

Travis was out front with Matt, unloading a surfboard from the back of a Jeep Wrangler. He noticed as I approached and greeted me with a handshake, locking our fingers for a moment before letting go.

"'Sup?" he asked.

I lifted my chin. "What's up with you and Shayne?"

Travis looked to Matt, who shrugged. "Mancini? Nothing, you interested?"

"Definitely not."

"Shayne's been ducking Travis since freshman year." Matt clued me in. "The girl's an obvious beauty, but Trav's been good about it."

Travis's gaze flickered to the Smiths' house. "We just got back from surfing. We're about to hit the Crab Shack, you interested?"

I was hungry. "Sure."

Together we all got in Matt's Wrangler and took off for the Shack. From the first three songs that played on the radio, it was obvious Matt had a thing for country, something that was even less tolerable than Nandy's taste in music.

The Crab Shack was on the boardwalk, and, according to Matt, it was a hub for the local teens, offering more than just seafood, including varieties of burgers, pizza, tacos, and chicken. It even had an outdoor seating area for those who wanted to soak in the sun with their meals while they got a good view of the ocean.

The place was obviously popular, because I spotted Chad, Warhol, Ashley, and a few of Chad's friends sitting at a table outside.

"Fucking great," Travis muttered as we got out of the Wrangler.

"Be nice," Matt warned.

"Where's Ben?" I asked, noting that Matt's boyfriend was missing in action.

"His family likes to travel during the summer. We won't be seeing him until September when school starts."

"Sorry about that."

Matt shrugged. "We FaceTime when we can, but what else can you do?"

Matt led the way to Chad's table and greeted all the boys. Travis stood back with me and gave a poor attempt at a wave.

117

Chad examined me, studying me from head to toe. "Tyson, we meet again."

"It's Trice," Travis corrected.

Chad clearly didn't care. "Sit down, take a load off."

Travis sat on top of the table next to theirs, and I took a seat on the bench beside him.

"So, you're Nandy's new houseguest," said Chad.

"Something like that," I replied.

"How well do you know her family?"

"Nandy and I used to play together when we were kids."

"I bet she's different now, huh?" Ashley asked.

"She definitely wears a lot less clothes than she did back then." I thought of earlier when I'd given her my copy of *The Color Purple*. She'd been on her balcony topless and texting, acting as if it were no big deal when I came into her room. Besides that, from the moment we met, it had been obvious she was comfortable in her skin, from her bikinis to her small tees—not that I was complaining.

Travis snickered and held out his fist for me to pound.

Chad watched as we bumped knuckles, his eyes lifting to mine, his annoyance clear. "Just exactly how close were you two?"

"We were five, six, and seven. We were as close as kids could be. We just used to run around playing outside and stuff."

"And that's it?"

"That's what he said," Travis interrupted.

"I'm not talking to you, Catalano," Chad said.

"Well, I'm talking to you, and if he says they were just friends, they were just friends. Get off his nuts." The boys at the table fell silent as they faced Travis's direction.

One look at Travis had me taken back. I'd thought he was

just a joker who ran off at the mouth, but as I took in the hard expression on his face, the look in eyes, and the way his jaw was set, it was clear—Travis wasn't to be fucked with. His gaze bored into Chad, as if daring him to say something or stand up and do something.

And I'd thought I was the only one who found Chad to be a dick.

"Cool off, Trav." Matt was sitting between Ashley and some other friend of Chad's. With a look in Matt's direction, Travis stood from the table.

"I'm going to order," he said as he walked off.

Chad turned to me, giving me a smile. "Hey, man, I'm just trying to scope you out. My girl's never mentioned some long-lost friend before. Where you from?"

"Lindenwood."

His brows rose and his mouth made an O shape. "Gotcha."

Warhol, Ashley, and Matt were decent about where I was from, but Chad's friends all wore the same uncomfortable expression.

With the fresh smell of seafood in the air, the cool scenery of the beach nearby, and the warm sun beaming down on us, I wasn't in the mood for this shit. I stood up and followed Travis.

"Sorry about that," said Travis when I caught up. "Chad's always annoyed the hell out of me."

"No offense taken, he lost me at the bonfire."

Travis smirked. "Chad thinks he's God and we're all his faithful servants. Nandy can do better. He really thinks he's the shit since he bagged the hottest girl in school. What kind of name is Chad Bradley anyway?"

A shitty white-boy name.

If Nandy loved Chad, I didn't see the point in sticking our noses in her business.

I was about to reply when my phone rang. When I dug it out of my pocket, I was surprised to see Prophet calling.

"Something wrong?" Travis must've noticed the expression on my face.

"I'm about to find out." I stepped away from the line, going and leaning against the rail on the boardwalk and staring out at the ocean. "Yeah?"

"Hey, I'm sorry to be calling you," Prophet began, "but something came up."

"What happened?"

"Khalil's goofy ass messed up his ankle."

I knew where he was going, and I let out a sigh. "Oh yeah?"

"And I wouldn't be asking you this, but you're the only one I trust, and you know how Mexico don't like new drivers."

I hung my head. "Yeah."

"We need a driver for the car he picked up."

It was too good to be true. Of *course* I would be forever tied to Lindenwood. Prophet was right, though—I knew he was calling only because of Khalil's screwup. Our crew was too tight-knit for him to ask for outside help.

Even if I was more than likely going to do the run, I'd be an idiot to take the job blindly.

"What's the make and model?" I asked.

"You're looking at…at least nine hundred. It's a Camry."

Nine hundred wasn't bad, but just how hot was the car? "How many days are on it?"

"Three."

"Was it a crank or a lift?"

"He lifted it. This is a clean run, Trice. Khalil definitely messed up. He's not getting anything, this is all on you."

Even if I was taking the risk, I wasn't taking the entire profit. Khalil was like a brother to me. Mishap or not, he was getting a cut.

I faced the boys. Ashley was telling some story and the others were listening. Travis was getting some girl in a bikini's number, and then there was me. The outsider who just didn't belong.

I didn't need the money, but it went beyond that. This was where I came from. This was where everyone accepted me. This was who needed me.

This was family.

"I'm in," I confirmed.

12 | *Nandy*

The beach was peaceful after all the chaos.

I'd finished *The Color Purple*, while in between her own reading, Shayne had gawked at boys. She was reading *The Notebook*. Despite her flirtatious habits, Shayne was very much a romantic.

"Ugh, so good," Shayne said as she bookmarked her page. She'd read the book numerous times, so much almost all the pages bore creases from being dog-eared so much.

I was quick to agree. "This was great."

Shayne stood and put on her sunglasses.

We started gathering our things just as Kyle Frogge walked by. He was dressed all wrong for the beach in a flannel top and T-shirt, as well as jeans and sneakers. Under one of his arms, he was carrying a Stephen King novel.

Kyle wasn't in our group, but I liked to think that summer made everyone fair game. Most of us lived in the same development anyway, and we'd ridden the same bus to elementary and middle school together as well. Shayne lived around the corner, Erica lived a few blocks away, Edi lived two houses down, and Kyle lived down the block from me.

So I smiled. "Hey, Kyle."

Kyle offered me a tight-lipped smile and a wave, and then he looked to Shayne. "Hey, Shayne."

Shayne was busy packing, barely paying Kyle any attention. "Froggie," she at least said.

Having failed yet again at gaining Shayne's attention, Kyle frowned and turned back to me. "Hey, Nandy."

"Enjoying the beach?"

Kyle studied our surroundings. "Mostly. I'm really just Sasha's ride."

Sasha Frogge, his younger sister. I remembered hearing one of the gossiping moms mention her a few times during the school year, saying how she'd fought her way onto the boys' soccer team at the local middle school. I thought that was admirable.

Kyle didn't play sports, and when I thought about it, I couldn't figure out what it was that he did. Why didn't I know Kyle Frogge better? Even though I didn't, I felt sorry for the way he practically worshipped the ground Shayne walked on when she clearly didn't notice. Kyle wasn't hideous. Beneath his shaggy dark hair, he was cute, adorable even. Sure, he wasn't as buff as some guys. Even tall as he was, he was more average than anything. But that was okay. From what little I did know, Kyle was always polite and courteous to everyone. Extra brownie points there, especially when I thought of how rude some guys could be, namely guys like Dickie Carter and Oliver Stein.

That take-charge part of me was almost tempted to play matchmaker.

"How's she doing?" I asked of his sister.

Kyle shrugged and looked in the distance to where a young blonde girl with long curls in her hair stood talking with a boy carrying a surfboard. Sasha was appropriately dressed in a bathing suit with a shawl tied around her waist. "She's making the most of her summer."

From the way Sasha was smiling at the surfer, I got a sense of déjà vu and nostalgia. "She just discovering boys, huh?"

Kyle grimaced. "Unfortunately."

I knew it all too well. Jordy had a crush on Manuela Gómez, and I suspected that half the time he spent at the Gómezes' house wasn't just to play with Hector.

"Don't tell me you're that overly protective brother," I teased.

"Not really. Sasha's the favorite. Anything she wants, she gets."

"Jordy has our parents wrapped around his fingers. I know the struggle."

Shayne came and stood beside me. "At least you're not an only child." The smile on her face showed how disinterested she was in continuing the line of conversation. "Can we go now?"

I bid Kyle farewell and grabbed my things, then led Shayne back to my car. Inside I cranked up the radio and drove toward Shayne's house. When we hit a red light, a familiar song came on and I reached down to turn it off.

"No, just let it play. Today was nice, okay?" Shayne held

her hand out and blocked me from turning from "Say It Ain't So." Back when she was Shayne 2.0 and her parents got divorced, and her mother was sent to rehab for the first time, Shayne had locked herself in her room and listened to the Weezer song on repeat for hours. I could never hear the song without thinking of how depressed she'd been and how scared I'd been for her.

I let the song play as Shayne began to sing along. Soon I joined her and agreed that the MoZella cover was just as good and a little more intimate from a girl's perspective.

At Shayne's house, we were barely in the front door before we bumped into Shayne's father. He seemed to be in a hurry and almost didn't acknowledge us.

"Daddy, hey," Shayne said as she placed her hands on his chest to stop him from colliding with us.

Mr. Mancini lifted his head from his phone and offered us both a smile. "Evening, girls, coming back from the beach?"

"Yeah." Shayne's voice fell flat as her gaze landed on his briefcase in his hand. "I thought we were having dinner tonight?"

Mr. Mancini gave her a sympathetic smile. "Can't, Bambi, duty calls. Rain check?"

Shayne pouted. "This is the fifth time you've canceled, Daddy."

"You still have Marge."

I winced. He seemed blind to the fact that Shayne despised her stepmother. She always had.

"I don't want to have dinner with her, I want to have it with you," Shayne whined.

Mr. Mancini appeared helpless as he glanced at me and then back to his daughter. "I'll make it up to you, I promise. Hey, take the AmEx card and go wild, it's on me." Instead of continuing the conversation, he placed a kiss on her forehead and quickly went around us and down the front path to his car.

Shayne turned, her luscious lips trembling as she watched her father pull out of the driveway to go back to the hospital.

"Doesn't he have a vacation coming up?" I asked, trying to find something to take the hurt from her face.

Shayne's sadness morphed into anger. "Yeah. He's spending it in Cancún. With *her.*"

Instead of going inside, Shayne parked herself on the front step and rested her head in her hands.

I sat beside her and rubbed her back. "He'll make good on his word. He promised."

Shayne looked into the distance, shaking her head. "Wouldn't it be nice to just run away? Go to Paris and experience the people and French stuff?"

"I don't know, Paris is cliché, Shayne." I'd never cared for Paris or French. I'd always wanted to learn Spanish and visit the Caribbean islands. Something about the beautiful beaches and the tropics made me want to run around naked. Most girls in PH wanted to see Paris and talked about it all the time at Cross High. Me, I wasn't interested.

Shayne nodded dejectedly. "I guess you're right."

Together we went inside and watched *Clueless*, one of Shayne's and my favorite movies. And then we watched *Legally Blonde*, another favorite of ours.

As much as I wanted to stay for dinner so that Shayne wouldn't be alone with her stepmonster, I had to go home because my parents had instigated a rule of us eating together as a family to get Tyson acquainted with routine. Really, I knew this would last about a month before my mother started missing dinner due to work and my father got something at the office. But I applauded their effort to try to make our home all idyllic for Tyson.

Except, when I stepped into the dining room, only Jordy was there setting the table as my father helped my mother unload the takeout at the island in the kitchen.

"What's going on?" I asked, noting Tyson's absence.

"Trice said some friends needed help back home, so he won't be joining us for dinner tonight," my mother explained.

My father made a face. "I'm going to have a talk with him when he gets back."

"Why?" I wanted to know.

My father faced me. "Nothing to worry about. He just doesn't look me in the eye and his attitude is cold."

My mother frowned. "He looks me in the eye."

He looked me in the eye as well. Not trying to get too deep, I said, "Maybe it's a personal thing. With the way his dad was…maybe it's hard for him to get close to males."

My parents glanced between each other, as if surprised that I knew of Tyson's past.

My father went back to unpacking the takeout. "Perhaps that's something to take into consideration."

"I wish you'd warned us about what happened to him." I was old enough to know this about Tyson.

My mother sighed. "It was hard for us to digest, and it didn't feel right telling something so personal about him to you and Jordy. It's Trice's story, and I see that he felt comfortable enough to tell you."

"It's nice to see you opening up to each other," my father agreed. "Why don't you go wash up for dinner?"

On the way out of the room, I noticed Jordy looking at me with approval. Some of my friends wouldn't have cared how their younger siblings viewed them, but in Jordy's eyes,

I wanted to be the best older sister I could be. He'd been right earlier to call me out about Tyson, and I was glad for it.

I didn't make it to wash up for dinner. Instead, when I saw the light on and the door ajar, I headed to Tyson's room.

He was inside, with his back to me and his shirt off as he went through a bag on his bed. From my stance in the doorway, I got a glimpse of how muscled and toned his body was. Though it was only a view from the back, I saw that his dark brown skin was void of any tattoos. My breathing hitched in my throat; Tyson *did* work out a lot.

He must've felt me watching, because Tyson turned around and stared at me, a questioning brow lifting.

Caught, I blushed as I stepped into the room. "My parents said you were leaving."

Tyson said nothing.

Not that I was paying attention, but the view from the front wasn't half bad, either. Again, I found his skin vacant of tattoos and his chest showing plenty of muscle. I didn't admire his build for long before taking notice of something on his right shoulder. It looked as if he'd been burned. The wound wasn't too big, about the size of the pad of my thumb, and it was then that I realized it was the bullet wound.

Moving automatically, I went closer to him and inspected it. My hand shook in front of me as I watched myself reach out and touch it. Tyson closed his eyes, wincing underneath my touch. I took in his handsome face, feeling terrible for what he'd been through. Drawing my gaze back to the wound, I found myself leaning closer and placing a kiss on it, as if that could make it go away or be better. By some instinct, I knew it was an exit wound, and I went around and placed a kiss on the other side, too.

Funny thing about exit wounds: they were such a paradox.

Sure, the bullet exited the body, but its path left a scar, a lesion, a memory of its existence, forever becoming one with that person and never letting them go, permanently embedding itself in that person's worst nightmares—or so I thought.

"They're my tattoos of that night," Tyson said as I came back around and stood in front of him.

I knew exactly what he meant. "I'm sorry you had to go through that."

Tyson pulled a shirt over his head, covering the wound. "Shit happens."

I held out *The Color Purple.* "I finished it at the beach."

He accepted the book and placed it in another bag he had on the floor. I wanted to ask him why he hadn't unpacked, but I left it alone.

"So, where are you going?" I took a shot and asked.

"Lindenwood."

"What for?"

Tyson looked over at me speculatively. "Why?"

"Just curious."

"I'm helping some friends out."

My gut told me he was up to no good. First he spent the night there, and now another trip back? "Doing that thing you used to do for money?"

Tyson didn't hold my gaze, and I knew I had my answer.

"Ty—Trice—"

He held his hand up. "Just call me Tyson."

"But you hate it."

He leaned against his desk, folding his arms across his chest. "Not so much when you say it. It reminds me of when we were kids, when things weren't so bad and I was kinda happy. I was always *Tyson* with you."

His words touched me, but they didn't distract me from

the matter at hand. "You can't go back there. All that's waiting for you is trouble."

His mind was made up. "I've gotta do a favor for someone, Nandy. I'm not really worrying about what could happen."

"Why not?"

"I have nothing to look forward to either way. I can take it or leave it. I'm doing this because someone needs my help."

I hated that he was so apathetic about whether he lived or died or ever got better. I hated that he'd given up on himself.

"Tyson, you have to believe in something."

He wasn't hearing me. "No, I don't. I'm just going with the flow. You won't change my mind. I'm leaving."

"What exactly is it that you're doing?"

"Going for a ride."

Vague, much?

"I—I could tell my parents."

"Even if I believed you'd do that, do you really think that would stop me?"

"What makes you so sure I won't tell?"

"Because you just got back on my good side, and I don't think you wanna piss me off again." His hard eyes challenged me to argue, and I conceded.

Looking down at my hands, I said, "What's the point of this ride?"

"I'm dropping something off and collecting a fee, but it's not about the money. A friend of mine can't do it, and I have to take his place. He'd do it for me."

"You won't get hurt, will you?"

"More than likely no."

"Promise me this is the last time you'll do something like this?"

"I can't do that."

"Why not?"

"Because if they need me, I'm there, no question."

"You can't ever prosper with one foot still in the streets, Tyson!" His carelessness was beginning to aggravate me.

He smirked. "'Streets'? You've been watching BET, huh?"

There was no use in arguing; he was bound to go regardless of what I said. Stupid Lindenwood, trying to bring him down with it.

I glanced at the bag on the floor, the one filled with other books.

"Do you consider yourself black or African American?" I wondered.

Tyson squinted and scratched his head. "*Black-American*, I guess, why?"

"You seem so gung ho about Africa."

"It's different. You can meet a Mexican or Asian who'll speak English and know all of our pop culture, but still have their hands in their roots. Us, we've been here for centuries, and little by little our touch with Africa has been lost. Africa is a continent. I can't even begin to imagine which country or nationality I'm from. We're American, as is our 'black culture' and history."

I liked his answer. Even though my parents had shown me movies like *Roots* and I'd learned about slavery in school, I didn't feel or like the term *African American*, because, like Tyson had said, nothing about me or my family was African. We were very much Black American and didn't practice any native customs or share links to the motherland. Edi and the Gómezes would go to Mexico on trips, and their household was very bilingual. Not to mention there was Erica and the Mandarin she would often speak around her cousins Geordan and Xiu.

"I do think it's nice that you're taking Jordy to Thailand. I like and respect that about your parents," Tyson went on.

"Do you ever wanna see some of Africa?"

"I don't have a passport, and I've never been on a plane," Tyson admitted. "But I guess it would be nice. Maybe I'd feel something. I don't do a lot of that these days."

"Feel?"

He shook his head.

It hurt to know that he felt empty. It was probably why the idea of dying didn't bother him. In his eyes, with his family dead, he had nothing left. He was a nonbeliever, someone in need of faith and hope.

I only hoped the summer wouldn't fail him and he wouldn't fail himself by continuing on the dark path he was following.

Tyson stood up from his desk and settled his gaze on me. "If I don't come back—"

I held my hand up and stopped him. "You will, or else."

He gave a soft smile. "Nice to see your ass is still bossy."

I smirked. "In my recollection, you seem to like this bossy ass."

With a quick flicker of his eyes measuring me out, Tyson said, "Yeah, I do."

His confession made my insides hot, and I couldn't fight my smile. "Well—"

"Nandy?" I recognized my boyfriend's voice as he called to me from the first floor.

Tyson glanced out his bedroom door and again he smirked. "I've gotta go."

He led the way down to the first floor, where Chad stood poised to climb the steps. At the sight of us together, he stopped short and took a step back to make way for us to enter the foyer.

"What's up?" Chad asked as he looked between Tyson and me.

"I'm going out," Tyson briefly offered before stepping around Chad.

"Lindenwood?" Chad continued.

"That'd be right."

"Oh." Chad bobbed his head. "Maybe you could take… Travis with you. He could stand some *realness*."

It was a known fact throughout Cross High that Chad and Travis didn't see eye to eye. Chad was what one would call the head honcho, but Travis was never fazed by Chad's popular status or ranking at Cross. Sometimes he'd do or say things just to piss Chad off, and Chad always took the bait. It was a stupid masculine thing that I never cared to take part in.

Tyson rolled his eyes. "Travis would be fine in Lindenwood."

"Oh? Is that so?" Chad didn't seem so sure.

"Real recognizes real in the 'Wood. Travis doesn't strike me as the bullshit type. He doesn't seem to scare easily either, so he'd be fine."

Chad didn't seem satisfied with this answer. "Well, good for him."

Tyson returned to me. "If—"

"Just come back, okay?"

Tyson nodded and slipped out the door, leaving me in the foyer with my boyfriend.

"What was that about?" Chad asked from behind me.

"Nothing." I stared at the floor. "He just has something to do."

"Should I have gone with him?"

"No."

Chad turned me around and smiled at me, reaching out

and touching my cheek. "Things are going to be real interesting once the school year starts."

"I know."

"He needs to know who's in and who isn't around here. Hanging with certain parties could ruin his reputation."

Travis Catalano wasn't part of our circle. He was a charming guy with a great face and smile, elements he used to lure people in. But when it got down to it, those who were wise knew to stay away from Travis. His I-Don't-Give-a-Fuck attitude often got him in trouble and some girl hurt. That and his frequent arguments with guys like Chad led to fights. Chad put up with Travis due to Travis's friendship with Matt and Ben. Both were on the lacrosse team with Chad, and that made Travis tolerable—if barely—by association.

I patted my boyfriend's chest. "Let's just see how the summer turns out, okay?"

He shrugged. "I missed you, figured I'd stop by."

My parents were fond of Chad, and with Tyson skipping out on dinner, I was sure they'd be more than happy to have Chad over. "Good, let's get to dinner, I'm starving."

13 | TRICE

It was nothing to go back to Lindenwood. Prophet and Khalil needed me, and there was no hesitating on my part to help out.

At the Crab Shack, Travis had asked what was up and if I needed his assistance. When I gave a quiet shake of my head, he left it alone and told me to "handle my business" before switching the subject. Warhol, Ashley, and Matt had joined us, and it hit me that there were definitely cliques established. Chad had his group, one Travis was clearly not invited into— not that he gave a fuck. Travis seemed to stick close to Matt. As Warhol and Ashley joined us, it was clear that they were more comfortable with Travis.

For a moment, I allowed myself to wonder how things

were at Cross High. Warhol and Ashley played football and didn't care where I was from. Matt and his boyfriend both played lacrosse with Chad but didn't quite seem up his ass like the others. Like Travis, Matt and Ben seemed to do their own thing. At least, that was the vibe Matt gave me. And then there was Travis, self-confessed trouble, yet he was in the marching band.

I liked the heterogeneity of Travis's group more.

Not that it mattered. As I pulled up to Prophet's house and parked, I knew I wouldn't be in Pacific Hills long enough to get comfortable or for its residents to get used to me.

The door opened before I could reach the porch steps, and the boys piled out of the house, but to my surprise, Asiah was with them.

Prophet met me first, placing his hand on my shoulder. "Five minutes."

The boys hung around the porch while I stood back where I was, staring at Asiah for the first time in six months. Nothing had changed much about her appearance. She was still casual in a simple T-shirt and jeans and a fresh pair of kicks on her feet. The ends of her dark hair were still dyed blue from the time she'd wanted to do something different. Even in the night, and after so much time, everything about her called to me. Her beautiful face, her mocha skin, and her petite figure.

It had been too long.

There was a small smile on Asiah's face as she came over and stood in front of me, hugging her arms around herself. Even after so much time, she knew not to just come out and touch me.

When I'd been shot, we were off-again. Before that night, I'd told her I needed space to get things together for my mother and me. She hadn't taken it well, deeming me a coward for not letting her help me. That a real man was one who knew he couldn't do it all on his own and wasn't shy to go to a woman for help.

I'd just wanted my mother to be safe and hadn't had the energy to focus on a relationship.

"So, I heard you got a new girlfriend," Asiah announced.

I knew she was referring to Nandy, and I knew Pretty, Money, or Khalil had blabbed.

"Oh, don't blame them," Asiah continued. "Tasha told me all about her."

"It's cool now," I said.

Asiah lifted a brow. "She pretty?"

We both knew my answer to the question and the rest of the inevitable questions that would follow.

Yes, Nandy was pretty, but she wasn't my type.

Asiah was my first and only. All my friends, excluding Prophet, thought it was better to mess around with more than one girl, but it wasn't like that for me. Asiah was the only one I'd ever attempted to let in, who meant more to me than just some random. Though we never got there—I was never able to fully share the extent of Tyson's dominance and cruelty. I'd told her he was strict, and though she'd pushed for more information, I hadn't revealed the truth. I owed her more than what I was giving her, another reason I'd let her go. Asiah was down from day one, and I knew she'd do more than take a bullet for me. That was why I'd always stayed loyal after we broke up, because Asiah was too real to be easily replaced.

So no, Nandy wasn't my new girlfriend. It had been…

I stopped to recall the moment in my bedroom when she'd pressed her soft lips to my scar. I'd known what she was trying to do, and I was grateful for it, not that it had worked. The damage wasn't there. The irrevocable ties to feeling again weren't where I'd been shot but were somewhere deep in my heart, my mind, and my soul. No amount of kisses could fix what was broken. The bullet had flipped my world upside down, and there was nothing to be done about it.

Besides, Nandy had Chad, and even if she hadn't, she'd changed. I couldn't be with a prissy girl from the Hills.

"She's just an old friend," I said.

Asiah accepted this. "I thought I was going to have to make a trip down there to let her know what's up."

"You'd do that?" It was a stupid question. Of course she would. In another life, I would let myself believe she was in love with me, and maybe, just maybe before that night, I could've loved her back.

"You never called," Asiah went on. "I waited and waited, but you never called. I get that it was tough, but I was worried."

"I wanted to be dead. I *am* dead."

She bit her lip and looked elsewhere, shaking her head. "I hate what he's done to you, what he did to you from the start. He's the reason you never let me in."

"Doesn't matter now. Things are different."

"Yeah, you're there, living all 'lifestyles of the rich and famous.'"

"More like lifestyles of the rich and *fucked up*."

Asiah smiled, though I could tell she didn't want to. "Do you like it there?"

Now that my beef with Nandy was settled, the Hills were decent. "It's okay. It's just for five months."

"Good. I'll be here."

"Five months is a long time to wait, Asiah."

"I've already waited six months, what's five more?"

Behind her, I caught Read stealing glances her way.

I wasn't in the mind to be with her, to make her happy and to feel with her, but she was a good girl, one who deserved someone whole and together.

Reaching out, I pulled her into a hug and held her close for just a moment.

Maybe, just maybe, I could've loved her.

Whenever we stole a car, we'd drive it to the Garage, a spot in town where Prophet had the hookup. The owner let us store our cars there until we were ready to make the run. From the Garage, we all drove uptown to Mexico's shop. I think his real name was Carlos, but since he spoke a lot of Spanish and employed a lot of Mexicans, we had taken to calling him Mexico, a nickname he had taken a liking to.

Since I was fourteen we'd been stealing cars together and driving them to Mexico's chop shop. The profit always varied, depending on the make and model of the car, but the business was quicker than that of a regular job.

Prophet had taught us the trade and its rules. We were never to steal a car twice from the same area within a two-month period, we were not to resort to bashing in a window or doing anything stupid to draw attention to ourselves, and we were not by any means allowed to make a run alone. We were a family, and when we went to Mexico, we went as a unit.

Usually, we stole cars about twice a month, although sometimes went a while without it. The easy thefts were called lifts, when we were able to find the keys and just cruise. Otherwise they were called cranks, where we'd have to use tools to get the job done. We stole from all types of areas throughout Los Angeles. Sometimes we'd venture to other cities or towns if we were itching for a good steal. Sometimes we'd pair up and split the profit, and others we'd all steal our own car and store it at the Garage and wait for the day to make the run.

Prophet had told me Khalil had cased a parking garage and found his car sitting and collecting dust, with the doors unlocked and a spare set of keys in the visor. Having Khalil's car be an easy steal made the idea of accepting Prophet's request not too hard at all.

Together we rode in an inconspicuous van to the Garage, and all the while, Money and Pretty sat inspecting their guns. They always carried heat with them on their runs, because we all knew in our situation, if we got caught by the police, there was only one way out. For us, going to jail was a death sentence. Nobody wanted to be locked up, so why not go out your own way instead?

I didn't bother with a gun. I never had, thinking that my going out in a hail of gunfire would upset my mother more than my stealing to begin with. Now that she was gone, I still didn't feel right about it.

At the Garage, we stood inside in a circle with the doors closed, all facing Prophet as he began to speak. Both Money and Pretty smoked on blunts, as they did before each run, never knowing if it'd be their last.

"Okay, let's go over the rules," Prophet began. It was a part of tradition: before each run we laid down the ground rules. "No loud music, no driving above the speed limit, no smoking, no personal items—" he turned to Pretty and Money "—and no drag racing."

Money and Pretty both exchanged grins.

The rules were pretty much for them anyway. Read, Prophet, and I always lay low. Khalil went with the flow, or whatever Pretty and Money were in the mood for. Sometimes when they knew they had a good car and were about to make a good profit, Money and Pretty liked to race to Mexico's, calling out bets to see who could get there first. Khalil would join in while the rest of us would shake our heads. But if they got caught, they knew to keep quiet. Death before disloyalty.

"Act natural," Prophet concluded.

One by one we turned to one another and did our group's handshake, hooking our thumbs together and forming a W with our hands, symbolizing where we came from and where we'd more than likely die.

Prophet opened the garage door and gave the go ahead to start for Mexico's, where he'd catch up.

I got in the Camry and drove off. We were allowed to listen to music, but I wasn't in the mood. Even though some would say the silence could drive you insane, I craved it. I'd spent six months being examined by doctors and therapists. Six months of steady buzz about the shooting had done me in. Pops had never asked about it in great detail; he'd told me he was sorry for my mother and for how he'd failed Tyson. I didn't want Pops's apology. He had a good heart and was an honest man; it wasn't his fault his own son had turned to shit.

The second therapist I saw asked if I wanted a family of my own someday, and when I'd told her no, she'd asked if I was afraid of turning into my father. I'd never feared that growing up. My mother used to tell me that someday, when I had a wife and kid of my own, my job was to do better than Tyson and be a better man regardless of whether I had a family or not.

I sat back as I continued up to Mexico's shop, almost laughing. Tyson was a monster, but he never stole.

No, I didn't want a family. I'd seen what it was like to love someone and to lose them. I knew what it was like to feel empty and emotionless. Having a family required a connection and, after losing *her*, I wasn't sure I could connect ever again.

I always drove the scenic route to Mexico's shop, taking less of a chance of being spotted by the local police. I was at Mexico's twenty minutes later just seconds behind Read, soon followed by the rest of the guys.

By day, Mexico ran an auto shop specializing in fixing cars and/or customizing them to someone's liking. At night, he'd take in stolen vehicles and chop them up for profit. He made good money, enough to where one look at him, and we knew he never missed a meal.

We stood outside our cars, watching the heavyset Mexican come down from the second floor of the shop, where his office was. He was dressed in his usual light blue jumpsuit with his long, dark hair matted under a trucker hat. A lit cigarette hung in the corner of his mouth, and as he came closer, he appeared jubilant.

He came to a stop a few feet in front of us and took us all in. Money and Pretty rolled their eyes, tired of the bull and ready for the pay.

Mexico stood with his arms open wide. "Ah, my five favorite *hermanos*, come to drop off more presents." He lifted his chin at me once he eyed us all over. "Long time no see, where's the other one?"

He was talking about Khalil. Of our group, Khalil and I were the only two with dark skin, while the rest ranged from brown to golden in Pretty's case. Mexico being Mexico he thought Khalil and I were related due to this common trait, and assumed I would be the one to know where he was; I ignored his ignorance.

"He got injured, couldn't make it," I said.

Mexico sucked deeply on the cigarette before letting out

smoke through his nostrils. "That's too bad. I heard he got me something good, too. The last car he gave me was a little dinged up, didn't make much off it."

I examined the Camry, knowing Khalil had done good with the steal.

Mexico liked to bullshit for just a bit before getting down to business. He gathered his clipboard and inspected all the cars and made comments on what would bring in customers and what was useless. In the end, he got out the cash and paid each of us our car's worth. Just as Prophet had guessed, I'd made an even nine hundred.

Standing back with Prophet, I counted out five hundred dollars and handed it over.

"Make sure Khalil gets this, okay?" I asked.

Prophet pocketed the money. "This won't happen again."

I shrugged. "You need me, call."

"You've got a pretty nice setup over there. This was just a one-time thing. Next time, we'll wait it out."

"I'm coming back," I told him. "I'm not staying there forever."

"The girl will get used to you."

"Nah, it's not even that. We squashed all that. This is where I belong."

Prophet's disdain for my determination to return was palpable. "You could live a better life than this."

"Maybe I don't want a better life."

"You're talking crazy. If I could have a good life without doing this, if I could take my mom, Gerald, and Cherish away, if I could picture Rain growing up safe, I would take whatever opportunity I had. This place ain't it for you, Trice." Prophet peered at the others, where Money and Pretty were counting their loot and where Read was standing back and waiting for us to go. "We've accepted our fate here. You died here already—don't let it happen again. Go, be happy. That is what she would've wanted."

He got me there, knowing that I couldn't argue against him. My mother would've wanted me happy in Pacific Hills. She would've wanted me to make the most of my opportunity for a better life. She would've wanted me to make something of myself and let her rest in peace.

And for that I didn't say anything. I went outside and waited for the others, to get in our stashed car and drive back down to the Garage and then get back in the van and go back to Prophet's house, where we'd separate for the night.

Parker was up when I got back to Pacific Hills. It was a little past eleven, and I met him on my way in the door. He was probably going up to bed by the way he was dressed, in a T-shirt and pajama bottoms.

He took a look at the clock on the wall and drew his gaze back to me. "Everything all right?" he asked, studying me.

For me, it was easier to trust a girl, or a woman, before a man. I knew Parker wasn't a bad guy, but my guard was up, and it probably would always be. Max approached me with care, and Parker did as well, but he wasn't fake about his intent to raise me like one of his kids. I wasn't sure I wanted to be told what to do or be bossed around by him. I wasn't sure I wanted to submit to anyone.

"Yes," I answered as I made for the stairs.

Parker reached out as I was passing, going and patting my back. He drew his hand away once he realized how stiff his touch made me. "I want this to work, Trice. I know what you've been through has made it hard for you, but I never intend to do that to you or my own family. I want you to be at peace here. I want this to be your home."

It would be home, if only temporarily. "Can I think about it?"

"Staying?"

"Yeah."

"I know you're here because of your grandfather's request, but I still think this could all work out."

"You do?"

"You were happy here once, as a child. Let yourself be happy again. Nandy will come around, and Jordy's always wanted a brother. Let us be your family."

"My interpretation of family is a little fucked up right now, Parker." Outside of Prophet and the boys, I just wasn't sure I could extend myself to be a part of another family.

"I won't pretend to know where you come from, or what it's like, but I do know it can get better."

"And how's that?"

"Because I like to believe after a person goes through that, it can't get any worse. Life's not that cruel."

I faced Parker, seeing an honest and good man in front of me. He was doing more than offering up his home and food for me; he was giving me a place in his family, a new shot at a place called home and a new future. In that moment, I let my guard down, knowing—hoping—that I wasn't wrong about him.

I held out my hand. "Okay."

Slowly Parker smiled as he shook my hand. "Welcome to the family."

Nodding, I turned and headed upstairs and into my room. I wasn't there for a second before I realized Nandy was in my bed, asleep, clutching what looked like a DVD in her hand.

I closed my door and made my way to her, angling my head to read the DVD's title.

"Oh hell no," I said as I realized what she was holding. When we were seven, she had this obsession with *You Got Served*, and she'd made me watch it hundreds of times, forcing me to watch her gawk at all the male leads in the film.

My words caught Nandy's attention and she leaned up, rubbing her eyes. "You came back."

"We're not watching that." I pointed to the DVD.

Nandy examined the film in her grasp. "You said you don't sleep much."

"I'd rather try than sit through that again."

A heavy look passed through Nandy's eyes, and she was silent for a moment. "Well, tell me about your night."

I rolled my eyes and kicked off my shoes before going and lying back on my bed.

"It was fine," I said.

Nandy lay on her side beside me, facing me. "Please don't do it again."

"I told you I can't promise that."

"Promise me you'll always come back, at least? I don't want you to leave again."

In her eyes, I saw hurt from before. "I don't know where I belong, Nandy."

"Tyson," she said softly, "please try."

I turned on my side and faced her. "I don't know how to try."

Nandy reached out and touched my cheek, caressing it and saying nothing.

I didn't like to be touched. I should've told her to stop and to leave my room. But I didn't, and we lay like that for a while before finally putting in the DVD.

14 | *Nandy*

Tyson didn't sleep. Twice I fell asleep in his room. The first time had been during the movie, and I'd woken up to see him scowling at the screen. The second time, the TV was off and he was reading beside me. That time, when I woke again, I stared up at him, wondering what it would take to change the cold expression on his face.

I scooted closer and wrapped an arm around him. He stiffened.

"Please stop," he said.

"Why?" It shouldn't have, but it burned to hear him reject me.

"Because I want you to."

"I can tell it's been a long time since you've been touched with affection."

"So?"

"So I'm giving it to you."

"Give it to Chad." He moved away, but not too far from my reach.

"You gotta let someone in, Tyson."

"I'm sick of being examined."

"Maybe you should just let the past be the past and let people in where you're at now in life."

Tyson stared at me, his hard eyes softening before he shook his head. "Damn, you're still bossy."

I started to smile, but then I noticed the time—eight fifty in the morning.

There was somewhere I had to be, somewhere I dreaded to be.

But that didn't take my mind off what Tyson might have done the night before.

"What'd you do last night?" I asked.

Tyson rolled his eyes. "Telling you would make you an accessory after the fact."

Now it was my turn to roll my eyes. "Technically I'm an accessory before the fact since I knew you were up to no good."

"Vaguely."

He wasn't going to tell me, and I couldn't stall what I had planned for the day.

I sat up and sighed. "I guess I better go get ready."

"What's up?" Tyson asked.

"I have to meet up with Mrs. Bradley, Chad's mom, to discuss cotillion and hang out."

"You don't get along?"

"It's not that, it's just…a lot, you know? I'm always worrying about something with her. It's nerve-wracking. Must be a Bradley thing."

"Chad makes you nervous?"

I ran a hand through my hair, wondering how to say what I was about to confess. Tyson sat beside me, so calm and quiet, letting me know he could handle whatever I had to say. Despite reconciling with him only two days ago, I felt comfortable enough to open up.

"Chad's sorta a big deal, as well as his family. I'm always worrying about how I look, stand, and come off," I confessed. "It all just keeps me on my toes."

"Chad must be an idiot, then," Tyson spoke up.

I chewed on my lip. "It's not that he does *it* or anything on purpose, really."

"Still," Tyson said, "I don't think I'd be happy if my girl wasn't sure of herself around me."

I was intrigued by the word he'd let slip out. "Your girl?"

Tyson dropped his gaze. "Not anymore, but, if we were together, I'd feel bad if I wasn't someone she could be herself with. You're already beautiful—you always have been—and I'm sure you're just fine articulating yourself as well as your posture."

I couldn't understand the thoughts swirling in my head. When we'd talked about Lindenwood, he'd mentioned his friends and how he hung around a bad crowd, but he hadn't mentioned a girl. It had been ten years—at seventeen, of course he'd moved on and explored girls, just as I'd moved on myself. I wondered if he loved her.

His words sank in, and I felt like he'd said, *beautiful*.

"Is she pretty?" I wanted to know.

"Who?" Tyson asked, appearing confused.

"Your girl."

His expression turned blank. "Yeah, very."

"Did you love her?"

"I could've." He sat back against his headboard and stared off. "One thing my mother taught me and showed me was how to love a person unconditionally. I could get caught for ditching school or doing something bad with one of the boys, and she would never lose her temper or look at me different. She'd lecture me, sure, but she loved me no matter what. I think if she knew what I'd been doing with Prophet, she'd still love me with her whole heart." He lowered his gaze to me. "That kind of thing is scary. I loved her just as much back, and she's gone now. It feels like I needed her to breathe, because I'm barely hanging on here, Nandy. I think I loved her more than life.

"I'm just not sure I can do that again with someone else. People our age switch partners like the latest trends. I don't wanna put my all into something just to end up back at square one alone, and I don't wanna risk hurting someone by not emotionally investing."

He started summer school on Monday, and I prayed Lydia would talk to him more. He needed therapy just as bad as Shayne had. It wasn't right to be cold and detached from people. I admired his strength in telling me the truth, that he was afraid to love another person and to lose them or hurt them. I admired that a lot.

I stood from the bed and stretched. "If you ever need a place to go, if you're lost or in trouble, just know that the model home is there for you, too. I keep a spare key under the mat on the back patio."

Tyson nodded. "Maybe you should show Chad one day."

His repeated rejection stung deep in my chest, but I tried to let it go, unsure why it even burned to begin with. "Why?"

"You should see the look on your face when you're there. You're so comfortable and confident, especially when you talk about decorating for a living. Maybe if he saw you like that, it would help."

I was too embarrassed to tell him that showing Chad the model home could backfire. Sure, Chad might like and respect it, but he might want to take advantage of it and use it as a place to have sex or to party. I didn't want to risk finding out. It was my sanctuary, my place for peace.

"Maybe if you tell your girl how you feel, it'll help," I said.

"I don't think so. She can do better."

"What's better than you in Lindenwood?"

Tyson appeared thoughtful. "You'd be surprised."

I squeezed his hand. "I hope you try, Tyson. Not for you, but for your mom. I don't think she'd want you to give up. I think some of the things she loved most about you were your strength and determination. If you try, you can make it here and be happy and live. But it's all on you."

"I'll think on it," Tyson said, noncommittal.

"Good. Tonight we'll help you out a little bit. We're all going to the Hook. Maybe you'll come, too."

"The Hook? What's that?"

He was in for a treat. "Wait and see."

I was thankful Shayne was with me as we sat at a table with Mrs. Bradley and *Ms.* Ray. Edi had to babysit, and Erica hadn't been able to make it. Shayne and I knew Erica wasn't in the mood to get out of bed to talk with "a bunch of nosy gossips," as she liked to describe all the Pacific wives in our community.

Mrs. Bradley and Ms. Ray were organizing cotillion, and they were telling us about previous cotillions as we sat in the dining hall at the country club. I was nervous about debuting, but Shayne's excitement kept me going.

"Oh, I certainly hope Naomi was able to talk that girl out of debuting," Ms. Ray said between sips of her cappuccino.

Shayne turned to face me as I did the same. They were talking about Erica's cousin, Xiu Yee. She was our age and somewhat quiet, and also a little clumsy—once she'd spilled red wine all over herself at an all-white charity event. Unlike her older brother, Geordan, or Erica, Xiu wasn't as cool or outgoing. On weekends whenever Erica would deejay at a party or club event, Geordan and his crew of dancers would show up and do a routine, while Xiu would watch.

I frowned at Ms. Ray. If anyone deserved to debut, it was Xiu. Erica was only doing it because her mother was making her, and I was sure the same went for Xiu.

"The girl can barely hold eye contact. It's sad," Mrs. Bradley said in response. She shook her head and looked at us, smiling, but the smile didn't reach her eyes or appear warm. "At least you two will make us proud." She patted my hand, and even her touch felt cold.

"Daddy's excited," Shayne spoke up. "I really can't wait."

Shayne was the smartest of my friends, which for some outside of our circle was a surprise. While she wasn't a genius, she was far from ditsy or dumb. It was no wonder she was being honored for her academic achievement—that, and the community service she did with Erica and me during the school year. In Pacific Hills, you learned early that extracurricular activities were favored more than good grades. Together my friends and I organized school events, helped out at charities, and stayed on top of our grades. Cotillion was a graceful reward, one we'd definitely earned.

Mrs. Bradley turned to me. "It's a shame your mother couldn't tear herself away from work to be here."

It was a jab. My mother hated the Pacific wives and their judgment of her. Most women in Pacific Hills were housewives who spent their days at the club with friends and shopping, spending their husbands' money. My mother was the anomaly, choosing to work and get her hands dirty rather than sitting back and playing some cliché role while my father worked. My mother inspired me. I loved seeing her work, even if it meant less one-on-one time. I hated the wives for mocking her.

"She's developing an important project, but she sends her love," I said, forcing a smile. Under the table, Shayne squeezed my knee, and I reached out and squeezed hers back.

Ms. Ray adjusted her jeweled brooch. "Well, someday you'll marry a successful man, and you won't have to worry about missing out on social priorities."

"But then he'd be the one away all the time," Shayne said.

Mrs. Bradley gave her faux smile. "The price you pay these days. What else could you ask for in a partner but a hard worker, dear?"

"Oh, I don't care for much. Just as long as he makes me smile and laugh, I'm great," I said. My husband having a fancy career where he was away all the time didn't seem appealing. And what was I supposed to do all day if not work?

Mrs. Bradley cleared her throat, taking and bringing her mug to her lips as a sour expression briefly marred her face. "Well, that's cute and all, Nandy, but we mustn't think childishly. After all, you can't live on smiles and laughter."

I focused on my hands. "Right, I want a guy with goals and a career in mind, and great genetics for our children."

Mrs. Bradley perked up. "Much better."

I was being sarcastic. I suppose she hadn't caught that.

Mrs. Bradley faced me, appearing serious. "You must ask yourself, what can a boy do for me besides offer up a good time."

Ms. Ray tapped Mrs. Bradley on the arm and could barely contain her smile. "Remember last year, when Nicole Hudson said she aspired to be happy?"

They laughed before Mrs. Bradley said, "What a shame she wasn't able to debut."

A shiver ran down my spine. Of course, they had the power to knock me out of debuting.

Shayne squeezed my knee again, and I looked over, finding a scowl on her face and a pool of tears in her eyes. Her father had the type of job where he was always on the go, and she was never a priority for him. She hated it, and I could only assume how much the line of conversation was hurting her.

"Excuse me." Shayne stood up and beelined for the restroom.

Ms. Ray watched her go. "I wonder if Taylor will sober up enough to make it."

Mrs. Bradley smirked. "Doubt it."

It was as if they'd cut me with their words. How could they say those things? I was glad Shayne was gone, because if there was one thing that made her self-destruct, it was talk about her parents.

I opened my mouth, prepared to scream—

A hand came down on my shoulder, and I jumped and turned around to find Chad standing there.

He gave me a smile that erased my angst. He leaned down and kissed my cheek before going and doing the same to his mother.

"Good morning," he said to us all.

"Chad, what brings you by?" Mrs. Bradley asked.

He braced his hands on the shoulders of my chair and leaned his weight onto it. Having him behind me made me feel better. "I just had to stop by and ask Nandy something. It's important. I'm sorry to interrupt."

"Nonsense." This time when Mrs. Bradley smiled, it was genuine and full of love for her son. She turned the smile to me, and it was real. "Nandy and I were just planning your futures. Weren't we, Nan?"

I forced a laugh. "Yeah, watch out, Chad, she's got you working sixty hours a week."

"Sheesh, all work and no play, Mom?"

"That's what now is for." Her gaze was on me as she spoke. "Live while you're young, because once you're an adult, the fun's over. All work and no play."

My stomach felt on the verge of imploding.

I would rather be poor than stuck in a marriage with no fun or passion.

"But if you must speak to her, go on," Mrs. Bradley said.

Chad took my hand and led me out of the room, passing Shayne on the way. In the hall, he was quick to press me against the wall and kiss me. I giggled against his lips and rested my hands on his shoulders.

"Let's get the hell out of here," he said.

"Yeah?"

"I'm sure you could use the escape. We all know how neurotic my mom can be."

This was why I loved Chad Bradley. He'd come here just to rescue me from enduring more of his mother and her friend.

I wrapped my arms around his neck and kissed him again. "You saved me."

Chad smiled. "That bad, huh?"

"The worst."

"Well, let's go. We can watch that movie you love so much. Sound good?"

"Sounds perfect."

I sent Shayne a text, telling her to fake an emergency so she could escape as well—no one deserved to go it alone with those two ladies—and walked away with my savior.

Half an hour later, Chad and I were in his bedroom, lying back watching something on the large flat-screen mounted on the wall. In Chad's arms, I felt safe. It definitely beat suffering through Mrs. Bradley's torture.

Chad held me close, and I lay back against his chest. It felt good. It felt comfortable. It felt like home.

"This'll all be over as soon as you debut," he said.

"No it won't, it'll only get worse. There'll be more events and more mentoring," I replied.

"I'm sorry she's like that. It's this town, you know?"

"I don't ever wanna be a Pacific wife, Chad. I wanna do more with my life than breed the next class of bitch."

He kissed my cheek. "You won't. You're going to be some hot career woman, and I'll mooch off of you."

I laughed. "And what do I get out of this?"

He wiggled his brows. "I'll compensate in my own special way."

I bit my lip and went back to looking at the TV. "We'll build our own future, something more than this."

He wrapped his arms around me and held me closer. "Got that right." It was quiet for a while until he spoke again. "Trice make it back in one piece?"

I thought of the illegal activity he might've participated in the previous evening. Whatever it was, it hadn't fazed him. "Yeah."

"He's gonna be okay, Nandy. He just needs some guidance."

"Tonight we're all going to the Hook, right?"

"That was the plan."

"Maybe he'll come out."

"Maybe."

Chad was a great guy, the best guy I knew. He had his flaws, but they made him more human.

"Can you look out for him, be his friend, and show him around?" I asked. At least Tyson couldn't easily scare another guy into backing down. I wanted him to warm up to Pacific Hills. I wanted him to belong.

Chad kissed me once more. "Sure thing."

15 | TRICE

I was in the middle of *Roots* when a knock made me look up. Parker entered through the open door.

"Doing some homework?" he asked.

"Yeah. The assignment's not due until the end of the semester, but I like the book."

Parker examined my room, his gaze stopping on my still-packed bags. "You getting along with the boys around here?"

I thought of Travis. "Yeah, a little."

"Good. Nandy was telling us she's going out tonight with her friends to the Hook. Maybe you should join them."

"Not interested."

"You sure? They've got great live music, alcohol-free

drinks, and good security so there's no major brawls. You could have fun."

I fiddled with my book. "I'm having fun with Kunta."

Parker's forehead creased. "It doesn't end well for Kunta."

I disagreed. "That's an interpretation. The way I see it, his blood saw freedom through Chicken George. He got out—Kunta's lineage didn't die in slavery."

Parker looked impressed. "I admire a good scholar." He again eyed my luggage. "Planning on getting comfortable?"

I glanced at the bags in question. "I am comfortable."

"Maybe you'll be *more* comfortable if you unpack one bag at a time."

Knowing that the point was to try, I conceded. "Good idea."

"So you're really staying in, huh?"

"Yeah, I'd rather get my reading done." Not that I was otherwise interested in associating with Nandy and her friends out on the town.

Parker sighed. "I just feel bad for Nandy."

"Why?"

"If you're not going out, neither is she."

I lifted a brow, closing my book. "You are aware that this is blackmail, right?"

By the grin on his face, he knew exactly what he was doing. "Lucid."

Stifling the urge to roll my eyes, I asked, "And Jordy?"

"Is far too young to go to the Hook." Parker moved to the doorway but stopped and looked back at me for a moment. "Get dressed, Trice, you don't wanna be late. Go out and have some fun, live a little. It's summer."

His idea of fun included my going out with Nandy and her clique of friends? Honestly, I would've rather hung out with Travis. At least with him, there'd be no bullshit. While I had no direct reason to dislike Nandy's friends, I just wasn't interested in trying with them. Erica was okay and Shayne wasn't too bad, but still. Nothing beat home.

I went and poked my head into Nandy's room after knocking and getting the green light to open the door, finding her zipping up a purple strapless dress that clung to her curves.

"We're taking separate cars," I told her, catching her attention.

Nandy lit up. "You're going?"

Unfortunately. "Looks that way."

Shayne, who was sitting on Nandy's bed wrapped in a towel, perked up. "Hey, Trice!"

I shifted my attention to her. "I'm thinking about growing a beard, Shayne." I left the girls to get ready, already knowing there was far more fun to be had with Kunta Kinte.

Chad came and got the girls, and I followed them to what was apparently a teen nightclub. When we'd left the Smiths' house, I'd heard the girls mumbling about some indie singer who was showing up, and how they were ecstatic about it. That, and the fact that Erica was also deejaying, with her cousins set to do a routine.

This oughta be interesting.

We weren't in the door a full minute before we bumped into Travis and Matt. Travis said something to Chad, and Chad glared at him before taking Nandy and Shayne away.

Travis seemed happy with himself. "God, I love that momma's boy."

Matt rolled his eyes, and I managed to laugh. At least I wasn't the only one who disliked Chad.

"So, you showed up," Travis said as he greeted me with a fist bump.

"I didn't have a choice," I said.

Travis rubbed his hands together deviously. "Boys, it's gonna be a long night." He turned to me first. "We're going to find a girl for you to make out with." He faced Matt. "And I already know your type—tall, blond, athletic, and sweet."

"Geez, Trav, can we wait a month until you start trying to get me to cheat on my boyfriend?" Matt sighed, pretending to sound exasperated.

"Who dates during the summer?" Travis asked as we moved farther into the club. "I mean, look at the endless possibilities in front of you. Ben left—you two should've taken a break."

Matt appeared apologetic as he faced me. "Don't let him get to you, we all mostly ignore him."

"If he loves Ben, three months shouldn't mean anything," I told Travis.

He wasn't interested. He was already scanning the club, looking like he was itching to score.

Matt watched as his best friend took off toward the dance floor. "Let the debauchery begin."

Matt followed Travis, and I took my time, measuring the club out. The vibration of the loud music made me feel alive, and the heat from the packed space almost made me feel claustrophobic. The scent of sweat mixed with a medley of body spray and cologne hung in the air as I made my way around the establishment.

The decor was that of a pirate's ship, where all the wood was made to appear old and moldy. A rope hung from the beams of the ceiling, and there were fake parrots all over the place, along with hooks. The over-twenty-one crowd were walking around wearing neon-orange wristbands made of rope to establish their ability to drink alcohol, while the rest of us underage were bare.

On the second floor, I spotted Erica on a makeshift balcony designed as a plank, deejaying. Ashley stood beside her talking to Warhol, who seemed to be shouting over the loud music.

Waitresses, and even the bartender, took part in the Hook's pirate theme as they were dressed in costume to play the role.

I found my way up to the nearest lounge on the second floor, doing my best to meander through the crowd and block out the awful pop music that was playing. When I got to an empty sitting area, the lights in the club dimmed and a spotlight shone onto the center of the club.

"Get up out of your seats, folks!" Erica's shout could be heard through the house speakers. "Show some love for my favorite cousin and his crew, DEFCON Yee. They're about to tear this place down and kick it old-school!"

Everyone on the second floor stood and headed to the railing to get a good view.

Down in the center of the club, on the dance floor, stood six Asians and a Latino. Four boys and three girls, all clad in matching colors. The girls wore black short-shorts with gray vests and red bras, while the boys wore black shorts, red vests, and gray tank tops. Every member of the crew had something unique about their hair or the accessory they chose to wear with their outfit, but together they were a unit.

The lights went out and flickers of red, yellow, and blue light shone through the club as the remix to Busta Rhymes's "Touch It" began playing and DEFCON Yee started their routine. The girls left the unit first, crip-walking to the side before turning to point to the boys, who took it as their cue to begin break-dancing, popping and locking.

The crowd buzzed with cheers and chants for more as the

crew reacted to the beat of the song, feeding off it. When a second Busta Rhymes song came on, "Pass the Courvoisier, Part II," the crowd's animation heightened, and I was almost surprised no one rushed the dance floor to join in as bodies around me began bouncing to the song.

Watching the people react and seeing DEFCON Yee kill it, I couldn't stop myself from smiling.

Maybe there was some action in Pacific Hills after all.

After DEFCON finished their set, Erica took the mic and thanked them for the show, then loudly kicked off the start of summer vacation. Everyone cheered, raising their drinks in the air.

Maybe Parker had been right in forcing me out of the house. The atmosphere was too jubilant to dwell on anything negative, and being left on my own made it easier to begin to transition to this fresh start.

About twenty minutes later, Shayne found me, coming over to where I was kicking back in the lounge area and sitting on my lap. Deciding to play along with her game, I wrapped an arm around her. This caused her to smile and lean into me.

Shayne reached out and stroked my jaw, rubbing the back of her hand on it. "You'd look awful with a beard, Trice."

Shayne was mad pretty in her little black dress. She had some of her dark brown hair pinned back, leaving a light dusting of her baby hairs against her forehead, and the rest of her hair falling in curls around her face and dropping to her shoulders. With her big brown eyes and admittedly cute smile, Shayne wasn't so bad at all.

Even if it was all a facade. This bad girl act wasn't fooling me a bit.

Sitting back, I stared up at Shayne's impish grin. "Some may say that beards are the new mustache."

Shayne wrinkled her nose, appearing adorable. "I didn't like that trend, either. I guess I just like my guy clean-shaven. I mean, if I endure painful waxes for you, might you shave for me?" She again caressed my jaw. "Of course, I do like scruff."

"Yeah?"

Shayne nodded. "Uh-huh. It's sexy, but then you got the guys who go full beard, and it's gross."

"Some might say that scruff can be quite...*sharp*," I said, feeling playful. "Might even stab you between—" I dropped my gaze to her thighs "—your knees."

Shayne's flush was all the confirmation I needed in our game.

She giggled and slapped my chest. "You can't hold that against me, I was only talking to Nandy."

Despite Nandy's warning, I got the sense that Shayne was a nice girl, and it wouldn't be a big deal to hang out with her, much like it wasn't so bad hanging around Travis.

"You don't want a guy like me," I came out and told her.

She frowned. "Why not?"

"Because there's no love in me."

"Who says I'm looking for love?"

I chuckled. "I'm not like the others, Shayne."

"That's the point."

"So let's not pretend I'm fooled by your act like they are, okay?"

"Act?"

"Act."

"Okay, then." Shayne sat up straight on my lap, reached out and procured my hand. "And let's also not pretend that I'm fooled by *your* act, Trice."

I lifted a brow. "Act?"

She nodded. "I don't think for a second that you're this big and scary guy. I bet you're very sweet, considerate, and nice."

"What makes you so sure?"

Shayne shrugged. "You've got a handsome smile. When I first saw you, I saw this tall, angry-looking guy, and then I saw you smile, and it was so genuine and contagious. I don't think a person with such a smile can have only darkness in them."

"If you believe in the devil, they say he was the most beautiful angel."

Shayne's laughter caused me to laugh, too. "Stop it."

I was beginning to reply when I glanced over and spotted Nandy. She stared for a moment, taking in Shayne on my lap.

Instead of saying anything, Nandy walked on by.

Shayne returned to me. "Let me guess, you don't dance, do you?"

"Nope."

She stood and straightened her dress. "I'm going to catch this set from Erica. Maybe I'll see you later."

I continued to sit back and enjoy the music until Erica switched genres again and I felt like walking around. Going to the railing, I could see down below that Nandy was on the dance floor in Warhol's arms. Chad was nowhere to be seen.

Shayne thought I was genuine from a smile, but it was Nandy who looked genuine with Warhol as they moved to the dance track. It was obvious as she moved that she had no inhibitions with Warhol and was being herself. There was no pressure to be this person that she wasn't, and she looked at peace.

"Beautiful, isn't she?" Chad was standing beside me, shouting over the music to be heard.

"Yeah," I told him.

Chad offered a smile. "Having fun or what?"

"It's not so bad."

He cast his gaze down at his girlfriend. "This is going to be a fun summer."

Nandy was dancing with Edi and Shayne now, having a good time with the biggest smile on her face. She was beautiful when she was happy.

"How'd it go with your mom?" I asked.

My question took him by surprise. "Tough as usual. I came through and sorta kidnapped Nandy."

I thought of Nandy's words from that morning. "Take care of her."

Chad turned to me. "You don't think I take care of my girlfriend?"

I faced him. "I didn't say what I thought. I said take care of her."

Chad smirked, moving a step closer. "No offense, but you just got here. You may have known her before, but I know her now, and I don't need you telling me how to treat my girlfriend, okay?"

I had to hand it to him for defending himself, but I wasn't impressed. I might have been new, but all things regarding Chad just didn't do it for me. He watched TV while they were in bed, he made Nandy nervous, and his mother frightened her. No relationship was perfect, but he was missing the mark for me.

"I guess we'll have to agree to disagree," I said as I attempted to move past him.

Chad caught my arm. "Things would be a lot simpler around here if we all got along."

"Play my position and all that too, huh?" I thought about it for a second. Nah, it just wasn't my style to fall in line with the great crowd. Even back in Lindenwood, the boys never got me to do anything I didn't want to do. If they were drinking or smoking, I never partook, even if it was the "simple" thing to do. "I'll be seeing you, Chad." I patted his arm and headed downstairs, no longer interested in the Hook. Had it been an hour yet?

On the first floor, I bumped into Travis, who had succeeded in getting Matt to dance with some girl in heels high enough that she'd surely fall and break her neck if she made one wrong move.

"Trice! Where ya going? The night is still young, my friend," Travis said as he steered me away from the exit.

Chad had found his way to Nandy, and he was making her laugh.

"Take my advice." Travis spoke in my ear. "Don't fall for her. She's the prettiest girl in town, I know, but she's got Dipshit, and she's content. Plus dating her means doing all this social shit, going to events, smiling, and kissing ass. It's far better to fly under the radar."

"I'm not entirely sure she's my type," I said.

Travis grinned. "What is your type? I see a blonde at two o'clock eyeing you like a four-course meal." He gestured at some girl who was indeed giving me the eye.

It didn't matter, I wasn't interested. "All you, Trav."

"I've got bad luck with blondes, they tend to be a little crazy."

My expression deadpanned. "And you're not?"

He didn't deny it. "Let's see."

"I'm going home. I've seen enough."

"Lame."

I rolled my eyes. "Have a good night."

"Wait!" Warhol came over and slapped me hard on the back. "You going home?"

"Yeah."

"Can I bum a ride?"

I shrugged and led Warhol out of the club. He hopped shotgun in my car and fiddled with the radio, despite my briefly mentioning that I liked the hip-hop station it had been on. He changed it to some channel that played a mix of popular songs from many genres.

"Was it fun?" Warhol asked as we caught a light.

"Seeing Erica's cousin was."

Warhol bobbed his head and stuck one hand out the window, squeezing and opening his palm. "Don't let them get to you."

"Who?"

Warhol sat back, staring ahead. "The bastards, man. Don't let them get you down. I've seen some newcomers come and be eaten alive by this place. You're from the 'Wood—stick your chest out, don't let these people get you."

"They won't." If I stayed in town until I was eighteen, nothing was going to get me down. And I wasn't about to conform to fit in, either. I still couldn't give a fuck about Pacific Hills and its phoniness.

Warhol laughed as the light turned green. "The first thing people tell you when you get to Cross High is to stay away from Travis Catalano, but you know what? I think they're all just scared, because he's got it figured out. He's beaten this system placed on us. Chad's parents practically run this place, and they're complete fascists."

The poor kids. "Perhaps we'll rebel, spark a little anarchy, and overthrow the system."

Warhol caught my sarcasm and laughed as I pulled into the Smiths' driveway and parked.

When I got out of the car, I spotted Kyle down the block,

standing outside with a telescope and staring at the starry night sky. As I made my way over to him, Warhol joined me.

Kyle noticed me, and then Warhol. "Hey."

I gazed at the sky and back to the boy in front of me. "Hey."

He seemed guarded, but I didn't blame him. From the few days that I'd been in Pacific Hills, it was evident Kyle was the resident loner.

"Didn't see you at the Hook," I said.

"Frogger doesn't party," Warhol spoke up.

"*Kyle* has a tongue," I said.

Kyle shrugged. "Not really my scene, you know? I bet it was fun, though. Sometimes I go when they have good bands playing."

I noticed he had a camera attached to the telescope. "What are you doing?"

Kyle touched the camera. "I like photography, and space."

"Aren't you on the newspaper?" Warhol asked.

Kyle blinked. "Yearbook."

"Same thing," Warhol mumbled.

This was more awkward than it needed to be. Looking at Warhol, I gestured to Kyle. "One way to break the system is to break social barriers. Football players can hang with the… Kyle."

Warhol snorted, but he went over to Kyle's telescope anyway. "How's this work?"

They were such a contrast. Kyle, tall and lanky, and Warhol, tall and burly from football. Warhol didn't make any smart remarks as Kyle explained to him how to snap a photo.

Maybe this could work.

A call came through on my phone, and I glanced down at my screen. It was Nandy.

"Hello?" I answered.

"Where are you?" I could tell she was outside by the sound of cars driving by in the background.

"Home."

"Come to the Crab Shack, we're all grabbing a bite to eat."

I was about to turn her down when I got an idea. Warhol and Kyle were looking my way. "Is Shayne there?"

I now had Kyle's full attention as Nandy gave me my answer. "Uh, yeah."

"We'll be there." I hung up just as she was beginning to question who I meant by "we."

I pocketed my phone. "So, Kyle, you hungry?"

The Crab Shack was on the boardwalk, a few feet away from the Hook. Finding the place filled with people was no surprise.

As the boys and I entered the diner, we passed a few kids who mentioned a bonfire down at the beach. Warhol commented that people never slept in Pacific Hills during the summer; there was always something to do.

Nandy was sitting at a big booth toward the back of the diner with Shayne, Erica, Ashley, Chad, and a couple of Chad's friends.

She waved at me, as if she were waiting on me.

A few booths over, I found Travis and Matt sitting back and going over the menu.

The dilemma before me reminded me of a poem I'd once read by Robert Frost, "The Road Not Taken."

When I took a step toward Travis's table, Kyle put his hand on my shoulder, quickly recoiling when I faced him.

"The most popular girl in school is smiling at you, and she saved you a seat. You sure about this?" Kyle asked, seeming nervous for me.

This time I didn't hesitate before taking the spot next to Travis.

He turned from Matt and faced me, lifting his chin in acknowledgment. He soon spotted Nandy and Chad. Chad was watching with what looked to be a mixture of shock and curiousness, while Nandy did her best to hide her smile and listen to whatever it was that Shayne was saying.

"What's this?" Travis asked me.

If this was going to work, I was choosing my own friends. I shrugged and sat back, prepared to skim the menu. "Trying."

Warhol and Kyle joined our table, and we ordered food.

Travis elbowed me. "So, since you're new to the area and in need of friends, we may be of service to you."

That had *catch* written all over it. "And?"

"And we just need a tiny favor." Travis sat up and turned so that his whole body was facing me. "There's this girl, and we need you to take one for the team."

He was clearly the girl-crazy one. "Why can't you do it?"

"Because—"

"She hates him," Matt cut in. "With good reason."

Travis scowled. "Her name's Tamra, and she's got the best parents a kid could ask for. They own a medical marijuana facility, and sources say Tamra knows how to get her hands on the goods."

"So if you get in nice with her, you get the goods," Warhol added.

I wasn't interested in Pacific Hills girls, nor was I interested in free drugs. Seeing the boys anxiously awaiting my response was humorous, though.

"Okay, describe her to me," I said for the sake of hearing them out.

Warhol went first, holding his hands out in front of his

chest, imitating a set of breasts. "She's this redhead with a great set of—"

"She's got a lazy eye," Kyle cut in.

Warhol rolled his eyes. "She does not."

"Yes, she does, how could you not notice?"

"I don't know, the five-second rule."

"Five-second rule?" Matt repeated.

"Yeah, never look a chick in the eye longer than five seconds, or else they'll start thinking you like them or some deep shit," Warhol explained.

Kyle snorted. "Dude, this isn't food."

They commenced arguing back and forth while we watched. I took in all the guys around me, knowing without a doubt that they were nothing like the people back home. They weren't even the face of Pacific Hills, and maybe, just maybe, that wasn't so bad.

I was still feeling everyone out, but I'd known from jump who I liked and who I didn't particularly care for. With Travis and his friends, it was simple—they'd taken me into their group, despite my origin, and they stayed true to themselves around me. That I couldn't knock.

Travis patted my shoulder and then squeezed gently. "Welcome to Pacific Hills, bro."

16 | *Nandy*

When I came downstairs Friday morning, Tyson was sitting at the kitchen table, eating a large bowl of Fruity Pebbles. I took a moment to study his red T-shirt and crisp white shorts. He looked fresh, handsome, and whole. Maybe going to the Hook the previous evening had been what he needed.

Tyson caught me staring and lifted a brow.

I grinned. "Hey, Trice."

His face blanked. "Either Trice or Tyson. Pick one."

I managed to laugh as I sauntered over to the table. "So, what's on the agenda?"

Tyson shrugged. "Don't know yet."

"Hmm, feel like getting out of here?"

"For?" That suspicious eyebrow lifted again.

"To hang out," I said.

The previous evening I'd saved him a seat at the Crab Shack, and he'd opted for Travis and crew. In Pacific Hills, you just didn't do that.

Tyson didn't look convinced by my offer.

Of course, he was going to be skeptical.

I threaded my fingers together and rocked on my heels. "It's early, the beach will be mostly empty."

Tyson wasn't swayed. "The beach?"

Briefly, I wondered if pouting would work on him.

Probably not.

"Oh come on."

Tyson weighed his options and, in the end, gave in.

"We're not swimming, are we?" Tyson ran his hand down the material of his red tee before lifting his head to hear my response.

Underneath my tank and denim shorts, I was suited up for a swim, just in case. Though I couldn't picture Tyson in the water.

"I was thinking volleyball," I confessed.

Tyson made a face but said nothing as he followed me out of the house.

As early as it was, there were a few people out and about. Parents going to work, Kyle preparing to go to Cross High to volunteer, and even Travis, getting ready for a morning run on his longboard. He tipped his head toward Tyson, and Tyson responded with the same gesture.

They were going to be friends, despite my warning.

In my car, Tyson heaved a sigh.

"What?" I wanted to know.

Tyson eyed my stereo but said nothing.

I hesitated, then set it on a moderate volume as I listened to Billie Eilish.

On our way out of the subdivision, we passed Jordy and Hector skateboarding. Jordy had on his elbow pads, something he and his friends dubbed *lame*.

Tyson noticed the boys, too. "Sometimes I wish I was a kid again. Things were so much simpler back then in a way."

His words made me think of younger Tyson. The boy who was all mine. The boy who listened when I spoke. The boy who followed my lead and did whatever I told him to.

Life hadn't been kind to the boy I knew who was now a man.

A broken man.

I still felt awful for how I'd treated him. Surely not all people from Lindenwood were as terrible as the nightly news and the papers depicted. *We* in Pacific Hills weren't so nice as the pamphlets and magazines tried to flaunt.

Tyson was different now, but so was I. It didn't mean we couldn't be as good of friends as we were before. Though it'd be easier if he'd just go with the flow and hang out with my friends instead of forging bonds with trouble.

The beach came into view, and Tyson shifted in his seat, releasing a breath.

He was much more handsome now that he'd grown, but he was noticeably guarded.

Once I found a space to park, I unbuckled my seat belt before reaching out and squeezing Tyson's shoulder. "Ready?"

His gaze slid over my hand. "As I'm going to be."

I took that as my cue to lead the way out of my car.

In my hand, my cell phone rang out my special ringtone for Chad.

I ignored it. Today was about bonding with Tyson, and any of the others would have to wait.

"Going to get that?" Tyson asked, nodding at my still-ringing cell. He cradled my volleyball in his hand, eyeing my phone curiously.

"Nah, I'll call him back."

"Oh, it's the red—Chad."

Him and that nickname.

"Did you have fun last night?" We reached the sand, where I was quick to slip out of my sandals and burrow my toes. The sand was a little hot against the soles of my feet, but I reveled in it. I *loved* the beach.

Tyson was waiting for my next move, seeming interested in neither joining me barefoot nor getting more comfortable. "It was straight. Erica's cousin can really move."

"Geordan's been dancing his whole life. Most of us envy his swagger." Geordan Yee was effortlessly cool and at one with himself. Along with his dance troupe, he made all the local girls swoon and still managed to be on time to work at his family's restaurant, the Garden of Yee.

For a lot of girls in town, Geordan was their first crush. Mine was...

"You seem to be making friends," I blurted out.

"The point is to try, Nandy," Tyson replied. "I like Travis, I can tell he's real, and I need that in a friend."

Travis was something all right.

A cesspool of broken hearts and dirty underwear.

"Tyson," I sighed. "You gotta learn the ropes around here. Travis is bad news."

Tyson rolled his eyes and gave me a pained look. "There's nothing wrong with Travis."

I focused on the nearby lifeguard, who was getting some

girl's number instead of watching for swimmers about to drown. "If you want a social life, he's not the way to go. In this town, and at Cross High, my circle is the one to be in. We're the future of Pacific Hills."

The sound of Tyson's snort drew my attention to his scowl. "Fuck this town and your social cliché high school bullshit. I'd rather hang around Travis and Warhol than a guy like Chad. Who names their kid 'Chad Bradley' anyway?"

It's a heartthrob name. "Chad is a great guy."

Tyson narrowed his eyes. "Oh yeah? I can tell."

"He is," I insisted.

Tyson wasn't convinced. "What do you even see in him?"

I began to feel uncomfortable with Tyson's inquisition. He didn't get to do that, to come back and question everything. Not when…

"You don't have a right to question my relationship or my feelings for my boyfriend," I told him.

Tyson casually released and caught my volleyball. "Sounds like you don't have an answer."

"I do. If you were here… A lot of this would make sense to you if you'd grown up here."

"I'm here now," Tyson responded, leaning close to me, "and what I'm seeing…is a lot of corny shit. I'll take my chances with Travis."

His proximity was confusing—that, and the cute way he was both mocking me and standing up to me.

I coolly swept some hair behind my ear. "I'm just trying to help you."

Nothing more was said.

We walked along the beach, admiring the views in a comfortable silence. Every once in a while, I peeked up at Tyson, to gauge where his mind was—with me, or somewhere else.

He was focused on the ocean, watching the waves crash as they came to shore.

"Hey," I spoke up, "how are things?"

Tyson shifted his attention to me. "Just trying to get used to all *this*."

I peered down at the sand. "What's it like, in Lindenwood?"

Tyson sighed. "It's not entirely bad, but some days, it's chaos. You can get killed for your shoes, or just being in the wrong group of friends. Shit ain't a cakewalk like Pacific Hills, I'll tell you that. Sometimes I just lie in bed at night, soaking in the silence. Back home, there's always noise in the heat of the night."

My heart ached for him. I reached out and took his hand, squeezing it gently. "I'm sorry you had to go through that."

Tyson studied our hands as if taking in how they were entwined. If the physical contact bothered him, he still didn't let go. "Well, now I'm here."

Yes, he was, and I was happier than ever to have him back.

It was early, but a few kids home from college were out on the beach relaxing, as well as a few from Cross High.

Unfortunately, some of the latter noticed us and began to stare and whisper. Most notably a trio of girls.

I shrank back and dropped Tyson's hand. *Gossip.* I'd spent way too long building up my public persona to let idle gossip bring me down.

Tyson didn't seem fazed by the bitchy chatter. His impassive face said he wasn't bothered in the least.

He was probably used to being judged.

Not me.

I took off in another direction, very aware he was on my heels. "Let's grab our own spot." We found a place by some deserted volleyball nets, far from other people. Far enough that I was sure our faces couldn't be made out if someone attempted to do a photo op.

My fancy ringtone for Chad went off again.

This time, when I didn't answer, my phone rang again with Shayne's caller ID showing up.

I gritted my teeth. Chad was persistent; he wasn't above using one of my friends to get to me when I didn't pick up fast enough.

For a moment, I considered shooting Chad a quick text, explaining I was busy, but I wasn't in the mood to argue if he didn't like that answer, especially when it came to who I was busy with.

I seriously hoped those nosy girls weren't about to hit up social media and blab about seeing me with Tyson. It wasn't like we were doing anything wrong. We were just—

"You're worrying too much."

"Am not," I replied, easing a hand through my hair.

For the first time that morning, Tyson furnished a smile. One that cooled my nerves.

He leaned over, as if to tell me a secret. "Are, too."

I couldn't fight my own smile as I gave in. "Okay. I don't like gossip, especially about me. This place can be brutal sometimes."

Tyson shrugged his broad shoulders. "Fuck it. Let them talk. Who gives a shit what people think about you?"

Easy for him to say.

I gazed up into his eyes. "Tyson, it's not that easy."

He shook his head. "It's not that hard, either. You're smart, beautiful, and people already admire you in town. A little gossip ain't gonna hurt you."

That was the thing—it would. I didn't want there to be "a little" gossip about me. Beyond dating Chad, I was the It Girl of Cross High, and the ideal girl of Pacific Hills. I worked hard for my academic and public service records.

The last thing I needed was a stain on my name.

I had cotillion coming up, and debuting wasn't a small thing—it was everything.

My cell buzzed, this time with a text from my dearest boyfriend.

Tyson's nostrils flared. His hand shot out and snatched the phone from me.

"Hey!" I snapped. "Give it back."

He pocketed my phone and shook his head. "No. Your ass dragged me out here for volleyball. I'm not about to sit here and watch you text your fuck boy."

Now my own temper was flaring. "He's not a fuck boy."

"No?" Tyson dug into his pocket and procured my phone. "Then text him you're with me."

I leaned back, almost stuttering. "No."

"No?"

"I mean…" I gave up in a loud *hmmph*. "It's complicated, okay?"

Chad wasn't exactly the jealous type, but I could tell he wasn't the most comfortable with my being so buddy-buddy with another guy, especially one I had history with. Even if we were only kids the last time we'd seen each other.

"Why did you even invite me out?" Tyson asked as he shoved my phone back into his pocket.

"Because I want you to have a nice day, enjoy yourself, and take a load off."

He was still doubtful. "Why?"

"Everyone should feel welcome." I thought of what my brother had said to me when I was being a total bitch before. "Everyone should feel like they belong. I want you to feel like Pacific Hills is where you belong. I want you to feel at home here, Tyson."

So that you never leave me again.

The thought came out of nowhere, and I almost pressed a hand to my chest to still my heart.

The first time he left me, I had missed him terribly.

Now that he was back, I wanted him settled and satisfied with his surroundings. Was that so much to ask?

Tyson stared at me good and hard, with no tell of what he was thinking. He tossed up the volleyball and caught it again. "Girls aren't as athletic as boys."

It sounded so childish. So asinine. So much like the old Tyson. The one who used to tease me. The one who took me on adventures out in the yard. The one who challenged me over the silliest things, like being a girl.

He was still in there.

There was still light in all that darkness. Tyson Sr. hadn't stolen it. Maybe in time, it would overcome all the pain.

Fixing Tyson with the toughest look I could muster, I said, "Game on."

17 | *TRICE*

Nandy was acting salty.

We'd spent pretty much the whole day at the beach playing game after game of volleyball, and I'd beaten her each time. During our last game, I'd let her win, something she was smart enough to catch on to and sulk about.

Once the beach started getting more traffic, we climbed back into Nandy's ride and drove on home.

We were sitting side by side on the family room floor having a movie marathon over pizza. It was nice to know Nandy could still pig out every once in a while.

The theme of our marathon was older movies we'd grown up watching. It was my turn, and I'd chosen *Juice*.

"God, those clothes," Nandy said in between sips of her pineapple soda. "I'm so glad we live in the present."

I chuckled, grabbing another slice of pizza. "Trust me, I'm sure in the future your kids will mock you for... You know, never mind."

Nandy faced me. "What? Go on."

I couldn't pass up bringing up the elephant in the room. "You never wear clothes. I'm sure your kids will be too busy asking why you're nearly naked in all your old photos than judging you on your fashion sense."

Nandy scowled and returned to the movie. "Ha ha."

I was beginning to laugh at her stale persona when her phone rang for the millionth time.

That redheaded fuck boy was persistent.

"Ugh." Nandy groaned as she rose to her feet and paused the movie. "One sec."

She slid her finger across the screen of her phone to unlock it as she stepped into the hall.

It was going on four in the afternoon and no one was home yet. Jordy was probably still out with Hector while Parker and Max were both out at work.

I almost wanted to get a job to busy myself, but in this town, I shuddered to think of the possibilities. Serving the spoiled youth at some eatery? Or slaving away for the stuck-up aristocrats and their prejudices at some retail store?

How was I ever going to get used to this place?

In the hall, Nandy's conversation was anything but hushed.

From her angry pacing to her rising voice, I knew Chad was giving her shit.

"It's not a date, we're just hanging out...We're not getting close like that...He's not my childhood sweetheart, we were just kids, Chad...Do not make this a big deal...well, of course I'd feel some type of way, but this isn't like that...Ugh!" She huffed and seconds later returned to her position next to me.

Fuck boy.

"Trouble in paradise?" I quipped.

The frown on Nandy's face ceased my taunting.

One thing I noticed, she cared too much about what people thought of her.

Life was too short for that.

It was beyond clear people thought highly of her already. She didn't need to continue to jump through hoops. Nandy was the princess of Pacific Hills.

"Just drop it," Nandy said with a shake of her head.

I pushed Play on the DVD.

"Dang." Nandy peered at the screen and pulled her knees to her chest, securing them tightly with her arms.

"What?"

"I forgot how cute these male leads were. Can we rewind to the part where Tupac's in his underwear again?"

I grimaced, shaking my head. "Didn't know you found guys like that attractive."

Nandy deadpanned, "What's that supposed to mean?"

"Just thought you had a thing for redheads."

She reached out and shoved me. "Shut up, Tyson." Soon her eyes were back on the screen. "Omar Epps was like boyfriend goals in every movie he did in the '90s and early 2000s." Nandy peeked at me. "You know, you sorta look like him."

I rolled my eyes and gazed at the screen. "And you're a regular Sanaa Lathan."

Nandy giggled, and I allowed myself to admit I liked that sound far better than her berating me, bitching at me, or whining at me.

She was different from what I remembered, but some of that old girl was still there.

Pacific Hills was a place people in my position used to

dream of. The land of the riches. The place to settle down and enjoy one's wealth. Where I was from, knowing it was just a dream made you smart. Thinking it could ever be a reality made you a fool.

Could this be *my* reality?

Travis wasn't so bad; Warhol, Ashley, and the guys, neither.

Having Nandy at my side would make things bearable. She was the only person I truly knew here, even if I barely knew her anymore.

Time had a sick way of changing everything.

I'd grown up fast and harsh, while she was still easing into adulthood.

I could almost envy that softness of hers, that naive and optimistic viewpoint she had.

Fingering the rug, I decided to at least truly try to be friendly and make it work.

What was the worst that could happen?

Ding-dong.

The front doorbell rang out in the foyer, yet another interruption of our film.

Nandy sighed as she paused the movie before going and getting the door.

I leaned back on my arms, curious to see who it was.

Shit.

Chad breezed into the house like he owned the place, and at once my mood sank.

"I just can't see why we *all* can't hang out, Nan," he was saying as he came into the room and hung in the doorway. His gaze fell upon me, and no hint of a friendly aura came off his person. *"Tyson."*

He wanted me to break his neck. He had to.

Refraining from calling him the moniker I admired for Nandy's sake, I settled with, "Chad."

He scratched his head, eyeing the screen before me. "Movies? Sounds like fun."

Nandy came and tugged on his arm. "Fine, you win, we'll do something at your house."

A slow smile curled onto Chad's mouth. "Yeah?"

Nandy rolled her eyes. "Yes. I'll hang out with Tyson some other time."

The smile disintegrated. "Sure thing."

Nandy pivoted on her toes and faced me, frowning. "Rain check? We have been together all day. I'm sure we can finish this weekend or something?"

There was no use in throwing a fit. Chad *was* her boyfriend. I told myself maybe in some other universe, I would've felt some type of way about Asiah spending too much free time with some other guy.

Besides, Nandy and I had the whole summer.

I let it go as I bobbed my head. "Yeah."

Nandy offered me a small smile. "Thanks for understanding."

Chad had had enough. He boldly took Nandy's hand and steered her out of the room and soon out of the house.

I faced the large flat-screen, wondering if I wanted to even finish the movie.

Loud footsteps sounded in the hall, and I just barely caught a glimpse of Jordy and Hector racing up the steps for his room.

Another figure came into my line of vision, and I realized it was Shayne.

She didn't look so good as she entered the room and plopped herself down beside me.

The night before, she'd been so bubbly and flirty, and now the crestfallen state she was in brought even me down.

Shayne gathered a slice of pizza and looked at the paused movie before facing me. "Hey."

Something told me she needed it, so I smiled at her. "Hey."

I restarted the movie, and we sat in a comfortable silence.

18 | *Nandy*

Jeff Bradley exuded wealth and power. I felt his presence every time I had an encounter with him, even if we were merely standing in the same room together. His wife and his son sometimes made me nervous, but Mr. Bradley was all things intimidating.

Time equaled money, so he was more out of the house than in. Running into him as Chad and I were entering the house after hanging out at Oliver Stein's had me on my toes.

"Nandy, good to see you," Mr. Bradley greeted me with a warm twinkle in his eyes as he seemed to be sifting through the day's mail.

While he was tall like his father, with matching eyes, Chad resembled his mother more.

"Hey, Mr. Bradley." I lifted my hand in an awkward wave.

He seemed amused at the gesture as he faced his son. "She just refuses to call me Jeff, huh?"

He had given me permission on several occasions, but people in his position earned the "Mr." title. It felt more respectful, not to mention Mrs. Bradley never let on that I could call her *Laura*.

Chad and I eased more into the house, getting comfortable in his family's sitting room as we sat together on the sofa. Mr. Bradley hung back in the doorway, continuing his browsing with the mail.

"Save the date," he mused, waving a flyer and reminder for cotillion next month. He appraised me. "So, Nandy, I hear your parents adopted another boy."

If gossip wasn't already a pain in the ass, *false* gossip was worse.

"Um, no," I spoke up to clarify. "They didn't adopt him—he's a longtime friend of our family who's staying with us now."

"Oh yeah? Where's he from?"

Chad snorted. *"Lindenwood."*

Mr. Bradley frowned. "Oh."

His reaction and Chad's judgment were unsettling. They didn't know Tyson. Had *I* been that awful in the beginning?

"He's really nice," I said in Tyson's defense.

Chad made a face. "Sure, babe."

Mr. Bradley wasn't convinced, either. "Your parents are ever the generous people, aren't they? First with the Vietnamese boy and now this one."

It was hard to keep my face even. "Jordy's Thai, as in Thailand." And he wasn't a "boy," he was my brother.

"Right," Mr. Bradley responded with what was surely a

phony smile. "All set for your big day? Cotillion will be here before you know it."

The idea of shoes, makeup, tulle, and hair came to mind, not to mention wearing a tiara. "Can't wait."

Mr. Bradley came and tapped Chad with the mail, eyeing his son with pride. "You should be honored, taking the prettiest girl in town with you." He returned to me, as if remembering something. "Oh, thank you for agreeing to help out with Charlotte."

It didn't feel like I had a choice, but I smiled anyway and pretended to be extra benevolent about the venture. "No problem."

"Who knows, if these pieces are good and take off, this could launch your modeling career."

Chad snaked his arm around me. "Oh yeah, my girl could be the real top model."

I wrinkled my nose. "Actually, I'm considering interior design."

Mr. Bradley boldly chuckled. "My son and the interior decorator, how cute."

He left us alone, and an *ick* I couldn't shake off settled on my shoulders.

Me wanting to decorate houses wasn't cute or funny, but almost a rite of passage. My mother developed residential properties, and my father built commercial and private aircraft. It was in my blood. I found joy in painting and picking out furniture and designing a room. I was more than a pretty face.

I looked to Chad, wondering if he'd say anything.

He didn't; he simply shrugged as if his father's blasé behavior was acceptable.

Oh. "I think I'm going to head on home. My parents want us to have dinner together and I forgot."

Chad frowned. "Because of that kid?"

"Yes, to welcome Tyson."

Chad heaved a sigh. "Listen, Nan, I know you love taking these newbies in and showing them around, but I don't know about this one. He was an innocent kid when you knew him, and now—"

"Now, what? What makes him not so innocent now?" I challenged. "Dickie does coke, Chad! Coke! Don't talk to me about innocent."

Chad backed away. "It's not like that, it's just… You know what, never mind."

I let him come and kiss me, and then I saw myself out.

Erica was right. We were privileged, coming off entirely disgusting for judging Tyson based on his city. It was important to learn, but it was even more important to *un*learn. Judging people by their pasts or origins was weak.

The whole thing made me want to apologize again to Tyson.

Only, when I saw the carefree smile on his face as I got in and hung in his doorway, I decided to let it go. He was standing by his dresser, his bag nearby, and he seemed to be finally unpacking. Or he'd been unpacking before he focused on his phone.

"Hey," I said.

Tyson lifted his head and noticed me. "Oh, hey."

Things had been rocky earlier, especially with his calling me out over Chad. But I didn't want to think about that. "You're unpacking."

Tyson shrugged. "One bag at a time."

A chime came through on his cell phone and he was back to it.

Dread settled deep in my belly. "That isn't Lindenwood, is it?"

Tyson released a laugh as his fingers danced across his cell phone screen. And then, as if he realized I was still in the room, he faced me. "I'm sorry, what?"

"Your phone—you're not texting Lindenwood, are you?"

Tyson was confused but then he got what I meant. "Oh, no, it's just Shayne."

I blinked. "Shayne gave you her number?"

Tyson shrugged, like it was no big deal. "Yeah, we watched *Juice* together, and then some movie where two people try to drive each other crazy in ten days or something."

They'd watched *How to Lose a Guy in 10 Days* together? Better yet, two movies?

"Cool," I said, even though deep inside I felt it wasn't. At all.

First it was Travis, and now Shayne?

Tyson's ease with Shayne was random, but highly evident after catching them all buddy-buddy at the Hook the previous evening. Now they were texting?

Maybe I should've just stayed with Chad.

"Cool," I said again, leaning away from the doorjamb. "I'm going to see what's for dinner."

Tyson was barely paying me any mind as he was deep into his phone.

Whatever.

In the hall, I bumped into Jordy. The only person I was genuinely happy to see. "Hey, what's up?"

Jordy pulled his attention away from his own cell phone. "Mom and Dad said they're getting Mexican for dinner, with extra guac this time."

I chuckled as I nuzzled Jordy closer. "Good, I'd hate to have to fight you 'til the death for it."

Jordy smiled. "Mom says I can redo my room."

"Yeah?"

"Yeah, I really like how you did Trice's room. I've been thinking mine is bland and I kinda want to paint it bloodred or maroon."

A project. The mere proposal of it had ideas popping up inside my head. Color schemes of maroon, black, and white, or even maroon, black, and gray.

Perhaps it had started with Tyson. When we were young, I'd gotten joy out of bossing him around and making him smile—*helping* him. I'd liked our forts, liked taking turns in creating our hideaways.

I decided to block it all out—the Bradleys and their snootiness, Tyson and his intent to go against the grain, and especially the fact that he was now texting my best friend.

"Jordy," I said, "you've come to the right person."

19 | *TRICE*

Monday morning came all too soon, and it was time to start summer school.

Pacific Hills was home now, and my first step in transitioning was completing my summer credits. So I got up early and packed my copy of *Roots* along with some school supplies as I got ready for my first day.

The night before, Travis and I'd made plans to hang out later and hit the subdivision's gym, so there was that to look forward to.

Maybe this could all work.

I was on my way down to the first floor when I passed by Jordy's room. Inside, I caught him and Nandy up still from the night before, rearranging his room. After ditching me

Friday for Chad, Nandy had come back slightly irritated, and she and Jordy set out on the task of redecorating his room. They'd stayed up Friday night moving furniture, and Saturday they'd painted his once white walls a matte shade of maroon. Neither Max or Parker had said anything, seeming to welcome this change and spark of creativity.

I'd stayed busy with Travis and the guys, and texting Shayne, all weekend, but a part of me had wanted to help out. Still, it was obvious they were fine on their own.

Standing in the hall, I watched Nandy laugh and play with her younger brother. In all his joy and glee, I could tell he really loved Nandy. That she had made this place a home for him and was a loving older sister.

Once upon a time, Nandy had been my Neverland, my memory of something good and true. Seeing her be that for her brother let me know she was still that same Nandy I'd once known.

We hadn't talked much since her boyfriend's intrusion Friday afternoon, and while I could tell it danced on her nerves when I questioned her status with him, I still wanted to patch things up and try this rekindling of our friendship.

That could wait for after school today.

In the front foyer, I bumped into Parker. He was clearly off work, lounging in his T-shirt and pajama bottoms. In his hands was a remote control, and in the air, buzzing about, was a model jet plane.

"Is this what you do all day?" I joked as I came down from the last step.

Parker knew no shame. "Don't listen to what anyone says, Trice, the nerd does get the girl."

Feeling playful, I said, "Nah, you must've had a lot of game."

"Oh, no, I asked Maxine out ten times before she gave in. Once she did, she realized your boy wasn't so bad."

They felt so normal and ordinary. I liked this.

"You meet in high school, or college?" I wondered.

Parker fiddled with his controller some more before safely landing the jet farther down the hall. "We met in college. She was the sorority queen, and I was captain of the debate team."

"Smooth. No wonder you won her over."

Parker wore a proud smile. "For sure, and get this—when I proposed, I built this tiny mechanical heart-shaped box. Totally had her swooning."

I guessed sometimes the nerdy guy did get the girl.

Maybe there was hope for Kyle and Shayne, who seemed oblivious that the guy existed.

"You'll have to tell me more sometime. I'm going in for school," I told Parker.

He nodded as he went back to his plane. "Have a good day, and again, I'm sure this'll all work out."

Like his wife, I was growing to trust and believe in Parker. His sincerity matched Max's.

I slipped outside and made my way to my SUV, aiming to start my day with optimism. This could work.

"Trice!" Warhol came jogging over from where his estate was two houses down. "Hey, let's carpool. I'll drive tomorrow, okay?"

"Sure."

Warhol hopped shotgun, and this time as we rode over to Cross High, he left my radio alone, agreeing with me on who was the best rapper out of LA.

We'd started a debate on who was top ten in the game when I pulled into the student parking lot fifteen minutes later.

"Look, all I'm saying is, beats beat lyrics," Warhol said as we climbed out of my car.

Across the lot I spotted Ashley, who was quick to join us by coming over and dapping us both up.

"Ashley." Warhol tapped his chest. "What do you think, man—beats or lyrics?"

Ashley made a face. "Erica and I argue about this all the time. Beats get the party bumpin', nobody cares about content."

I sighed, squinting at him. "What does she see in you again?"

Ashley snorted and shoved me.

Kyle soon climbed out of a nearby car, and the guys at once set off on him.

"Hey, Frogger, you wanna start a carpool?" Warhol asked.

"I probably shouldn't, in case one of the teachers needs me in early or later," Kyle declined.

"All work and no play, boy," Ashley said with a shake of his head. "You ain't ever coppin' a girl with that mind-set."

"Like Mancini," Warhol snickered.

I studied Kyle, awkward and innocent in his own way. Thinking of Parker, I thought he had a shot, if even a little.

"M-maybe I'll invite her out to the Hook. I hear Sour Pineapples are playing a show," Kyle spoke up.

Warhol wrinkled his nose. "Sour *who*?"

"It's, uh, an indie band. They're local, but so good."

Ashley and Warhol shared the same look of confusion before waving Kyle off.

"You just make sure you get back on the football team. Can't stay hydrated without you," Ashley said.

They poked fun at him, but it seemed more playful jest

than cruelty. Hopefully Nandy was wrong and this social circle bullshit wasn't real, because Kyle seemed okay to me.

"Welcome to hell, boys," Warhol drawled, spreading his arms out as he gestured around us at Cross High.

These kids were really making me dread the actual school year come September. "Let's get this over with," I said.

We entered the school as a unit before going our separate ways. Warhol had chemistry, Ashley had algebra II, Kyle was an errand boy, and I had both English and algebra II to make up for.

Along the way to my first class, I spotted more school posters littering the walls, one featuring the sports crowd and Cross High's football team. In all the photos of the green football field, the marching band stood out to me.

The school, much like our suburb and subdivision, was very multicultural, I was quick to realize. In the official marching band photo, Travis and a few other white students were easy to spot among the group heavily composed of Asian and Latino faces. While most of the group chose to do corny poses or facial expressions, Travis hung back in a corner staring straight at the camera, smile-free. If it weren't for his matching blue-and-black uniform, I would've questioned his presence in the photo.

The guy was really in the marching band.

I made a mental note to clown him for it later.

"Ah, there he is."

Behind me, Lydia was coming my way, seeming happy to see me.

"All ready for school?" Her perkiness was almost infectious.

"As ready as I'm going to get. We both know I have a habit of ditching."

Lydia shook her head, boldly reaching out and squeezing my shoulder. "Well, then, allow me to walk you to Mrs. Copeland's room. She'll be your instructor for English, where I hope you're a fan of the classics. If you didn't like Shakespeare, Jane Austen, and the Brontë sisters before, you're in for a treat, because you meet again."

I threw my head back and groaned as I walked with her up toward the second floor. "Can't wait."

Lydia patted my arm and chuckled. "So, it's been a week. How are you adjusting?"

I had to hand it to her, at least she genuinely seemed to care beyond my academics. "Not so bad. I'm making friends, I think."

"Good. There are a lot of nice kids in this school with plenty of character and personality."

She wasn't lying. The suburbs of Pacific Hills weren't what I expected.

"You might be right about that," I let her know.

"It wasn't until I got away from where I was from that I realized how far I could go."

We walked to the third floor, where Lydia led me to room 335 and stood back. She threaded her fingers together, an honest look in her eye as she peered up at me. "Tyson—*Trice*—I hope this all works out for you. A part of your English course is writing, and I mean it when I say you've got a gift. No pressure, but free yourself and relax. If you can, write something that feels familiar—write something that feels true."

She left me with these words and, as I faced my English class, I wondered if I could. If I had it in me. If the pen was mightier than the sword.

It was the start of summer, and we would see.

20 | *Nandy*

The first month of summer blew by quick as routines set in and relationships blossomed, and friendships stayed the same.

With cotillion at the end of the week, I was both anxious and excited for my debut. My friends were preparing—and complaining, due to some of their mothers nagging them about every little thing. I didn't mind; it was all going to be worth it. Friday was going to be my night.

Things were perfect…well, almost.

"Can you pass the salt?" Tyson asked. Then, as if to annoy me, he added with a sickly-sweet smile, "Please."

Poking at my baked potato, I avoided his eyes. "Get it yourself."

"Nandy!" my mother scolded. She glared at me as she passed Tyson the salt shaker. "What's gotten into you?"

Tyson was enjoying my reprimanding. *Bastard*.

"Nothing," I muttered.

"I thought you two were getting along."

"We aren't," I said, as Tyson replied, "We are."

My eyes met his and, like always, I couldn't hold his gaze for much longer than a moment.

Tyson had been with my family for a month now. We'd gotten past our rocky beginning, and things had been fine, but now they weren't. I couldn't quite place why I was so mad at him, but one day I woke up and everything he did incited me with anger.

I didn't know how to articulate it, but the anger was deep inside of me, bubbling up to the surface, and just when I thought I could grasp the reason, another part of me shoved it back down.

My mother rolled her eyes, standing from the table. "Figure it out."

She dropped her plate at the sink and left the room. With my father working late at his office and Jordy over at the Gómezes', that left only Tyson and me.

With my gaze on the remains of the evening's dinner, I could feel him staring at me.

One look up confirmed it. He liked this. It was hard to miss the taunting gleam in his eye. "You look nice, Nandy."

I scowled. "Screw you, Tyson."

This caused him to smile. "Can't take a compliment?"

"Leave me alone."

"And here I thought we were working on our friendship. *Tsk-tsk*."

He had gotten on my last nerve. I grabbed my plate and washed the leftovers down the disposal.

Heat caused the hairs on the back of my neck to stand up.

When I turned around, Tyson was right behind me. Too close. I could smell his cologne. Rich, intoxicating, and delicious.

He set his hands on either side of me on the counter's edge, blocking me in. His smell was suffocating me.

"Wanna hang out?" he asked.

It was a stupid question. One he definitely knew the answer to. "No."

"Come on, Nandy. You, me, and the TV. I'll even watch some reality shows you love." He seemed sincere and genuine, but the answer was still no.

"I have, uh, stuff. Call Travis or something." I pushed him aside and went to my room, ignoring whatever he was saying behind me.

Inside my room, with my back pressed against the door, I reminded myself that I despised all there was to Tyson. Tyson hung with Travis, and I hung with Chad. Tyson goofed off with Warhol and sports, while I sunbathed with the girls. Tyson played video games with Jordy and asked my father how his day was, while I snuck in and read *Roots*. Tyson. Tyson. Tyson. Ugh.

As if to piss me off further, I heard him go into his room and start playing rap music loudly. Some catchy chorus with a wicked drum beat was blasting, and I had half a mind to storm next door and…

Fuming, I went to my bed instead, buried my face in my pillow and screamed the thoughts away.

I hate you, Tyson Trice.

A hand came down on my shoulder and I shot up, panicked that he'd come into my room, somehow able to hear the thoughts running around in my head.

It was Shayne.

She held her hands up. "Hey, I knocked, but clearly you couldn't hear me."

I sat up. "Yeah. He's being a dick."

Shayne frowned. "Ty's vibing some good stuff."

Ty? Since when had she been put on the exclusive list of calling Tyson by his real name, let alone a nickname?

"You mean Trice," I corrected as I stood up.

Shayne shrugged as she followed me out of my room. "Whatever. He doesn't seem to mind."

Her confidence grated on my nerves, and I blocked out the annoyance as I went and pounded on Tyson's door.

He must've been ready, because the volume decreased and he came to the door with an easy smile. "Hey, Nan."

He was doing this on purpose.

"Mind keeping that crap down?" I snapped.

Tyson gestured toward his room, appearing wounded, but only in mock. "That's not crap."

"Yes, it is."

"Actually, I thought it was good. Who was it?" Shayne stepped forth and asked.

Tyson smiled toward my best friend. "OutKast."

"Oh, I like them!"

"Really, Shayne?" I had the decency not to roll my eyes.

"Yes. They're good."

"You really know OutKast?"

"Yeah, they're the ones who sing that 'Black Beatles' song, right?" Shayne's face fell flat as she let her own annoyance show. "Honestly, Nan, give me some credit." She faced Tyson. "To be fair, I only know 'Hey Ya!' but it's like the best song ever."

Tyson agreed. "I dare anyone to listen to it and sit still."

They shared a smile as if I'd disappeared.

"Scarlett's going to be so amazing," Shayne said.

He agreed. "She's gonna be dope."

I had no idea who Scarlett was, but the fuzziness between my best friend and the enemy was nauseating. And the fact that they had this inside joke? It was all so stupid.

"Too bad we can't say the same for Nandy," Tyson teased with a peek at me.

Oh, now I was allowed to be included in their dumb conversation? "I'm just not a big fan of rap, is all."

"That's the problem." Tyson shook his head and went back to Shayne. "I got the new Lana Del Rey, you should hear it."

As my mouth dropped open in shock, my best friend practically jumped for joy. "Really? I've been meaning to hear that. You gotta come over tomorrow after school and we can jam."

"Definitely."

Now Tyson liked Lana?

"Seriously? *You* like Lana Del Rey now?" I'd played her countless times over the past few weeks, and he'd voiced his opinion against her from the beginning.

Tyson shrugged. "Yeah. I mean, at first it was annoying, but I like her sound. It's tragic, it would kill over a hip-hop track. Like Dido and Em."

"Oh my God, yes. Dude, tomorrow we're gonna chat and make more plans for Scarlett." Shayne held out her hand, and I watched in horror as Tyson high-fived her, and worse, reached over and gave her a hug.

"Shayne, let's go to your house. I'm sure your stepmonster's figured out the childproof lock on the medicine cabinet by now," I said.

Shayne groaned. "You're right, let's go. 'Bye, Ty."

"Catch you later." He went back into his room and shut the door, and I grimaced as I led my best friend out to my car.

The whole way to her house, she babbled on about Tyson and how funny he was, how smart he was, how strong he was, and how he just got her.

"Daddy loves him," Shayne was saying as we walked up to her front door. "He thinks he's funny and good for me."

Mr. Mancini was tough on guys—when we were thirteen and Shayne wanted to have a party with boys and girls, Mr. Mancini had wagged his finger and strictly told her, "You are not to think of boys until after med school." If he liked Tyson, then that said a lot.

I told myself I didn't care as I stopped in the foyer at the sound of my cell ringing.

Shayne went to the family room, and I sat on the last step on one side of the dual staircase to answer Chad's call.

"Hey," I said as I picked up.

I could hear guys in the background. He was somewhere with his friends, probably hanging out and getting amped for the final season of football.

"What's up?" he asked.

"I'm with Shayne," I said. *To avoid being near Tyson.*

"Oh, cool. Speaking of that, my mom wants to know if you've got your hair and shit together," Chad said with mock exasperation.

I'd already gotten my relaxer along with my extensions. Our makeup was being taken care of, and I'd bought the perfect dress. "All's squared over here."

"I cannot wait until this hell is over. It's bad enough we've gotta deal with homecoming, the luau, and prom."

"Don't you like seeing your girl all dressed up?"

"I saw you dressed up last year, and the year before that," Chad admitted. "I always see you dressed up for something."

My mouth fell agape. I knew this was all driving him crazy, but this was my big day. *My* cotillion.

Blinking, I let it go. "Well, it's almost over."

"I'm just hoping when it's done we can have some fun again." The tone of his voice oozed with innuendo.

Defeated, I gave in and said, "Yeah."

"Sweet. Let's talk later, the guys are getting restless. Love you."

I mumbled a response before hanging up and staring at his contact photo. It was of us at the beach. He had his arms around me, and I was doing my best to smile despite how cold I'd been that day.

Me and Chad. Chad and Nandy. Nandy Smith and Chad Bradley. *"Candy,"* as my friends and a group of freshmen took to calling us. There were countless photos of us together online and of me sporting his jersey number and jumping around at games in support. We were ideal. We were perfect.

I found Shayne in the family room on the couch, curled up as she texted ferociously on her phone.

"Let me guess, Tyson says hi?" I said as I went and sat beside her.

It was like she hadn't even heard me. She was too engrossed in her phone, smiling all big and cheesy.

I hate it.

Shayne soon was busy flipping through the channels on the TV. "Ooh, I like this song! Ty showed it to me."

On-screen, some guys with dreadlocks were rapping and preparing what looked to be stir-fry. I didn't admit the fact that the beat was kind of catchy.

Shayne sat back, in awe at the video before her. "We're just making plans for Scarlett. She's going to know all genres of music."

Gritting my teeth, I did my best to calm down. "Who is Scarlett?"

"Scarlett's the redheaded baby girl Trice and I are going to adopt one day when we're married," Shayne explained ever so casually. "We'll have our own son and name him Dante, because we agree that it's a good ethnic blend. We're going to spend our vacations in Italy so our kids can learn their heritage, and Trice can work on his Italian. Now he's adamant on me being Shayne Trice, but I'm all for hyphens because Daddy only has me, and I like being a Mancini."

My blood boiled. Not only did they hang out on the regular now, they had gone as far as to make up this fictional future together filled with adopted redheads and baby boys? I hated it.

"Or maybe we'll have more than two kids. I mean, look at him, Nan, he's a total babe. We're gonna have an army of little babies." Shayne squealed with delight at the idea of birthing Tyson's future offspring.

Dear freakin' God.

She was staring at photos on her phone, talking in a dreamy voice about the future of her and Tyson. "What I really like about him is how he can be soft—he can let his hardness go and just relax. He's incredible." She admired a photo in her phone of her and Tyson. Shayne was sporting a bikini, and Tyson was shirtless as they mushed together. Shayne was doing her best impression of a *grr* face and Tyson had his nose scrunched up. My stomach jolted at the reality of them looking...*cute* together.

I hated Tyson. I hated how he bonded with Jordy. How he won my parents over. How he cooked for us once a week. How he stole my friends. How he went from laughing or smiling on a rare occasion to doing it all the time with his "friends." How he had become this totally carefree person. How he was smart, deep, and thoughtful. How that damn haircut had had a major effect on his appearance. How he knew how to get under my skin with just a look or a smile. How the summer before senior year had morphed into the summer of Tyson Trice.

Most important, I hated how he probably knew I held no real contempt against him at all. Not even a little.

"I'm thinking about asking him to be my date for cotillion," Shayne confessed.

I felt sick. "It's totally last minute, Shayne."

"I know, but we can make it work. I never like guys, but I like him."

My best friend liked Tyson. *My* Tyson.

I was wrong. I was selfish. But still, he was mine, had been since we were younger. He couldn't be Shayne's.

But as I watched her go through more selfies of her and Tyson, it became painfully clear that he already was.

21 | TRICE

Lydia wanted to talk to me Tuesday after class let out. I was supposed to go to Shayne's, but something about the tone of Lydia's voice and the expression on her face made me think something was up.

After four weeks, my semester of summer school was coming to a close and, according to my teachers, I was doing well, but Lydia managed to unnerve me.

"Something wrong?" I asked as I sat in front of her desk.

Lydia cooled me with a smile. "No, no, everything's great, actually. I just wanted to talk to you about English."

I sensed a straight setup. In the beginning of the semester, English had been about book reports and writing prompts. Now, the topics were screaming that we were being watched closely.

I sat back in the hard plastic chair, eyeing the woman in front of me. I was curious as to how long we'd bullshit before coming straight out with it. "Yeah?"

Lydia nodded. "I'm in love with your prose. I love the way you described young boys from your environment and how they feel the need to beat this inferiority complex by proving how tough they are."

Where I was from, and maybe this went for everywhere, it wasn't cool to be weak or soft. Boys weren't allowed to cry or express their feelings. It was about being hard and surviving.

It was this hardness that so many of us radiated that also became our demise, or our fatal flaw. In my latest paper, I'd written about envying women and girls for their abilities to express emotions without shame. I wrote that it wasn't fair that women were taught it was okay to be human and have feelings, while boys weren't taught the same. I wrote that teaching boys to be strong and hard was the very trigger ruining a generation.

I didn't wish to be emotional, but I wondered how many of us from the 'Wood would've fared differently if we didn't go along with the crowd. If we didn't want to prove we were tough. If we weren't afraid to say we cared about a girl. With guys like Khalil, it was all about acting tough enough or hard enough, and then you had guys like Money and Pretty, who were so far gone that it was no longer an act but the real deal. Maybe I was somewhere in between. After being in the Hills, I knew that, without the Smiths, I probably would've hardened in the 'Wood. I probably would've let my flaw eat me alive.

But that was just me writing in English.

I'd known something was up when my English instructor went from asking us to compare the symbolism in the book to our lives to switching it up and having us write about ourselves.

No one else in class had picked up on it, but I had. And here was Lydia, all but confessing.

"You've been monitoring me?"

She shrugged, guilty. "We were discussing how the summer semester was going, and you came up. I guess you can say we got greedy for more."

I lifted a brow. "And now?"

Lydia opened a drawer and pulled something out. She set a brand-new composition book on top of her desk and pushed it toward me.

"Now the rest is up to you. I love your writing, Trice. It's honest and real. You write about realizing there was no God when you lost your mother, and I found that to be brave."

Nearly flinching, I played it off with a shrug. While I was growing up, my family wasn't really religious, but they'd expected or assumed that there was a higher being, as much as my mother spoke about a God. Pops too, and sometimes Prophet would say something about Him as well. After the shooting, I'd known in my heart that I didn't believe, nor did I want to. "I would rather believe in nothing and die than believe in something and die anyway."

Lydia bobbed her head. "That's what I'm talking about. You're not afraid to say how you feel. So many kids around here are whining about useless social media BS and being cut off from credit cards, and you've got something to say. I would love to see you continue, even if it's just to get this story out."

"You just wanna read about what happened."

"I'm not going to pretend that I don't want to know," Lydia admitted, "but whether or not you wanna show me is up to you. I just want you to keep expressing yourself in this way. You're a survivor, and you've got a heck of a story to tell."

I didn't have to take the composition book, but as I stood to leave, I found myself grabbing it.

In the hall I bumped into Kyle, and we made our way to the student parking lot.

"Hey. Wanna come over and play some games?" Kyle asked.

"Uh, sure. Maybe later, though. I'm supposed to be hanging out with Shayne right now."

Kyle perked up, shaking his hair out of his eyes. "S-Shayne? My Shayne?" He blinked a couple of times, catching himself. "Well, not m-my Shayne, but… Because you know… Just Shayne, Shayne, you know? Everyone knows Shayne and…" He blinked. "Shayne Mancini?"

This was where things got awkward.

I liked Shayne.

Kyle liked Shayne. *Really* liked Shayne.

"That'd be the one."

"Oh, oh, okay. You guys have fun or whatever." His shoulders slouched in defeat. "I'll get started on the box."

"What's your take on redheads?" I came out and asked.

"I have a few in my family. I'm sure there's some Irish connection or something, but I'm not partial, why?"

"Just keep that in mind." I reached out and patted his chest before heading to my car.

Going home wasn't an option with Nandy probably there. It had been a month, and she had completely flipped the script on me. One minute she was friendly, and the next she acted like she couldn't stand to be in the same room with me. If she was watching TV in the family room and I came in, she would turn it off and leave. If she was lying out by the pool and I came outside, she would cover up and ignore me. She didn't invite me to the Hook or the Crab Shack. If Travis wanted to go somewhere and we bumped into Nandy and the gang, she would ignore me.

At first it had been annoying, but the part of me that stopped giving a fuck a week later thought it was cute, and then I began to mess with her just to set her off. I hadn't done a thing to her, and yet she'd gone back to despising me.

So I started going to Shayne's after school.

Shayne Mancini had just kinda happened. Once, she'd sought my opinion on this summer blockbuster that was showing, asking if I thought it'd be interesting for her and her dad to see. I'd said yeah, and the next weekend she'd come over upset, wanting to see Nandy, because her dad had canceled on her. But Nandy hadn't been home, so I'd taken her to the movie and we'd grabbed dinner after.

We sorta fell into place after that. I liked Shayne, on a different level than I liked Travis. With everyone else, Shayne was this one way, but with me, she was herself. She was goofy. She was girly. She was stuck-up, but she was smart, opinionated, and so much more than what was on the surface.

It was funny that Nandy had told me to stay away from Travis and Shayne, because there wasn't a thing wrong with either of them.

Shayne met me at her front door, wearing a bathing suit. It hadn't taken much time to learn that most girls in Pacific Hills lived in bathing suits. Shayne swore she rarely saw the sense of owning underwear due to the fact that most girls wore swimsuits under all their clothes.

Now, she was wearing a black bandeau bikini top with a pair of jean shorts.

She grabbed a fistful of my T-shirt. "Come on, let's go out back. I wanna get you topless."

That was another thing about Shayne—the shameless flirting never ceased. At one point, I'd started flirting back, and the next thing I knew, we'd created this imaginary life together complete with a redheaded daughter and a son with an Italian name and bright future.

I liked that about Shayne. She didn't push, but she made me think of a future, even if it was just pretend.

In the Mancinis' backyard, I sat back on a beach chair and Shayne sat between my legs, telling me about her day.

"Oil me?" she asked as she held out a bottle of sunscreen.

I took to oiling her back as she carried on. She was talking about something she'd heard on the news about the water supply in Africa and how she wanted to spend the summer before college going out and helping.

Once, she told me she wanted to join the Peace Corps when she was younger, but then the idea of becoming a doctor had inspired her just the same.

A part of me wanted to visit Africa to find my roots and to connect with my heritage. Shayne wanted to go help. The thought made me smile.

Dr. Mancini came into my line of vision as he stepped out into the backyard. With my hands lathering sunscreen onto Shayne's back and shoulders, I thought to stop.

But Dr. Mancini didn't seem to mind.

He greeted us both with a smile. "Hey, kids."

Shayne sat up. "Daddy! You're home."

"Yeah, just for a bit." In true Dr. Mancini fashion, he was scrolling through his cell phone. It didn't take long to learn that once his phone came out he was no longer in our universe.

"I was thinking maybe we could go sailing this weekend," Shayne suggested.

"Uh-huh." He put on his glasses to glance at something on his phone.

I watched as Shayne's eyes slit. "I read that book I said I was going to read. I even wrote the report for you."

"Sounds good, honey."

Her nostrils flared. "I had sex with Ty in the pool, total raw dog."

"Glad to hear you're having fun."

She threw her hands up as her pretty face twisted in anger and sadness. "You're canceling tonight, aren't you?"

Somehow these were the words that registered to Dr. Mancini as he finally faced his daughter. "Oh, I'm sorry. I'm on call all weekend. You know how that is."

Shayne let out a breath and I knew she was crushed.

I wrapped my arms around her from behind, holding her and feeling her relax into me. I knew she was still upset, but I could sense her fight was over.

"I'll have dinner with you," I said.

In front of me, Shayne bowed her head as she simply nodded. Dr. Mancini smiled at the rescue and mouthed a *thank you* before going back inside.

Moments passed, and I attempted to massage Shayne's shoulders, but she kept silent, looking off into the distance. On the outside, this seemed pretty regular for them. Dr. Mancini canceled on her a lot, and she would always find something else to do to avoid doing anything with her stepmother, who seemed heavily medicated most days. Shayne's mother was reportedly in rehab.

I guess it was true, what they said. The prettiest people sometimes had the ugliest lives.

"How was summer school, Trice?" Shayne asked.

"Lydia wants me to write about my life in Lindenwood."

"Maybe you should."

Maybe I would. It would give me something to do. But that wasn't the entire issue. Once I filled the book with my tale, then what?

Shayne's silence called to me.

"Something wrong?" I asked.

"Do you ever just wish you could go back and change your life?"

"You have no idea."

"I just wish… I just wish my mom could be here and my dad… They wouldn't even have to be together…" Shayne stopped to think. "No, they would. I just wish they were together and it was all fine, you know?"

I nodded.

"What are your parents like?"

I was surprisingly relieved to know that Nandy hadn't told anyone about my situation. "They're dead."

Shayne turned around, reaching out and rubbing my arm. "I'm sorry. Can I ask how?"

I felt numb. "My dad killed my mother, shot me, and killed himself."

Shayne read me right, because she didn't offer any more affection than squeezing my shoulder and frowning. "I hope it gets easier here, Trice."

Maybe it would.

"Your dad has good intentions. He just sucks at showing it," I said.

"I don't want him to have good intentions. I want him to be my dad."

At the Smiths', both Parker and Max worked long hours during the week, and even then they'd come home and check on all of us. With Dr. Mancini, it seemed as though he expected Shayne to be okay with taking care of herself.

It had to be tough on her. He was tangibly the only parent she had left.

I didn't want to talk about our parents, not when it was a trigger to upset the both of us.

"Can I ask you something?" I asked.

"What?"

"Last night, with Nandy, what'd you guys do?"

"We watched TV and did our nails." Shayne held out her hand and wiggled her fingers. "I did cobalt blue, you like?"

The color did complement her. "Yeah. About Nandy—has she said anything to you, about me?"

Shayne appeared thoughtful. "No, not really. Why?"

I wasn't about to whine about Nandy's mistreating me, but I did want a hint as to what I'd done to deserve it. "No reason."

Shayne gathered her phone and sent a text. "I wonder what she's up to."

"Probably at the beach kicking sand in kids' eyes."

Shayne snuck me a disapproving look as she smiled.

Her phone pinged and she read her text. "She's at Mrs. Stone's helping bake cupcakes for some charity drive. We should go. Mrs. Stone always lets volunteers keep a dozen for themselves."

While I wasn't in the mood to bake, the opportunity to seize the day and talk to Nandy had presented itself, and I knew I had no choice.

Standing, I gathered my keys. "Let's go."

22 | *Nandy*

Leave it to my mother to volunteer to help Mrs. Stone bake cupcakes for charity and then drop out due to work. No, leave it to my mother to do all that, and then force *me* to fill in for her. Honestly, I hadn't been doing anything, so I didn't mind going and spending my Tuesday afternoon packing and labeling cupcakes with a ninety-year-old woman who scolded any girl who dared to show an ankle or their midriff.

It was for a good cause, as the proceeds were going to the nearest children's hospital, and it got me out of the house. Not to mention as I bumped into Kyle Frogge, it gave me an opportunity to get to know the quiet guy from down the street.

In a room full of girls and older women, he was the only guy who had shown up to volunteer. Mrs. Stone was using this to her advantage and had him carrying boxes of baked goods to her Suburban for each trip she took to the venue to set up.

I caught Kyle alone across the dining room labeling cupcakes, so I made my way over to him. "Hey, Kyle."

He appraised me for a second before responding. "Hi, Nandy."

Kyle seemed surprised that I'd approached him. His slight suspicion made me laugh and nudge him. "What's up?"

Kyle shrugged and labeled a pack of coconut iced cupcakes. "Oh, you know, not much. You?"

"Same. My mom got caught up at the office and volunteered me to take her place," I said. I leaned back against the table, eyeing the boy beside me. "So, what are you into and what do you like?"

Kyle perked a brow. "Really?"

"Yeah, I feel like I don't talk to you enough."

"We've been neighbors since we were nine, and I think we've had all of three conversations our whole lives."

"So, let's change that. Tonight's battle of the sexes. You should totally join in. It's cotillion tradition."

Kyle frowned. "Chad and his friends aren't really my scene."

I couldn't blame him there. I think it was loyalty and sports that linked Chad in with the likes of Oliver and Dickie. But I wanted Kyle to belong, and not sit home alone while most of us were having a good time at the beach later.

"You can miss *Star Wars* for one night," I teased.

Kyle deadpanned, "It's *Star Trek* actually. Big difference."

"Really? Is that the one with the hand thingy?"

He snorted at my attempt to do the symbol as he bobbed his head, peeking at me from beneath his shaggy dark hair. "They just both happen in space. *Star Trek* is more about exploring the galaxy than a war. A few guys at school formed a club I'm a part of. We mostly watch reruns and shoot the shit, but it gets me out of the house twice a week."

It sounded nerdy but adorable. "I'll have to check it out once school starts. Hey, maybe I could talk to Shayne about joining."

Kyle's face lit up with the biggest grin. "R-really?"

"Yeah, it wouldn't hurt to try new things."

Kyle held up his arm between us. "Pinch me, because I *have* to be dreaming."

I pushed his arm away and laughed. "Oh come on, I'm for real. You know, you're really cool now that I've gotten to know you better, and maybe you could school us on *Star Trek*."

Kyle's smile disintegrated. "Okay, now I know I am dreaming. Any minute you're going to morph into Uhura and I'm going to be Spock."

I felt my brows furrow at the reference. I sorta got it. Chad had dragged me to see some remake of the iconic science fiction show in theaters. "Why wouldn't you be the captain guy?"

Kyle made a face as he gestured to himself. "I'm not exactly the leading man."

Kyle wasn't the quintessential beefy lead in an action movie, true, but he was cute in his own way. Like Joseph Gordon-Levitt cute. Plus, his wit was endearing, and I found his interest in space and science fiction unique.

I patted his chest. "You just need confidence. Girls love confident guys."

"Kyle!" Mrs. Stone called from the doorway.

He faced me. "I'll consider tonight."

Because I was actually thinking about checking out his

club, I asked, "Hey, Kyle, about the club, you guys don't dress up or anything, do you?"

Kyle backed away, looking around as he clasped his hands together. "I will have to talk to Brady about that."

I stifled a laugh as I heard my phone sound out of my pocket.

A picture message came in on my phone, and I looked down to see it was from Shayne. It was a photo of her in a bikini top leaning back into Tyson blowing a kiss. The caption read: On our way :)

A selfish sickness lined my stomach, and I set my phone facedown.

She was doing that a lot lately, using pronouns like *we* and *ours*. I hated that I noticed and cared.

Most of all, I hated that I couldn't control it. It started as a tick and turned into a full-blown itch that wouldn't go away.

There was a little Nandy inside of me that would jump up and down whenever Shayne spoke of Tyson, going *mine, mine, mine!* The more Little Nandy jumped and shouted, the more I caught myself almost letting the words spill from my lips.

Chad materialized out of nowhere, causing me to jump and almost drop the pack of cupcakes in my hand.

He chuckled as he reached out and caught them before they could hit the floor. "Nervous?"

"Oh, hey." I accepted the pack of cupcakes. Seeing they were peanut-butter-and-jelly flavored, I grabbed the roll of labels that accompanied the flavor and quickly made them ready for sale.

"'Oh, hey'? Geez, it's great to see you too, Nan," Chad said as he attempted to help. "Even if it has been practically forever."

"What's wrong, Chad?" I let out a sigh as I put down my labels.

His brows furrowed as he did the same, facing me with his full attention. "Um, how about the fact that I barely get to see you? You're always busy with the girls or helping out at stuff like this. We barely have any time together."

"You know I've been busy getting ready for cotillion."

Chad rolled his eyes. "You know what I mean."

"Is this about sex again?" It was my turn to roll my eyes and get back to work. He'd complained before about our not having hooked up at all that summer, and really, I just wasn't in the mood to argue over it. It felt like I was getting a migraine from it all, Chad and his complaining, and then that stupid text.

Chad scoffed. "Yeah, that's exactly what this is about."

"You'll get your rocks off whenever I have enough free time on my hands to blink."

"This is not about that," he snapped. "This is about you and the space that's been wedged between us. I seriously doubt you have to spend every waking second with the girls, talking about dresses, hair, and makeup. Or out doing things like this."

"Like *this*?" I repeated. "We're helping out a good cause, Chad!"

Doing things like *this* was what I enjoyed—helping people in need because I was more fortunate than others.

Maybe I didn't have to spend as much time away from him as I did. As awful as it sounded, being at Mrs. Stone's helping out was exactly where I would've rather been than with him at the moment. It all fed into that selfish part of me that I was losing control over.

"That's not what I meant," Chad said.

"It's almost over," I said finally, as I thought of cotillion.

Chad grimaced and his shoulders sagged. "Did you tell *him* about tonight?"

I managed to lighten up. "Not that I talk to Tyson, but telling him wouldn't do me any good, now, would it?"

Chad shifted moods, too. "I promise to be nice. I don't think Catalano's getting involved, so it should be easy."

"No offense, but I think Travis would make tonight a little bit more fun," I admitted. "Think of the steps he'd take to win."

My boyfriend chuckled. "The guy's a loose cannon."

"Some might say that excites a girl."

"True, but that lifestyle is bound to catch up with you."

And that was Chad—he always stayed in line and did as he was told. Once, the boys had been playing flag football with Travis, and when Travis had gone rogue and not passed the ball to Chad, and scored on his own, it had set Chad off.

Travis didn't live by rules or care what people thought, and people in our circle sorta did. Sure, we broke the law, drank underage, and partied, but we stayed mostly in line to appease our parents and to look good. Travis was fearless. And Tyson flocked to him.

To think, here I was stressing and glorifying my debut as if it really mattered. I had to jump through hoops for these old ladies in town just to debut in an expensive dress and prove myself worthy.

Looking at the likes of carefree Travis Catalano, I couldn't help but wonder: worthy of what?

"Do you ever think we worry too much about image and our parents, and what's planned out for us?" I came out and asked.

Chad appeared thoughtful, but then he shrugged. "Where's this coming from?"

I shook my head. "Nothing. I'm just talking crazy. Ignore me."

Chad stepped closer and kissed me, quick and chaste. "The guys were talking about hanging out at the beach after. You in?"

It wasn't like it was anything special—it was tradition after the events we had planned for the night.

Still, I put on a smile. "Yeah. I invited Kyle Frogge, so be nice."

Chad wrinkled his nose. "That weird kid?"

I shoved him. "He's not weird."

"Sure, babe. Here comes controversy," Chad mumbled as he looked across the room to where Shayne was entering with Tyson. She was holding his hand and leading him into the crowded room. The sickening thing was, they seemed to match, with their clothing color scheme of black and dark gray.

I could see Mrs. Stone scowling at Shayne's choice of a crop top and a high-waisted skirt with a slit in the side, exposing her from the thigh on down.

Chad was staring at me. He looked down at a pack of cupcakes and fingered the messed-up label. "I guess I'll see you later."

"Yeah, I'll see you."

He left, and Erica and Edi came over, Erica studying me and then looking after Chad.

"Trouble in paradise?" she quipped.

"No, we're fine," I insisted. I focused on Edi's hair, which was all ready for cotillion due to her recent trip to the salon and added extensions. "Nice locks."

She giggled as she ran her fingers through the tresses. "New hair has me feelin' like Rapunzel and shit."

We laughed, and my mood lifted gradually.

"Got that right. We can't all have flawless hair like Erica over there," I teased.

Erica smirked and tilted her head, jiggling her curls. "Oh, this is just God and conditioner."

We all had long hair, but Erica's was perfect. She could've gotten extensions, but really, she didn't need any.

Shayne came over, almost seeming to glide and glow.

"Hey," she said as she greeted us all.

"How nice of you to show up when it's basically over," Erica said.

Shayne waved her off. "We totally decided to come last minute. Now we're in the mood for a burger run. You guys in?"

The girls agreed.

"I'm actually still full from my kale salad earlier," I spoke up.

"Ooh, the one with the yams, cranberries, and raisins?" Shayne asked.

"Yeah." As much as I wanted to pig out, I was forcing myself to eat healthy so that I could still fit into my dress.

"Is there any left?"

I nodded.

"Save me some?" Shayne moved on to the girls and soon held up her phone. "Look what Ty got me."

It was a new case. One of the little mermaid, Ariel, sitting backward with a big blue bow in her hair. The emphasis was on her great head of hair for sure. I got the gist of the gift right away.

"That's so sweet," Edi said as she examined the simple case. "Did you ask him to cotillion yet?"

Shayne peered over at Tyson and smiled with a shrug. "Not yet. I'm thinking I'll do it tonight after all the mayhem."

Tyson was talking with Kyle, oblivious to what was in store.

Biting on my lip, I frowned at it all. "It's so last minute, Shayne. He's missed all the practices and wouldn't know how to waltz."

My best friend stopped smiling. "So?"

"So, what if he says no?"

She narrowed her eyes. "Why would he say no?"

I focused on labeling the last pack of cupcakes. "You don't have to have an ego about it, I was just saying."

It got quiet, and I could feel the heat from their collective stares.

Shayne huffed. "Wow, I thought you'd be happy for me. Guess I thought wrong." She walked off, heading straight for Tyson and Kyle. Immediately she demanded Tyson's attention and was blind to Kyle's smile and stare.

Erica frowned. "That wasn't nice, Nan."

I threw my hands up. "What? I'm just saying it's not right to ambush, is all."

"What's with you lately?" Edi asked. "You don't seem like yourself."

"Yeah, it's like you're on permanent PMS or something," Erica added.

"I'm fine," I insisted with a little edge in my voice. It was one thing to notice myself how alien I had become, but for my friends to notice as well was a tad bit too much.

I was losing it.

And I lost it even more when Tyson came over.

"Can we talk?" he asked.

In the background I could see Shayne standing with her arms crossed, glaring our way.

Oh great, did she tattle on me?

Instead of giving me a choice, Tyson took my arm and led me out to the hallway between the dining room and the Stones' back study. I stood against one wall and him against the other. He stared at me, and I hated it.

"What?" I snapped.

Tyson frowned. "What's wrong with you?"

Crossing my arms, I shook my head. "Right now? You stopping me from working."

"Nandy... I just don't get it, okay? Cut me some slack, I'm trying to meet you halfway here."

"Well, don't." *Stop it*, I told myself, *you're being a bitch and he's done nothing wrong.*

Tyson stood straight, his expression changing to cold. He studied me as he shook his head. "I guess it's a good thing I don't care about you, or your attitude would be a big deal to me."

If he'd said it to hurt me, it worked.

Staring down at the floor, I forced myself to let it go. "Yep."

"I guess I'll get out of your way, then."

"Yeah, do that."

He was quiet as he remained where he was, and I felt my insides collapsing under his heavy scrutiny. I knew I was wrong. There was no one to blame but myself for being so jealous of my best friend and hating the sight of her and Tyson together.

The little hallway got tinier, and if I reached out, I could've touched Tyson. But I didn't.

Instead, I squared my shoulders and straightened, preparing to go back to what I was doing.

"See you at home," he said from behind me as I walked on by him.

My cold front dropped at the sound of his voice.

Like an addiction, I found myself looking back, only to find him doing the same. His expression went stoic as he gazed at me gazing at him. He turned away as I did and I went back to my station.

The girls were gone, and Kyle was in their place, packing the cupcakes to be taken to the event.

He was watching as Tyson met up with Shayne. Kyle studied her, the way she smiled, laughed, talked, blinked—everything. He tilted his head, shaking his hair out of his eyes, watching the girl who had it all and yet had nothing. "The only thing worse than existing in a world of notoriety is knowing that you don't matter to the one you want the most."

I peeked over as well and watched as Tyson placed his hand on Shayne's shoulder and smiled at her, then gestured to the door for them to leave.

Frowning, I went back to my cupcakes. But they were all packed. "Shut up, Kyle."

23 | TRICE

Shayne had disappeared. One minute we were watching TV in the Smiths' family room; the next she was going to the kitchen to get something to drink, and then she was gone.

It wasn't like the Smiths had a mega mansion, but searching the first floor left me coming up short. Shouting her name garnered me silence.

Something was wrong.

I figured she wasn't up on the second floor with Nandy, because they'd had a weird vibe between them at the cupcake charity. Shayne hadn't told me what was wrong, but if looks could kill, she and Nandy were gearing up for war. I didn't get it, and it was beginning to aggravate my last damn nerve. It was one thing for Nandy to treat me some type of way, but to treat her friends like shit?

The doorbell rang, stopping me en route to search the second floor.

It was nine thirty, and everything reeked of too much quiet.

Through the translucent glass on the side of the door, I could just make out Warhol's burly figure, which let me know that either Ashley or Travis was ringing the bell.

It was Travis.

When I opened the door, Travis walked in, Warhol and Matt behind him, both managing to greet me whereas Travis just stood waiting.

"Well?" I asked as I shut the door behind the troops.

Travis grinned, reading of pure mischief. "Dude, come on, it's Boys Versus Girls night, let's go."

"Boys Versus Girls?" I questioned.

All of them shared the same look of confusion before Matt took the initiative to speak up. "Every year before cotillion, the boys and girls have a battle of the sexes to make up for the girls bleeding our ears about the event. It's our way of getting back at them and having some last-minute fun before the big day. It's basically capture the flag. They got theirs, and we got ours."

"It usually ends at the beach, and we all have a bonfire. There's even a big water balloon fight," Warhol spoke up.

I turned to Travis. "You're going to cotillion?"

"My parents forced me to take pity on a family friend." He shrugged. "I wasn't going to take part in tonight's excursions, but what the hell? It's worth it to cause some mayhem for a night. So let's get started. We gotta join the others, even Bradley." Travis made a face at the mention of Chad. "We aim to be inclusive."

I wasn't interested in the idea of pranks and mayhem, and I was going to decline the whole thing until an idea hit me.

"Anything goes?" I wanted to know.

By the devious expression on Travis's face I had my answer. "Pretty much."

"I'll meet up with you guys later. I have an idea," I said as I stood back.

Travis bobbed his head. "All right, I gotta go make nice with Chad. What should I tell him about you?" He tossed me a walkie-talkie.

I fiddled with the device. "That we're going to win."

A half hour passed after the boys left before I was finally able to put my plan into motion. I was beginning to think my stakeout wasn't going to work, but then I heard her door open.

Nandy came out of her bedroom with her gaze glued to the carpet. I took her aloofness as my cue to seize the moment.

I grabbed Nandy and pushed her against the wall, turning her around so she couldn't see me.

"What the hell, Tyson?" She protested, trying to wriggle away, but it was no use.

"It's Boys Versus Girls night, which you conveniently didn't tell me."

"Travis—"

"You did it on purpose, and now you're mine." I pushed her legs apart and began patting her down.

"Really?" Nandy asked as she peered down at me while I patted her calves and ankles. There wasn't much covering Nandy in her sheer hoodie and shorts. Looking at her, I knew she wasn't carrying, but I had to go along with the role.

"You can never be too sure."

Nandy smirked as she turned around after my search. "Oh gee, do I get to check you for weapons, then?"

I stepped closer to her, invading her space. "I'm always packing a weapon on me."

She swallowed, as if unable to reply for a moment. "I thought you didn't care about me."

"I lied."

Nandy slowly bit into her bottom lip. I noticed that her two front teeth were slightly longer than the rest, not that it was a big abnormality. She was no longer that pretty little girl from my youth, but someone who had blossomed into a beautiful woman. Her hair was up in a disheveled bun and her face was bare of makeup, except maybe that banana lip balm she was always rolling across her lips. She was staring up at me with pure wonder in her dark eyes, and it was distracting, just as it had been when we were kids.

I recovered quickly and focused on the task at hand, finding guilty pleasure in tying her up.

I pulled the string from my pocket and gathered her hands and tied them together.

"Seriously?" she questioned as she looked up from her hands to me. "What are you going to do with me?"

"Don't worry, Chad won't be too upset about it."

From there I grabbed hold of her arm and helped her down the stairs, out the front door and into my truck.

Once we were on the road, my walkie was paged.

"Yeah?" I asked as I answered it.

"Chad wants to know what's going on," Travis said over the radio. "He's being a bitch about waiting."

In the background I could hear the whiny redhead swearing at Travis.

I rolled my eyes. "I'm kidnapping Nandy."

There was some arguing, and then I was greeted by the

sound of Nandy's boyfriend. "What the fuck are you doing, Tyson?"

In the passenger seat, Nandy frowned and bowed her head.

"I'm going to let that one go," I told her before holding up the walkie and pressing on it. "Deaf much? I said I'm kidnapping her, we have to capture her flag, and I'm going to make her tell me where it is."

Chad still wasn't on board, and I could hear the boys arguing over the walkie on their end. I tossed mine in the back seat and kept driving.

"Why couldn't you take Shayne?" Nandy asked from beside me.

"Because Shayne disappeared," I replied. "Besides, Shayne's cool, you're not."

"All the more reason to be with her."

"I just need some answers," I said. "I deserve to know what the hell's wrong with you, and if I have to use this shitty night as an excuse, so be it."

Nandy merely sat there, facing forward. "Where are we going?"

"To the model home," I told her. "No one would know to look there."

Nandy sighed. "I don't even care about this damn game. I'll tell you where our flag is if you take me home."

I shook my head and pulled onto the street where the model home was located. "I don't give a fuck about the battle, I just care about you. Okay?"

Her silence should've been enough to turn the car around and take her ass back home, or leave her on the side of the road, but deep down, I knew something was wrong. Lydia wanted me to care despite my body shutting down and refusing to absorb or emit emotions. I hadn't spoken to Prophet or any of the others in a minute, making my entire world Pacific Hills.

It was new and it was different, but I liked hanging out with Warhol and watching movies, or playing video games with Kyle, or shooting the shit with Travis and Ashley, or hanging with Shayne. They were safe, they were normal, they were my friends.

But none of it felt right with things on the outs with Nandy.

Nandy came before all of them, and if I was gonna endure life in the Hills, I wanted to do it with her. Who else was gonna show me around but the princess of Pacific Hills herself?

I snuck a glance at her. Or maybe she was, as her name suggested, the queen of the Hills.

At the model home, I led Nandy up the stairs and explored until I found the master bedroom. The rest of the rooms were empty, but the master was set up with furniture to allude to how the room would look if someone moved in. There was a four-poster bed, and a couple of chairs by the fireplace in the room, and a couple of nightstands, and that was it.

Nandy sat on the bed, and I grabbed a chair and sat before her, staring her down.

"Aren't you going to tie me to the bed?" she questioned with a smirk.

I rose to my feet, going and hovering just over her, planting my hands down on either side of her. I watched as she inhaled, her pupils enlarging as she gaped up at me. Her lips—her tempting lips—were parting. For some reason, I wondered if the redheaded fuck boy was kissing her right, or—

"Don't tempt me," I told her, stepping away from her.

Nandy quickly recovered, looking elsewhere. "Perv."

She had the prettiest brown skin, reminding me of this song

"Brown Skin" by India Arie that my mother used to play. Nandy was hella distracting. No, she wasn't that same little girl I once knew, she was every bit a woman.

"Start talking, Nandy," I ordered. "What's your problem? What did I do wrong?"

She pursed her lips and remained quiet.

It wasn't a surprise that she was choosing to be stubborn. If she wanted to play it that way, we could take all night. I had no other plans, and no one knew where we were.

"Why does it even matter?" Nandy asked after a while.

"Because it does."

She glared at me. "Why? You've got Shayne, Travis, Warhol, and the rest of them. Why me?"

I shrugged. "Because you came first. Now, I'm sorry if I've done anything to offend you, but you gotta let me in."

Nandy frowned, and I just didn't get her angst. Something told me that was the problem—she expected me to be a mind reader and know what I'd done to ail her.

She shook her head and sighed. "It's not you, it's me."

At least we were getting somewhere.

I leaned over, holding her attention. "What's up?"

She seemed ashamed. "At first, it was because you chose the wrong group. I had a seat ready for you with us, with our group, *the* group to be with around here. And then, you never cared if you were on the outside and I watched you be happy with them, with her. And it burns."

"Burns?"

She wouldn't look at me anymore. "I'm jealous."

As much sense as it made, I was still surprised. I didn't push it, not wanting to make her more embarrassed than I could see that she already was.

"Really?" I asked.

She bowed her head. "You surrounded yourself with my friends, my people, and they embraced you. And then you took Shayne and made her obsessed with you, and you became obsessed with her. Before all this, when I was a kid, all I had was you. You were mine, and then you left. After you came back to me and we were okay again, I thought you'd still be mine, but you're not. You're theirs, and Shayne's. No matter how hard I try, I can't hack it, I can't control how I feel. I don't wanna share you, and I don't want to see you with her. I want you to myself."

I stood from the chair and went and sat next to her on the bed. I untied her hands and massaged away the imprints the string had caused.

"All to yourself?" I repeated with a perked brow.

Nandy nodded. "I want to be your favorite, Tyson."

For the first time since we'd become reacquainted, Nandy was vulnerable. Yet she had never been stronger to me.

"I like Shayne," I confessed as I reached out and placed my hand on hers, "but I like Kyle more. I don't really know this town or these people, and I'm not about to step on anybody's toes. He's completely into her. I have a lot of love for her too, but I'd rather just be friends."

"Just friends?" Nandy repeated.

I nodded. "Only friends."

"Okay."

I moved closer to her, calculating my moves and assessing the situation for what it was and how far it could go. "Now, what are you willing to do to become my favorite?"

Nandy opened her mouth and I held up my hand to stop her.

"Are you going to stop giving me attitude and be nicer to your best friend?" I wanted to know. "You and I can be friends, Nandy, but I'm also going to choose who I want to kick it with, and it's not about to be that boy you love so much and his crowd of friends."

"Chad isn't—" The sound of her cell phone going off interrupted her, and she reached into the little pouch of her hoodie and got out her phone. "What should I tell him?"

"That your clothes are on." I stood from the bed, deciding that she and I could talk later. We had a game to continue. I grabbed her phone from her and answered it. "Hey, Chad."

"Seriously, dude, what the hell are you doing with my girlfriend?" he demanded to know.

Looking at Nandy, I asked, "Where's your flag?"

She rolled her eyes. "At the Crab Shack, taped to the back of the building. Erica and Edi are guarding it at the front."

I recited the info into her phone and hung up after agreeing to meet up with the boys at our territory, which was just outside of the Hook.

"We can talk after all this, okay? I know that when we were kids, it was just me and you and no one else, but it shouldn't matter that Jordy's here, or the others—we can still have our time. You're important to me, Nandy, more important than anyone else in this situation."

She offered me a smile and gestured to the door. "Come on, before we're late to the show."

And that was the end of it, if only for the moment.

By the time we made it to the boardwalk, the others were chasing each other around and the boys had declared their victory. The night was still young and, according to Travis, the mayhem had just begun.

Chad took Nandy's hand and led her toward their friends while I stood back with Travis and Matt.

"He was being a bitch the entire time," Travis whined. "You should've just taken Shayne."

"It wouldn't have been as much fun if I just took Shayne, you know?" I elbowed Travis as I joked around. Things weren't quite squared away between Nandy and me, but it was nice to know the reason behind her cold shoulder.

She was jealous.

Jealous.

I was beginning to wonder just how jealous when I caught sight of Shayne waving to me as she headed my way.

"Hey," she said as she stopped in front of me. She looked around us and back to me before tucking a few strands of her hair behind her ears. "Can we talk?"

"Yeah, sure." We started walking away from Travis and Matt. "What's up?"

"Well, I know it's crazy last minute and all, but I've been wanting to ask you to be my date for cotillion," Shayne came out and said.

Just a few hours ago, I would've said yes, but thinking deeper, I could see the hole I was digging for myself as far as Shayne went. Soon—or maybe it was too late—she would grow feelings, and I feared her reaction when she realized I didn't have any beyond friendship. It wasn't like I *couldn't* like her. She was amazing, but there were other factors stopping me from going there.

"I'm not sure that's a good idea," I came out and said. "Maybe we can meet each other there and have a dance, though."

Shayne stopped walking and studied me. "What?"

"I want us to be friends, and I think going to this event together like that could come off the wrong way."

Her mouth dropped open and she looked shocked.

Shayne was beautiful, and smart. She had this thing about watching "gray movies"—because calling them black-and-white proved to be too difficult for her. She would watch the same movies over and over, even though she knew the outcome of boy gets girl or sister goes insane. Beyond that, she would volunteer at homeless shelters when she got a chance, or donate some of her allowance to charity. Shayne was a good girl, which didn't surprise me when I'd called her out for her purity and she hadn't denied the fact. She was special.

She was definitely the type of girl you took home to your mother, and then your mother would look at you and then her, and question why she'd gotten with you, because you clearly weren't on her level. Only, I didn't have a mother to accompany the scenario. I couldn't exactly give Shayne the ordinary. I knew she considered herself motherless as well, due to her extreme abhorrence of her stepmonster and her mother's being facilitated in a rehab clinic, but still, it was different. I *was* different.

I liked Kyle because he was nice, genuine and normal, far more than I would ever be—far more worthy of Shayne than I could ever be.

"B–but, Scarlett." Shayne sounded defeated, and I hated to be the cause.

It was hard, but I did it. "Someday you're going to change this world and leave your mark, Shayne. Someday a great guy's going to be by your side and watch you take off. I'm sorry, but I'm not that guy."

Shayne shook her head, and I feared she would cry. "I don't understand." Her head shot up and she glanced past me, and I looked over, catching her eyeing Nandy, who was with Chad. Shayne came back to me. "It's not fair."

"It is," I said. "I don't want to hurt you."

"So you do *this* to me? From the moment we met, I never treated you like a criminal or a leper. I never treated you like shit for a month and ignored you. We hung out, and you let me think this was going somewhere. You filled my head up with images of Scarlett and Dante, and now you wanna be *friends*?"

I hadn't intentionally led her on. It was all messed up, because I hadn't thought we'd move forward. At the time, it was all just harmless flirting.

"I'm an asshole for that. I shouldn't have talked about those things and ignored the possibility that you could want more." I gestured to myself. "I can't give you more. I can't be that guy. I've got a lot of issues and problems, and I can't bring you into them."

Shayne's eyes watered. "It's just cotillion."

"Maybe…maybe you should ask Kyle."

She wiped her eyes and blinked at me. "Who?"

"Kyle. Kyle Frogge."

Shayne scoffed and rolled her eyes. "Froggie?"

"He's a nice guy, Shayne."

"Whatever, *Trice*. Just reject me, don't try to pass me along to the next person to make yourself feel better."

I started to apologize, but she wouldn't hear me as she walked off. She didn't stop by her friends but headed past them and kept going, toward the beach.

Matt and Travis came over and looked in Shayne's direction.

"You just passed on a crazy beautiful girl, for what?" Matt asked.

I'd meant it when I said I wasn't that guy for her, but deep down, I knew there was another reason.

I shrugged it off. "I just got a lot of things to sort out, and I don't want to ruin our friendship."

Kyle sauntered over but he kept peering back, watching the path that Shayne had taken. "Hey."

"You should go ask her about cotillion," I suggested.

Through his shaggy hair, Kyle peered up at me. "I… I don't think that's going to happen. She wouldn't— She doesn't know I'm on this planet, man."

"She knows your name."

"She calls me 'Froggie' when my last name is Frogge."

Travis reached out and slapped his back. "Close enough. Take what you can get at this point."

Kyle looked among us, bouncing his hazel eyes from Travis, to Matt, and finally to me. He cracked a shy grin. "I've been in love with her since the sixth grade, when she was the only one who cared to get the combination to my locker after Warhol shoved me in. I joined the football team, because when we were fourteen, she said her favorite movie was *The Waterboy*. I see her for more than just her looks, I see her for her good soul." His smile dimmed, as did his gaze. "But seeing doesn't always go both ways. She doesn't see me, probably never will."

I braced his shoulders, staring him dead in the eye. "Talk to her."

Kyle frowned. "Yeah?"

"Yeah."

With a nod of approval from Matt, Kyle took off, determined to speak to Shayne.

"Think he's got a chance?" Matt asked as we all stood watching Kyle descend the pier.

Travis grinned. "No fucking way."

The chances were stacked against him, but I felt optimistic. "Come on, guys, the night is still young."

Travis pulled what looked to be a water balloon from out of nowhere. "Got that right."

I watched as he reached back, threw his arm forward and released the balloon, sending it soaring in the air and then splattering at the feet of the group of girls huddled around Chad and his crew. They screamed and looked our way, glaring and stepping away from the boys.

The games had begun.

24 | *Nandy*

I was soaking wet, utterly drenched. Though the material of my hoodie and shorts was thin, they lay against my body heavy and sagging.

I should've worn a bra.

Not only was my peach hoodie semi-sheer, the added water left no imagination as to what my breasts looked like. As cold as it was, my nipples beaded through to make things worse.

Nudity didn't bother me; I was as free as they came in that department, but out of respect for Chad, I covered up with my arms as much as possible while trying to avoid the water balloon bombs being thrown about. Travis Catalano might not play on the football team, but I had to admit, the guy had an incredible arm.

From behind, someone seized me and pinned my arms behind me. "Got her!" I heard Warhol shout.

Travis grinned and reached back before releasing a water balloon in my direction, hitting me in the chest.

So much for keeping covered.

Warhol ran off before I could retaliate, leaving me squeezing more water from my hoodie.

We were all having fun, as if we had no care in the world, except for Shayne, who was sitting by herself far off down the beach. She was staring out at the ocean and wouldn't come play with us no matter who tried to talk to her.

I couldn't help but stop to look at her. I felt awful for not talking to her. Awful, and selfish for hogging Tyson from her when she had done nothing wrong.

A few feet away I spotted Kyle standing and observing Shayne, seeming to debate about going over to her or not.

Maybe…

I went over to Kyle and nudged him with my shoulder. "Hey."

He offered a small smile. "Hey."

"You know you should just go talk to her," I suggested.

He took a step forward like he wanted to, but then he recoiled and shook his head. "Nah." He faced me. "You go."

"Me?"

Kyle nodded. "She looks like she's having a bad day, and the last thing she needs is some guy hitting on her. In fact, I'm pretty sure she could use her best friend right now."

I gazed at my best friend. "You're a sweet guy, Kyle."

Kyle went bashful as he tried to hide his smile. "According to Travis, that's the problem."

"What would Travis know about girls anyway?"

"He has a lot of them vying for his attention," Kyle replied, "but I'd rather have *the* girl than a lot of girls. Call me crazy."

The thing about Kyle Frogge—sure, he wasn't mega gorgeous or extremely confident, and maybe he was on the outside of our group and world, but he was a genuinely good guy. Beneath his shaggy dark hair and shyness, he was adorable. Any girl would be lucky to have him, because he seemed to be the type of guy who would value a girl and respect her and listen.

It was such a shame too many of us wanted the bad guy before the right guy.

Taking Kyle's advice, I went over to Shayne and tried to reconcile.

I stood in front of her instead of sitting, because I wasn't sure how that would go. Once she noticed me, her expression turned sour.

"Hey." I tried to smile and wave at her. "You're missing out on all the fun."

Shayne shrugged and hugged herself.

"Come on, you know we're a team. I can't defend myself without my best—"

"Why couldn't you just say you liked him?" Shayne cut to the chase as she glared up at me.

I couldn't reply right away. It was awkward and embarrassing for her to call me out on that.

I scoffed. "Seriously?"

She narrowed her eyes. "Seriously, Nandy. From the moment he got here, you treated him like shit, and I liked him. I was always nice to him, and then all of a sudden, you care and turn into a complete bitch on me. And now he just wants to be friends with me, and you two show up together tonight all smiles."

"That's not fair."

"No, it isn't. Especially since you're the one with a boyfriend, and you're crushing on some other guy—one *I* liked."

"I never said I liked him." My voice was too shaky and defensive for me to even believe myself.

Shayne threw her hands up. "Who are you trying to fool? You know me, Nandy. You know that Trice was the one guy I genuinely liked, and then he turns out to be like everyone else around here." Her eyes were watering and she was beginning to sob, but I didn't get it.

"Everyone else?"

"Everyone loves you. It's all I ever hear. You're so smart, beautiful, and you've got amazing parents. Nobody wants a mess like me."

I immediately sat next to her and wrapped my arms around her. "Shayne, you're gorgeous. Plus, way smarter than me. Like, by a lot. I don't even know all fifty of my states, and I always confuse them with cities."

"That's because you're an idiot," Shayne said between a chuckle and a sob as she wiped at her nose. "If I'm so smart and pretty, then how come no one ever likes me? It's always Nandy, Nandy, Nandy."

I thought of Kyle and the fact that he was in love with Shayne, with all his covetous staring and awkward attempts to talk to her. "Not everyone likes me."

Shayne rolled her eyes. "If Matt wasn't into Ben or vice versa, they'd both like you, too."

It was hard not to laugh at that statement. I elbowed my goofy friend. "Oh stop. You're amazing, and I'm just saying you'd be surprised at who's noticed this."

Shayne stared down at the sand before her. "Why couldn't you just tell me you liked him? We're supposed to be friends."

"Because I'm the one with the boyfriend, remember? I'm not supposed to like him."

Shayne shook her head. "It's not fair, Nandy. It really isn't."

"I know, and I'm sorry I'm being completely selfish here. I hate myself for how I feel and how I can't control it."

"You should go for it," Shayne said. "You know I never really cared for Chad."

As if it were that simple. "Chad's the one."

"And Trice is amazing."

"That wouldn't bother you just a bit?"

She frowned. "It would, but at least you'd be happy."

Now my eyes were watering. She wanted me happy before herself, and that made me feel even worse about my feelings for Tyson. Shayne and I'd been friends since middle school. She had always been supportive, protective, and loyal. She had always been the one having rough patches at home, the one who depended on me when things got worse, and here I was, being a leech and demanding attention from the one boy she actually liked. Taking her one source of happiness, and I felt completely awful about it.

But he's mine; he's always been mine. My subconscious was just as greedy as my heart and I hated it. "I'm sorry, Shayne."

She offered a bitter smile. "Promise me something?"

"Yeah?"

"You'll dance with me at cotillion?"

The floodgates broke and I found myself crying as I leaned over and hugged her tight.

We sat like that for what seemed to be forever before screaming broke our union.

Travis was sprinting down the beach holding some girl's bikini top, and the girl was chasing after him while doing her best to conceal her goods.

"Who wants to go skinny-dipping?" Travis hollered.

I shot up, gearing for the fun of it, but caught sight of Chad and a look of disapproval from him.

Shayne snorted. "Really?"

"What? It's fun."

In the end, Travis gave the swimsuit top back and joined the others at the nearest bonfire.

I met up with Chad and settled down next to him.

Shayne remained seated by herself, but I promised I would give her a few more minutes of her lonesome before I intervened.

"We're going to play a little game I call Truth, Shot, or Dare," Travis announced as he held up a flask.

"Truth, Shot, or Dare?" Tyson repeated.

"Yes. The objective of our game is simple. You pick truth, you answer. If you don't, you take two shots. If you're not into truth or dare, you take a shot. You pick dare and you refuse to do it, you take three shots."

"So the point is to get drunk," Matt concluded.

Travis grinned. "Pretty much."

"This is why we avoid you, Catalano." Chad spoke with obvious disdain.

I was leaning into him and had to look up to scold him. "Be nice." Travis was being cool for once, and there was nothing wrong with a little harmless fun.

"So, Edi, how about you go first?" Travis suggested.

Edi shrugged. "Sure."

"Truth, Shot, or Dare?" Travis prompted.

After a pause, Edi answered, "Truth."

"Why won't you hang out with me one-on-one?"

"Ooh!" A few of us chimed in on his putting her on the spot.

Edi wrinkled her nose. "Because you're a creep."

Travis huffed. "Martin Luther King Jr., did not die on a cross for you to reject me this way."

Edi clicked her tongue. "He ain't die on no damn cross, Catalano."

"The man had dreams about us, Edi!"

By now all of us were laughing at Travis's mock angst and a few pointed out that Edi didn't exactly fit the description of MLK's dream.

"Whatever, I reject you and you run off with someone else," Edi pointed out.

Travis snorted. "Well, yeah, I'm not going to sit around waiting forever for you."

Warhol shoved Travis, and the game went on.

"Bradley, you go," Travis said as he eyed my boyfriend.

"Uh, truth, I guess," Chad said.

Travis got this naughty look on his face and I knew Chad had chosen the wrong option. "Does Nandy ever talk dirty or get kinky in bed?"

All of the guys eagerly anticipated Chad's answer, and I cringed.

"Travis," Matt chastised in my defense.

While I let it go with a shrug, I was appreciative of the gesture.

"I mean…" Chad stopped to laugh. "She definitely gets more fun when she's a little drunk."

"Wow, I'm boring when I'm sober, huh?" I mumbled as I picked at my nails.

It was no big deal, right? It was just a stupid question with a stupid answer. Only, I felt weird about Chad's answer. He was all that I'd known, and if I got more fun only when drunk, what did he think of me when I wasn't?

Chad leaned down and kissed my temple. "It's not like that, Nan. I'm just saying you let go a little when we're wasted."

I rolled my eyes.

"Nah, you meant that, man." Oliver egged him on, causing Chad to flip him off. "Your girl's a prude."

"Screw off, Ollie!" Chad warned.

I sank lower into my spot against Chad, feeling more uncomfortable.

"Or maybe Nandy has to get drunk to go there with Bradley," Tyson spoke up in my defense.

The air got cold and silent quick as everyone froze.

I couldn't believe Tyson had said it, even as I looked at him, seeing the defiance in his eyes as his gaze met mine.

He should not have said that.

Chad's arms tightened around me, and I could only assume he was shooting Tyson a matched cold glare.

"Nandy, wanna go next?" Travis quipped, moving things along.

"Shot," I decided, not wanting to take a chance with truth and too lazy to accept a dare.

"My type of woman." Travis passed his flask to me.

Upon taking a sip of the harsh liquor, I found myself coughing. Call me a lightweight, but I was a cooler type of girl, something fruity and simpler than beer, straight liquor, or even worse, vodka. Yuck.

"Now, how about—"

"I'm calling who's next," Chad cut Travis off. "*Tyson*, how about you go?"

Tyson lifted a brow as he peered at my boyfriend. Despite him hating being called by his first name by anyone other than me, he kept his cool. "Truth."

"Why the hell are you here? Why aren't you home 'chilling with the homies' in Lindenwood?" Chad's tone was icy.

I sat up and held my hand out to Tyson. "Don't answer that."

"Why not? We all wanna know," Chad went on.

Everyone looked between Tyson and Chad, waiting for an outcome.

"That was two questions," Tyson finally said.

Chad shrugged. "Take your pick."

His jaw clenched, but Tyson answered, "I got shot, and had to move."

The confession gathered a few murmurs and looks of judgment around the bonfire. None of us had known anyone who had dealt with such an extreme. Looks of doubt ran across some faces, namely Chad's.

Chad snorted. "You got shot? I'm guessing they had bad aim, then, huh?"

He'd gone too far, especially considering Tyson's father's aim had been deliberate in killing his mother.

Tyson's nostrils flared as he kept his focus on Chad. Chad sat nonchalant, unafraid of the enraged bull he'd just flashed red at.

The more the two of them stared at each other, the more it seemed like they were silently daring the other to make a move.

Eventually, it was Tyson who suddenly stood and walked off, leaving the bonfire.

"If you can't take the heat," Chad mumbled as he looked at his friends.

Fed up, I pushed my boyfriend. "You didn't have to do that. You're being a jerk!"

Chad glared at me. "Well, you're *my* girlfriend, so I guess I'm your jerk."

I got up and went after Tyson, who had stopped a few yards away and seemed to be collecting himself. "Hey."

With his eyes closed, he inhaled deep then slowly exhaled, as if focusing to calm himself down. "Hey."

"Listen, he's just an asshole sometimes. I'm sure if you two actually talked or something…" But then, I wasn't so sure. From the moment they'd met, there'd been tension between them.

Tyson opened his eyes. "Would you be mad if I hauled off and beat his ass?"

I shouldn't have, but I laughed just a little. "Maybe a tiny bit." I displayed the amount with my thumb and finger.

Tyson cracked a smile. "I don't belong here, and I'm never going to fit in."

"That's not true."

His gaze was on Shayne. "Only a few people don't care. The rest, they do."

I bit down on my lip, watching him watch her. "Go."

Tyson shifted his attention to me. "Huh?"

"Go and be with her," I told him. "She doesn't care about Lindenwood, or any of this. I'm sure sitting there with her would be a whole lot better than sitting there with us."

Tyson appeared thoughtful before he nodded his head. "See you at home?"

My heart sank. "Yeah."

He walked away and sat with Shayne. She laid her head on his shoulder, and they stayed like that, remaining quiet, it seemed from where I stood.

With nothing else to do, I put my tail between my legs and went back to my group.

25 | TRICE

The Smiths were running around in a frenzy. It was the night of cotillion, and everyone had descended into madness. Max kept yelling out things from a checklist as she meandered through the house, and Parker and Nandy were like a couple of marionettes obliging.

I sat in the family room, writing in my composition book about my youth. I had to admit, Lydia might have been onto something. It felt calming to get my thoughts out. Chronicling my earliest memories put everything into perspective for me. From what I could recollect, I started with preschool and how I vividly remembered being the quiet one, how Tyson and my mother once sat down with a counselor to see if anything was wrong with me, because I was so introverted. My mother thought I just needed to come out of my shell on my own and meet someone who was going to help me. Tyson thought I was strange.

By the time I turned five, things had gotten bad between my parents, and Pops came and started taking me with him into Pacific Hills to landscape. I could remember being dressed in a sweater and khakis and feeling out of place. Pacific Hills was full of the uppity type, the kind of folk you had to stay polite and clean around. I followed Pops silently as he went from house to house doing yard work and greeting the few friends he'd made.

Then came time to do the Smiths' yard.

I would remember it for as long as I lived. Pops had me standing beside him, strong and up-front. Max had come to the door prepared to go somewhere, but she'd stopped to smile at Pops and then at me, and unlike the others from Pacific Hills, Max had meant her smile. I didn't smile back, but I nodded and greeted her with a hello.

Then, I looked over and I saw her.

Peeking out from behind their front door was a little girl. Her curious dark eyes lingered all over me, as if she had never seen a boy before, and I had to admit I was curious to see what she looked like as well.

Thank God for Max, because she looked back and opened the door wider and revealed the little girl who had been spying.

And there was Nandy.

The cushion next to me filled with a body, and I pulled away from my writing to find Jordy joining me on the sofa. We were both dressed and ready to go, but Jordy's hair was kind of a mess. I just knew that Max was going to throw a fit about it. She had stressed all week about wanting us all presentable, one reason that I'd gotten a haircut from the local barber with Ashley on Tuesday. Though I admired Jordy's careless approach as he lay back on the couch revealing that he was wearing sneakers with his dress pants.

"Writing in your diary again?" he asked as he began thumbing his handheld.

I shook my head. "It's not a diary."

"Do you write your thoughts in it?"

"Some."

"Tales from events in your life?"

"Yes."

"Then, dude, it's a diary."

I eyed the little pest beside me. "No, it's not."

"Say it's a diary and I'll let you play with this during the ceremony," Jordy said as he waved an extra handheld.

I snatched it from him and tossed him a smile. "You were saying?"

Jordy grinned and went back to his game.

We both were going to be bored out of our minds.

I tried refocusing on my composition, but I was stuck on Nandy. Where to begin. How to describe her. How to give depth to what I felt—and *felt* for her.

Even if the composition was for my own personal viewing, I wanted to write Nandy right. She was my past and my present, and the words needed to do her justice.

As if summoned by my mind's jumbled confusion, Nandy appeared in the doorway. She had gotten her hair done Monday morning, and she stood before Jordy and me with all the added length pulled up in a bun as she wore a dress that hugged every bit of her, accentuating her hourglass figure. Her brown face was void of makeup at the moment, making her look more youthful and pretty.

Quickly, I jotted down a note in my composition about Nandy's features.

"What are you two doing?" Nandy asked as she eyed her brother and me.

"Trice is writing a diary entry," Jordy said as he snuck me a clever smile.

I shook my head. "It's not a diary."

"What are you writing about?" Nandy wondered.

"You."

Nandy took in a breath, and I had no clue what she was thinking as she stood there, staring at me. Things were once again off between us. She wasn't upset this time, just distant.

To be honest, it felt like one big mind fuck. It was like Nandy wanted something from me, and I had no clue what. Everything I did was wrong, and it was frustrating walking on eggshells around her all the time.

The doorbell rang, and the three of us migrated to the front door, just as Parker and Max also headed in that direction.

The bell rang a few more times, as if the person behind it was in a rush to get inside.

Parker opened the door, and in a blur of white fabric, Shayne stormed in.

Her hair was a mess. Tracks from her extensions were falling out, like she'd pulled on them. Her face was wet from her tears, and she was carrying a big ball of white puff that was probably her cotillion dress.

Like the mother figure she was, Max stepped forth and went in close to console Shayne. "What's going on?"

Shayne's pretty face crumbled. "He canceled."

I frowned. Her father had ditched her, on a night like this, *her* night?

She began to sob and wipe her eyes. "He promised, Max!"

Parker went over to rub Shayne's back. "Hey, it's okay. Why don't you come with us? I'll be your escort."

Shayne's shoulders began to shake with her melancholy. "I'm not going."

Max sighed. "Shayne—"

"No! I'm not going, because nobody wants me. Nobody cares about me!" She took off for the staircase, her sobs echoing behind her.

Max, Parker, and Jordy stared at the staircase, while Nandy and I both took the initiative to go after Shayne.

Max cut us off, facing the both of us. "You can't be late."

I went to step around her. "I'm not debuting."

Max cut me off once more. "But Nandy is. You two go on, and I'll stay here with Shayne."

Nandy frowned. "Mom, I can't. Shayne would drop cotillion in a heartbeat for me. It won't be the same without her."

"And just like I would with Shayne, I'd be highly disappointed in you for missing out on this. You are going to your cotillion." Max turned to me. "All of you."

Saying no more, she turned and went up to find Shayne.

Parker scratched at his head. "She'll handle that. Let's get going so Nandy can get ready."

"Can I take my own car?" I asked.

Parker opened his mouth, but Nandy stepped up beside me. "Yeah, can we ride together?"

Parker studied the both of us and held up a finger. "You better show up."

"We will," Nandy assured.

Parker took Jordy and led him out of the house, and I calmed myself down from the annoyance of Nandy bogarting her way into my car.

She gathered her dress and met me at the door, stopping to study my face.

"You were gonna stay and be with her, weren't you?" she asked.

I fished my keys from my pocket. "Doesn't matter now, does it?"

Nandy frowned and stared down at the linoleum. "Go. Be with her. I'll hitch a ride with Edi and the Gómezes."

I rolled my eyes and made my way out to my car. "Just drop it. You've already ruined it. If we don't show up together, I'm fucked."

Nandy's frown increased, but she said nothing as she went and got in the passenger side.

She had pissed me off. I couldn't stand her constant games. She barely spoke to me, and when Shayne came around, she got needy and selfish. She couldn't have her damn cake and eat it, too.

In the car, I turned the radio to a hip-hop station and hoped to drown out my annoyance with the emcee's rhymes.

"Who is this?" Nandy asked in a small voice.

I blinked away some tension. "Wale."

She looked at the radio. "You like him?"

I bobbed my head. "He's poetic, has a message, deeper shit than what's poppin' on the radio most days."

Nandy gave a small smile. "You sound like Erica. She's stuck-up with her hip-hop."

That was one thing I liked about Erica. She was bougie with her music, and I didn't blame her. It was nice to be around someone who didn't care about the beats and was more for the lyrics.

"Yeah, she has good taste."

"I like this song," Nandy said as she started to nod along to the radio. My anger lessened at the fact that she was off-beat, but it was kinda cute that she was trying.

That was another thing about Nandy—she was too damn cute. That was why I had always done whatever she said when we were kids.

"Yeah, he's pretty dope," I said.

"I'm sorry I ruined your plan." Nandy fiddled with her hands in her lap. "I wanted to stay too, but I do have to go. My mom would kill me. We spent so much on my dress, not to mention all the preparations and planning I helped out on all year. I can't *not* go."

I shrugged. "It's whatever. Max'll take care of her."

The car went silent, and the hip-hop station remained playing to fill the void.

"This summer has been a mess and it's my fault," Nandy confessed. "I've been so hot and cold, you must think I'm insane."

Got that right. "Summer ain't over yet. Still time to turn into a normal person."

"Stop it."

"I'm serious." To ease the tension, I flashed her a smile.

We'd arrived at the venue, and I was behind a row of cars waiting to be checked in. Seeing all the families heading inside caused me to sigh and wish I'd grabbed Jordy's handheld before I left.

"Has the summer been completely awful?" Nandy wondered.

Despite being in the Hills, my summer was straight. I had Travis and the guys. Shayne as well, not to mention late-night video game contests with Jordy. It felt so normal and healthy compared to before. It was like I'd fallen into a parallel universe and was a new Tyson Trice.

"No," I admitted, "it hasn't."

"Wh-when are you happiest?" Nandy asked without looking at me.

I shook my head. "That's not fair."

Finally, she faced me. "Why not?"

"Because I feel like you want me to say when I'm with you, and it's not fair. Shayne has been there for me, Travis too, and—"

Nandy opened her door as I pulled up to the valet. "Just forget I asked."

She was out of my car fast, and I had to race to get to her as I handed off my keys to the valet.

I had my arms around her waist, halting her en route as I finally caught her inside the entrance. "Stop."

Nandy frowned. "Just let it go, Tyson."

I made her look at me. "What do you want from me, Nandy?"

She peered up at me, her lips parting as she took in my face and her gaze trailed to my mouth. Just as quickly as she examined my lips, her gaze darted back up to mine. Her lips trembled as if she wanted to say something.

"What's going on?" Glancing over, and I found Chad assessing Nandy and me.

Nandy wiped her eyes and moved away from me. "Nothing. Shayne came over and was upset, and it was just this thing."

At first Chad seemed skeptical, and then he nodded. "Yeah, what can you expect, she has a flare for the dramatics."

I *really* did not like him. "Shayne isn't dramatic."

He smirked at me. "Oh?"

"No, she's not."

He rolled his eyes. "I don't get it. First you're defending

my girl, and now you're defending your own. Make up your mind, Tyson."

That was the last time he was going to call me that.

I began to walk over to him to knock the sneer off his face. Only, Travis appeared and held me back.

"Easy," he said gently. "This is a big event, and people know where you're from. They expect this kind of shit. Don't feed into it."

"That's right, teach him how we do things outside of the streets," Chad said as he glared at me.

Travis closed his eyes and took in a breath through his nose, trying to hold his composure. And then he shrugged. "Fuck it." In seconds he was nose to nose with Chad, insulting him with a few choice words. "Why don't you go fuck yourself, Firecrotch."

I was both amused and baffled at Travis's insult, but not distracted enough to let him get a lick at Chad before me.

Quickly, I pulled Travis back. "I can't kick his ass, but you can?"

He smirked. "I've hated him longer."

Chad puffed up his chest, planting his hands on his hips as he took a stance. "You know what, Travis?"

"What, Chad?"

"You're really starting to—"

"STOP IT!"

Nandy's shout paused the fight brewing between the three of us as all eyes were on her.

She stepped away and glared at Travis and me before fixing her eyes on her boyfriend. "Enough already. I've had it with your little digs at him." Now she was focusing on me and Travis. "And for peace's sake, can't you two just—"

"You know what, I don't need any of this shit." Chad undid

his tie and threw it on the ground as he shot a finger in Nandy's direction. "I'm over it, Nandy."

People were still entering the venue, some stopping to see what was going on, while others hurried off to get ready.

"Wh-what?" Nandy's voice was barely above a whisper as she almost appeared childlike before me.

"Bradley—" Travis tried to intervene.

Chad waved Travis off. "Fuck it, I'm done playing this game. Choose right now, Nan, me or 50 Cent over there."

At my sides, my hands balled. The spectators began to whisper in shock and awe. This was mere entertainment for them, but one look at Nandy, and I could tell it was her undoing.

Her eyes glistened with tears as she looked between Chad and me. Not stopping there, her attention landed on the crowd surrounding us. And then she let out a sob before rushing past Travis and me, taking off into the night.

26 | *Nandy*

I wasn't sure what day it was, or what time. I just knew that I had a wicked headache from crying some moments and being sleepless the next. I lay in bed waiting for the Excedrin to kick in, or make me drowsy enough to where I wanted to just sleep. Whichever took me from this depressing state of consciousness.

After Chad's ultimatum, I fled the scene, hailing a cab and then going straight home, only to get in my car and take off once again. No one knew where I was, and that was how things were going to stay. The model home was my sanctuary, and I needed its privacy more than ever.

To think, I'd spent practically the whole summer fussing over my big day, just to lose it over petty drama. All I'd wanted was to debut, and as I gazed online at my friends' social media pages, at their photos and videos of the event, my heart ached at what I'd given up.

The more I lay in bed thinking it over, the more upset I became at the ugly facts.

This was entirely my fault. From Shayne, to Tyson's angst, to Chad's brutal way of publicly ending things with me.

Chad Bradley was the king, and I'd thought life would be easier as his queen. And it had been…until Tyson came back.

For the longest time, I'd felt like I needed to be perfect, because Chad's family was perfect. I'd wanted to fit in, because his family was *in*. Chad had always felt like the safe choice, because everybody liked him. It was easier to be a part of the crowd, or to lead it, than to be against it. I didn't want to be alone again.

But that's exactly where I was.

I curled into a ball and refused to sob again, feeling some relief as I realized my headache was lessening.

A sudden burst of music startled me, and I shot up in bed, turned and discovered Tyson at the foot, gyrating his hips as he held up his phone. It took me a moment to recognize Omarion's voice and the old B2K song that was playing. It was the goofiest, random sight, and I actually laughed.

At once he stopped and shut off the song. "Yeah, you better laugh. I watched four videos to memorize that move."

I made a face. "If you watched four B2K videos, it was your own idea, just admit it."

Tyson lifted a brow and I quieted down, knowing that this was the very reason I was in my current position. I was very much into Tyson Trice, and the people who were closest to me knew it and saw it, too.

Tyson stepped around the bed and stood in front of me,

observing me in the silent, serious way that only he could. "I'm surprised there's no fort."

"Fort?"

He nodded. "I remember when we were kids, if you were mad or in trouble you'd build a fort in the living room and hide. We used to do that and lie there for hours. It was just you and me against the world."

Him and me.

"I could really use a fort about now," I said, as I thought of making one to hide in like he'd said, and to see if he'd join me.

"Or if you weren't feeling well we'd lie on the couch and watch *Arthur* all day," Tyson went on.

"You remember that?"

He shrugged. "I remember everything about you, Nandy."

Every summer from when we were five until we were seven, he was mine. And then he wasn't.

I remembered everything about him too, so much, one day it just hit me. I literally spent a day questioning which version of him I liked more, the boy, or the man. The man made me nervous and inspired me to dive deeper, and the boy had done whatever I wanted and always was by my side. Now I wanted every version of him, just for myself.

I was being selfish again, and I couldn't find it in me to hide my shame, not with him standing in front of me, looking at me and making my insides melt.

"I don't think *Arthur*'s going to make me feel better this time, Tyson," I admitted.

Tyson sighed and hung his head. He peeked up at me, remaining quiet and making me nervous. "You gotta get out of here."

"Do my parents know where I am?"

He shook his head. "No, but they suspect I've known where you've been for the past two days."

"Thank you. I know we're not on the best terms, but you're here and you didn't tell them."

Tyson bobbed his head and took a step closer. "So go home and fix everything."

"I don't want to. Not right now, at least."

He blinked, as if trying to stop himself from becoming irritated.

And then he took another step closer, practically hovering over me.

One moment he was leaning over me, staring intently, and the next he was closing the distance and bringing our lips together.

He pressed his forehead to mine, peering into my eyes briefly, measuring my reaction and taking in my wanton soul. His pause was too long, as my arms shot around his neck, beckoning him closer as I reunited our lips. Tyson came closer, his arms sneaking around me, his fingertips grazing the thin material of my tee. His touch was powerful, as was the feel of his kiss.

Oh God I wanted this, I wanted this so bad.

Tyson.

When he started to pull away, I was left grasping at his shirt to keep him near me, on me.

Tyson reeled back and just stared at me again.

"What was that?" I asked, noting that my chest was rising and falling.

"A hunch." He stood up from the bed and tossed what I hadn't noticed was in his hand—a bag—beside me. "Get dressed. We've got someplace to be."

How could he go from kissing me to talk of going somewhere? "But…"

"You have a nice one," he finished for me. "Now let's go."

"I told you I wasn't ready to go home."

"I know," Tyson said. "Prophet called me and told me they're having a cookout and, no offense to your family, but I've missed some good old-fashioned soul food. Not to mention can't nobody touch Alma's pound cake."

"You're taking me to Lindenwood?"

"The way I see it, you haven't eaten, and you could use the getaway. We're gonna go eat, listen to some old-school, and just have a nice day," Tyson declared.

I felt my heart warm and my face smile. "You're taking care of me?"

He shoved his hands into his pockets. "You took care of me."

"I did?"

"It wasn't too long ago you brought me here and got me talking, Nandy. Now let's go, before Pretty's greedy ass eats up all the food."

I sifted through the bag and found a T-shirt and pair of shorts. He must've just grabbed anything, because the top was striped and the shorts were floral print. Thankfully the black-and-white top meshed well with the black floral shorts, nothing too crazy or bizarre.

I sat up and pulled my shirt over my head, and noticed how Tyson turned away.

"When did you start hating clothes?" he asked.

"According to my mom, I've always had a thing for running around naked, ever since I learned to walk. She said once, I was being changed and as soon as I was naked, I took off running around the house."

"That sounds like you," Tyson said. "I'm going to go wait downstairs."

I replayed his kiss over and over as I got dressed, wondering if it meant that Tyson wanted me, too. Possibly. Maybe. Hopefully.

In Tyson's car we listened to hip-hop and said nothing the first twenty minutes on the road. The more we kept silent, the more I swelled with questions.

"Are we gonna talk about it?" I finally came out and asked.

Tyson shrugged. "Chad's always been a bitch."

Oh. We were talking about him. "I was awful to him. I don't blame him."

Tyson shook his head. "You know what your problem is, Nandy?"

"What?"

"You always get what you want."

I bowed my head. "Does that mean I get…?"

"It means you're taking your ass to Chad as soon as we get back so you can talk."

"That's done, Tyson."

"You sure about that?"

"Yes."

"I guess you're free."

He was playing games with me, and I didn't like it.

"So we're just going to act like you didn't kiss me?" I snapped.

"Like I said, it was a hunch," he replied with a lazy shrug.

"So this is nothing?"

For a moment Tyson was quiet, and I felt myself begin to feel ill at a reality where it was all one-sided, where he would never like me the way I liked him. I had lain in bed for two nights, feeling upset about what Chad had said, but more upset with myself for what I felt for Tyson overall.

As bummed as I was about missing cotillion, I cared more about my predicament with Tyson.

Chad had embarrassed me, but he'd been right to call me out.

Chad was all I'd known, and then Tyson came back, and everything changed.

I loved one, but liked the other. It wasn't supposed to be that way.

I was an awful person.

"Right now, I really don't know. You're the only one who makes me so damn mad and irritated. Back there in the bedroom, I figured if I kissed you, you'd get your shit together." Tyson shook his head. "But I know it's only a matter of time before you pull some other stunt that leaves me going crazy."

"I'm sorry, okay? I didn't mean to fall for you. I had a boyfriend, and this just happened. Do you think I enjoy this? I feel like I have no control. You make me nervous, Tyson. Watching you and Shayne, I feel inadequate. I hate myself for being envious of my best friend instead of happy for her. I shouldn't want you, but I do."

Now Tyson appeared apologetic. "I'm sorry I can't say the same."

"Because of someone else?"

"I don't know, maybe."

"So you felt nothing when you kissed me?"

"I didn't say that." He glanced my way. "I'm torn between wanting you and wanting to strangle you. The thing is, I don't even know you anymore. You haven't given me the chance to this whole summer. Now you want me, and I'm supposed to come running? It's just like when we were kids,

Nandy—you'd flash those looks, and I'd do whatever you wanted. Not this time. I don't know how I feel, but at least I'm admitting that."

It felt like I was drowning in my feelings and would never surface. One minute my heart was beating hard, and the next it was sinking low in my chest.

I kept quiet for the remainder of the trip to Lindenwood. I was a little nervous to be around his old life, especially because I knew of the illegal activities he'd done with his friends— that, and the harsh realities shown on the news about Lindenwood as a city.

"Before we head to the spot, there's a place I want to show you, a place that reminds me of the old me," Tyson said as we crossed the city line.

I sat up and kept a lookout for any special landmark or place.

When we stopped, I noted we were on the street by a local park and across from a library. Tyson got out of the car and I followed, figuring we were there.

My eyes skimmed the library before focusing on the park. It wasn't what I expected in a place like this. It was breathtaking. The sign, naming the place Ashby Park, was freshly painted and stuck up out of the green, nicely trimmed lawn. That was what stuck out—the lawn over the stretch of land was a bright and healthy green. Not only that, there were flowers planted along certain areas, vivid yellows, reds, lavenders and pinks that prettied up the park even more. On the playground were a few families or single moms or dads with their children, who seemed to be having the time of their lives as they played on the unblemished equipment. There was no litter, no graffiti, no monsters in sight.

"Surprised?" Tyson asked as he gauged my reaction.

Honestly? "Yes."

He snorted. "Lindenwood ain't all bad, Nandy. We've got nice schools and public places, but don't let the media tell it." He gestured across the street at the library. "When I was a boy, my mom used to take me there all the time. That was my favorite place in the world, besides being next to you in Pacific Hills."

Touched, I said nothing as I looked at the library. That explained his stance on reading and possibly writing.

"She used to have me read two books a month and give her a full oral review on them." Tyson tapped his temple. "To keep my mind going."

I admired his mother for this. Clearly she'd had a big impact on who Tyson was.

"This place is beautiful," I said.

Tyson agreed. "We used to either read in the kid's section in the library or sometimes out here in the field, or at a picnic table. I put up a fight about coming when my friends started kicking it on me."

I frowned. "Tyson."

He chuckled at my scolding. "You sound just like her. If I could go back in time, I'd change up and stick with her. For always."

The thought of his mother made me curious. "Is her grave near here? Do you want to go?"

At once Tyson visibly tensed. "I—I… I can't… I can't go. I can't see her…like that. I can't. I can't." The sound of his voice caused me to step closer and lean into him for support as my heart tore in two. This wound was still fresh, still sore, and would probably never heal.

I rubbed his back. "It's okay, Tyson, it's okay."

It wasn't, but someday, it would be.

"Don't blame yourself, okay? Your mom would be so proud of who you are and what you're becoming," I assured him.

Tyson regarded me deeply, silently, intently.

He soon blinked and looked elsewhere. "Let's go, I'm starving."

We got back in his car and rode over to the cookout.

"You'll be fine," Tyson insisted after we'd made it to a house that was surrounded by cars.

I kept close to him, and he let me. "I'm nervous."

"You should be." He flashed me a smile and put his arm around me.

The house before us was all one-story. By the chipping paint on the concrete porch, I could tell the family who lived here had been here for years. There was a bed of flowers in the yard, a personal garden of white roses that made me smile.

"What kind of name is Prophet anyway?" I asked as he led me up the driveway.

"It's a nickname," a third voice cut through the air. A guy Tyson's height was coming our way. He was definitely older than us, and had a friendly aura about him as he came to a stop in front of us. He stuck his hand out. "Prophet."

I placed my hand in his and shook. "Nandy."

He smiled. "Named after Queen Nandi of the Zulu clan?"

I felt myself brighten, hearing the reference. I was growing to appreciate my name more and more. "Yes."

He faced Tyson and bobbed his head. "I like this one, but Asiah won't."

"She here?" Tyson asked.

Prophet made a face. "You know Momma love her some of that girl. Plus, you know, Read's been around."

Tyson said nothing, and I wondered what was going on.

Prophet turned back to me. "Anyway, Prophet's a nickname. We all got one, it's a crew thing. Trice is the only one whose real name I actually remember."

"What's your real name?" I felt brazen enough to ask.

If my question was too personal, he didn't let it show. "Hakeem. People started calling me Prophet due to my teachings, among other things. You come on back here, and we'll work on your nickname."

He led Tyson and me toward the backyard, where the smell of barbecue billowed in the air as classic R & B played loudly and Al Green sang about staying together. Everyone was enjoying themselves as they talked and ate at picnic tables and goofed off. One boy, with vibrant golden-brown skin and natural curls in his hair, was dancing around an older woman, trying to coax her to dance with him. It was goofy and so genuine.

Tyson nudged me. "That's Pretty. We call him that because, well, it's obvious." He placed his hand on my hip and pointed to each person and named them. Asiah stuck out the most, the girl who was shorter than me, shared my skin tone, was super pretty in a hard and tough way, and was sporting a plain black T-shirt and camouflage capris. She had a don't-mess-with-me look about her, and I didn't even think about going and introducing myself to her, especially as Tyson said she was his ex.

Asiah got one look at us and stopped what she was doing, her gaze lingering where Tyson's hand was on me and how close we were standing. Attitude lit up her face, and the boy next to her, Read, stared at her and then glanced our way.

That girl who'd cut Tyson's hair, Tasha, was nearby as well, entertaining a young girl and a baby.

"Is that Trice?" Alma came on over and was quick to hug Tyson tight, and he hugged her just the same. "Oh, it's good to see you, baby. Just because you don't live here anymore don't mean you can't call us."

Tyson brightened up, showing how happy he was to see her. "I'm here now, Alma. Especially for that pound cake."

She narrowed her eyes and pretended to swat him before turning her attention on me. She sized me up. She was maybe a few years older than my mother, her hair holding more gray and her expression more tired, yet friendly. "And who is this?"

Tyson stepped to the side and left me to speak for myself.

"Nandy," I said, going and holding my hand out.

Alma looked at my hand like it was a foreign object before leaning over and pulling me into a hug. Where I came from, we shook hands, but I liked how she felt the need to actually hug me, as if she knew me.

"It's nice to meet you, Nandy. Trice, why don't you get this girl a plate, she looks hungry."

And suddenly I was embarrassed for the top I was wearing, which gave a nice peek at my belly button.

I took Tyson's hand and followed him to where an older man, Gerald, was grilling by a table full of food. It was like nothing we had back home, so much sauce on one portion of the barbecue, and then there was the fried food. Not to mention the array of desserts, cobblers, the pound cake, and what looked like banana pudding.

"Help yourselves, kids," Gerald said with a friendly wink.

Prophet and Asiah came over, and I leaned more into Tyson.

"We got some dogs fresh off the grill," Gerald pointed out. "We got beef, we got pork, pick your poison."

"Does it matter?" I asked.

Asiah rolled her eyes while Prophet politely smiled.

"Some of us don't partake of the swine, so beef is more

adequate. Or it's a taste thing, like pork ribs are far superior than beef ribs," he explained.

Asiah grabbed a paper plate and faced Tyson. "I'll make your plate, Trice."

I squeezed Tyson's hand and pulled him toward me. "No, I can do it."

Asiah lifted a brow as her nostrils flared. "You don't even know the difference between beef and pork, and you think you can make his plate?"

Her accusatory tone made me bite my lip, feeling uneasy over my lack of knowledge about the foods before me. In Pacific Hills, I didn't back down from anyone or anything. Then again, I didn't have to, because no one questioned me. Here in Lindenwood, I was out of my element.

How could I question this girl? A girl who Tyson once knew fondly and intimately.

Prophet looked between me and Asiah as Tyson appeared caught in a war. "Nandy can help Trice, Asiah. *You* can make Read's plate, since y'all came together."

"I think I want dessert first." Tyson finally spoke. "Just to get it out of the way. Who made the carrot cake?"

Asiah took a step back. "I did." She tossed the paper plate aside as her voice got a little hollow. "Prophet told me you were coming, and I wanted to make it, just like your mom used to."

Things got quiet as she walked off and took her seat next to Read.

Tyson dropped my hand and eyed the cake, frowning.

"You better eat a slice," Prophet said. "She spent all week making different versions of it to get it right."

"I don't want any."

"Trice." With anyone else, I had the feeling Tyson would've

gotten mad and argued, but one look at Prophet, and Tyson kept quiet.

"I just lost my appetite," Tyson said softly, eyeing the cake.

"Cool off," Prophet instructed.

"Come on over here with me, Trice," Gerald added. "You got far too many people to greet."

Tyson leaned close to whisper to me. "Guess."

Together he and Gerald went around the party, while I was left to guess what he liked to eat.

There was so much food before me, but I refused to back down from the challenge.

It wasn't that Trice couldn't make his own plate, it was just something I noticed couples sometimes did for each other. My father for my mother and vice versa. It was a love thing.

"Beef hot dogs are the best," Prophet said as he came and stood beside me. "Pork ribs are better than beef, and—"

"I wanna guess," I told him. It felt like a test. Tyson didn't know how he felt about me, and I didn't want to lose him before I had a chance to show him who I was and could be.

Prophet held up his hands and stood back to observe me as I began making Tyson's plate.

"I hope you don't mind me crashing," I spoke up. "I got dumped back home, and Tyson wanted to make me feel better."

Prophet seemed to understand. "He spoke of you when he came to see us last month. Now I see why Trice puts up with you."

I stopped making Tyson's plate and stood back. "What's that supposed to mean?"

Prophet smiled. "Have you looked in the mirror lately?"

Oh. It was almost comical. I was a mess. "Didn't you hear? I just got dumped."

"You shouldn't sell yourself short."

"Why is that?"

He gestured to where Tyson stood holding a boy I learned was named Rain, Cherish's son, and looking absolutely adorable as he played with the baby. "I never thought I'd see him smile and be genuine and happy. You're doing something right down there in the Hills, Nandy. Keep at it."

I wasn't doing anything for Tyson; instead, he was just frustrated with me. "But then you called him to come back."

"I know, and I apologize for that error. It won't happen again. He can do more than this, more than us. He got too much pain here, too much struggle." He began making his own plate. "And what I meant was, beyond the fact that you're pretty, you've got spice, an attitude—no, *fortitude*. He's always had a thing for that."

I bowed my head. "He doesn't like me. He says I make him crazy."

"You might, but you're the only person I've ever seen call him by his first name." He studied me with compassion as he threw me a bone. "And he let you hold his hand. I don't remember him ever being so touchy before."

Cherish came over, and Prophet said something playful to his sister before joining Tyson and the other boys.

Asiah was watching Tyson as well, and having caught me watching her watch him, she mean-mugged me before turning back to Read.

Cherish nudged me as she peeked between Asiah and me. "I don't know why she acting like that," she said. "Anybody can tell y'all ain't doin' nothing."

"We're not."

Cherish went on. "Trice is cool people, Nandy. I just hope while he's up in the Hills he's opening up. I want him to believe in something again, something good. He was so dark the last time I saw him. I hope it all works out."

Tyson was smiling and making cute faces at Rain, and I felt like Prophet was right. A month prior, I wouldn't have pictured Tyson smiling or playing with a baby, but here he was, so cute and carefree.

Cherish went and sat down at a table, and I cut Tyson a slice of the carrot cake for dessert, smiling at the sight of it. I wanted to know him. To be able to know things about him and to go out of my way to do them for him, like Asiah had done with the cake. I couldn't recall doing a personal thing like that for Chad, and I felt bad about it.

Chad was so normal and clean-cut, and I'd expected to be with him forever. Tyson was a newfound mystery who needed help and compassion, and I finally felt the drive to give it to him.

Perhaps that was the biggest difference, the thing I felt with Tyson that I hadn't with Chad. I loved Chad, yes, but not enough to where I could stop myself from crushing on Tyson. It was something to learn from. I wanted to go home and talk things out with Chad, but I still wanted to explore Tyson and to learn about him. I hadn't given him a chance to know me, but we still had enough summer left for us to get there. I hoped.

I made our plates and set them down at the table side by side, and Tyson soon joined me while Prophet and Gerald took their places as well. Tyson took one look at his plate and tossed me an appreciative smile before digging in.

Everyone was talking as "Ain't No Woman" by the Four Tops serenaded us in the background. I didn't have anyone to talk to, so I ate and listened to bits of conversation going on, admiring the group's closeness and the way that they spoke and lived. Tyson rubbed my knee, letting me know he was there.

When Prophet spoke, Tyson really listened and looked on with admiration and respect. I loved seeing that expression on his face. Home in Pacific Hills, the closest he seemed to content was when he was with Travis, and that was probably because Travis wasn't like my friends and me—he wasn't afraid to just *be*, fuck-up and all.

Across the table I could sense Asiah shooting daggers at me. After growing up in Pacific Hills, I knew how to put on a mask and act fearless. So I put up a cold front and ignored her.

"Man, when I go out, I'm going out like Scarface. I'ma be a godfather with mines," a guy they called Money was saying as he and Pretty rambled on about nothing.

"Hell yeah," their friend Khalil ad-libbed. I'd been shocked to learn that he was seventeen, because he seemed so much younger as he went along with whatever Money or Pretty were saying or doing.

Pretty pretended to have a gun and shot at Money multiple times, and Money died dramatically as a result.

Ugh.

Both Prophet and Tyson shook their heads.

"You guys don't like those movies, do you?" I wanted to know.

Prophet shrugged. "The thing these young brothers fail to realize, as they're idolizing those men, is that the Italians were racists. They didn't like our black asses, and yet these rappers, and fools like them, are paying them homage and treating them like gods."

Tyson looked at me, and I felt my heart stutter when I stared back.

"Do you wanna get out of here?" he asked, whispering the

question in my ear. His lips were so close to my skin, causing me to shiver.

"Where?" It didn't really matter where, I was ready to go anywhere with him.

"Somewhere to learn," he said, "later."

I nodded.

"Shit, it ain't about the Italians, Proph," Money spoke up. "It's about the image, the power, the empire. That's what we want."

"And then they all die or live constantly watching their backs," I said.

Money smirked as he glanced at me. "So? You gotta die for something."

"Why not go out on top?" Pretty added.

"You two are so stupid." Asiah sighed as she leaned into Read, who was also shaking his head in disdain. I liked Read for his quiet demeanor, unlike the three of his friends, who were loud and apparently clueless.

"You can be so much more," I mumbled.

"Not all of us come from the suburbs like you," Money said with a meanness to his tone, stilling me. "Don't sit there and act all high-and-mighty with them diamonds in your ears and on your wrists. The world wasn't handed to us, so we gotta take it."

"Money," Tyson cut in. "Stop."

Money clicked his tongue. "For what?"

"Stop it before I body slam you in front of the girl you're trying so hard to embarrass." He spoke so calm and level that the threat seemed even scarier.

Money stared at Tyson and then at me. "Okay, you right. My bad."

"I just don't think aiming to die is a way to live," I said.

"It's not," Prophet agreed. "You just gotta understand that around here, Nandy, living ain't promised. It ain't easy, and I'm glad Trice got out."

I felt disheartened. Rain was just a baby, and the idea of him having to grow up in a world aiming to die hurt my soul. No child, boy, or man should have to live in a reality like that. I thought of Tyson's mother and these people around me, and hoped maybe, just maybe, there was more out there for them.

"Maybe all of our daddies will shoot us and we'll all get a ticket out," Money mumbled.

A curtain of silence settled over the table.

Oddly, Tyson smiled, like the comment amused him.

And then he shot up from the table, despite my pleas not to do any damage.

It was Prophet who got through to him and caught Tyson, stopping him from laying a hand on Money, who sat back, enjoying the drama he'd just orchestrated. Gerald got involved and took Tyson into the house while Prophet went on to reprimand Money.

Lindenwood wasn't as ugly as I'd always thought, and it probably wasn't as bad either, but it was clear to me that not everyone was happy for Tyson, not everyone had his best interests at heart.

Tyson had to get away and stay away.

Something had to give.

27 | TRICE

Gerald was weak. Old and weak. It would've taken little to no effort to overpower him and go after Money.

But because of one thing, I didn't. I would admit it only to myself and to my composition book, but I was *angry*.

Tyson had killed my mother and nearly me before getting away with it with one shot to the dome.

It left me feeling powerless and angry.

That was why I didn't fight Gerald or Prophet, because deep down I knew I wouldn't be able to control myself. It would be the first time I let the anger out, and I feared I would love its release if I went to town on Money.

Still, as I sat in Alma's kitchen, I found my knee bouncing, giving way to my overpacked rage. From Chad to Money, it was building, and knowing there was no way to let it out made me distraught.

There was blood in my eyes, and no amount of blinking could clear my vision.

"He's an ass," Gerald assured me as he patted my back.

I stiffened, and he moved away.

"Don't let him ruin your good time, boy. You're here with a nice-looking girl, and you live in a better environment. Don't let him get you down."

I continued to sit in silence.

Destruction. I craved it.

Prophet came inside a moment later, and Gerald and he exchanged a nod before Prophet took over.

"You know how Money gets. Fool never knows when to shut up." Prophet shook his head. "You straight, or do you need another minute?"

"I think I should go," I decided.

Prophet frowned. "It's probably for the best."

"I can't come back here."

This place, it wasn't so bad, but the company I kept, and the world I involved myself in, wasn't good for me. Prophet and his family would always be supportive and a crutch for me, but the others, not so much.

"I know, and it hurts. You're getting out." He gave a dry chuckle. "Shit, take Khalil with you."

Khalil wasn't as far gone as Money or Pretty. There was still a chance for him, but the thing was, he had to want it. The stealing, the girls, and parties—Khalil lived for it all. He had accepted this town for what it was, and more just wasn't in the cards for him.

I hung my head, staring down at the tiled kitchen floor. This was it, goodbye. Ever since I was nine, it had been about these guys and this world. We grew up watching *Menace II Society*, pretending to be that shit. And even though we knew the fates of our favorite characters, it was what it was. This was our city, this was our destiny, there wasn't supposed to be a way out.

And yet, *I* was getting out.

Prophet sat at the table with me. "Hey, at least you got her." He thumbed a finger over his shoulder toward Nandy. "We oughta call her Feisty. I like her."

I couldn't find it in me to lighten up. "She'll drive you insane if you get to know her."

Prophet made a face. "That must be your type, considering Asiah."

"I hope Read takes care of her," I said.

"He will. He's had a thing for her for a while. If anyone will do her right, it's him. I'll be around to make sure things are on the up."

The back door opened and Money came inside, holding a cup more than likely filled with beer. He came to the table and gave a smug smile as he reached out and shoved my shoulder. "Man, you know it wasn't like that. I ain't mean it like that, Trice. You know me, man. I was just buggin' because I swear that's ol' girl you was clownin' a month ago."

I didn't care to get that deep with Money. "Things change."

He chuckled. "I'll say. Dude moves area codes and acts like a whole new person." He tilted his head back and drank from his blue plastic cup. "I'm sorry for what I said. It was low, and I know you hate him and it wasn't right."

Money's tone changed as he spoke to me, going from playful to serious. In some ways, we were like brothers, able to fight and argue, but still be down for each other no matter what.

But I still couldn't stay or come back. Crabs in a bucket and all that.

Letting it go, I bobbed my head. "It's whatever, man. We straight."

"Come on back outside, then." He tilted his head toward the door. "Ain't seen you in a month, we gotta catch up."

I shook my head. "I gotta get going. Her parents are looking for her."

Money smirked. "Bet they is." He peered out the kitchen window, where Nandy sat holding Rain as Cherish seemed to be arguing with Pretty. Everyone else was carrying on and fussing, and Nandy was just playing with the baby. I had suspected in the beginning that she might recoil upon meeting my people, but seeing her adapting and making light of the situation almost made me smile.

"I'ma holla at you next time, then." Money came over and slapped my hand, and we did our group's handshake before he headed back outside.

Prophet stood and I did as well, knowing what was coming next. He scratched his head, half smiling. "I'm not good at these things."

"I usually never get a chance to say goodbye, except for in Pops's case," I said.

Prophet pulled me into a hug, slapping my back before stepping away. "It was nice knowing you, Tyson Trice. Maybe you don't believe in God anymore, but if you start to…maybe we'll meet up there someday." He gestured toward the ceiling, but I knew he meant more. "Maybe they'll make a little hood just for us. We can all get together and play cards, and joke around like we used to."

"And if we go to hell?"

Prophet shrugged. "Then hopefully some fine-ass angels sneak out and meet us and we'll have a party."

I cracked a smile. "I'll bring the ice."

Prophet stared at me a moment longer before nodding and going back outside.

Though I'd said goodbye to Prophet, I knew I had to be respectful and pay the same homage to Alma, Gerald, and Cherish.

Outside I allowed all three of them to hug me and say goodbye.

As Nandy and I prepared to go, while Alma was shoving Tupperware into Nandy's arms, Asiah pulled me aside. Read was at the table talking with Khalil, and I spotted him eyeing us.

"So this is it?" Asiah asked as she crossed her arms.

I nodded. "It has to be."

Her brows furrowed. "What happened to five months?"

"Reality."

She eyed Nandy. "So you're choosing the uppity bitch?"

"You've got Read."

Asiah frowned. "I lost my virginity to you. I gave my trust to you, I fell in love with you." She almost seemed to be pleading.

"And I tried to love you back. I do care about you, I have love for you, it's just that—"

She took a step back, not wanting to hear me. "You don't want to love me. You never did."

"I gave an honest effort. It's not like I have a lot of experience outside of you and what we had."

"You act like you were ashamed to let me in."

"I'm sorry, Asiah. It's not only you I'm like that with."

She peeked at Nandy, who was looking our way now. "I

doubt that." Asiah peered into my eyes, and I could see just how much I'd hurt her. She swallowed, gathering what was left of her pride. "I guess I should wish you both luck, you're going to need it. Goodbye, Trice."

Asiah went back over to Read and leaned down to whisper something in his ear, and in moments they were getting ready to leave as well.

Nandy came over to me and reached out to caress my bicep. "You okay?"

I moved away from her. "We're heading out."

She gathered the Tupperware and said her goodbyes before following me out to my truck.

I tried to let music blur out all the tension, but of course Nandy wanted to talk.

"You don't look so good," she noted.

I glanced her way. "I bet you wouldn't look so hot either if you never got to go home again and see your friends. If that option left you homeless altogether."

Boldly, she reached out and placed her hand on my free one. "You're not alone nor homeless, Tyson. Your home's with my family back in Pacific Hills."

It wasn't the same, and so I didn't reply. Not that I had to, because it was always a short drive or walk from Prophet's place to my house.

Nandy stared at my house, and it didn't take a rocket scientist to figure out where we were.

When she let out a small gasp, I took the initiative to get out of the car.

Nandy got out as well and came to stand beside me, looking up at the three-story home. "Do you wanna go inside?"

From the street it looked like the house was completely boarded up. "There's no way in."

Nandy tossed me a smirk as she took off toward the back-yard, where the grass was overgrown due to being unkept for months.

"Correction, I don't think this is a good idea," I said as I followed her.

Nandy wasn't hearing me as she jogged up our back-porch steps. To my surprise, someone had beaten her to the punch. The board that had been nailed over the back door lay on the porch, as if someone had come by with a crowbar to make their way in.

"Probably was some looters," I told her as I opened the back door and peeked inside.

Nandy went on by me into the house, and I couldn't grasp her bravery or brashness.

Soon I wasn't paying attention to her as I took in the abysmal state my former home was currently in. Furniture remained, but trash littered the floor, giving me an idea of kids or the homeless using the place as refuge. Not to mention the repugnant odor that hung in the air.

"Ugh," Nandy complained as she covered her nose. "Smells like—"

"Something died in here?" I challenged as I looked her way. "Well, guess what, you're right."

She frowned. "That's not what I was going to say." She peered down at the floor. "I have more sense than that."

Nandy observed the decaying kitchen, and I watched as disgust overtook her expression.

"Asiah doesn't know anything about my family's history before the shooting. Neither does Shayne," I spoke up. "I didn't want Asiah to know about my parents or demons. Shayne, either. With you, I just feel like I have—*need* you to understand me. You drive me insane, but the only reason we're here now is because I obviously like your crazy."

"I'm happy you brought me here."

She took out her cell phone and turned on her flashlight to guide her from the kitchen to the front room, the living room.

My nerves did me in as my steps became heavy.

There were brown stains on the white carpet. Brown, rust-like stains from their blood…our blood. I could see the spot where my mother had died and where Tyson had lain after he'd shot himself. I could see where I'd been, too far from her to save her. Before I could stop myself, I leaned against the wall farthest from the faint memory of the massacre, my breathing becoming harsh.

I could see it, playing in my head again. As the scene unfolded in front of me, I was left feeling the way I did every morning when I woke up, and every night while I lay in bed trying to get some sleep.

Angry.

Weak.

Powerless.

Guilty.

Lonely.

I closed my eyes and rocked back and forth for a moment, trying to fight the sensations churning through me, trying to push forward.

"Th-this is where it happened," I let out as I opened my eyes to find Nandy staring at me with worry and wonder. "I came here that night you pissed me off, and I swear I could see it. Being here now, I can see it all over again. I was standing where you are when he got ready to shoot her. I was so far away."

"He had a gun," Nandy tried to reason with me.

She couldn't see it. "Years—I had *years* to do something to protect her, and I failed." I shook my head and stood from the wall. "I don't sleep much at night because of this room, and the scene I see in my head right now that you will never understand. I don't feel anything good, because I can't. I carry this room with me all the time, and the scene never stops. It's like an endless loop."

I stared down at the spot where I was supposed to have died before our neighbors burst through the door and called the police. "Sometimes it gets better, and then nights like last Tuesday happen, where Chad throws it in my face, or today. Just when I think I've escaped it, it creeps back up on me."

Nandy cautiously moved closer to me. "You can't continue to relive this. It's not fair or healthy."

"Healthy?" I chuckled to myself. "None of this was ever healthy."

She opened her mouth but soon shut it and bit down on her lip. She looked up toward the staircase and soon had her phone out once more as she moved on to the second floor.

I took another glimpse at the stains and the scene of that night before following her up the steps.

My room was the first on the right, and she had guessed accurately as she stepped inside it.

My room was simple, almost vacant. There was the bed, the dresser, the closet, and a desk and a small box TV. No pictures, posters, or other artifacts showed who I was—or who I used to be. It was as if I'd been preparing for the life I lived now, a life with a void.

Nandy held up her phone and peered around my room, and I could see the dissatisfaction on her face.

But then she went toward my tiny closet.

"Hmm," she said as she peeked inside, and my breath

caught. Just when she was about to shut the door, she saw it, and to my embarrassment, she raised her light to illuminate my corniness. Nandy looked back at me and barely hid her smile as she nodded toward the T ✛ N carving I'd made years before. "Most people do that kind of thing on trees."

I smirked. "Don't worry. I got a good ass-whupping for that when Tyson found it."

To this, Nandy frowned and ran her hand over the inscription. "You'll get better, Tyson."

That was what every therapist I'd seen had said, as well as Lydia. "No, I won't."

Nandy faced me, appearing serious. "There are five stages to grief. It takes a while for you to get to acceptance, but you *will* get there, and you will heal. Right now, I know that you feel—"

She was psychoanalyzing me, which pissed me off as she sounded just like the rest of them.

"You don't know how I feel," I snapped at her.

"I bet you blame yourself."

"I blame God, I blame Tyson, but most of all, yes, I blame myself, and I'll never stop. There will never be a day where I don't feel like I let it happen. Lydia thinks this—" I gestured to myself "—is fixable. But you know what, it's not. This is it, Nandy, get a good hard look. You should make it work with Chad, because *we* will never be. I can't be that guy, and I don't want to be."

She frowned. "You don't want to try to move forward?"

"No."

"Why not?"

"You should really watch *Shaka Zulu*." I paced the floor, feeling everything come back. It was like irony was taunting me the moment Nandy entered my life.

"Why?"

"Nandi was Shaka's mother and his Achilles' heel. When she died, he lost his mind, and that was the beginning of his downfall." I took a step back and gestured around us. "I'm hanging on by a thread. I loved her—" my voice strained with the hurt of it all "—and she's gone. I don't know what to do with myself anymore. Everything I ever did, it was all for her, and I don't know what to do now."

I turned my back. "I always thought I would die before I turned twenty-one, and now that I've got the opportunity to excel, I'm not sure I want to see twenty-one. I don't have a purpose without her." Bowing my head, I let my shoulders sag. "I can't do that again. I can't get that attached to another person. I can't feel loss again. I'm not built for it."

There was nothing more weakening than having something in your grasp one moment, and having it snatched from you the next without you being able to put up a fight. I didn't want to fall in love, I didn't want to have companions who were close to me like siblings, I didn't want connections. I didn't want to feel, because feeling led to pain, and I'd carried too much of that on my shoulders since the night my father shot me.

It was inevitable.

I was just like every other guy out there. I had given in to my hardness, put up a front to avoid revealing my vulnerabilities. I couldn't be that guy, and I wouldn't be. Not for anyone.

"I guess my town's a perfect fit for you, then," Nandy said bitterly.

"Why's that?"

"You're a knight, Tyson. You've got armor on over your heart and mind, and you won't take it off. Your damaged soul is impenetrable."

"Yes, it is."

"Funny, it didn't even take collagen or Botox to give you such a mask." She walked past me, ready to go.

"I'm sorry, Nandy."

"I know."

It wasn't supposed to be this way. I had brought her to my house to show her who I was and where I came from, and yet I froze up the moment I revealed a wound and she tried to touch me. It was like we had taken a step forward only to jump a hundred back. I couldn't help it, but with Nandy, withdrawing didn't feel right. She was probably the only person whom I felt the need to push further with, to explain myself so that she could understand.

There was a part of me that, whenever I saw her, wanted to be a kid again, free and happy like I used to be when I visited her in the Hills.

But I was seventeen, and I couldn't get those days back.

It wasn't fair to her, and it wasn't fair to me, but she had to understand that this was how it had to be.

Nandy paused in the doorway, pity and hurt in her eyes. "Can I ask you something?"

"Yeah?"

"Are you afraid?"

I didn't bullshit her and ask of what. "Yes."

"So am I." Nandy looked around my damaged past. "I'm so afraid of starting something new outside of Chad, the norm, everything, but I can't be stagnant, Tyson. I feel like I have no idea where I'm going in life anymore. The page is unwritten, and that scares me, but I'm going to be strong and face it head-on with a pen, not a pencil. Mistakes are bound to happen, but that's life—you grow and you learn from it. Hurt, that's inevitable, and so is growth. You have to let yourself grow and be happy—you can't wallow in this state that you're in."

"I'm mad," I told her.

"You will be, for a while."

I shook my head. "I want to break things. It's building inside of me, and I want to let it out."

Nandy came to me and placed her hand on my chest, above my wound. "I think you just did."

"It's not enough."

"What do you write about in that composition book?"

"I went back to the beginning."

"And how does that feel?"

"Calming."

"See?"

It stunned me to realize she had gotten through, had touched me far deeper than her hand on my chest.

I placed my hand over hers. "You know what your problem is, Nandy?"

The corners of her lips began to turn up. "What?"

"You always get what you want."

28 | *Nandy*

My parents were waiting for me in the foyer when we got home. Tyson slipped on by me to go to his room, the traitor.

"Oh thank God." My mother heaved a sigh of relief and placed her hand to her heart as she set eyes on me.

My father looked momentarily comforted before his expression morphed into anger. "There you are!"

I folded my arms as the weight of the past two days settled on my shoulders. "I'm sorry about running off and wasting your money on cotillion."

"Is that all you have to say?" my mother asked.

"Seriously? We couldn't care less about the money," my father fumed. "We were worried sick you were lying in a ditch somewhere. And honestly, I have half a mind to wring Trice's neck, because I know he's known where you've been."

My mother stepped up to pacify my father's angst. "Nandy, what has gotten into you? This behavior you've exhibited all summer isn't you."

How could I begin to tell them I was into Tyson? That my world had tilted upside down the moment he'd stepped back into my life? That my heart felt as if it had been on pause for him all this time? It was so treacherous, I hadn't wanted to believe it until it was staring me right in the face as everything I thought I knew and cared about blew up in front of me.

"I'm sorry, Mom, Dad, I really am. I was lost for a minute, and now I'm finding my way. If I'm grounded, I understand. I should've called," I said. "I was just going through a lot. Chad and I broke up, and I felt overwhelmed and had to get away."

My father's anger seemed to lessen with this explanation. "And you couldn't tell us?"

"I should've," I agreed. "It just happened so fast. Don't blame Tyson, this is all on me. I had a rough start to my summer, and now I'm going to work on communicating better and *being* better."

My parents faced each other and spoke with their eyes, seeming to come to some silent agreement.

"This won't happen again, Alyssa," my father stated adamantly. "The shit you've been pulling this summer has gotten on our last nerves. Think about the example you're setting for Jordy."

I should've behaved better for my brother, but really, Jordy was already on the right path. He'd accepted Tyson without question. Jordy was a saint.

"I know, I'm going to be better, I promise," I said.

"Honestly," my father huffed, "you owe me big. I had to deal with Laura Bradley and Charlotte Ray and all their incessant whining about you not being there."

From experience, I knew that there was nothing worse than that duo coming down on you. "Sorry, Dad."

"Not yet you aren't. I promised them you'd make it up to them. Whatever schmoozefest charity event they throw together next, you're theirs."

Cringing, I conceded. "I deserve that."

"You deserve GPS tracking, but I'm just glad you're okay."

While I was sure Mrs. Bradley and Ms. Ray would be unbearable due to my skipping out on cotillion, at least what mattered most to my parents was my safety.

"I know this is asking a lot, but I really need to talk to Chad," I told them.

My father folded his arms, inhaling deep to practice the utmost patience. "You know what? Go ahead. I'm sure he's been worried, too. Let him know you're still breathing before we ground you until graduation."

I blinked, knowing he wasn't serious, but still. Talk about extreme. "Thanks, Dad."

My mother released a sigh, at once appearing sympathetic. "Now, how are you?"

My father softened as well. "Yes, how are you dealing with this? You worked really hard toward cotillion."

Sure, in a way, I was bummed I'd missed out. We'd all worked hard for that night—a night neither Shayne nor I could ever get back.

"It sucks that I missed out, but I guess it never really mattered," I said. What did I gain from putting on that dress, that tiara, and presenting myself in front of most of this snobby town? It would've been cool to have that moment with my friends, but we'd have more moments come the school year and life in general. I would be okay. There was more to life than image.

Yes, I would be okay.

★ ★ ★

Xiu Yee was out walking her family's dog as I took a stroll through my neighborhood.

She came to a stop in front of me, offering a polite wave as her cocker spaniel, Penny, came closer and sniffed at my legs.

The girl in front of me scoffed, tugging on the leash in an attempt to get her dog away from me. "Sorry about that."

"It's nothing." I noticed that I'd arrived at my destination. "So," I turned back to Xiu, "I meant to tell you, you looked amazing at cotillion."

I'd seen pictures online, along with an impressive video.

Xiu's cheeks reddened. "Oh, thank you."

Xiu was usually just Erica's quiet and shy cousin, but at cotillion she'd been a showstopper. With a gorgeous white dress, red lips, and curled hair, Xiu was a star that night.

Her brother, Geordan, had been her escort, as Xiu also didn't have a boyfriend, but that didn't matter, because they'd done a cute little dance come time for their skit after Xiu's debut.

"You had the best skit," I told Xiu. "I didn't know you danced, too."

Xiu immediately bit into her lip. "I… I don't. I mean, not like Geordan and DEFCON Yee."

"Looks like they need to add a new member to the crew."

Xiu fiddled with her leash. "Geordan would never let me dance, and neither would my parents." She offered me a half smile. "I'll see you around, Nandy. I gotta get Penny to hurry up and pee."

I said goodbye and walked over to the Bradleys' house. Doom and gloom seemed to wash over me. I wasn't ready to face either Mrs. Bradley or her son.

I didn't get the chance to brace myself or prepare what

I'd say after I rang the doorbell. On this rare occasion, Mrs. Bradley actually came to the door instead of her housekeeper.

She wasn't thrilled to see me. "Oh look, you do know how to show up for something."

I would have to endure. "I'm sorry, Mrs. Bradley."

She rolled her eyes. "Are you? You were the most important deb, and you let us down."

She knew how to rub it in.

"Leave her alone, Mom." Chad's voice, tired yet strong, broke through the awkwardness, sending goose bumps across my flesh. This was it.

He came to the door, wedging himself between me and his mother.

Mrs. Bradley put up no fight before leaving us be.

"She's just giving you shit because it's convenient. Like three other girls didn't show up for various reasons." Chad offered a lazy shrug. "I think Mischa Wilson's pregnant or something."

So Shayne and I weren't the only ones who'd missed out. It wasn't the end of the world.

Chad stood before me looking drained but comfortable in his T-shirt and sweats. The shirt was one I'd gotten him, and I forced myself to stare into his wounded blue eyes.

"Can we talk?" I asked.

He surveyed the area behind me before coming back to me, crossing his arms. "About what?"

Being brave, I said, "Why it's over."

Chad pulled his front door shut and sat on his front step.

"I'm sorry," I said from behind him.

No matter what, I should've been honest with him when my feelings started to change.

Chad rested his elbows on his knees as he stared out at the street. "Sorry doesn't change a thing."

Never the emotional type, I was shocked to find myself tearing up and choking on my words. "I am, Chad."

"Fucked him yet?"

It was a jab. *"No."*

Chad looked down. "What's stopping you?"

"Give me some credit here. It's not about that."

"You sure stopped messing around with me. Shit, that I don't mind, but when you emotionally and mentally checked out on me, that's when I knew we were over. You started avoiding me, Nandy, making up shitty excuses to keep us apart. And don't get me started on that kid. One minute you hated the guy, the next you were all about him and pouting over seeing him with Shayne," Chad said. "I knew I lost you the night of Boys Versus Girls. But I was so stupid, I thought we had a chance to be us at cotillion. But you showed up with *him*. You constantly defend him. You were out of this relationship a long time ago."

"I fucked up, and I'm sorry. Do you think I like this? I feel awful about what happened between us." There were no words or gestures that could fix what I'd done and how I felt, and that's what hurt us both the most. It was done, irrevocably.

"I don't care." He stood and prepared to go back inside.

"Chad," I pleaded, trying to keep it together and avoid a breakdown. I'd known he would be angry, but I wanted to make amends. I wanted it to end better than this.

His eyes glistened in the night as he glared at me. "What do you want me to say? And don't think this is me wishing you the best, because I don't. I hope it crashes and burns and it hurts just as much as this does. I loved you."

"And I loved you," I said back. "I don't know how this

happened, but I'm sorry that it did. I'm sorry that you got hurt and that you made the choice for us on how to handle the situation. I'm sorry our friends probably blame you. I'm sorry I fell for someone else. You deserve better, and so do I. I can't be what your parents want."

"I never asked you to be," Chad said.

I shook my head. "But we never fought it, either. We went with the image and the flow. Tyson and I might crash and burn, but I'll learn from it. We have one more year to be kids, and then we're on our own. I wanna prepare to live a life on my own, doing what *I* want, not what I think is expected of me. I wanna work on that most. You should, too."

There was nothing more to say, so I turned and prepared to head home.

"Hey, Nandy?" Chad asked from behind me.

I faced him one final time. "Yeah?"

"I said I want him to hurt you, but I don't mean that. Maybe he's better for you, maybe not, but if he does hurt you, I'm going to kick his ass, okay?"

I managed to smile and left with a lighter step. Despite it all, he still cared, just like I still cared for him. If Tyson hadn't come to Pacific Hills, maybe we would've made it. Even if we'd ended on our own, at least we would've given it an honest effort.

Tyson's serious concentration face was adorable. Back home, he was at the kitchen table scribbling in his composition book, and I kept sneaking peeks at him. I had my own notebook out, but really, it served no purpose beyond an excuse to be in the same room as him.

Being playful, I went old school and wrote down the age-old question: *Are We Friends?* And then I drew three boxes, one for *yes*, another for *no*, and a last one for *maybe*.

I slid him the sheet of paper and laughed when he mean-mugged me.

Instead of checking a box, Tyson scribbled a note and passed it back to me.

Friends don't kiss

He had a cocky look on his face as he continued to write in his composition book.

"Do you want to go for a swim?" I asked. It was late, but the day had been long and emotional. Unwinding in the pool sounded perfect.

Tyson shut his composition book. "Any excuse to not wear clothes, huh?"

"Don't act like you don't like it," I teased as I stood from the table.

The thoughtful expression on his face left me wondering what he was thinking as I went up to my room. At the model home, he'd told me my butt was cute, which also left me wondering what all Tyson had noticed about me and my body. I could admit that everything about his left me intimidated. So broad, so tall, so manly, and not to mention his intellect. The attraction wasn't all about hormones and getting physical with Tyson. I was most obsessed with his personality and mind-set. I admired all that he'd become.

In my room, I dug out a navy blue bikini and quickly put it on before going down to the pool, where Tyson was already waiting. I turned on some music at the entertainment center, and we were soon serenaded by an R & B song that was cozy and great.

The pool was warm enough for a few laps and maybe some splashing around, but I didn't want to play around or get fully wet.

Tyson was relaxing against the pool wall, watching as I waded over to him. "How'd things go?"

I didn't want to talk about Chad. It was obvious Tyson would never understand him, and Chad would never get Tyson.

"He's hurt," I said. "I really messed this up. I can only hope that in time he can forgive me and we can be friends or something."

Tyson made a face, as if thinking over his words. "He probably does need more time. This'll smooth over. You live and you learn."

I agreed. "Thanks for taking me to Lindenwood."

Tyson recoiled. "Nah, I'm sorry about that."

"No, I get it now. It's a place with real people, and no matter what the media says, it's not all bad. There are good people and good things happening. You're living proof. I can see why you'd want to go back there. I liked Alma and her family, especially Prophet. But I can see why you can't, either."

"Temptation is a powerful drug."

There was a chance that Lindenwood could still be a haven for Tyson. Although, with its painful memory of losing his mother, I could see why Tyson was better off someplace new.

"What are you doing tomorrow?" I asked.

"I've got a meeting with Lydia to work out my schedule for senior year, and then I'm supposed to meet up with the guys."

School was approaching fast, and I couldn't help but imagine Tyson roaming the halls of Cross High. Or better yet, needing someone to show him around, and I was the go-to girl for that kind of thing.

"Are you good in school?" I wanted to know.

Tyson shrugged. "When I *go* to school."

Oh yeah, he lived a different life before. "Well, you certainly will be going to school here."

I didn't miss him rolling his eyes. "There goes that bossy ass again."

His smart mouth caused me to park myself in front of him, staring him down. "And you like this bossy ass."

"I don't recall saying that."

He never did admit to having feelings for me in the way that I had feelings for him. He'd told me he liked my crazy and wanted me to know him, more than he ever had Asiah or Shayne. I knew that counted as much as the words he hadn't said.

He'd told me I always got what I wanted, and that had been true when we were younger. If he really believed it for a fact now that we were seventeen, well...

I moved closer to him and wrapped my arms around his neck.

Tyson instantly had his hands on my waist, almost pushing me away, but not with enough fight. "What are you doing?"

I smiled, eyeing his mouth. "Getting what I want."

This time I kissed him, and it wasn't for a hunch.

Tyson leaned back as I hovered over him, his gaze locked on my mouth as he licked his lips as if to tempt me. "I can't."

My heart fluttered. "Why?"

He peered up at me. "I don't want to be a rebound."

I came closer. "Then it's a good thing I don't play basketball."

Tyson bore an adorable expression on his face. "You're corny."

"And you're cute."

I went in for another kiss, one he was willing to return.

Tyson was a tease, playing with my lips slowly before giving in and relinquishing his self-control and just kissing me back with all that he had.

Still, he tried to fight it. "This is wrong."

"Yeah, I know," I said before going in for more.

His arms circled my waist and held me in place, and I enjoyed the feeling of being brushed up against him as the power and intensity of his lips sucked me in. He kissed me deeply so that my heart and soul could feel it and tingle, too. His strength and gentleness were two contrasts that made me admire him to my core. Tyson was such a complex individual that it was no wonder I'd fallen for him the moment he returned to me.

"We really shouldn't be doing this," Tyson said as he pulled back once more.

Deciding to play along, I kept back. "Why not?"

"Because you might get caught." A third voice entered the pool area, bringing an icy chill to the heated moment I was sharing with Tyson.

I looked up to discover my father standing at the edge of the pool. He looked every shade of pissed off, and I knew to back away from Tyson even as I felt his grasp leave my body.

"You, up to your room, now," my father said as he pointed at me. He faced Tyson, and his anger increased. "You, in my office, now."

My father didn't wait for either of us before storming inside.

29 | *TRICE*

Parker was pissed.

Nandy got out of the pool first, shaking due to the cold air her father had left behind. She gathered her towel before looking at me one final time. I could see the fear in her eyes as she turned away and slipped inside.

Watching her walk away, I didn't want, nor like her leaving. All I could think about was her lips on mine and the feel of her body against mine. That hadn't been just a taste, like at the model home. It had been more, so much more. I'd known we were exposed, but fighting the temptation was hard, especially with her eagerness to latch her lips to mine.

Now Parker was upset, extremely.

I should've gone to Parker immediately, but then I thought

maybe it would be more appropriate to dry off and put on a shirt before facing his reprimand.

And perhaps I could think of what I would say to him, to ease his angst against what he'd seen.

Although…I wasn't exactly sure what it was that Nandy and I had. One minute I wanted to kill her; the next she was making me face the reality of a future, of progressing after what I lost. I wanted to be angry, and she was patient enough to tell me I *would* be angry, but not forever. This was different than with Shayne, where everything we'd talked about had felt like make-believe. This was real.

I just didn't know about Nandy, and kissing didn't make it any less complicated.

Parker was waiting for me in his office, too riled up to sit still. The moment I stepped into the room, he stared me down.

"Sit," he ordered. When I didn't, he lifted a brow as if questioning my being insubordinate. "Sit, Tyson, now."

I guess I had an authority issue, because still I stood. He had every right to be mad, but the magnitude of his anger made me cautious and curious. "Are you kicking me out?"

Parker squinted, as if confused. "Because you kissed my daughter? No." He shook his head. "Now sit down. I won't ask again."

This time I sat, calmed knowing that he wasn't going for the extreme. "So you're mad," I pointed out. "I get it."

Parker breathed out through his nose, his shoulders rising and falling. He was beyond mad. "That won't happen again, do you understand? You two are not about to start messing around."

"Why?" I asked.

"Because you live in this house, as a member of this family.

We took you in to be with us. You and Nandy can't be together like that."

"Family?"

Parker nodded. "If you were a year younger, we would've officially adopted you."

I knew Parker meant well, but he was pushing it. "You're a little late to the party to rescue me and be my parents, don't you think?"

Parker sighed and sat on his desk, scratching his head. "Listen, Trice, I'm not trying to replace your parents and what you had, but I want to give you a true fresh start. It was always a pleasure having you around when you were younger, just like it's been this summer. We're building a family here, and that means Nandy is off-limits."

"No disrespect, Parker, but I'm not going to look at Nandy like my sister."

He shrugged. "That's on you, but like I said, it's not going to happen. Whether you view her as a sibling or not, that's how we're looking at it in our eyes. Do not touch her again, are we clear?"

His reasoning sounded so simple, and yet I held some doubt. "If I lived in Lindenwood, would this be a problem?"

Parker made a face. "No, because you wouldn't be under this roof. You'd be her boyfriend who lived elsewhere."

Maybe it was that simple for Parker. He didn't want us messing around, because he wanted us to be family. If that was his only reason behind being against Nandy and me, I could understand.

"You care about what the neighbors would think, don't you?"

"Along with the fact that I just don't think it's appropriate, yes. I'm not running a house that operates loosely, and I don't need it to appear to be, either."

It was funny how life worked out. We had freedom of choice, but we didn't have the freedom to make said choice without judgment or having to explain. *Ain't that fucked up?*

"Well, I'm sorry for disappointing you and kissing your daughter, Parker," I said as I stood from the chair, ready to go on up to bed.

Parker stood, too. "I mean it, Trice."

"Yes, sir."

"There are nice girls in this town. When school starts you'll be so busy you won't even remember this night," Parker insisted.

He meant well, but it wasn't going to happen that way. Other girls? I had tunnel vision for one girl only. Somehow, I had to make it work so that we could see where things could go.

I went up to my bedroom and tore off my shirt, aiming to take a shower. Maybe it would help clear my head, or maybe not.

Between kissing Nandy and Parker's warning, I didn't know what I was doing.

My bedroom door opened, and I turned to see Nandy coming inside. She closed the door behind her and pressed her back to it, staring me down with nothing but curiosity.

"It's all my fault," she said.

"Nothing we can do about it now. He doesn't approve and just wants us to be family. That's what he wants to build here."

Nandy looked at the floor, her shoulders sagging. "What do you want to do, Tyson?" She already looked defeated.

"Well, first I wanna refrain from being homeless," I told

her, "and second…" I stared at those nice lips of hers. "I wanna kiss you again."

My confession took her by surprise.

I liked and respected Parker, but I couldn't leave Nandy alone. "I like you, Nandy. Going forward as friends or family is not an option."

"Maybe he just needs more time."

I shook my head. "He's completely against this. He probably thinks I plan on knocking you up with a bunch of nappy-headed babies or some shit."

Nandy wrinkled her nose. "I'd make sure their hair was tamed. God knows your braids are forever embedded into my memory."

I rolled my eyes. "I was recovering from a bullet wound and taking care of my grandfather. I ain't have time to be looking cute."

Nandy came up on me. "You were still cute, Tyson."

"Uh-huh, sure."

Nandy wrapped her arms around me, staring up at me with a smile. "You've always been cute." She kept moving closer until I backed away and fell onto my bed. She sat on my lap, appearing victorious in her stance over me. "I know my dad pretty well. We have ten minutes before he comes up here to give me my round of a lecture. So for the time being, you're mine."

She leaned down and brought her mouth to mine, taking the lead.

My arms tightened around her and held her body closer; I knew that what we were doing was both inevitable and dangerous at the same time.

A part of me found it sexy as hell when Nandy was bossy and in control, and another kinda got the tick and urge to—

I grabbed her by her waist, seizing her and laying her down beneath me, pinning her in place with my hips.

Nandy put up no fight.

She lay back, running that pink tongue of hers over her bottom lip. "Nine minutes."

The air between us had gotten hot quick. The material of our clothing was thin, and *parts* were close. With my hand on her shorts, I could feel that she wasn't wearing anything underneath them, along with her braless state in her T-shirt.

It had been too long.

I leaned back and stared down at her. "We should cool it."

Her brows pushed down in confusion. "Why?"

"It's been a *long* time since I've been physical or messed around, and I'm pretty sure I'm going to need longer than, what, eight minutes to get the job done."

Nandy's eyes widened and she sat up. "Oh." She bit down on her lip. "Promise not to get mad?"

"Sure."

"I like you, a lot. I like the way you talk, the way you carry yourself, the way you move in this town. I like it all. The thought of having sex with you sorta…scares me. I just haven't with anyone but Chad, and we didn't really hook up this summer. You'd be a new feel, and I'm kinda nervous about that. I don't want to rush it until I'm sure, okay?"

Her response put everything in perspective for me.

"Do you still think of the future?" I wanted to know.

"What do you mean?"

"Do you still wanna have two girls and name them Miracle and Mexico?"

Nandy closed her eyes and groaned. "I was seven!"

I smiled at the sight of her embarrassment. When we were kids, she was determined to have two daughters and stick them with those names. And at one point, she'd demanded that we all call her "Nay." Nandy had been a precocious little girl and I couldn't wait to keep learning what type of young woman she'd grown into. "You wanna see where this can go?"

Nandy nodded. "Yeah."

I leaned over and gave her a quick kiss. "Me, too."

Nandy was at the kitchen table the next morning eating a bowl of fruit while I stood at the island counter eating Fruity Pebbles. Max stood at the counter across from me, sipping on coffee and going over spreadsheets. The room was quiet except for the sound of Nandy's fork hitting her bowl and my spoon digging into my cereal.

Max cleared her throat as she began tucking her paperwork into her bag. She turned from the counter and eyed me and then Nandy. "Let's not pretend that I didn't speak with Parker over what happened last night, shall we?"

Nandy gave her attention to her mother. "How do you feel about it?"

Max shrugged. "Honestly, I thought it was bound to happen once you two started pestering each other. At first, I thought you'd never get along, but once you did, I'm not surprised this is where things ended up. But Parker's right. We're building a new family, and it would be inappropriate for you two to see each other."

Nandy made a face and poked at her diced pineapple. "This is completely unfair."

"Correct me if I'm wrong, but didn't you just break up with Chad?" Max challenged. "I don't think you're making sound decisions right now."

"I am, Mom."

"If Trice never came here, would you have left Chad?" Nandy didn't respond, and Max seemed to take that as her cue to go on. "It would be foolish to hurt someone over temporary feelings. You and Chad had a nice thing, and you were good together." Max turned to me. "And Shayne's a lovely girl. You two have just been cooped up in this house together too long. You need to get out and explore."

Max seemed a little more understanding than Parker. For that, I took a stab at explaining our situation. "You're not against us, but you're siding with him, I get it. I don't think it's right to patronize us, though. We've barely spent a minute together without fighting, and now we just wanna see what's beneath the surface beyond the initial attraction. Shayne's my friend, and Chad's just a redheaded—"

"You're right, Mom," Nandy cut in. "I did just end things with Chad, but that doesn't have anything to do with what's been lingering for Tyson since I was a kid. It's not about a rebound, it's about curiosity, and like he said, seeing what's there. Like it or not, we *don't* see each other as family. The least we can be is honest with you and Dad about that."

Max pursed her lips, staring between the two of us. "It'd be wise to take my advice and heed my warning. Parker does not approve, nor do I. This could get very ugly, very fast, Nandy." Max regarded me. "Dating is hard enough, but under one roof? There's too much temptation, let alone risks. If you two were to date and it ended badly, that would spoil the atmosphere. Besides—" she gathered her bag to go "—we're not running a free-for-all around here. Take my advice and let it go."

Max left the room and promised to see us after she got off work. The only beauty of the situation was the fact that she and Parker both held impressive careers where the hours were long and varied. Their laborious work ethic often kept them away during the week, and they'd be blind to what was going on between Nandy and me.

At the table, Nandy sat poking at the remains of her fruit, her face twisted up.

"They'll just take more time to convince," I assured her.

She only looked at me, and I knew she was upset from more than just Max's words.

"What?" I asked.

Nandy rolled her eyes. "Enough with insulting Chad already."

Now I was smirking. "I don't like him."

"Clearly." She scoffed. "Technically you already won, so this little pissing contest between you two can stop at any time."

Her annoyance made me curious. "You agree with your mom, that this is temporary and Chad's more long-term?"

Nandy shook her head. "Do I want to be with you and explore? Yes, but I'm not about to put up with you insulting Chad. It's rude and uncalled for. He tried to be nice to you, and you always saw him as nothing. High-fiving Travis over my lack of wearing clothes and being standoffish. Don't put him down when he at least tried."

I was surprised at the prickle of jealousy I felt at the reality before me. Nandy actually loved Chad. She had sacrificed a lot to give in to being with me. She hadn't been miserable and he hadn't been an asshole to her, she just wanted me more. I hated the idea of Max being right, that Nandy was giving up her relationship for something fleeting. I didn't know about forever and the long run, I just knew about the now and the moment. The more I thought about the situation, the more I hated feeling inadequate compared to Chad.

Standing from the counter, I was suddenly ready to go and speak to Lydia, anxious to talk about anything else.

"Tyson." Nandy sighed.

"Don't," I replied. "Let's just let it go for now."

She got up and stood in my way. "You have to meet me halfway with this."

"Why were you with Chad?" I wanted to know.

Nandy took a moment to think. "Honestly, because he was popular and safe. It was easy to be with him, blend in, and be part of the crowd. He liked me, and I liked the feeling of being wanted by him. It made me feel worthy, like cotillion."

"So Chad was just convenient? I don't want to be convenient."

"You're not—you're someone I don't have to put up a front with, someone I don't have to worry about looking perfect next to. You make me feel flawless just as myself."

Maybe I had been an asshole to Chad. From the first moment I'd seen him, I'd deemed him a fuck boy, and his own snide remarks hadn't helped, either. "If you were standing here talking shit about Asiah, I wouldn't like it. I guess I can see where you're coming from."

Nandy nodded. "I just want the best for the both of them, and for us."

"Asiah has that with Read."

"Yeah? Do you think he's safe?"

"Not everyone's doomed to die there."

"I'm glad she has someone. She seems like a very thoughtful girl."

"And Chad's a nice guy?"

Nandy narrowed her eyes. "You just can't say anything nice, can you?" She shook her head. "I hope he finds someone better for him than me, someone who can be herself around him and his parents, and who makes him happy."

"You being yourself would've made him happy."

"How can you be so sure?"

"You make me happy."

Nandy's lips turned up. "Really?"

I wrapped my arms around her. "When you're being petty or bratty, I kinda just wanna laugh and kiss you. I mean, when I first got here, you really thought a box of cornflakes was going to shield you from me?"

Nandy laughed. "Leave me alone."

"Nah, that was straight childish."

Nandy stood on her toes and kissed me. "I like that you're tall."

She was probably five foot nine or ten, not too far down from me, which I liked as well. Asiah was much shorter than Nandy.

"I don't know what I'm doing, or what you want from me," I admitted.

Nandy ran her hands up my chest. "I just want *you*. It's okay to be yourself and not this tough guy from Lindenwood. I've seen you act so genuine and kind with Travis, Kyle, and Shayne—be that way with everyone. Or at least try."

I still didn't care for Chad, but out of respect for Nandy, I would stop talking shit about the guy. In a way, Nandy was right. I had the girl, my own friends, and I was making my way. Our paths wouldn't have to cross, and that was more than fine by me.

At Cross High I sat before Lydia, marking down my courses for the upcoming school year while she sat behind her desk reading my composition. Every once in a while, she would emit a response, an "oh," a laugh, or a sigh. I tried not to let her reactions distract me as I picked out each class I wanted to take. Cross High seemed like one of those schools where you had to excel in something and do more than just attend class. Smart or not, I just wanted to graduate. Extracurriculars did not interest me.

"All finished?" Lydia asked as she peeked up from my book.

I handed her the course catalog and my selections and sat back as she read them over. I knew by the way she looked at me upon finishing reading that she had something to say.

First, she held up my composition book. "I love this."

"Thanks." I'd felt weird about her reading it, but then, I figured, why not.

"I love how you've written it as a story and not a journal." Lydia leaned over and winked at me. "Bonus points for writing in first person. I hate the feeling of a third-person narrator when I'm reading a book." She flipped through the pages of my notebook, having so much left to read from her place toward the beginning. There were plenty of nights where I'd stayed up writing, and I had nearly filled up the entire book. "I just love how you paint the world that Tyrin lives in and his family and friends." Lydia looked up at me. "Can I ask who Queen's character represents in real life? I admire how you describe her."

Despite my best effort, I couldn't fight the small smile that managed to escape my stoic expression. "She's just a brat."

For the first time in my life, I found myself leaning on someone to guide me, because with Nandy I was completely vulnerable, trusting her with my thoughts, fears, and anxieties. With Asiah, I'd been closed off, and I'd come to realize that I hadn't a clue how relationships were supposed to work. With

Nandy, I still wasn't sure, but it was a relief to have someone to confide in, to be there and listen, and to comfort me.

Beyond writing the story, having Nandy had kept me sane after Lindenwood and my final goodbye.

Lydia made a face. "You describe her as always getting what she wants when she and Tyrin are seven. Now that time has passed, I wonder if there's a possibility that they'll be more. Her character really brings out the boy in him." Lydia fingered a page of my book. "It feels like Tyrin was forced to grow up too fast and has emotional issues, yet with Queen he's finally able to be a kid and be happy. I wonder what lies ahead for when he's seventeen."

I was just writing my world as a story; I hadn't seen it like Lydia described. I couldn't help but be curious about what lay ahead of me as well.

"Who knows," I said.

"Nandy's a nice girl, Trice. She does a ton of after-school work for this school and I'm sure she'll be the one who shows you around more once school starts." She flipped a page of my book and began reading aloud from one passage. "'My childhood was full of history lessons and self-awareness. At one point we started in Africa. We were kings and queens, as Mom said. She told me that, one day, I'd meet my very own queen, and I would be her king, and we would reign together. Staring at Queen for the first time in ten years, being around her, felt more than just familiar, it felt like kingdom come. I'd always remember Queen. She was home.' That's probably my favorite line so far. Not only is this a coming-of-age novel, it's a love story you can't help but root for."

The smile she gave me made me feel embarrassed for the way I'd had Tyrin's character describe Queen's. The way he looked at her, the way he listened to her, the way he felt about her, the way he did whatever she wanted—it was all written out, as if the pages were linked to my veins and thoughts, bleeding out what I wouldn't say.

Beneath Tyrin's coldness, after the haze that had been his childhood, his emotions were coming to life. He felt angry, passionate, crazy—he *felt*, despite believing that his heart had shut down the moment he lost his mother. With Queen, whether she was driving him crazy or making him smile, he felt alive, with every pitter-patter of his heart beating deep within his chest.

It was autobiographical, and Lydia could see it, clearly.

"You have a way with words, Trice." She handed me my book and held up my course selections. "You need at least one or two more electives for your senior year. Might I suggest either literature—there you will read and discuss classic novels—or creative writing, where you can explore an emphasis on fiction writing. Or both."

I didn't want to add another class, especially one that wasn't essential, but I had a feeling there was no fighting Lydia.

With a scowl, I grabbed the course catalog, flipped through the pages and pointed to Creative Writing. "This one."

Lydia smiled. "Nice choice."

She typed on her laptop for a while before turning back to me. "Well, you've completed your semester of summer school and aced your exams, and that makes you an official Cross High Knight. I look forward to seeing you during the school year, Trice. And I especially hope you continue with your writing. I like the story—let's see if Tyrin gets that happy ending."

I was due to hang with the guys after my meeting with Lydia, and a quick text confirmed they were at Matt's.

The Smiths' location was very convenient. Everyone lived so close together—Travis and Warhol were next door, Kyle across the street, and Matt right around the corner along with Ashley. It made driving redundant, and the walk was quick enough that I didn't mind.

The only thing, though, was that not only did Matt and Ashley live around the corner, Chad did as well—right next door to Matt.

Chad was in his driveway washing his car when I walked by. He noticed me, and I noticed him.

Nandy wanted me to try, and for her sake, I offered him a nod.

Chad kept staring, squinting at me into the sun. He shook his head and went back to washing his car.

"For what it's worth, I'm sorry," I told him.

Chad shrugged. "Don't say sorry. Just enjoy the ride, man."

"It's not like that."

"Yeah? I doubt that."

"I get that it was hard for you to break up with her, so I'm sorry about that."

"Or maybe I just beat Nandy to the punch. The way I see it, we broke up, but whose shoulder is she crying on, Shayne's, Erica's, or yours? Sometimes there's no getting around the inevitable."

"You should've fought for her," I came out and said. The thing about Asiah, I knew she loved me, and it was harsh, but I knew I didn't love her, at least not in the same way she loved me. Or I would've fought for her.

If Chad really cared about Nandy, he would've fought for her, or at least broken up with her less dramatically. Instead, he'd chosen to be petty. Hurt or not, he'd acted childishly.

Chad's eyes blazed as he glared at me. "It's pretty fuckin' hard to fight for someone who's eyeing another team."

"Again, I'm sorry about that. And about the way I've treated you since I got here. We don't have to be friends, but it doesn't have to be an issue, either."

Chad's angst dissolved just a little and he went back to his car, saying nothing.

I took that as my cue to move on toward Matt's house.

"I'm sorry, too. See you around school," Chad said from behind me.

I turned back and lifted my chin at him in acknowledgment. We wouldn't be friends, but for Nandy's sake, I didn't want to hate the guy or keep on with the bullshit.

Matt's mother answered the door and let me in, telling me the boys were up in Matt's room.

Matt was at his desk, Skyping Ben. Travis was lounging in a chair watching videos on the flat-screen.

I waved to Ben and greeted Matt and Travis before taking a seat on Matt's bed.

"Chad still out there?" Travis asked as he tossed a foam football in the air and caught it. "He was getting ready to wash his car when I came over."

I nodded. "Yeah, we had a few words."

Travis frowned. "Prick."

"Be nice," Ben said from Matt's laptop. "The guy just lost his girl. He's going through a lot. No offense, Trice."

I shrugged. "None taken."

Travis rolled his eyes. His hatred for Chad ran deep, just like Chad's for him. "Ask me if I care. The guy acts like he owns this place and I'm supposed to bow down to him."

Travis was wearing a tank top, accentuating his arm muscles

and ability to protect himself. The way he and Chad often bickered, I was surprised they hadn't brawled.

Ben sighed. "Chad's made it clear he doesn't want to be friends—"

"Then fuck it."

"Yeah, but you could still be nice," Ben insisted.

Travis smirked and gestured toward Ben. "Ben's a pansy."

On-screen Ben flipped him off. "Blow me, Trav."

Travis scrunched up his nose. "I would, but then what would Matt say?"

That was one of the first things I'd learned about Travis. You couldn't outtalk him. You couldn't win in an argument no matter how hard you tried, because nobody talked shit like Travis did.

Travis stood from the chair and threw the football at Matt's back. "Come on, Trice, let's get out of here. I can tell Ben's anxious to whip it out, so let's give them some space."

Ben was somewhere out of reach, so because I liked him and Matt, I shoved Travis for his bluntness as we exited the room.

"I'm starving. Wanna hit the Shack?" Travis asked as we headed to his car.

"Definitely."

He let the top down so we could bask in the hot July summer sun. Travis sat back and relaxed as he drove with one hand while Kendrick Lamar killed his "Control" verse through Travis's speakers.

Travis bobbed his head, looking my way. "This shit right here, this is real music." He shook his head. "I don't get to listen to this at home without headphones. My mom straight trips when she hears swearing, or any type of hip-hop beat. I guess it helps to like a lot of alternative stuff too, and some

R & B. But when I'm in my ride, I make sure to blast this shit as loud as I can."

Another song came on, and he immediately turned up the volume. I recognized "Switch Up" instantly and admired Travis's taste in music. I could only imagine his mother clutching her pearls at the likes of Big Sean's raps or even Kendrick's.

Travis knew all the words and rapped a few lines as he continued to cruise through the streets of Pacific Hills' quiet community, blasting music that had those on the sidewalks staring at us with wide eyes.

I admired Travis's fearlessness. He wasn't afraid to be himself and didn't put on an act for anyone, even if he garnered disapproval. With no ties left to Lindenwood, I liked having someone genuine in the Hills.

It took a lot out of me not to laugh when he pulled into the Shack's parking lot and an elderly couple looked ready to die of a heart attack at the sound of Travis's music. The husband held his wife's waist as she held her hand to her chest, mouth open as she stared at Travis. To make it funnier, he shut off the car, and instead of opening his door, he simply leaned up and jumped over the side.

The elderly couple were quick to hurry to their car as we walked by them to the front door.

Travis was oblivious.

"I gotta stay out of the house for a while. My mom's interviewing potential babysitters," he told me after we put in our orders.

"Landon and London ran another one off?" His twin brothers were a terrible duo; it would take a lot of cash to keep a babysitter for longer than a month.

"Landon's not bad until London coerces him into some shit. They're just kids, though. It can't be *that* hard to find a sitter."

"That Catalano blood ain't a joke."

Travis smirked. "What's up with you? Summer school done?"

I nodded. "I'm officially a Knight."

"Bet the Smiths are happy that shit's done and out of the way."

"I'm sure that's the least of their worries," I said.

Our food came and we grabbed a booth and sat on opposite sides.

"What's going on?" Travis asked.

"Parker caught Nandy and me kissing, and he doesn't approve. Max isn't so against it, but she's siding with Parker. They want us to be a family, but I don't see Nandy that way. There's always been something there."

Travis bobbed his head, taking in my words and thinking to himself. "Okay, before you screw up a good situation, ask yourself, do you just want to smash Nandy, or jump into something serious with her? If this is all just for a taste, well, you may wanna back off. If it's for something real, why not? Parker's a chill guy. He may eventually change his mind, as long as it's real." He shrugged. "If you want my opinion, go for it. Mancini's a nice girl, but you turned her down for more than just Kyle. You're curious about Nandy, so why not?"

It was honest and genuine. I could only respect all of Travis's words. I held out my hand. "Thanks for the support."

He grinned as he slapped his palm against mine. "Always. You ride for me and I'm ridin' for you."

Loyalty. I could rock with that.

I spotted Shayne sitting at a table by herself, reading a book.

"Be right back," I said as I stood and went to Shayne. Just

like Nandy, Shayne had taken out her extensions and was back to her usual self, only she seemed down. Perhaps partly from her father, and partly from me.

She looked up and barely offered a smile as she noticed me. "Hey."

I sat across from her, noting she was reading what looked like a love story. "Hey. I finished summer school. I'm officially one of you." At least on the outside.

Shayne nodded. "It's going to be an interesting school year, I can already tell."

"Oh yeah, think of all the fun we're going to have." I tried to sound cheery, but it didn't catch on with her.

I stared at her as she stared at me, the impact of my rejection etched across her face. From the second I'd met her, she was always smiling, flirty and happy. Now, not so much.

Shayne chewed on her cheek as she bookmarked her page. "A-are you happy, Ty?"

"I guess I am."

"Then that's all that matters." Shayne got this sad smile. "Scarlett O'Hara Trice was just a fantasy anyway."

"Nah, I'm sure there's some guy out there who can give you a true Scarlett you won't have to adopt. She can still be all those things you imagined."

I could see the doubt in Shayne's eyes. In her mind, I saw her differently than other guys, so the idea of meeting someone else who could see the true Shayne felt flawed. But I knew it wasn't.

"I'm thinking about asking Max if I can stay with you guys for a while. Maybe just a week, though," Shayne said.

"Why?"

"I'm still mad at Daddy. Between him being gone all

day and my stepmonster's antics, I'd just rather be with the Smiths." Shayne shrugged. "It's not like I have anyone else."

She had her friends, and me—if she'd let me—but I wished she had someone else. It was becoming clear to me how a relationship worked, because when you needed affection and love, a significant other could be just as important as family and friends.

The type of bond that love brought could heal tension and pain. I could tell by looking at Shayne that she felt alone, and I wished more than anything that she could open her eyes and see—

Speak of the devil. Kyle sat down beside me. He nodded at me before focusing on Shayne. "Hey."

She smiled politely. "Froggie."

It was like she was blind. Kyle's mother could be in the room, and Kyle would still greet Shayne first.

Kyle flicked his hair out of his eyes. "I, uh, got some shots from cotillion if you want to see. I know you missed it, but I figured you'd want a look."

He held up his phone, and Shayne's gaze fell upon it and lingered.

Her own phone let out a chime, and she read its screen before shaking her head. "Sorry, I have to go." She waved her phone. "SOS from Erica. I'm sure your pictures came out nice, though. I bet they're going to look real good in the school newspaper."

"Yearbook," Kyle corrected.

Shayne smiled, and Kyle's eyes lit up at the sight of it. "Yeah, that." She faced me and waved. "'Bye."

Kyle was on cloud nine as he followed me back to Travis. You would have thought Shayne had agreed to go out with him or something.

"Things still awkward?" Travis asked.

"A little," I confessed.

Travis shook his head and peered at Kyle. "Dude, you gotta put your foot down and make Mancini yours."

Kyle blinked. "I—I mean… You know… She's like…complex. You don't just walk up to Shayne Mancini and ask her out, you have to have flair."

"I was once like you—skinny, terrible taste in clothes—and then I got laid," Travis said.

I rolled my eyes. "Trav."

He cracked a smile. "Actually, I'm kidding. I was never like you, but that's a good thing. Guys like you, you notice stuff. People like when you notice the small things. You should talk to her one day and casually bring up books or something."

Kyle toyed with his phone. "Maybe."

I reached out and patted Kyle's back, feeling hopeful. Going forward, nothing was certain, but I was beginning to realize that there was beauty in uncertainty. Maybe Nandy and I would make it and be strong, and maybe Shayne would see Kyle and realize he was perfect for her. It was the third week of July, and we still had all of August. There was a lot of summer left—who knew what could happen.

30 | *Nandy*

I'd been in the middle of lying out by our pool when Erica sent me an SOS text, leaving me to drop everything and race to her.

After stopping by the store to grab two quarts of Moose Tracks and some of Erica's favorite soda, I went straight to her house, where her mother let me in.

I grabbed some spoons from the kitchen before making my way up to Erica's room. She was sitting on her bed with music playing in the background.

"What's up?" I asked, taking in the scene before me. Erica was surrounded by the girls: Shayne, Edi, and Xiu. And on the surface, I couldn't tell something was wrong.

But then they all looked at me and I realized what was up.

Edi patted the space left for me on Erica's queen-size bed. "Come on, Nan, we gotta talk."

I brought over the ice cream and soda and set it in the middle of us before sitting cross-legged between Edi and Shayne. "So..." I stretched out the word. "What's up?"

All at once my friends mirrored the same look of annoyance.

"Really?" Edi asked.

"What?" I asked innocently.

"Don't 'what' me. You weren't at cotillion, and then you were off-the-grid, not returning texts or phone calls. What's the tea, sis?" Edi demanded to know. "And for the record, I always told you Captain Ginger was no good."

All eyes were on me, and I wasn't sure how to explain the end of Chad and me, and the possible beginning of Tyson and me.

"Chad and I are done," I announced with finality. "I realized that I was more into the idea of him than actually being with him. I mean, his parents are so overbearing and overwhelming, and Chad's worst wasn't something I wanted to be around. Tyson's been shot, and Chad mocked it?"

None of the girls disagreed with my decision, but none of them had ever liked Chad to begin with.

Xiu reached out to offer support. "It's okay, you just needed time away. This was a big moment for you."

It was more than that.

"I sorta have this thing...with Tyson," I confessed.

Edi and Erica both looked shocked as Shayne picked at her nails.

"That's foul, girly," Edi spoke first. She patted Shayne's back as she shook her head at me.

"I know," I agreed. "My parents don't even approve."

Shayne frowned. "No judgment, okay? This isn't about Nandy and Ty, they're happy, let them be." To prove her support, Shayne scooted next to me.

"At least you're big enough to admit your faults, and the two of you aren't fighting," Xiu reasoned.

"See, no," Erica stated, holding up an acrylic fingernail, "we don't fight over boys. All it does is tear us apart and make them look like kings."

"Got that right," Edi chimed in. "We do queen tingz over here."

Together my friends and I laughed, all reaching out to high-five one another. Nothing, especially not a boy, could come between us.

"Ashley's hosting this Throwback Thursday event this week. Why don't we all be each other's dates? Screw the boys for one day," Erica suggested.

I was in, and so were the others.

Shayne sat up, appearing extra perky. "Okay, we need a candle."

"For…?" Erica prompted.

"To symbolize us burning away all the bad energy and bullshit, and moving forward with positivity and fun," Shayne explained as she stood from Erica's bed. She grabbed the black candle from Erica's dresser and crossed back over to us before lighting it. "Let's all burn a strand of hair and say what we're burning, and what we're moving forward with."

It was kinda of strange, and also kind of neat.

I reached into my hair and pulled out a strand as my friends did the same.

Erica went first. "I'm burning away any doubt that I've ever had in myself with this DJ thing." She placed the strand of hair in the jar and sat back. "And I'm moving forward with the four best friends a girl could ever have."

It was cheesy, but the feeling was beyond mutual.

Edi went next. "I'm burning the drunken mistake of sending Travis that nude."

"Edi!" We all yelled in shock.

Edi shrugged. "Do not drunk text, ever." She placed her hair into the jar. "And I'm moving forward by steering clear of guys with freaky colored eyes."

Xiu went next. "I'm burning my fear, and this year I'm going to move forward and do something that's been scaring me for a while."

Erica eyed her cousin as if waiting for her to continue. Xiu blushed but remained silent.

Shayne cradled the candle in her hand and carried on. "I'm burning away all guys who disappointed me. And I'm moving forward by being happy for me and embracing my singleness."

I was last, and I had so much to burn.

I placed my strand of hair into the jar and sat back, thinking over what I wanted to say. "I'm burning my image. I'm not going to be who anyone wants me to be. I'm just going to be Nandy. And I'm moving forward by taking risks and learning from them."

Done with the ceremony, Shayne blew out the candle and waved it around like sage. "This is the good energy and vibe we have placed into the universe. We will not think of the bad and what we burned. We are moving forward together, and we will enjoy the rest of this summer."

It was like a toast, so I reached up and touched the candle. "Hear, hear."

Soon, Edi, Erica, and Xiu followed suit. "Hear, hear."

We were all different with different hopes and dreams, but

at the end of the day, we had each others' backs and tried to relate and understand each other.

Nothing beat friendships like this.

31 | TRICE

Travis led the way to his car. The elderly couple was long gone, leaving no one to gasp as Travis jumped into his ride without opening the door like a civilized person.

Before I could get in, a patrol car pulled up alongside Travis. A tall guy dressed in a black uniform got out and approached him, staring at him as he gripped the front of his utility belt.

Travis didn't look fazed one bit. He merely nodded casually at the officer. "What up, Wendell?"

Wendell grimaced, breathing in through his nose and letting it out. "Easy, Trav. You staying out of trouble?"

"Always, sir," Travis replied. "I'm all about being a law-abiding citizen."

And then, because Travis was completely reckless and ignorant, he set his key into his ignition and brought the car to life. Once more, sounds of hip-hop loudly emitted from his speakers as some old 50 Cent tune filled the area.

I could see the annoyance on Wendell's face as Travis flashed him a shit-eating grin.

Travis straight didn't give a fuck. That was often humorous, but not with five-o.

I got into the car and turned down the music. Anything to avoid getting in trouble.

Travis groaned. "Aw, man, he was just getting to my favorite part."

He set the car in Reverse and backed out of the space while managing to wave to Wendell before pulling away.

"Some of us don't want to get arrested," I said.

Travis smirked. "Wendell's just a rent-a-cop."

From what I knew, he was local security for our development. Wendell guarded the gate that kept our little community exclusive. Sometimes he would patrol the neighborhood, flashing his light to see if anything shady was going on. I knew this from my many restless nights.

"Any cop is bad news," I said.

Travis shrugged. "He gets off on harassing me, so sometimes I enjoy feeding into it. Don't worry about it—you just focus on Nandy."

"It's going to be interesting," I confessed. "Dating's never been my strong suit."

"Nah?" Travis pulled into his driveway and sat back, looking my way.

"When you love someone and they die, sometimes you close yourself off. You don't wanna love anyone after that, because the pain of losing them hurts too much. I didn't

want to feel after my mom died. I didn't want to love anyone, not even Pops. It's like a piece of you goes when they
do. Love makes you vulnerable, and vulnerability is not for
me. I had one girlfriend, and I wasn't good to her, because I
could never let her in."

Travis stared at his house, thinking over my words. "I
don't like being controlled." He faced me. "My parents, the
teachers, Wendell, the man, they're all on my back, telling
me what to do. The last thing I want is some girl doing that
shit, because that's just another person to answer to.

"Nandy's a core for a lot of people around here. In school,
she sticks to her circle, but this summer she's been down with
everyone. I think if you allow yourself, you could open up to
her. She runs a lot of stuff for school. She's the nicest person
when it comes to the new kids, she makes these little welcome packages complete with a little personalized teddy bear.
Hell, she's the first to step up and help anyone around here.
She's Miss Social, but I don't think she'd try to control you."

To that I had to snort. The girl was always telling me what
to do, ever since we were five. I'd never let Asiah run me,
never let anyone tell me what to do except for my mother,
but with Nandy, it was always just her. She was different from
the girls in my neighborhood, and hella bossy, but so cute
that I never really cared.

I guess, deep down, I knew. From the moment I'd laid
eyes on her again, I was carrying a ten-year torch for Nandy
Smith. I liked her for her, and because she made me happy
when all I'd felt when I was younger was anguish.

"Nandy knows when to take charge and when to fall back.
Maybe she's good for me."

"Just don't turn into J. Crew on me, a'ight?" Travis teased.
"You can like this town, but don't let it take you."

"Warhol said the same thing. It's different here, phony at times, but it has character."

Travis examined our street and the neighboring houses. "We'll see once school starts."

The front door to the Catalano house opened and his mother stepped outside. Her hands instantly glued to her hips as she eyed her oldest son with annoyance. "Travis, did you teach London to throw up gang signs?"

Travis clicked his tongue as he snatched his keys from the ignition. "I'm a white boy from the suburbs, what gangs do I know?"

His mother narrowed her eyes, not buying it. "Get in here this instant."

Travis rolled his eyes and jumped out of the car. "Duty calls, Trice. Catch ya later."

I got out of the car and went home to the Smiths' house. Inside, Nandy was just making her way to the staircase, her earphones in her ears and her hair swept up in a loose bun. She looked adorable in her tee and shorts.

Upon seeing me, she removed her earphones and greeted me with a smile. "Hey."

I'd missed her, the realization causing me to smile, too. "Hey."

She came over to me and stood in front of me. "Have fun?"

"Mostly." I held up my bag from the Crab Shack. "I grabbed you a lemon chicken almond salad sandwich."

Nandy eyed the bag with glee. "On a croissant?"

"The only way to eat one."

She greedily snatched the bag and peered back at me appreciatively. "Thank you."

"How was your day?"

She held up her phone. "Erica and I—"

The front door burst open, immediately causing us to jump apart. Jordy entered the house. His hair was a mess, his shirt torn, and he was breathing hard as his eyes glistened with unshed tears.

Shit.

"Jordy!" Nandy rushed for her brother, too quick for me to seize her.

This only upset Jordy more. "Leave me alone!" He went past us, storming up the staircase and wiping at his eyes.

Nandy wasn't hearing it.

I caught her before she could go after Jordy. "Stop."

"He's my brother!" she said, gesturing toward the staircase.

Jordy was embarrassed, and the last thing he would want was Nandy babying him. At eleven years old, he was still a kid, but at the age where he didn't want to be *deemed* a kid or treated like one.

"I'll go," I told her. "Just wait here."

She frowned, a fight in her eyes, but surprisingly she conceded.

I went to Jordy's room. When I knocked, he allowed me to enter.

He was sitting on his bed, head down, shoulders shaking.

I sat next to him, knowing better than to reach out and touch him. "Wanna tell me what happened?"

He didn't speak, his gaze glued to the floor.

"It's okay if you don't," I went on. "We can just sit here."

We sat silently for a while before he got the courage to open up to me.

"I—I was at the skate park," he began. His voice was heavy, as if he wanted to cry, but he pushed it down and covered it up, because that's what boys do. "I was talking to Mani and

Hector, and this kid from my class, Louis, he was trying to impress Mani and so was I."

"You got in a fight?" I asked.

Jordy nodded. "I did this trick on my skateboard and Mani liked it, and Louis couldn't do it. He started making fun of me. He called me an adopted freak." Jordy peered up at me. "He told me my real parents didn't want a freak baby, and soon my mom and dad wouldn't want me, either. I tried to hit him, but he's bigger than me."

"And Mani saw?"

Once more Jordy nodded, his true hurt out on display. It had to be rough to be bullied in front of a crush.

The thing that bothered me most about Jordy's story was how he was telling it, how he was holding back his emotions.

"You wanna cry, don't you?"

He shook his head, though his voice gave him away. "No!"

I hung my head, shaking it. "It's okay to cry, Jordy. He hurt your feelings. Hit you in a weak spot. It's okay to let it out."

"I'm not a baby!"

To the Smiths, and even to Jordy, he wasn't adopted—he was their son, as natural as Nandy was. To the outside world, at first glance, the Asian boy with the black family would seem strange, but anyone who saw their family interact would understand that it wasn't strange at all.

I reached out and touched Jordy's shoulder. "Can I tell you a secret?"

"Yeah."

"I never got to cry over losing my mom. She's been gone for almost a year, and I never cried over it. As bad as it hurt, I never allowed myself to sink to my knees and cry. Where I'm from, you gotta be hard, tough, a man. Crying's for the weak. But between you and me, I bet it feels good to let it out. I wish I could, you know? It hurts every day, but I'm so cold I can't even shed a single tear.

"Crying doesn't make you weak. People rant all day about equality, but we allow women to cry and be emotional, yet we paint this picture of men being strong and that tears are not acceptable. I'm not saying you should cry over everything, but if something pierces your soul, it's okay to let it out. You're human, you feel pain, so go ahead and cry. You love your parents, and that kid hit below the belt. It's okay to cry, Jordy."

Still, he peered up at me, tears in his eyes, but not falling. "You never cried once after losing her?"

I shook my head. "I allowed my hardness to take over, and emotions aren't my strong suit. I miss her every day, but I don't cry. Sometimes I feel guilty, because it's like I didn't love her if I don't shed a tear. I don't want that for you. Being tough isn't about not showing emotion, not crying. It's really all intellect, and clearly you're smarter than Louis if you know better than to pick a fight over a girl."

Jordy looked away. "I really like Mani, and I didn't want her to see."

The thought of crying in front of Nandy made me wince. The image even made me feel weak and pathetic. I didn't want that for Jordy. I didn't want him to shut down like that. "I'm willing to bet she likes you more than Louis. Only stupid girls like bullies, J."

A single tear rolled down Jordy's cheek, and he was quick to wipe it away. He sniffled and offered up a half smile as he glanced my way. "I know what all you said, but can you please not tell Nandy, or my mom? I promise I'll cry later, just don't tell, okay?"

I cracked a smile as I reached out and tousled his hair. "It's just between you and me. You can come to me for whatever, you know that, right?"

He bobbed his head. "Yeah, I know. I always wanted a brother, and now I have you."

My smile broadened with warmth. It was nice to feel this close to Jordy. "I have an idea on how you can get Mani's attention."

"Yeah?"

"Definitely. You like Mani, and I'm going to help you make a move."

Jordy appeared thoughtful. "And maybe you can get Nandy's attention?"

I chuckled. "I sorta got that on lock already."

Jordy narrowed his eyes and nudged me. "Dude, that's my sister."

I stood from his bed. "Noted. Tonight I'll drive you and Mani to the movies. You gotta get one popcorn and two drinks, though. Plus, you gotta see something scary—that way you can protect her during all the scary parts."

"All the scary movies are PG-13, though."

"I got you covered." Someone in town had to have a connection with the local movie theater.

Jordy seemed to like my idea regardless. "Okay. I'll text Mani." He gathered his phone and was quick to commence to texting. "Oh, and Trice, thank you. I'm really glad you're here."

Stopping in his doorway, I looked back at him and nodded. "Me, too."

Out in the hall, I found Nandy waiting against the wall, obviously having overheard our entire conversation.

I meant to say something, to explain, but she threw her arms around me.

"God, I love you," she said as she hugged me tight.

I froze, unable to process those three words.

There was a cracking inside of me. A layer of ice eroding deep inside my chest.

Somehow, those words chipped away at my hardness, and just as they did, a new layer of ice emerged, strong and sturdy, fully reinforced.

32 | *Nandy*

Shayne came over with a bag around five, right around the same time my mother got home from work. Tyson had been in his room ever since our hug in the hallway after his talk with Jordy. He had made some comment about having to write something down, and I hadn't seen him since.

Shayne lay on my bed reading some teen romance that featured a black couple kissing in the rain on its cover. She kept chewing on her thumb, worry etched on her face the more she read.

Looking at the cover, I questioned whether Tyson and I would ever have that.

Sighing, I told myself to calm down.

"What's wrong, Nandy?" Shayne set her book aside.

My door was shut and I knew we could talk. "Beyond the fact that it's 'forbidden,' I was just wondering if this thing with Tyson is worth it. If we'll ever be…" I gestured to the hardcover in her hands "…that."

Shayne glanced at her book and back to me. "You two fighting?"

I pulled my knees to my chest and hugged them close. "No, not really, at least not yet. From the moment he got here, we've been fighting one moment and fine the next. I just keep messing up with him. I make him crazy, and I don't want to. We definitely have more spark and flames than me and Chad, but I don't want it to fizzle out. I want more romance than bickering."

Shayne was my best friend, and I loved her for the fact that she would tell it to me straight no matter what. When I vented to her, I knew her commentary would be sincere.

She reached out and put her hand on my knee, and I briefly admired the color of her pink nails. "You want a storybook romance, Nan?"

"Basically. That's what we all want, right?"

"But Ty's not your average hero, he's been damaged and is trying to rebuild. That's the downfall of all fairy tales. They make it all about the princess, when sometimes it'd be nice to get to know the prince and his story and journey. I mean, *Aladdin* is like the best Disney movie ever for a reason."

Her comment made me laugh, though due to Tyson, I had to say I was obsessed with *Tarzan* due to all the times we'd watched it.

"Thanks, Shay. I guess I just don't want us to end up disappointing each other and wasting our time."

Shayne offered a sympathetic pat on the back. "I think you're overthinking it. You're caring too much about things being perfect. You just need to go with the flow and let it be. Just roll with the homies."

I frowned. "I love you, but never say that again."

She wrinkled her nose and waved her book around. "Sorry, this story is just really good. Can't help but pick up some of the lingo." She stared at the book in her lap and shrugged. "Before, you were a brat to Ty, Nandy. Now, you're both trying to work your shit out. You won't make him mad, because you have no reason to be fickle and pull away."

"True." With Chad out of the picture, nothing stood in the way of me getting what I wanted.

"When half these girls get back from vacation and school starts, you're going to have to worry about fighting them off, and because I'm your best friend, I gotta fight with you and resist at the same time."

"I hate you."

"You better." Shayne pulled me into a hug. "Just relax. Don't rush it. Stop and enjoy the ride."

"A lot happened in ten years. I feel like we need a day to just pick each other's brains."

"What was he like back then?" Shayne asked curiously.

A smile crossed my lips. "My slave. I used to decide everything we did, and he would let me. Sometimes he would demand we do things his way, but that was mostly when we were watching TV or a movie. I think, back then, I knew his home life had to be different than mine, because he had this dullness to his eyes, but when we were playing or hanging out, he'd be so happy. Now I don't think he's like that too much. I don't think he's going to let me always have my way, and it's fun to see him being more aggressive."

It was fun, and downright sexy. Before, it was innocent

between us, even if we'd kissed once or twice, but now, our friendship had every opportunity to blossom into more.

I decided that Shayne was right and I had to let it be, or else I would stress myself to death and ruin what I had with Tyson.

Shayne set her book on the nightstand and stood and stretched. "I'm starving. Let's go see what Max ordered."

"Probably Chinese," I said as I stood from my bed as well. "Did you tell your dad you were staying here?"

Shayne shook her head as we headed for my bedroom door. "Let's see how long it takes him to notice I'm gone before he starts calling me with the 'Bambi, please' routine."

"Shayne—"

"My stepmonster totally makes up for my absence. They're going away next week." Shayne stuck her finger down her throat and pretended to gag. In the hall, she reached out and knocked on Tyson's door. "Come on, Ty, Jordy, let's go eat!"

My best friend merrily turned and skipped down the staircase and I followed, wondering how long it would take for her father to realize she wasn't home.

My mother had gotten chicken from the Crab Shack, and together she and my father were in the dining room setting up the options from fried to baked as the sides of mashed potatoes, corn, and macaroni and cheese sat in the middle of the table.

"Hey," I greeted my parents.

Tyson and Jordy entered the room, and my father observed him and then me before speaking. "Hey, yourself. How was your day?"

Tyson sat next to Jordy on one side of the table, and I sat next to Shayne on the other. "Melodramatic."

"You know, the usual," Shayne added, causing my father to loosen up and smile.

The dinner conversation was light and humorous, and all the while I noticed Tyson didn't look at me or speak to me as the others carried on. I wasn't sure if that was for my parents' benefit, or if something was wrong.

Jordy was busy scarfing down his food, barely taking a moment to breathe.

"Done!" Jordy declared. He grabbed his glass of water and drank it in two gulps.

"What's the rush?" my father asked with a chuckle.

Jordy stood and grabbed his plate. "Trice's taking me to the movies." He faced Tyson and eyed him and his plate. "You done yet?"

Even though he wasn't finished, Tyson nodded and stood as well. "Yeah, we can go."

Underneath the table Shayne kicked my ankle, and one look at her found her making a face as she bobbed her head toward Tyson.

"Can I come, too?" I spoke up.

Tyson barely glanced at me. "Uh, sure."

"Is Shayne going with you?" My father spoke up, eyeing all three of us.

Tyson shook his head. "It's not a group activity. Jordy's taking Mani to see a movie, and I'm his ride. If Nandy wants to see a kiddie flick, I don't mind, but it's not anything inappropriate, Parker."

"Besides," Shayne cut in, "I'm going over to…Froggie's to see his pictures from cotillion since I missed out."

My parents were confused.

"Who?" my mother asked.

"Exactly," said Shayne.

I nudged my ignorant best friend.

"I mean, you know Froggie—tall, skinny, kind of a dweeb, awkward, trips over his own words a lot, sorta—"

"Kyle Frogge," I offered for Shayne's sake.

"Oh," said my father. I could tell he wanted to protest, but Shayne had been smart in bringing up how she'd missed cotillion, because my father's angst dispersed and he softened up. "Well, okay, but no funny business. I mean it."

Tyson appeared tired as he looked from me to my father. "Yes, sir."

"Are you ready now?" Jordy asked, sounding exasperated. He peered up at Tyson. "Come on, you can help me pick out what to wear."

My little brother took Tyson's hand and tugged him out of the room, leaving their dishes at the table.

My brother's anxiousness was amusing. I gathered my plate and theirs and brought them to the sink. It wasn't a surprise when my father joined me in the kitchen, no doubt to give me another warning about Tyson.

"Why don't you invite Chad over tomorrow? I'm sure there are things you two can talk about," my father said as he began filling the sink with soap and water.

"Chad and I are done, Dad," I said.

My father sighed. "I mean what I say about Trice, Nandy."

"If we do see each other, what are you going to do?"

"We'd have no choice but to put him out." He said it so coolly, as if it took no thought to go there.

I hadn't a reply, at least not one quick enough.

"Then you're not the father I know and admire." I wanted to leave, but he caught my arm.

I could understand how my parents felt about Tyson and I messing around under their roof, but for my father to threaten to exile Tyson was too far. My parents were who I looked up to; they were loving and giving. No matter what, they'd always opened our home to my friends, which was why it was no big deal that Shayne had come to stay with us, or Tyson. It was who they were, it was in their nature. For them to feel so negative about my feelings for Tyson and his for me painted them in a bad light. It disappointed me more than anything.

"You ready?" Tyson entered the room and I turned from my father, taking my arm back.

"Yes," I said.

"Nandy," my father called out from behind me. He came forth and handed over some money. "For Jordy. He's going to want to feed his date."

"They're eleven, it's not a date," Tyson spoke up playfully. "They're just 'hanging out.'"

My father smiled. "Uh-huh, sure."

He left us alone, and I went with Tyson to meet Jordy at the door. He was growing more impatient by the second.

"All right, let's go already," he said.

He had changed into a pair of khaki shorts and a navy blue polo top. It was simple and not too much.

"He had like five options," Tyson told me as we followed Jordy into the night.

My brother was adorable.

Together Tyson and I watched as he walked briskly over to the Gómezes' house. It was fascinating watching Jordy this way. He, Hector, and Mani hung out nearly every day, and now this was his first crush and his first almost-date. He would be starting middle school in the fall, and those years would fly by so fast that soon he'd be in high school. It was that pivotal time when he would discover himself as well as who and what he liked.

Studying Tyson as he peered at my brother, I knew deep down what *I* liked—what I'd always liked.

Jordy knocked on the Gómezes' door, and soon Warhol answered, followed by Mani.

She was wearing a pink tank top and a cute little layered purple skirt. Her hair was curled and held back by a headband with a flower on it. As cute as Mani looked, I just knew Edi had helped her get ready for her night out with Jordy, just as Tyson had helped him.

"Don't go running off too fast," Warhol said to his younger sister. He faced Jordy, sizing him up as if he were a threat. He gestured with his head as he said, "C'mere, Jordy."

Nervously, my brother approached Warhol, and then, in a lightning-like movement, Warhol had him up against his house. Jordy's hands were splayed against the house as he gazed back at Warhol in shock.

"Spread 'em," he said as he kicked Jordy's feet apart. Warhol began patting Jordy down as his sister complained behind him. "¡*Cállate*, Manuela! He's not getting out of here without a cavity search."

"They're eleven," Tyson spoke up beside me. "Trust me, J's clean."

Warhol pulled Jordy from the house. "You can never be too sure." He pulled out a flashlight and aimed it at Jordy. "State your full name for the record."

Jordy looked to Tyson and me for help. "Uh, Jordy Smith."

Warhol stepped closer, shining the light right in Jordy's eyes. "What are you, one of those freaks born without a middle name?"

"I–it's Martin," Jordy said.

"Uh–huh, likely story." Warhol whipped out his phone and snapped a photo of Jordy. "My dad's a cop, and he as well as every other officer on his force will be getting a copy of this." He pointed to Mani. "That's my little sister, so there are gonna be some ground rules for you taking her out. One, no R movies. No nudity, either."

"Again, they're like eleven," Tyson said.

Warhol flashed his light on Tyson next. "You trying to influence my sister to take her clothes off, Trice?"

"You're embarrassing me!" Mani cried out.

"So?" Warhol shrugged and went back to Jordy. He dug into his pocket and pulled out a funny-looking device. "First, breathe into this. I gotta make sure you're sober enough to take her out."

Tyson reached out and moved Warhol's arm away from Jordy. "Seriously? A breathalyzer? He's *eleven years old*, Warhol."

"Hey, my mom let me drink soda at eleven, I know all about the hard stuff." Warhol eyed Jordy with menace. "I got my eyes on you, kid."

Jordy backed away. "Dude, it's just a movie."

"It better be rated G." Once more Warhol dug into his jeans, this time pulling out a folded piece of paper. "Now, I drew up a seating chart for the film, in case you try to get cute. You do live next door to Travis Catalano."

The seating chart had Mani sitting on one end of a row of seats and Jordy far over on the other end.

Warhol was insane. He hadn't even gone this bizarre when Edi first went out on dates, although he did have the football team to back him via threats of bodily harm if Edi ever got her feelings hurt.

Tyson snatched the seating chart and shook his head. "We got it, can we go now?"

Warhol held up a finger. "Just one more thing." He leaned

over and whispered something in Jordy's ear, causing my little brother's eyes to bug out of his skull.

He appeared almost ashen as we finally headed for Tyson's truck.

"He's just being a brat," Mani insisted as she looped her arm through Jordy's and pulled him close to her.

As crazy as Warhol was, there was no telling what he'd said to my brother.

Tyson drove us all to the boardwalk where the local movie theater was located. The marquee over the theater listed what was screening and the ratings.

"Ooh, *Zombie Cadets III* is playing!" Jordy exclaimed as he saw the gruesome-looking poster on the side of the theater.

Mani stuck her head between the front seats and peered at the theater. "No way, I wanna see *Animals Loose*." She pointed at the poster with the animated group of animals, something definitely more suited for their age group.

The two began to bicker, and I undid my seat belt, preparing to get out of the car.

A hand came down on my thigh, stopping me.

It was Tyson. "We gotta have a conversation." He said no more before facing my brother and Mani. "Why don't you two play Rock, Paper, Scissors for it?"

The three of them got out of the car, and I watched as Tyson led them to the theater.

I sat back, then peered in the visor to check my appearance. In the back of my head I could hear Shayne telling me I was overthinking it as I frowned at the state of my bun and plain attire. I *was* stressing about things being perfect.

I decided to take a calming breath and let it be, just as Tyson came back to the car.

"What's up?" I asked as he closed his door.

Instead of talking, he leaned over and pressed his lips to mine, kissing me gently.

His lips brought me to life, and it didn't take much effort to lean over and meet him halfway, kissing him back.

Tyson pulled away far too fast as far as I was concerned. "Nothing, we got better things to do than watch *Animals Loose*."

"That's what they settled on?"

Tyson made a face. "You Pacific Hills girls always get your way."

"Don't front like we didn't grow up watching your movies," I shot back. "You had me watching the *Mighty Morphin Power Rangers* movie like every weekend, not to mention *3 Ninjas*."

Tyson chuckled as he started up his car. "And don't you front like you wasn't feelin' it, because you was always down for those movies."

"Well, the '90s did have some classics," I replied. "I'd rather watch that than some zombie flick. I don't think I'd survive the zombie apocalypse for all the wrong reasons."

"Why's that?"

"Because I wouldn't be able to straighten my hair, or bathe for that matter. Plus, don't get me wrong, but the main reason I wouldn't wanna die by a zombie is they're so damn dirty."

Tyson cracked up. It was such a pleasant sight, seeing him unwind like that.

He held up his phone. "I figured we can ride around listening to this instead."

"What?"

"A little of your music and a little of mine," he said. "I made a playlist of a lot of that Sara Cara girl you like so much, and some Florence and the Machine, as well as some of my favorite rappers. It's back-to-back—that way we can take turns listening to our favorite artists and explaining if one of us gets confused."

Sara Cara was like my favorite alternative artist. She was so mellow and intense. We needed more black girls like her in alternative music. It meant a lot to me that Tyson took the effort to try her out.

"You were putting that together the whole time you were in your room?" I couldn't help but smile at the gesture.

"Yeah, and I was writing."

"I thought something was wrong."

"Why?"

"I don't know, you seemed kinda distant until you kissed me."

Tyson faced me, appearing serious. "You said you loved me."

"Oh, well, I do. I always have, since I was younger. Don't you love me?"

He seemed wounded suddenly. "Like a friend?"

"Well, yeah."

Tyson shook his head. "I don't want you saying that again unless you really mean it, okay?"

I tried to understand what could've upset him, but I failed to grasp it. "I did mean it, Tyson."

"No, I mean, *really* mean it, Nandy."

I got it then. He didn't want me to tell him I loved him unless I meant I was *in* love with him. I didn't get what the big deal was, because I did love him as a person. The thing he'd done for Jordy was just another reason for that.

"The last person who said that to me was my mom," Tyson spoke up. "She's the only person who would say it. Asiah tried, but she knew it made me feel weird. As fucked up as it may sound, I gave it an honest effort, but couldn't fully go there with her. The only woman I've ever felt that strongly about is my mother, and if I'm going to say those three words, I want it to mean more than just 'friends.' I don't play games, I want it for real. Friends doesn't do it for me, okay?"

I bit hard into my lip, trying to contain all that I was feeling. He wanted to love me, like, *really* love me. Full-blown love, deep love, more than friends love, romantic love. Me.

I made a mental note to have a little freak-out in my room later, when no one was around. For now I kept calm and played it cool. "Okay."

He set up his Bluetooth, and I was rewarded by the sweet sound of Sara Cara.

"The title of this song reminded me of you," Tyson explained, as Sara described a poor little rich girl.

I tried to roll my eyes but ended up smiling. I was a tiny bit difficult, so what.

Tyson didn't frown or show any distaste for Sara Cara, and I happily sat listening as it appeared we had a winner for our first song.

Soon the song was over and a rap song came on, or hip-hop, as Tyson was quick to point out that it was by Nas.

Nas was rapping and inciting a message. There was one line telling girls that, whether they wanted an athlete or a rapper, whoever they chose, it was essential to make sure he was a thug and intelligent, too. Tyson wasn't a thug, but he was tough and smart.

As Tyson continued to drive around, we listened to each other's taste in music, both soaking in the vast differences. Tyson admitted he admired Sara Cara's sound and even a little Florence, while I couldn't help but vibe his favorite rappers, from Nas to J. Cole, and soon Kendrick Lamar. I liked it all. They weren't like those rappers who talked dirty, reckless and illegal; they were smart, more than just brolic—funny, and deep.

There was even one song disclaiming Christopher Columbus and his discovery of America.

"Dude was the first terrorist, he and them pilgrims," Tyson spoke up. "Yet he gets a day for discovering shit that wasn't new. Ain't that America?"

I could never get bored or tired of hearing him explain his viewpoint.

I reached out and held Tyson's free hand as he drove with the other.

"This is everything," I told him.

He looked down at our hands and squeezed gently, smiling over to me. "More."

We reached a red light, and soon he was leaning over to kiss me again. We weren't supposed to see each other, but there was no stopping us. We were inevitable.

Tyson reeled back and gazed into my eyes. "I think this is going to be my favorite summer yet."

33 | *TRICE*

On the patio Wednesday afternoon, Shayne sat across from me reading some book. I was reading over my composition book, peering down at it in frustration. I'd filled it to the last page and was debating whether the story was over or not.

I flipped through the ink-littered pages and wondered how thick it would be if it were a published book.

Nandy walked out and pushed my book away as she leaned over and kissed my cheek. "Enough already, I'm kidnapping you."

"Word?"

"Uh-huh. No more writing, you're coming with me."

"Where?"

"Not telling. Just be happy I'm not blindfolding you."

"Kinky much?" Shayne teased as she peeked up from her reading.

Nandy wiggled her eyebrows. She reached out and caressed my chin. "Oh yeah, couldn't you imagine how cute Tyson would look all tied up?"

Shayne blushed and laughed with Nandy at the idea of it.

Even if she was laughing at my expense, I enjoyed the sight of Nandy. After ten years, she had grown and blossomed. From her smile and her figure to her manner, even to her pushy and nurturing side, everything was on point. She was just too damn distracting to be platonic with.

Writing Tyrin's story, expressing his feelings and past with Queen, I realized one truth about my connection with Nandy after all these years. It was psychological. I'd always liked her, because I knew that she was the type of girl my mother would've liked, had she ever come with Pops and me to Pacific Hills.

Ten years later, I liked Nandy for more. When I'd gotten pissed and angry in Lindenwood, she hadn't backed down. She was stubborn, and she'd gotten through. I needed that, someone who wouldn't enable the hardness, but call me on it.

This was more than hormones; it was everything.

Nandy was still giggling with Shayne. "Look, Shay, he's considering it."

I might have liked her, but there was no way in hell I would ever let Nandy tie me up or down.

I tried to swat her as she headed back into the house to go get ready.

"So, how was last night with Kyle?" I asked as I turned to Shayne.

Her forehead adopted a crease. "Who?"

I rolled my eyes. "Kyle Frogge."

Shayne shrugged. "Oh, I went to Edi's last night. I only brought up Froggie and his pictures because I knew Parker would feel sorry for me and let you two go out alone. I can wait until the school newspaper comes out before seeing those pictures and remembering how I was supposed to be in them."

"Yearbook."

"Same thing." Shayne sighed. "Besides, last night was a total bust. Warhol wasn't even up for flirting with me—he kept going on and on about tracking Mani's GPS on her phone."

I frowned. "Why are we friends with him?"

Shayne chuckled. "Because he's Warhol and we love him." Her dark eyes soon fell upon my composition book. "So, how's *that* going?"

Again I frowned. "I think I'm finished."

"Can I read it?"

I shook my head, and she stuck out her lip in a pout. "Is that supposed to work?"

"Well, yeah. I'm me."

"Not going to happen." I flipped through the pages of my book, unsure if it was really done or not. "It's more of a story, about me, and Nandy."

"Come on, you can trust me. I'm a hopeless romantic, and I love a good love story." Shayne got out of her seat and pretended to massage my shoulders, for all of a second before going and snatching my notebook. "Besides, you've been agonizing over these pages for hours. It's time to get out of here and live a little. Let me see if sucks or not, okay?"

"Really?"

"Yes, really."

"I'd value your opinion. You do read a lot."

"Duh, I'm an expert on these things. You're in good hands.

Now you are going to hit the town with your smoking-hot girlfriend, and I have some beach reading to get into."

"You're such a brat, Shayne."

She blew me a kiss. "You know you love me."

"You're lucky you're my best friend, or I wouldn't let you get away with that cute crap." I stood from the table, still a little nervous at the idea of Shayne reading my work.

She held the notebook to her chest, staring at me. "I'm your best friend?"

I shrugged. "Outside of Travis, I like to think that, if I needed someone to talk to, it'd be you. You both never judged me or pulled any funny BS. I admire that."

Shayne smiled. "Nice to know I'm appreciated." She held up my notebook. "But I'm still not going easy on you if this thing totally sucks." She tossed me a sassy look and skipped her way into the house.

I shook my head. Pacific Hills girls were going to be the death of me.

Nandy was in control, which wasn't a surprise, as she led the way to her car and had me ride shotgun.

In the beginning, riding in the car with Nandy had been a pain due to our different tastes in music, but after a while, I'd grown to like her favorite singers and artists. Only, this wasn't one of those occasions.

She put on some song with a catchy beat, and when the artist started singing I realized she was playing some shitty mumble rapper. Nandy giggled at my scowl, and I soon found it hard to be angry at the sight of her swaying to the music and smiling. How could the devil be so beautiful?

Nandy sang along and swayed some more, using her free arm to wave her hand in the air—in my face.

"He's literally just listing shit," I pointed out.

Nandy shrugged and kept singing along to the song. I *thought* I'd fixed her taste. Clearly not.

She pulled into a lot that was attached to a strip of shops. We got out of the car, and I followed as she led the way to the first one.

"We are going on a day date," Nandy announced. "And what better day date than cooking?"

Warmth rushed through me. It sounded perfect.

We entered the small establishment. A few couples were already standing at workstations, and a man in a chef uniform was at the front of the room. The cool gust of the AC was welcome against the heat from outside.

Nandy made a fuss to pay for our experience, and I let her win before leading the way to an empty work area.

"Welcome, class." The man in the white uniform greeted us once we were all ready. "I'm Chef Tomas, and today we will be preparing cabbage rolls."

A collection of *ooh*s resonated around the room, and I was honestly eager to learn this dish. On some occasions, my mom had bought cabbage rolls, but being able to make them myself would be even better.

Nandy faced me with worry. "I was hoping we'd be making spaghetti."

Who couldn't make spaghetti? "This is even better."

Still, Nandy was apprehensive. "I'm going to suck."

She was being a baby, so I moved behind her and held her close, noticing at once how she relaxed into me as Chef Tomas went on. I listened closely, all while admiring the scent of Nandy's sweet-smelling perfume. I wasn't the cuddly type, but I could get used to this girl in my arms.

First, Chef Tomas had us Saran Wrap a head of cabbage and nuke it for fifteen minutes, and since that seemed an easy task, I left it to Nandy while I seasoned our ground beef and added in the pack of ready rice. When I was a kid, I used to love volunteering to hand-mix my mother's meat loaf just to get my hands all dirty with the egg, beef, and bread crumb mixture.

"See, this isn't so hard," I assured Nandy.

She widened her eyes. "Oh wow, I pressed buttons on a microwave."

I chuckled. "It's a step up from toast."

When the microwave went off, Nandy carefully grabbed the cabbage and placed it on the counter before her. The smell wasn't appetizing, warranting us each to wrinkle our noses. We let it cool down before I peeled off the Saran Wrap and a leaf for her and myself.

Chef Tomas was at the front of the class with his own demonstration. "All you need to do is supply a good amount of your filling in the center of each leaf. Roll the cabbage around the filling like a burrito and tuck in the sides, and then roll the cabbage all the way up."

I followed his method, perfectly making my first cabbage roll.

Nandy's was a mess.

She groaned as she went for a second attempt, and then a third.

Finally, I went up behind her. "Tuck and roll." She angled her neck to where I could rest my head on her shoulder as I guided her. "See."

Nandy nuzzled me close. "Not bad."

The class went on, but Nandy paused. "Hey, let's take ours home to bake. Maybe it could be for dinner and soften the blow some more."

"Maybe your dad will see it as a peace offering?"

That caused Nandy to frown as she gazed at our rolls. "Let's go grab something to eat?"

"Sure."

Chef Tomas was surprised at our willingness to take our raw rolls home to cook, but excused us from the class as we wrapped our rolls to go.

We dropped the rolls off back at the house to store in the fridge before heading to the Crab Shack, because Nandy was craving fish, and the idea of fish and fries sounded too good to pass up.

"So you let Shayne read your journal?" Nandy brought up as she sat on the other side of the booth from me.

"It's not a journal, it's sort of a story," I told her.

Her brows furrowed. "About me?"

Now I felt sorta shy. "About me, and…us."

"Oh," said Nandy. "And Shayne's reading it? Maybe she'll give you a critique?"

"Maybe."

Nandy was quiet as she poked at her fish. "I'm sorry about how that all turned out."

"What do you mean?"

"I mean, I was selfish and intruded on your friendship with her. I don't want things to be weird for you two."

"She's become my best friend here, besides Travis. I think we're going to be okay. It wasn't really all you. I like Shayne, she's a great girl, but before we became cool I was working on a friendship with Kyle, and he likes her."

"I'm glad you guys are still gonna be close. And who knows, maybe you can bring Kyle around and see what happens."

"Nah, he's gotta stand on his own two and step to her."

"Maybe tomorrow night at the Hook."

"Oh that, you're going?"

Nandy shrugged. "Of course. Erica wants us girls to go as each other's dates. You and the guys should come, it'll be fun."

"Sure. I'm going to need something to keep my mind off Shayne reading my book."

"Don't stress it, writing is just therapy for you," Nandy encouraged. "Unless writing is something you think you wanna do."

I sat back in the booth, staring at her. "What do you mean?"

"Have you thought about college and what you wanna study?"

College had never crossed my mind. My life had always been about survival and my mother, and half the time I never even thought about school. I used to cut school, a *lot*.

One thing I knew about the Hills was that its schools and parents bred Somebodies, meaning, everyone had a career in mind or was thinking about college or their future. There was no time to be stagnant, it wasn't acceptable. It was enough to make you feel defective, if you really didn't know what the hell you wanted to do with your life.

"I like writing, differentiating characters and settings, but as far as college goes, I never saw myself there. I had a different mind-set then."

"And now?"

A quote by Marianne Williamson came to mind, and I knew that I couldn't let the fear of not being good enough beat me.

"Now I'm sure that, between Max and Lydia, Ms. Gonzalez, college is very much going to be pushed on me. I don't know, maybe that's not such a bad thing."

"Whatever you decide to do, I'm with you."

I spotted Chad and his friends entering the establishment. Upon hearing the rowdy boys around Chad, Nandy soon noticed them, too. They didn't see us, but Nandy still sank into her seat.

It wasn't acceptable. We already couldn't be together at her house—out in town, we couldn't let anything get between us.

I reached out and squeezed her hand. "We're not doing anything wrong."

"I know."

"Then let's not hide it."

Nandy peered up at me, appearing unsure. "Do you think my dad will kick you out?"

"I don't know. I can tell he's adamant about not approving."

"It's just not fair, you know? You're finally happy, and he wants to ruin it."

"We'll be fine. It pays that he's hardly around due to his schedule. We'll find a way to show them that we're legit if we're…you know."

Nandy giggled. "Going steady?"

"Yeah, that."

"Okay." She looked thoughtful for a moment. "Are we, though, together in that way?"

"I've only had one girlfriend, and I wasn't good to her. I feel different with you, I always have. I don't know how to do this, though."

"You just go with the flow." She stopped to think. "And roll with the homies."

I shook my head. "Never say that again."

She came around the booth and sat on my lap, wrapping her arms around me. "We can do this, Tyson. We just have to trust each other."

I held her close, staring up at her. Trust and vulnerability had been weaknesses to me before; it felt scary relinquishing both to this girl who was stronger than me in this thing we were doing, this girl who had all the power.

There was this quote about a king bowing only to his queen, and how he wasn't anything without her, because like in a game of chess, she protected him and kept him focused.

My heart was fragile and timid; offering it up felt asinine, but I couldn't let anxiety get in the way. I couldn't be a coward.

Leaning over, I pressed my head to Nandy's shoulder and rested there. I felt secure when she ran her hand over my head, soothing me, probably knowing what I was thinking.

"Can we get out of here?" I asked as I looked up at her.

She was massaging my scalp. "Where to?"

We couldn't go home. We wouldn't be able to be together there. "The model home."

She stood and held out her hand to me, and I knew, as I accepted her outstretched hand, that this was what I wanted more than anything.

34 | *Nandy*

The girls wanted to go all out for Thursday night. The theme was Throwback Thursday, so in honor of that we made an effort to dress up. Erica looked amazing in her basketball jersey dress with Timberland heeled boots. Edi and Shayne wore matching Juicy Couture hoodies and shorts sets, Edi's baby blue and Shayne's pink. I kept it simple in a denim jumpsuit that offered plenty of cleavage and legs.

We were throwing it back to the early 2000s style, enjoying ourselves and the atmosphere. We hung out in a group, watching the boys we knew flirting with girls and using their best game. Warhol had a girl eating up his best lines as he danced with her to Flo Rida's "Low," and Travis could be seen getting number after number. Tyson was around, either talking to one of the guys or sitting back and enjoying the music. The girls and I stayed together until Erica had to go and do her gig.

All of the Hook was up dancing to the old Nelly song "Hot in Herre" as Erica played the tune at the DJ booth and couples ground into each other.

"Ladies!" Erica shouted over the microphone as the record ended. "How many of you love you some real hip-hop?" The crowd of girls screamed their agreement, egging Erica on. "How many of you rock with Nas? Eve? Q-Tip? How many of you love you some hot boys?"

I made sure to scream and holler my answer just as other girls were screaming, too. Erica put on a record by Missy Elliott called "Hot Boyz," and more dancing ensued.

Across the club, I spotted Tyson with Warhol and Matt. He was eyeing me, slitting his eyes, obviously having seen my cheering. I blew him a kiss, and he shook his head, still smiling nonetheless.

Travis came to the bar and got a bottle of water, and then sat back beside me, scoping out possible victims.

He slid his attention to me, wiggling his eyebrows. "'Sup?"

"You look like you're creepin'," I replied.

Travis smiled. "I am." He gestured his head toward the club floor, and I looked over to where Xiu was weaving her way through the crowd of dancing bodies. "She's dying for it."

"Geordan will kill you," I let him know, "and then Erica will revive you and kill you again."

Travis smirked. "It's just a dance. It could be us, but you know how that goes."

I frowned. "Do you think he'd care?"

"Trice?" Travis shrugged. "He doesn't seem like the jealous type."

Chad had never cared whenever we'd all gone to the Hook together and I danced with Warhol, Matt or Ashley. It had never been a big deal, because everyone knew where things lay. With Tyson, I wasn't sure if it was something he would like or not. Thinking of him dancing with another girl, I wasn't sure if I would like it myself. It was odd; I had never felt possessive or that attached before. There was this selfish part of me that wanted Tyson all to myself, and a greedy part that wanted to be the only one who savored the feel of his hands.

I took a sip of my Diet Coke, knowing I needed to loosen up. It was too fast to feel so much.

Travis eyed Xiu where she was standing with Edi and Shayne, moving a little to the beat. She looked a little nervous and shy, a little out of place. A slow smile took his lips. "God, she wants it so bad. I'm getting her next song."

The universe was on Travis's side, because as the beat to the next song came on, I cringed.

"Travis, no!" I begged at the sound of Ginuwine's "Pony" beginning to play.

Travis closed his eyes, taking in some air, as if he were inhaling the feel of the beat. "Done."

Without hearing my plea, he swaggered over to Xiu in a way that caused me to scratch at my neck. Watching him circle her, lean in close to her ear and whisper to her, peer into her eyes, I could actually understand the spell and appeal of Travis Catalano.

Somehow Xiu agreed, and I could read the words *don't be shy* on Travis's lips as he took her hand and led her into the crowd.

One minute Xiu was biting at her lip, the next she was feeling out the beat, and soon moving slowly with Travis's movements. She raised her hand to his shoulder and held herself there as her hips began to wind to the song, matching Travis beat for beat. He smiled at her kindly, encouraging her.

A wild look passed over Xiu's face, and a moment later she had turned around, her hair whipping in the air, as she pressed her back to Travis's chest, allowing him to grasp her hips as she danced into him. My jaw dropped. The shy look was gone as her moves became confident and sensual.

Was this really Xiu Yee?

I stood and joined Edi and Shayne, who also looked mesmerized by the sight of the once shy girl we thought we knew so well. Even Warhol and Ashley came over to watch the couple dancing. From the way Xiu was winding her hips and dancing onto Travis like it was a private show, she'd been hiding her talent from us all.

"Shit! Go Xiu!" Warhol cheered. He said it again and it caught on, and soon a crowd was cheering Xiu on as she put the moves on Travis.

Travis was practically the only person not stunned by the way Xiu was dancing. The way he danced with her, egging her on and matching her moves, I just about fell for him. It was so easy for us to deem Travis wild and trouble due to his reckless behavior, but from his friendship with Tyson to his encouraging Xiu to let go, I had to admit, Travis Catalano wasn't a bad guy after all.

Something told me that, come the school year, I'd be losing a good deal of friendships connected to Chad, but seeing the way Travis treated Tyson, Kyle, and now Xiu, I had a feeling I was going to gain a lot more in the aftermath.

The song finished and Xiu raised her hands to her face as it exploded bright red. Travis grinned and pulled her into a hug, saying something into her ear. She deserved the round of applause our group was giving her; she had killed it.

Shayne's mouth was still open in shock. "Looks like DEF-CON Yee just got a new member?"

Edi held up her cup. "What the hell did she drink that I didn't get?"

"I call next!" Warhol shouted.

"Hell no, I'm next," Ashley argued.

The two went off and joined Xiu and Travis, circling the poor girl, fighting for a dance.

Shayne shook her head, turning to me and offering me a half smile. "Can we pee?"

The expression on her face told me she wanted to talk and I agreed, following as she led the way to the women's restroom.

Inside, I adjusted my zipper as we stood in front of the mirror, briefly letting air into my jumpsuit.

Shayne was running her hands through her curls, yet even in the mirror her gaze kept flickering to me.

"What?" I came out and asked.

Shayne turned to me. "Do you think you and Ty are close to like, you know, hooking up?"

The question caught me off guard. At first the thought of it had made me nervous, but after spending so much time with Tyson and talking to him, it was becoming less and less overwhelming.

I took a step back. "What?"

Shayne came closer. "I stayed up reading his story, Nan. He's like crazy in love with you."

I didn't know what to say. The idea of Tyson's love...it stunned me. "Huh?"

"The story's about a kid named Tyrin, and how he grew up in this bad city, watching his father beat his mother, and his friends robbing and stealing, and one day he goes to an affluent town and meets this girl, Queen—you. They're both seven, and they hang out for an entire year before Tyrin's home life gets so bad that he doesn't want to leave his city anymore.

"Ten years pass and his father kills his mother in a drunken rage, and Tyrin ends up staying with his uncle in the affluent community, next door to Queen. At first, they fight a lot, because she assumes he's this thug, but then they talk and they connect. He's mesmerized by her beauty, just like he was when he first saw her, but beyond that—she's fierce, independent, and smart. She's everything to him, and he falls helplessly in love with her."

The parallels to our situation caused me to have to lean against the sink for balance and support.

"Go on, please," I insisted.

"I'm not going to spoil it. It's a really good story. I just…" She stopped and a tear rolled down her cheek. "It was just so beautiful, Nandy. The crazy thing is, I don't even think he realizes what he wrote and how he feels."

He'd told me it was about us, but I hadn't imagined how deeply rooted we—*I*—was in his story.

"Can I have a quote?" I joked to ease the tension.

Shayne appeared thoughtful. "'It was eminent. It stood against time. The love I felt for Queen was the closest I would ever feel for another person next to my mother. Looking into Queen's dark eyes, I felt peace and calm. I had found my kingdom. I was home.' I read that about a million times. He's in love with you."

It felt unreal. I needed to read the story for myself and to hear Tyson say the words himself for it to be true.

Shayne grabbed hold of my arm, causing me to look into her eyes. "Be careful, Nan. He's fragile. He may not admit it, but he's afraid to love. He's afraid of getting hurt and losing someone. You left Chad for him—he may question that, but don't let it frighten you. If you really care for him, fight for him, no matter what."

It sounded like a lot, pressure even, but it wasn't. Tyson needed to be pushed, loved, and led away from the environment and emotions he'd grown up with. He needed to know that he mattered, was important, and could beat his past. Being the one elected to the task, I welcomed it with no qualms.

I headed for the door. "Don't worry, he's in good hands. Not only does he have me, but he also has amazing friends."

We found the others huddled together, still discussing Xiu's dancing. Xiu deserved to be the center of attention. It took major guts to step outside your comfort zone, especially in public.

Tyson found us and wrapped his arms around me. Warhol had just begun to tell some obvious lie about this epic fight for Xiu's next dance he'd had with Ashley.

The music came to a stop, and we all turned to the DJ booth to see what was happening.

"I wanna dedicate this next song to my best friend, Nandy, and her new boo, Trice," Erica cooed over the microphone.

I wrinkled my nose in embarrassment at the sound of B2K's "Why I Love You" as it came on all throughout the club.

Feeling slightly giddy, I turned and eyed my guy.

Tyson smiled at me and moved to the melody, goading me to dance with him as others began egging us on.

Seeing how goofy he looked, thinking of the time at the model home, I loosened up and went closer to him.

I felt too much to dance. I just needed a moment to bask in his arms and feel him.

Resting my chin on his chest, I looked up at him, amazed

at how far he'd come. It was scary, from ten years apart to nearly two months reunited, and here we were. The lyrics of the song matched what I felt for him through and through. I loved his wisdom, his compassion, his wit, his bravery, his strength—*him*.

Tyson leaned down and kissed me, and I felt it deeper than he could've imagined.

"You know I waited ten years for this," I came out and said.

He smoothed my hair, swaying to the song, silently nodding. We were in sync, because I knew he felt it, too.

Soon Soulja Boy started rapping about kissing a girl through the phone, and the mood shifted, causing us to find a quiet spot in the basement section of the club, where everyone lounged around on couches, talking.

I lay against Tyson as he curled his arms around me.

"So," he said, running the tips of his fingers down my arms, "you down or what?"

I looked back at him. "Huh?"

"You liked the song, right?"

"Yeah, it was really nice."

"So, if I wanted to really throw it back and grow my hair out, sport some braids, you'd be down to braid 'em for me?"

I clicked my tongue, shaking my head. He wasn't that cute. "Um, no. Besides, I always had a thing for J Boog and Lil' Fizz."

Tyson leaned close to my ear. "Fizz had the twists, though."

I wanted to argue, but I could only smile. "I don't even know how to braid hair to the scalp."

"You can learn."

"You are *not* getting braids again, Tyson."

He chuckled in my ear, sending a shiver down my spine. The sound and the feel of Tyson was the best.

Travis came and found us. "Y'all chillin' now?"

"It's getting a little hot up there," Tyson said.

Travis grinned. "Can't agree more. I met a girl who wants to dip, so I'll catch you later, okay?"

He leaned over and he and Tyson knocked their fists together twice before pointing at each other. It was some sorta secret handshake.

"We should have one of those," I suggested after Travis had left.

Tyson smirked. "That's mad corny, Nandy."

Maybe it was.

I stood from the couch. "Let's get out of here."

"Where to?"

"Trust me?"

He regarded me with suspicion. "Partially."

I rolled my eyes. "Come on, before I find some other cutie to take with me."

Tyson narrowed his eyes and stood, coming up on me and wrapping his arms around me again, holding me close. "You want beef?"

I held up a fist. "Bring it."

He didn't put up a fight as I took his hand and led him up the steps, through the maze of bodies and out of the club.

The Hook was right by the beach, and I dragged Tyson toward it in a heated rush. I felt childish and giddy at what I wanted to do.

He had no idea what was going on, but he kept up with me and eyed me curiously as we raced down to the sand.

The beach was deserted, leaving just us and the cool waves and the moon.

I stood in front of Tyson, assessing him. He hadn't dressed up, sporting a simple gray tee and tan khakis.

"Come here," I told him.

Tyson came closer. "Yeah?"

I crooked my arm out. "Dance with me?"

Tyson got this amused expression on his face as he eyed my arm. "Seriously?"

"It's not quite the street, but it's just you and me."

"Just the way you like it, huh?"

"Square dance with me, Tyson."

If he thought the gesture was lame or corny, he didn't voice it as he hooked his arm with mine.

Together we skipped in a circle, laughing at how silly we were being at our age. We went around and around, and I didn't get dizzy, too high off the feeling of being with Tyson.

There was a lone towel someone had left behind, and together we fell back onto it. Me on my back and Tyson between my legs on top of me. It was here where I faced the idea of sleeping with him. With all the emotions and sensations I was feeling, I thought I could go through with it. What more did I need to know or feel about him? We were inevitable.

Tyson leaned down and kissed me, and I wrapped my arms around his neck to pull him closer as it deepened and intensified.

We were in the open, exposed, but I could tell neither of us cared.

Just as I was getting comfortable, Tyson pulled away and lifted up on his arms. "We gotta cool it. If I'm going to unleash the beast, it ain't gonna be in public like this."

"Beast, huh? You that confident?"

The cocky expression on his face caused a deep clenching beneath my belly. *Oh.* He reached out and ran his thumb over my lower lip.

He leaned down and kissed me quickly, and then again, and soon we were at it once more.

It felt good to just be together, no boundaries or rules. I trusted Tyson, and I knew he trusted me. In all that I was feeling, I knew deep down I wanted to go all the way with him.

Tyson gazed into my eyes, as if sensing where my mind had gone and what I was feeling. He almost seemed to blush.

The sight of his expression made me laugh, and that caused him to laugh and calm down.

He grinned down at me, loosening up. "I think we—"

And then his phone rang.

35 | *TRICE*

My phone was going off. I could hear it in my pocket.

Nandy didn't seem to care. She was quick to lean up and trace my bottom lip with her tongue, sending a very important member of my anatomy at attention. She did it again, and I was beginning to think whoever was calling could wait.

My phone stopped but then started again, and curiosity got the better of me as I reached into my pocket, keeping my eyes on the girl beneath me.

She stared at me, lifting a brow as she toyed with the zipper of her jumpsuit. I reached out and cupped a breast, enjoying the feel of her in my hand, wondering what her skin would feel like. Nandy's response was a low moan, one that sent a wave of pleasure to my groin.

My phone was still ringing for attention.

With our luck, Parker was probably calling.

I leaned away from Nandy and brought my phone to my ear upon answering it. "Hello?"

"Yo, T, what up?" Money's voice stilled me, and I knew something was wrong.

Immediately I got to my feet and walked away from Nandy. "Money? What's up?"

"Didn't interrupt anything, did I? Was you fucking on something?" Money asked with no restraint.

Almost. I eyed Nandy, who had sat up and was adjusting her zipper and cleavage.

"Is there something you wanted?" He was holding back, and the sense of it was driving my blood pressure up.

His silence confirmed it.

"Yo, man, Mexico out here trippin'," Money finally came out and said. "He's getting paranoid, talking about the feds is onto him."

My eyes shut as I swore. "Fuck." This wasn't the time or place to discuss the matter, especially with Nandy nearby. "Call me back in ten minutes."

I hung up and faced Nandy, who looked quizzical. "We're going to have to finish this another time. I've got something to do."

Nandy looked to where I was gripping my phone. "Who was that?"

"No one."

She stood and came over to me. "Tyson."

I took a step back. Fuck. The last thing I needed was her involvement, mixing her in with the mess of my previous life. "I'm going to leave. I have business to get into. I'll see you later, okay?"

"And you'll tell me later?"

I shook my head. "No."

She frowned. "I thought you trusted me."

"This doesn't concern you." In the distance on the board-walk, I could see groups and couples walking away from the Hook, laughing and carrying on as if nothing was wrong in their perfect little worlds. Me, I didn't have that luxury. I faced the girl who I wanted nothing more but to spare and protect in that moment. "Do me a favor and go and meet up with your girls and enjoy the rest of your night."

"Tyson—"

"Nandy, please, just mind your business, a'ight?"

She flinched, taking a step back and looking down at the sand. Knowing her, I expected a fight, but when she turned and walked away, I had to admit it stung. It wasn't about trust, because sure, I trusted her, but this, this life that I'd led before, I didn't want it to touch her. I didn't want to trouble her with the mistakes of *my* past. I'd rather her be pissed at me than concerned—at least until I could fix things on my own.

I got in my ride and returned Money's call as I rode on home.

"What the fuck is going on?" I demanded to know.

"Ay, Prophet got a call from Mexico's loony ass, talking about he's sure the feds are casing the place. They came by twice asking him if he knew about some missing cars, and now he's acting crazy. He's saying he wants one tricked out ride so he can coast, or he's turning us all in."

Fuck.

"He thinks the feds are onto him, so he wants us to steal a car so he can chop it?" He had to see the lack of logic in that. Mexico couldn't be *that* dumb.

"He says it's been quiet, but he's not taking any chances.

There are other garages in Lindenwood. He thinks they're asking everyone. He wants to coast before they come back for another round, is all."

It seemed sketchy, but I could understand Mexico's paranoia and see why he wanted to skip town. We stole from other cities and didn't stick to a pattern, making the odds of tracking us down less likely. But of course Mexico wasn't about to trust a group of misfits from the 'Wood.

"Why didn't Prophet call me?"

"You know you his favorite, T. He doesn't want to bring you into it, but I thought you had a right to know."

"Damn right I do." Even if Prophet wanted more for me, this concerned me. I'd stolen just as many cars as the others, met up with Mexico just as much. When shit went down, Mexico wasn't about to be lenient with me. If my crew was going down, he was saying my name as well.

Then again…

"He doesn't know our names," I pointed out. We spoke in code—shit, the only person's name besides Khalil's that I knew was Prophet's, and that was only because Nandy had asked him.

"True, Read said that as well, but I ain't about to sit here and call his bluff."

"What's the plan?" I pulled up to a red light. Prophet was smart. I knew he'd come up with something to get us out of this mess.

"Man, you know Prophet and them," Money went on. "They're thinking about areas to look, but Mexico wants something top of the line, something that cost a grip. They ain't about to find that so last-minute. We got until Saturday night. And you know what I wanna do."

The light turned green, and it took a moment for me to process that it meant Go.

Money was talking murder, and a dark part of me was almost siding with him.

But then, killing Mexico seemed risky, and wrong. There had to be another way.

"No," I spoke up. "We're not going that route."

Money clicked his tongue. "I knew I shouldn't have called yo' punk ass."

It was comical, lightening up the situation. "I'm glad you did. I'll handle it."

"Nah, I can't drag you into this mess, Prophet would beat my ass."

"We're family," I said. "Y'all looked out for me, it's nothing. I can't leave you hanging. Besides, I'm in the land of honey, remember? I can find a car worth the ticket out of town. Leave it up to me."

Money was quiet for a moment, as if weighing out his options. He was crazy enough to want to end Mexico, but I could only hope he would see things my way.

"I don't like this, T. Mexico was supposed to be cool, and now he thinks he can turn on us?"

"People do a lot of things out of fear. Just let me get him the car, and we'll see where we're left after that, okay?"

"You got one day to find a car."

"I'll find a car, Money. Just promise me you won't do anything stupid."

"No, you don't do anything stupid. Don't ruin your good chance, that's your new life. Don't fuck it up over us."

"Before this, it was about surviving, and we did it together. We got in this mess together, and we'll finish it together. This is the last run I'm going to do, and if it's to set us all free, then it's whatever."

"Word is bond, I respect that. Be careful."

"Always."

"I'll see you Saturday."

I hung up as I made it home.

Something felt off, and I had to call Prophet to confirm it.

"T?" he answered on the second ring. "Everything good?"

Possibly. "Yeah, how are things with you?"

"Everything straight over here."

"And business?"

He was quiet, and I hated to think he wouldn't tell me. "I'm thinking of falling back for a while. Hell, I may even think about college or something."

Closing my eyes, I shook my head. "You'd tell me if something was wrong, right?"

"And drag you into it?"

"Prophet."

"You're free, Trice."

"We're born in chains, remember that? We're never free."

"You got out, so stay out, okay? I'm about to head to bed now. Take care, and do me a favor and stay out of trouble. I love you, man, stay up."

Prophet hung up and left me in the dark.

I knew Prophet was looking out for me, and I was staying away from the city, but this was personal. Turning my back on them wasn't an option, so if I had to seek out a fancy car and steal it to secure our freedom, so be it.

36 | *Nandy*

I didn't get much sleep. It was strange how I couldn't find comfort in the model home anymore. Not since sharing it with Tyson. The last time I'd been here, I'd been in Tyson's arms, kissing him. At the time, it had seemed like he needed me, and now here he was, pushing me away. We'd taken a step forward just to take another back.

It was selfish of me to intrude into his personal life, but I got the sense that he was in trouble, and I wanted to know how much and what kind. If only to help somehow, someway.

After waking up in the model home, I gathered myself together and began walking home. It was a hot walk, but one that left me alone with my thoughts. Not that that was a good thing. Every thought that came to me was negative and scary. I didn't like not knowing what was going on.

Maybe Travis had gotten into some type of embarrassing trouble and called Tyson to get him out of it, and that was why he'd shut me out. I could live with the idea of Travis being the cause of Tyson's secrecy. Rebel or not, Travis Catalano was safe compared to what else lingered out there that could've been calling Tyson.

At home, I found that my parents were already gone for work, which was a breeze since I didn't have to explain where I was all night.

Jordy came into the kitchen, a soccer ball under his arm. He lifted his chin in acknowledgment. "Hey."

I held up the doughnuts I'd gotten on the way home. "I brought breakfast. Do Mom and Dad know I didn't come home last night?"

Jordy accepted the bag and browsed through my selections as he shook his head. "They kinda figured you crashed at Erica's or something, and since Shayne didn't come either, they're not too upset. Although you should've called. Trice came home." He nibbled on a cream stick before gesturing toward the fridge. "There's leftover Mexican in there. I sorta ate your nachos."

I forced out a smile. "It's okay. I'm not really hungry."

Jordy seemed indifferent. "I'm heading over to Hector's. Do you mind if I take these?"

While I'd bought them for everyone, I didn't too much mind giving them all to my younger brother and his friends. It seemed no one else was home.

"Sure."

I went up to my bedroom and over to my iHome. I set my phone inside and scrolled through my music and settled on a song that described all that I was feeling and going through.

I let the song scream from my speakers as I fell onto my bed, hugging one pillow and burying my face into another.

While it may not have been the end of the world, I couldn't help but question if it were the end of us, whatever *us* was.

About a third of the way into the song I felt another presence climb onto my bed with me, and soon I felt him wrap his arms around me. Against all judgment, I reveled in the feel of his body weight on me, and the sensation of being in his arms pulled me in against the current of anxiety and doubt.

I turned over and was face-first with Tyson. He lay against me adorably in another gray tee that hugged his body and gave an exceptionally good view of the bulges of muscle that were his arms.

I reached out one hand and rested it on his chest as I peered into his eyes.

Tyson whispered, close to my ear, "I don't want it to be just a kiss."

There were so many things I wanted to say, but once our lips touched, all questions blurred away.

He kissed me, and it was as if someone had pressed Play and we'd resumed our moment from the beach. Only, I could tell something was amiss. He kissed me desperately, as if he were determined to see each kiss through to distract himself.

When he reached for my zipper, I almost got lost in what we were doing. I let him unzip my jumpsuit as he kissed a trail from my neck down my chest. He kissed the valley of my cleavage as his hand slipped into the shorts of my jumpsuit.

I bit down on my lip as he cupped me and my back arched. *Oh God.*

I reached down and covered his hand with mine, showing him the way, helping him.

"Tyson," I let out in a breathy moan.

He watched me as we kept going and my breathing heightened with what was building up inside of me. Something about his attention and the look on his face pushed me over the edge and I was especially happy there was music playing to block out my screaming in the results of our activity.

I lay back as my body wound down, and Tyson brought his arms back around me and leaned down to kiss me. Kissing didn't seem like enough to him, because he was going deeper as he soon hovered over me and gripped my thighs in a way that sent electricity coursing through my body.

He shifted his weight off me as he propped himself up on his arms. His gaze fell over me and I could see the intent of his desire. I knew what he wanted as his hands slid down the measures of my curves, and I wanted with everything in the heat of the moment to give it to him, except a tiny voice in the back of my mind stopped me.

We were stalling.

The previous evening had happened, and we were skirting around the issue of the telephone call that had interrupted our moment.

I scrambled to sit up and held up my hand to keep him away. I got out of the bed and turned off my music before facing the boy in my bed looking at me with worry.

Clutching my jumpsuit together to keep my breasts from spilling out, I asked what had been on my mind all night. "What happened last night?"

Tyson studied me. "Nothing."

"Bullshit, Tyson."

He let out a sigh. "That's not what I want to talk about right now, or what I want to *do*."

"So you really think you can brush me off and then show up now and mess around with me?"

Tyson deadpanned, as if it weren't already obvious. "You weren't saying that a moment ago."

I stood straight, feeling guilty. Quickly, I zipped up my jumpsuit to hide the evidence of what we'd done. "I was distracted."

"Come on, I just wanna be close to you," he begged. He sounded needy and seemed anxious, making my knees feel weak.

Still I pushed to stop the charade. "And I'm trying to get close to you, but you won't let me."

Hardness covered Tyson's face. "Nandy, drop it."

"No. Tell me what's going on. I know it's something serious. I can help you."

Tyson remained silent.

He wasn't willing to share his phone call or his distress, and I wasn't in the mood to continue fondling each other, or have sex with him with such a big space between us. If it wasn't my mood swings between us, it was his secrets now. We just couldn't get the timing right, and I hated it. Every turn was another winding road, and I feared we'd never get it straight.

I gave up.

I needed space, and I went to leave.

"Where are you going?" He was up out of the bed and after me.

I paused at the door. "I'm going to take a shower, and I want you out of my room."

Tyson grimaced. "If I tell you what's up you're not going to like it."

"Not telling me has yielded the same result."

He cursed and stared down at the carpet. "Something came up back home, some trouble. I'm going to have to figure out a way to fix it."

"Doing that illegal stuff you used to do?"

He nodded.

"That's completely stupid and reckless, no!"

"You have no authority to tell me what to do."

"I'm not telling you, I'm strongly suggesting it."

"And you have no place to."

"I think as your girlfriend—wait, we never put a title on it, did we? I guess you're right." Defeated. I felt defeated.

Tyson appeared hurt as he tried to get close to me. "Stop it, it's not like that. You mean a lot to me, but this—this is bigger than you. I'm not turning my back on them. That's where I came from, that's what I know, and that's what I'll protect."

Even if it cost him everything?

I didn't cry, I just hurt all over.

Bowing my head, I shook it slightly. "I don't know 'Trice,' but I guess I just met him. Have fun going home and doing what you *have* to do."

"If I walk out that door, what does it mean, Nandy?" When I didn't answer right away, he touched me. "Look at me."

And I did, because I felt too much for him, too much to let him do what he was doing, and too much to support it. It was ruined and broken, and I did *not* feel okay.

"We were fragile from the start, the ground was never solid to walk on, and all it took was one step to break us. I just didn't think it'd be so soon." Just when I'd gotten him to myself, someone else came and took him from me all over again.

Tyson caged me against the door, reaching his hands out and planting them on either side of my head. He seemed determined and resilient as he shook his head. "I walked away from you ten years ago, and I don't plan on doing that again. I just need you to understand that this is something that I have to do."

He was risking everything he'd built to save a past he needed to escape. The thought seemed to rip my heart out of my chest at the possible consequences of such foolishness.

"I… I'm sorry, I can't." I ducked under his arm and opened my bedroom door, leaving my room and him behind.

37 | TRICE

She didn't even know the full story, and she was disappointed in me. Telling Nandy my intentions for the night would surely ruin any chance I had with her.

I almost wanted to call the whole thing off, but I couldn't go back on my word. I couldn't let my friends down.

Hours seemed to pass as I lay in my room, staring up at the ceiling. There was music in my ears, but its content wasn't reaching me. All I could think about was my moment with Nandy in her room on her bed, uninterrupted until she'd demanded answers from me. To think, if Money hadn't called, perhaps we would've been closer by now, maybe even truly intimate. It gave me chills to know that, between us, it would mean something—something real and something deep. In the beginning, I hadn't wanted to be close to anybody, but as my last hours of freedom possibly slipped away, all I wanted was Nandy.

But all she wanted was the truth.

I forced myself to come out of my room, only to discover that Nandy was long gone.

Being in the house wasn't helping. Outside with fresh air, I still couldn't think straight. I wished she were home. Even if she would more than likely ignore me, at least she'd still be in the vicinity. For the first time, I was in the wrong, and the guilt was weighing me down.

Matt's Wrangler came down the road and pulled to a stop in front of the Catalano residence. Travis hopped out and gave Matt a salute as he drove off. Travis noticed me and came over, wearing only a pair of sweats with a jump rope draped across his shoulders.

He came to a stop in front of me, and we did the little handshake we'd created one boring afternoon, before he sat with me on the front step.

"You should've joined Matt and me at the gym. One of my favorite pastimes is boxing." Travis demonstrated a few jabs as he grinned my way. "If you ask Matty, it was a tie, but just know that I kicked his ass."

I offered him a small smile and stared down the front walk.

Silence fell over us and I knew the hours of the day were winding down. I had to find a car before it was too late.

"Trouble in paradise?" Travis asked as he elbowed me.

"Something like that."

He patted my back. "Last night didn't go so well for me, either."

"I thought you took a girl home."

Travis looked at the street and shrugged. "Nah, we just didn't click like I thought."

I wanted things to be normal and calm, but a choice lay in front of me.

"This is deeper than your girl," Travis observed. "What's up?"

I shook my head. "Nothing."

"Nandy'll forgive you, man," Travis said.

"This isn't about Nandy," I confessed. Keeping it inside wasn't going to help, and at least Travis wasn't the type to judge. "It's something back home."

"Someone hurt or something?"

"We're different than you," I said as I faced him. "At least, they are."

Travis tried to be understanding. "We can't be *that* different."

I shook my head. "You guys have it set here. In the 'Wood, going to school, or even college, calls for a slow route to money. For them, they want money fast. When I was growing up, to make a little money, we'd get together and go around stealing cars. My friends did it for the cash and the high. I did it to save up for my mom and me. A month ago, I got a call that they needed another runner, because one of my friends got hurt. So I went back and delivered the car to the guy who chops them in exchange for cash. Living life like that was simple back then. And then I came here.

"Last night I got a call from a friend saying our chopper is getting paranoid. He wants us to find a top-of-the-line car to deliver to him so he can skip town, or else he'll turn us all in to save himself. Best case, this is just paranoia getting to him. Worst, the feds are closing in and he really could turn on us.

My friend wants to permanently shut him up, but I offered to find a car to deliver to him tomorrow night."

"Steal a car, you mean," Travis corrected. Unlike Nandy, he wasn't disgusted with me. He didn't even seem mad, he just accepted my story as if it were no big deal.

"Yeah, that."

Travis squinted into the distance where Kyle was getting into his car. "You steal from this area, you're the number one suspect. Big black guy from Lindenwood, who else could it be, you know?"

"If I don't steal, we're fucked."

Travis shrugged. "Could be the case either way."

"Yeah."

"You can't blame Smith for being upset. She's into you, left behind Bradley, goes against her parents, and this is probably a slap in the face."

"She doesn't the know the details, just that I have to do something illegal. The details would end us."

"Rightfully so."

"I don't have a choice."

"There's always a choice."

"Yeah? What other problem-solving choice do I have?"

Travis stared at me. One second he was studying me, and the next he was reaching into his sweats and pulling out his car keys. He tossed them my way. "Problem solved."

It was generous, but… "I can't."

"It's my dad's," he went on. "I'll just make up some story about it being stolen while I was out."

"Travis."

"I'm serious, Trice." Crazy thing was, he looked dead-ass serious. "Take the car."

It was here that I knew that he was lying.

I shook my head. "This is your car."

He gave me a half smile. "I probably would've crashed it or something anyway."

"Knowing your dad, he's gonna be disappointed you let it get stolen."

Travis didn't deny this. "My dad's always disappointed in me."

"I can't take your car, Trav."

"The way I see it, what choice do you have? You steal a car that's rigged to go off and you're fucked, and your bros back home are equally fucked. You take a car with a set of keys—"

"A lift," I cut in. "Breaking into a car with force is a crank, but easily stealing a car that's not rigged or has keys is a lift."

Travis nodded. "You lift my car, and you're home free. It's worth a lot of money—it's only a year old, top-notch navigation and Bluetooth. It's the dream steal."

Travis wasn't bullshitting me. He wanted me to take his car. He was giving me a free and easy run, but it was beyond a noble gesture.

"You barely know me."

"You have a second chance here, and I get that you want to free your bros and clear your history, but this car comes with a rule. This is your last tie to Lindenwood. After you deliver the product and everything's squared away, you're done for life. You're going to come back and build a new beginning with Nandy or whoever. You said it yourself—you got shot, and not everybody survives that, but you did. It'd be a pity to beat the odds just to land in jail or juvie. Do better."

"You're actually good at this," I said.

"Matt's like a therapist when I'm on a destructive path. I'm sure I've done something that caused him to say something similar to me."

"Still, you did a great job paraphrasing." I squeezed the keys in my hand, feeling speechless. "Thank you."

"I'm just here to be honest. You can't have your cake and eat it too, and the only cake you should want to eat is—"

"You were doing so well."

Travis managed to laugh. "We're not about to hug or some shit, are we?"

Closing my eyes, I really laughed. He couldn't be too serious for long. "Hell no."

I had a way out, an easy way out, yet still, it didn't sit right with me. Not at all.

Accepting Travis's car was simple, but even if it were the way through, another plan seemed to come to mind.

If I was going to bury my past, it was time to come to terms with everything and truly move forward. One way or another.

38 | *Nandy*

With the weight of my drama with Tyson crushing me, I went to Erica's to cope.

Coming to Erica felt just as natural as Shayne coming to my family with her angst. Erica was probably the calmest of my friends, and having her to talk to about Tyson felt reassuring.

When it came to my dilemma with Tyson, I felt left out. I couldn't believe he was willing to go back to the city that had nearly killed him.

I envied other girls. My final year of school should've been a big cliché, about stressing over what college I got into and all the traditional events. About finally deciding to sleep with the boy I liked, or not. About a first job or internship. Instead, I was stressing about Lindenwood and the hold it had over Tyson.

I thought of Tyson's friends and how they were all different from him, but the same in a sense. Khalil, with his tall height, dark skin, and hair braided in sections, was our age, but seemed so much younger. He was a follower, going along with the likes of Money and Pretty, two guys who seemed content with material things like money, weed, and sex. Read was hard to interpret; he was quiet and didn't convey much about his inner thinking. Prophet was their chosen leader, and I could tell he genuinely wanted more for Tyson, and even Khalil. He accepted that Money and Pretty were going to live and die by Lindenwood's honor and that Read could go either way. But Tyson and Khalil, he wanted more for them, a way out.

Tyson had gotten his way out, and yet he still had one foot back home.

I'd fallen in love with a criminal. I should've expected this to come with the territory. If my life were one of those rap videos, perhaps I'd toughen up and go with him, have his back and support him. That true Ride or Die persona. But I'd grown up in Pacific Hills and followed the rules all my life; this decadent way of living wasn't something I knew or could understand.

Erica frowned, noting my silence at the foot of her bed. "You and Trice are fighting already?"

We'd been up in her room, geared to watch a movie or two, but my mind was elsewhere, staring ahead at her TV absentmindedly.

"I'm not from his world, and I can't understand or hang," I told her.

I'd told myself I wasn't to blame for Tyson's actions, but the girl inside me who was in love with him…she felt every bit pessimistic.

"I think you not being from his world is what drew him to you. Don't get it twisted, Nan. You probably mean a lot to him. Ten years is a long-ass time to be carrying a torch for someone."

"It's different than that. He barely lets me in, and when he did, I can't just agree with this choice he's making. That's why I came here, I couldn't deal with it."

"I know it's hard and confusing, but try to meet Trice halfway to hear him out and express your feelings. Who knows, it might sway him, whatever he's dealing with."

Tyson had seemed so adamant about going through with his illegal activity. Maybe it was pointless to try to talk to him and steer his choice. Maybe it was pointless to try to be with him.

I loved him a great deal, but I couldn't condone his choices if they were going to be risky.

Everything had seemed simple when we were kids.

But it wasn't.

At least not for Tyson. Things had always been hard for him. This was just another wrench thrown into his life, and it was easy for him to decide what to do.

Maybe Erica was right, maybe talking to him could change his decision.

If only.

On the way home, I stopped at the local supermarket to pick up some groceries. I wasn't a cook, but the idea of making Tyson dinner—or at least trying to—put me at ease about the idea of talking to him again.

At home, I looked up several recipes for baked chicken and settled on one that required the chicken breasts to be pan-roasted and seasoned with a garlic rosemary rub. We had a meat thermometer, and I felt safe with the idea of roasting the chicken so long as it browned and came to temp.

With my phone in my hoodie pocket, I plugged in my earphones and jammed out to Mariah Carey as I picked out some sides.

Cooking wasn't so bad, I discovered as I wiggled my hips around the kitchen and prepared each portion.

Despite the sad breakup tunes, upbeat Mariah got the job done as I finished cooking about forty minutes later.

I was pulling the rolls from the oven when I looked over my shoulder to check the time. Tyson was standing in the doorway, watching me.

Quickly I ripped the earphones from my ears and stood back against the stove. "How long have you been there?"

Tyson shrugged as he came over. "Long enough." He peered at the food behind me. "This brings a whole new meaning to the term shake and bake." His grin caused my heart to stutter. "Smells good. What's for dessert?"

Feeling playful, I said, "I was thinking I'd put a bow on myself and you'd have me."

A hungry look passed through Tyson's eyes as he remained silent.

"Kidding, of course," I quickly added.

Tyson lifted a brow and came even closer. "I'm not."

All of my insides melted into a pathetic puddle of need. "I… I made you dinner, Tyson."

He blinked. "Really, for me?"

"Yes." I nodded, but then it hit me. "Shit."

He became concerned. "What?"

"I don't even know what you like. It's probably all wrong."

Tyson wrapped his arms around me. "I like baked chicken

most. And you made mashed potatoes and broccoli, even rolls, you're good."

"The potatoes are instant," I confessed.

Tyson didn't care. "Truth be told, I like real potatoes, but instant's just as good. No girl's ever cooked for me before, not that there's been many, but still, this means a lot."

Just as I was standing on my toes to kiss him, my father came into the room.

Tyson barely made an effort to move away from me. The sound of "Touch My Body" coming from my dangling earphones didn't help much, either.

I moved more away from Tyson as my father stood, assessing us. It was obvious we hadn't been acting like "pretend siblings" or whatever he wanted of us.

"Dad, I made dinner," I came out and said.

He held up the bag I realized was in his hand. "I grabbed Italian."

"Oh."

Tyson's hand found its way to my lower back as he gained my attention. "Do you mind if we take our portion somewhere private? I think we need to talk." I managed to nod before he faced my father. "If that's all right with you?"

My father was oddly calm. "Sure, okay. After you get back I think it'd be best if you packed your things and—"

"Dad!" I went and stood in front of Tyson.

My father noticed the gesture and appeared amused. "Like I was saying, I think it'd be best from here on out if Trice gathered his belongings and moved into the pool house. It's obvious you don't intend to stop seeing each other, and at least that way he's not technically under the same roof."

Speechless, I stared at my father.

The pool house was vacant, but it was a luxury. On the

main level, it housed a kitchen and living room, and on the second floor was the master suite. Moving Tyson into the pool house wasn't punishment at all, as he would now have his own private space.

"Understand?" my father asked of us.

"Yes," Tyson answered. "Thank you, Parker."

Tyson touched my arm and said he'd go and wait in the car, sensing my father wanted to talk.

I went about preparing a picnic basket for us to take to the model home. There was a mock dining room set up, so it served us well to go there for privacy.

"I don't want you to get hurt," my father said as he came over to the island.

"I don't want to get hurt," I said.

He touched me. "He's not the same person he was before. He came here angry and cold, and now that the summer's almost over, here we are."

"Travis and Shayne are to thank for that. They've been his rock."

"And you?"

"I just fell in love with him." I cursed myself for how I'd spent the beginning of the summer treating Tyson so harshly. But then, had I taken the time to get to know him sooner, I would've only fallen in love with him earlier.

My father massaged my arm. "Be careful, Nandy. Not only for you, but for him as well. He's still got a lot of healing to go through. Your mother and I were thinking therapy should be in his future."

I gathered my picnic basket. "I think that's a great idea. He has a lot of survivor's guilt he needs to work through."

My father offered me a quick hug as I prepared to leave.

Tyson was waiting patiently for me in his car. I set the picnic basket in the back seat before joining him up front.

"Do you think your curfew still applies?" he asked as he pulled out of the driveway and headed off for the model home.

The question made me stop and think. Did it still apply now?

"We'll see," I replied.

I was just happy that my father was coming around. He knew how we felt and no longer wanted to get in the way.

At the model home, Tyson took my free hand as we ascended the front walk together. The place didn't seem like my haven anymore; it felt like *ours*. Something told me Tyson felt that, too. He flashed me a smile as he unlocked the front door and led us inside.

The topic of conversation would be heavy for dinner, but at least Tyson was ready to let me in.

I set up plates as Tyson went around the table, removing the designer plates on display. The day the Pacific Hills Agency found out about the model home and began putting it to use would destroy me. I liked having a second home, and I especially liked sharing it with Tyson.

Tyson came up behind me and kissed my neck. "Damn, you really didn't make any dessert."

"Easy, we haven't talked yet," I told him.

"There's been a change of plans," Tyson came out and said.

The news lifted my spirits. "So you're not going now? Great. See, wasn't it easy?"

Tyson didn't return my joy. "That's not what I meant. I'm still going. I have to."

Suddenly I lost my appetite as I set down the Tupperware and backed away from him.

Erica had said I should hear him out, but it wasn't so simple. He was going off to do something illegal, and I couldn't stand by that at all.

"Just...forget it, then." I pushed past him and left the room, going toward the staircase.

With all my angst, I went into the master bedroom to do the one thing that could possibly make me feel better.

I made a fort.

I gathered all the pillows and made a little pallet on the floor, and then took the sheets and hung them up on the highest furniture before taking the comforter and lying down inside. If only the fort could hide me from my troubles, maybe things could truly be all right.

Lying there, I didn't exactly feel much better, not with thoughts of Tyson getting himself arrested swarming around in my head. I cuddled a throw pillow to my chest, wishing things didn't have to be the way that they were.

Time ticked by, and I noticed Tyson's absence. I wondered if he'd begun eating without me. It wasn't like he could do anything else to upset me.

Oh, well.

"Really?" I heard his voice outside the fort, and a moment later he was crawling in and joining me. He sat down beside me, appearing crestfallen.

Adorable or not, I just could not consent to his mission.

Tyson sorta frowned as he cleared his throat. "Growing up, I had it pretty nice. My dad made good money, but he worked a lot, and when he came home, the littlest things would set him off. My mom did her best to raise me as well as him. I'm not like my friends too much in that sense—maybe only Prophet and Khalil can relate to my situation with our upbringing. Or maybe just Khalil. He came from a humble background and some money, too.

"But anyway, after it got worse and I stopped coming to see you, I started hanging around Prophet and forming a plan to get money to save my mom. We were a group of thieves, Nandy. We went from city to city stealing cars and having them chopped uptown by this mechanic. It was the best way I could get quick and easy money, and enough to truly save."

"That's what they had you do last month?" I came out and asked. Stealing cars was wrong, no matter the reason, but having that be the revelation wasn't too much of a big deal. I'd thought it was something worse, something extreme, like drug trafficking.

"Yeah." Tyson nodded. "Khalil got hurt, and I had to do his run for him. I haven't always done what I should. I haven't always been a good guy. But there comes a point where you have to look in the mirror and decide which guy is gonna ensure your survival. The good guy, he wasn't cutting it. I was hungry, I was desperate, and I wanted to save my mom more than anything. It's not something I expect you to understand. It's not something you *can* understand.

"I'm not sorry for what I did. I'm only sorry I didn't act soon enough to move us away from him. Being in that situation is what made me. I had to do what I did to survive."

"And now? This thing you have to do, you gotta steal another car?"

Tyson shook his head. "I was supposed to, but I'm not. Our chopper, Mexico, he wants a big way out of town, because he's scared the feds are onto him. He wants one of us to deliver a car tomorrow night. I have another idea."

"What?"

Tyson smiled softly as he reached out and caressed my cheek. "Do you really need to know all the details? Just trust me on this, okay? Before, I was going to be stealing something. Now, I'm exchanging my past for my future. It's all legit and legal, I promise," he swore.

I clutched his shirt in hands. "You swear?"

"I swear, Nandy. If I get pulled over by the police, they're not going to arrest me or anything. I'ma be clean."

He *wasn't* doing anything illegal. There was no crime about to take place. The news calmed my nerves, even if I was still in the dark. "You scared me."

"I scared myself." He looked away. "I don't want to be that guy anymore. I have to go back and say goodbye. From here on out, I'm on the straight and narrow, and with you. I just have things to settle there, okay?"

"Okay."

He reached out and touched my face again. "If I don't make it home tomorrow night, I want you to know that I love you, okay? I want you to know that I don't regret this summer, that I've loved every minute of fighting with you and being with you. That I love you and your family for taking me in and giving me this second chance."

My vision blurred at his confession and the possibility of his not returning home from his trip.

"Don't." I struggled to speak. "Don't say that. You're gonna come back to me, okay? Promise me."

"I want to."

"Then promise me!"

For a moment, he just stared at me, and the terror of whatever he was planning scared me deeper than his getting arrested. "I promise, Nandy. I love you."

My heart swelled, and I didn't want any more words to be exchanged between us.

Tyson read my soul, and he knew not to speak but to act.

He leaned down to kiss me and I reached for the hem of his T-shirt, wanting it off him.

Tyson caged me against the floor, his arms on either side of me as he stared down at me. "No."

"Please," I begged.

"Say it," he demanded. "I need to hear you say it."

I was afraid to tell him how I felt, but I knew he felt the same. "I love you, Tyson."

My words must have been magic to his ears as he lowered himself to meet my body, and his hands seized my waist as he positioned himself between my thighs. Our kisses were impatient as rushed hands went about grasping at clothing, trying to rid our bodies of any material. It was like a race to see who could get the other completely naked the fastest. In the end, Tyson won, and the sensation of being nude felt completely daunting for the first time.

Lying naked beneath him, I felt shy and nervous. His gaze roamed my body as he took his time to become acquainted with all that I had. His exploration made me feel like a virgin again, like what we were about to do was so new to me that I was almost afraid. But I wanted him too much to be truly scared.

I reached out to touch him and he caught my hand, interlocking our fingers, the contact instantly warm. Skin against skin. We were like a dark chocolate Reese's. I liked the sight of us.

"It's okay," I told him. "We'll be safe, okay?"

Tyson nodded, probably wanting all of me just as I wanted all of him. He kissed the back of my hand before releasing me and removing the last of his clothing and gathering a condom from his wallet.

I watched him hover above me and gain his stance between my thighs. Anticipation prickled all over my skin as I let out a breath, if only to release some of the butterflies. All the while Tyson kept his eyes on me, eating up my nerves the longer he stared at me.

And then, without warning, he rocked into me.

Tyson leaned down and gave me a quick kiss. "You okay?" he breathed out.

I could only manage a nod, my breathing already jagged the more he moved.

Soon, we formed a motion, a rhythm, and got into a groove as our movements intensified.

It was better than it would've been at the beach or in my bedroom, because I loved him, and I knew he loved me.

I clutched the sheets around my body as Tyson leaned over and kissed my shoulder. We lay side by side under the fort, closer than ever. I felt giddy suddenly, as if everything was finally okay and settled. Well, almost.

"Hey," I said. "I want to apologize for how I behaved in the beginning. Even if we didn't end up here, I wish I'd been nicer. I'm sorry."

Tyson lifted his head from his pillow, at first slowly beginning to smile, but soon he was laughing at me.

It made me feel self-conscious. "What?"

Tyson grinned like an idiot. "Yo, that was all it took to get you to shut up and be nice for once?"

I bit at my lip as I reached out to nudge him. "Why did we even wait?"

"I should've just taken you down at the door, huh?"

I giggled. "Maybe."

Tyson caressed my cheek. "Nah, I think this was perfect. It was more."

It was.

"We're going to be fine," I insisted with extra hope.

Tyson nodded. "We'll go and enjoy senior year."

"I don't want it to just stop there. I want it to go beyond." He had disappeared ten years ago, but now he was back, and I wanted it to be for good and for always.

"We'll go off to college and later marry and all that, huh?"

"You'll be a great American writer and I'll work for my mom's company."

"And kids?"

"We'll have two kids, and a big house that I'll decorate."

"Two girls?"

"No, a boy and a girl."

He seemed to agree after a moment. "We'll teach them young that they're kings and queens and have all the potential in the world. And you're going to learn to braid so our daughter can run around with beads in her hair."

My eyes watered the more we spoke. "And we'll have to adopt from Thailand, in honor of Jordy."

Tyson wiped away my tears. "Definitely."

"You're going to come back, okay? What's a queen without her king?" I asked as I eyed him sheepishly.

He came and pressed his forehead to mine, staring into my eyes. "I love you."

"I love you," I told him. And I did, with everything in me.

39 | *TRICE*

In the beginning, when I was recovering, I'd considered killing myself. All I'd wanted was to be where she was, wherever she was.

I'd ignored her last request, wanting no part of it, until now.

When my mother died, I was given a letter she'd written well before she'd died, her last words. She'd known she was a goner, and that had upset me more than anything. It was like she'd always felt that way, always telling me that *I* would see a better future. That *I* deserved to be happy. I'd felt betrayed. Like all the private conversations we'd had late at night were lies. She had never intended to start a new life with me; she'd known he wouldn't let her, and she hadn't been willing to fight for it.

It had taken me a while to finally read her letter, and once I had, for the longest time, I'd done nothing. She had wanted me to find peace and happiness, to live to the fullest of my heart's content. But I was stubborn. So for months I'd left my bank account as it was, ignoring the sum of over fifty thousand dollars in it.

Some of it was my collection from boosting, and the rest came from my mother's life insurance.

It wasn't much, but I was willing to bargain with it to get Mexico out of town.

And then I'd be done with Lindenwood for good.

I showered in the pool house Saturday evening, preparing to start fresh. My mother had wanted the money to go toward good, and I couldn't think of anything better than freedom.

The sound of the shower curtain being pulled back shifted my attention. Nandy was standing there, dressed in a silk kimono.

"Before you go," she said with a coy grin.

In seconds, she was untying the string and dropping the kimono, revealing that she wasn't wearing anything beneath it. The sight of her naked body excited me instantly. Nandy could tell.

She stepped into the shower with me and closed the curtain behind herself.

"Going away present?" I joked.

"No," she said. "It's an early welcome home present."

Nandy lay on her stomach on my bed as I finished getting ready to go. She was wearing her kimono again with her feet kicked up in the air, eating a bowl of fruit. I almost threw caution to the wind and forgot the whole venture altogether.

"You could stay," Nandy said. "We could stay here, and like, do stuff."

I suppressed a smile. "Stuff?"

"Uh-huh." I watched her eat a piece of fruit, paying attention to the way her lips wrapped around the spear of pineapple before she took a bite. She knew she had me, and so, like the devil she was, she winked.

I had to go.

"Sounds promising, but you know I gotta do this," I told her.

Nandy made a face and set her fruit aside. She looked up at me. "Okay, if we make it in the long run as a couple—"

"*If*, huh?"

"—you're totally on cooking duty."

"You did all right, why just me?"

"Well, you're the writer, you'll be home."

"I never said I wanted to be a writer."

Nandy deadpanned, "Really, Tyson? You *just* wrote that story, or book for all I know."

"That was therapy. Besides, I might wanna be a basketball player."

Nandy wrinkled her nose. "No offense, but you're a bit… *much* for basketball."

I lifted a brow as I headed her way. "What are you trying to say?"

"Oh nothing, your build is just more football than basketball and—"

I took her down, lying on top of her and grasping at her sides.

Nandy giggled under me as she tried to push me off. "No, Tyson. No!"

With her thighs wrapped around me, I slid my hands up

her sides, enjoying her curves. "Did you just say no to me? Did you?"

Her giggles increased as well as the desire on her face. "What? You made a good breakfast. Can't take a compliment?"

My lips found hers and quieted her down. Kissing was one of the top things that could stop Nandy's mouth.

She knew I had to go, and for that she clung to me, kissing me deeper and tugging at my shirt to keep me in her grasp.

"Tyson," she whined when I resisted her power and pulled away.

"It'll be quick."

She pouted. "Like two hours, maybe even three."

I rolled my eyes. "I got business to get into, then I'm all yours. If you really wanna do me a favor, you'll stay here just like this and wait for me."

Nandy barely smiled. "Okay."

I stood from my bed and crossed over to my dresser, where I grabbed my composition book and walked it back over to Nandy.

"Maybe you can read this," I suggested. "I've been skimming it, and I'm pretty sure whenever I go to type it I'll be adding in more. Shit, it might be a novel or something when I'm through. Don't laugh, but I sorta feel accomplished. It's not a real book, but it's all my words, and I don't know, I just thought it was neat."

Nandy accepted the notebook. "You should feel accomplished. This is a lot." She sifted through the pages and admired my penmanship before going to the first page and beginning to read.

I leaned down to kiss her temple. "I love you."

She peeked at me. "You better."

I nudged her. "Say it back."

She chewed on her lip. "I'll say it when you get back."

It was just a simple trip, but I wanted to hear her say it just in case I got caught up. "Please?"

The look on her face almost made me freeze. She didn't want to say it, and I could tell she was putting up a front. Sure, she was letting me head back to Lindenwood—not that she had a choice—but her nonchalance was an act, and I could see in her eyes that she was afraid.

"Tyson, please." She lowered her gaze and fiddled with my book. "You're acting like something's going to happen. And I don't want to entertain the thought. You know how I feel, so come back and I'll say it, okay?"

As if a new life and fresh start weren't motivation enough, coming home to hear her say those words definitely inspired me more.

With one more kiss, I left her in the pool house and made my way outside.

Inside the main house, I discovered Shayne and Edi running around in sparkly dresses, giggling about something. Kyle sat out in the family room with Jordy on the sofa, awkwardly fidgeting as he took every other moment to peer at Shayne.

"Ty!" Shayne came over to me and squeezed my arm in an attempt for affection. "You coming to the Hook with us? Where's Nandy? She said she was going out to be with you."

"We're actually going to stay in and watch a movie," I said.

Shayne made a show to groan. "Lame!" She then flashed me a smile before facing Edi. "Come on! Let's go find some of Nandy's earrings to borrow!"

Together the terrible twosome raced out of the room to scavenge through Nandy's things.

Kyle came over to me and offered a nod, or maybe a gesture to get his hair out of his eyes. "Hey."

"So you guys are hanging out," I noted.

Kyle blushed. "Shayne said I did such a good job carrying their things yesterday at the beach that I can carry their purses at the club tonight."

I shook my head. "Hell no. Don't let her walk all over you. You gotta be more assertive, or she's never going to respect you."

Kyle chuckled and tugged on his collar. "I—I don't think I have it in me to be mean, you know, to her. Or anyone."

Not that it was a major problem, or a problem in general, but Kyle didn't have a tough bone in his body. He was right, he couldn't be mean, but he could be respected.

"Okay, when Edi gets down here you're going to tell her you're not holding her purse for her," I said.

Kyle was confused. "Okay, why?"

"You're going to say everything you wanna say to Shayne to Edi."

"But—"

"Listen to him," Jordy cut in as he stood from the sofa. "The dude's a chick guru."

Kyle blinked. "Even you have a girlfriend?"

"No, he's too young. He's just smart enough to get in now and stake his claim. That way, when they're of age, he's got first dibs," I replied.

"Sorta like you did with Nandy?" Kyle asked.

Jordy groaned loudly as he passed us by. "That's my sister!"

The girls could be heard coming back down the steps, and soon they were in our presence once more. I nudged Kyle to go on.

With his chest slightly puffed up, he walked over to Edi and stood firm. "Edi?"

She stopped comparing stolen goods with Shayne and faced the boy in front of her. "Yeah?"

"You look amazing tonight. That dress just compliments everything about your beauty."

Edi gushed and touched her chest. "Aww, thank you."

"Tonight, I don't want to hold your purse," Kyle said boldly. "I'd rather hold your hand."

Edi was surprised, as she looked to Shayne, to me, and then back to Kyle. And then she burst into laughter. "Sorry, Kyle, but not only would my brother fold you into a pretzel for talking to me, I just can't get into a *chico blanco flaco*, sorry."

She breezed past him with a small frown before exiting the room.

Kyle appeared defeated.

I said nothing, I just waited for it.

Shayne came over, and instead of walking by Kyle, she took his hand. Even in her heels, she couldn't reach his tall height. She was only five-two. On her toes, she swiftly pressed her lips to his cheek before standing back. "'Stop acting so small. You are the universe in ecstatic motion.' Rumi said that, never forget. Chin up, you did good. Kyle. I'll be in the car."

Shayne let go of his hand and followed Edi out of the room.

Kyle raised his hand to his cheek, as if to seal her kiss there. He faced me, eyes wide, smiling goofily. "She said my name."

"And now you gotta buy her a Sprite with a splash of cranberry, the only way to get it pink, and dance with her."

"Dude, I don't know what to say. But thank you," Kyle said, sounding both radiant and serious. "Before you got here, none of these guys ever really spoke to me. Now *the* girl, the dream, just said my name and kissed my cheek. Trice, I'm really glad you're here, and I'm glad you decided to stick by me rather than falling in with Chad and his friends."

It had been a gamble I'd won out on. "Nah, I'm just glad you're you, Kyle. This night is yours, man, go and get your girl."

Kyle seemed to be puffing his chest out. "I feel like a man now. I think I just grew a chest hair."

I chuckled. "I've got something to get into, but I expect to hear results tomorrow."

Kyle agreed, and together we headed out of the house. Out front, the boys—Ashley, Warhol, Matt, and Travis—surrounded the Catalano driveway as they talked shit back and forth. Kyle joined them, and I stepped over for a quick hello.

"Would you rather hook up with Mrs. McGreery or Ms. Foster?" Ashley asked, causing the boys to groan in disgust.

From summer school, I knew Mrs. McGreery was pushing a million. Ms. Foster had to be the better choice.

Matt frowned. "Why do I get the tough question?"

Warhol shoved him. "Quit stallin'."

Matt twisted his face. "Ms. Foster."

"Dude, she smells like she bathes in cat piss!" Travis frowned.

"At least she's young."

"This is what you're doing?" I was stupid enough to ask them.

Ashley shrugged. "Pretty much. We're heading to the club, but for now it's Warhol's turn."

"Give me something good, Catalano," Warhol said.

Travis rubbed his hands together, smiling deviously. "Would you rather catch your parents having sex, or...your grandma masturbating?"

Warhol's face twisted in revulsion. "Is death an option, because I'm totally all for that."

Travis shook his head. "Nah, you gotta choose. Your mom's got like eight kids. You know she's a freak."

Warhol shoved Travis. "She has one more than your mom, asshole."

"Yeah, but my mom had one set of twins. Yours had two because she was really getting it in."

Warhol went on to mumble some profanities Travis's way. "Why are we even friends?"

Travis flashed a crooked smile. "'Cause I'm funny."

"God, how long, and how much do I see?"

"At least a minute and you see *everything*."

"What position are my parents in?"

Travis shrugged. "I don't know, your mom looks like a doggy-style kind of girl."

Warhol almost gagged. "My parents."

The better question was, why was I friends with any of them? They had an odd way of having fun. Harmless, but odd indeed.

"I'm heading out," I said as I backed away and started for my ride.

"Wait up," Travis said as he jogged over to me. "You sure about this?"

"Yeah, I'm sure."

"My car's still up for grabs."

"I appreciate it, I really do, but I got it covered."

Travis stood back. "A'ight then, hurry back. Matt was at the store earlier and saw a girl who looks like Rihanna and heard her talking about going to the Hook tonight. I'm so in there."

I managed to smile. "That your dream girl or something?"

"Nah, I really don't have a specific type of dream girl, just as long as she's fine as hell and on birth control. Although, there's just something about black girls with green eyes that gets me every time. I swear that's my kryptonite."

I was with him on not having a specific type. Of course, black girls in general were my type, whether their eyes were green, hazel, or the common brown. "I don't know about the eye color thing, but I feel you on the birth control part."

"Yeah, I mean—" He stood back and crossed his arms. "You hit?"

"This is not a conversation I'm comfortable having, Trav."

He chuckled and raised his hands. "Fair enough. Congrats, though. You just hurry up. We have things to get into tonight and celebrate."

"Yeah, you get to that and just pray the girl don't end up looking like Deebo from *Friday* or some shit."

Travis smirked and held up a middle finger. "Matt knows me and my taste, thank you very much."

We did our little handshake, and I climbed in my car and drove off.

Lindenwood would always be a part of me, good or bad. It just was. This town made me, and I couldn't forget that, even if I was now choosing to turn my back on it and reside in Pacific Hills. I would never truly fit in there. I would probably always be that tough guy from the 'Wood to the ignorant, but as long as my people rocked with me, that was all that mattered.

Kyle's parents liked me. Travis's parents loved me and had dubbed me a good influence on their wild son. In fact, everyone's parents seemed to like me. Life in the Hills wasn't as bad as I'd thought it would be when I was first shipped there.

The best part, though, was Nandy and the Smiths. I hadn't

thought I'd fall in love with her. I hadn't thought I'd love her family as my own when I'd stepped foot in their door. I'd never thought I'd want something for myself, but I did. With Nandy, and just for myself in general. Waking up each day felt like a challenge, one I was becoming happy to accept. Maybe I would be a writer, or maybe I wouldn't. Who knew, but I needed to push forward. There was no going back, and there was no standing in place.

Shayne's little Rumi quote caused me to smile as I pulled into Khalil's driveway and turned off my car.

Prophet looked at all of us as brothers, and like him, I viewed Khalil as a younger brother, even if we were the same in age.

He came to the door a moment after I rang the bell. He was dressed in a large baseball jersey and black pants, a gold chain around his neck, and I knew he probably was sporting the gold bottom grill he liked to wear in his mouth.

"Yo, what's up," Khalil said as he greeted me with a hug.

"Can we talk?"

Khalil nodded as he stepped outside and shut the door behind himself. "What's goin' on?"

"How are things with Mexico?" I hadn't spoken to Money since our phone call, and I hadn't spoken to anyone about my plan.

Khalil sighed. "Prophet wants to lay low for a while. He's talking about school and how I should apply myself more. You know Prophet." He rolled his eyes and waved me off.

His words humored me for a moment. He never wanted to listen to anyone's guidance. I let it go.

I reached into my jeans, procured the envelope I was carrying and handed it over. "Here, it's for you, and your mom."

Khalil accepted the envelope and looked inside, his eyes growing. "Damn, fam, how much is this?"

I shoved my hands into my pockets. "Five thousand."

Khalil looked through the money anyway. "Word?"

"And my phone number and address are in there too, in case you ever need me. The Smiths don't judge. If you ever need a place, they'd take care of you. They took care of me." He was the only one I was reaching out to, the only one I wanted to save. Because of Prophet, and because Khalil needed it. "If things get tight, I want you to have that money."

Khalil gave a lopsided smile as he tried to hand it back. "My mom is doing better, T, man. I don't steal because we're poor or some shit. I do it because... I don't know, that's just what we do."

I knew he wasn't hard off, but whenever his mother was sick, which seemed often, she lost hours at work and money on her paycheck, making it hard to cover their bills. Khalil's father had stepped out when he was a kid, and it was just them two, though sometimes his grandparents would help. I almost wanted to take him with me to Pacific Hills, to show him a better life and to have him prevail.

"Keep the money, in case she gets sick again," I said.

"She quit her old job," Khalil said. "She's at the hospital now, making better money. You sure about this?"

"Positive."

"Good looking." He stared at the money some more. "Ay, can I buy some jewelry?"

Dude really had a thing for that flashy shit. I never could get into accessories.

"Yeah, man," I said with a shrug. "But save some of it, in case."

"Definitely. All gold, no diamonds. Gotta leave that to the motherlands."

"You just don't go around bragging. I don't wanna hear about you getting jumped. You know Money and them would bring havoc on whoever touched you."

We were like brothers, and if someone ever touched one of us, they were going down. Khalil was as tall and nearly as big as me, but I wouldn't put it past anyone to try him if he came around with expensive shit.

"Nah, that ain't me, T, man. Prophet would put a boot in my ass. You tryna come through, though? Mom's in here cooking up a late dinner before she heads off to work, and you know she can throw down."

I shook my head. "I just wanted to come and give you that. Stay out of trouble, 'Lil."

He slapped my hand and we did our group's handshake for the final time. I gave him a brief hug before beginning to go down the front walk.

"Ay, Trice," Khalil called from behind me. "What if I don't have an emergency, you know?" He raised the envelope in the air for emphasis.

"Call me up and come through anytime you want. It's a different world there, but it's not so bad."

"I don't think I could make it in the Hills. I'ma need me a hood girl with attitude every day of the week before one of them bougie chicks."

I managed to laugh, thinking of Nandy and some of her friends. If Nandy could hang out in Lindenwood, I was sure Erica, Edi, and Shayne could, too.

"We'll see. Stay up, okay?"

"Always. See you later, man."

I got back in my ride, the gears turning in my head. The

drive to Mexico's wasn't long enough, and the aura for this run felt far graver than any of the others. This time was different. This time was all or nothing.

The garage looked vacant when I pulled my car to a stop in front of it. Usually the place held a few lights when we were delivering cars.

The sign on the front door said the place was closed, and I almost believed that Mexico really had closed up shop and forgotten the deal. But that would be too simple.

The front door was unlocked, causing me to pause and wonder if something was up. Through the glass door the front room was dark, going along with idea of the garage being closed.

I headed inside, finding the lobby empty as well as the air. There was no talk, no music, and no sounds of cars being worked on.

Something didn't feel right.

I stepped around the front desk and went back into the garage area. Instantly, I froze.

Mexico lay on his back on the ground. From the blood pooling beneath him, I knew he was dead.

Still, I went to check on him, just to be sure. Had my neighbors assumed I was dead and left me that way, I wouldn't be alive now.

Feeling for Mexico's pulse, I found that he wasn't lucky. He was dead.

Shit.

"Ain't no saving him." Money's voice made me jump, and I looked up to see him stepping from the shadows.

I shook my head. "I had it covered."

Money tossed me a Cheshire cat smile. "Really?"

Gazing at him, I didn't want to be right, but I knew.

I hung my head, staring at Mexico. "How long have you been planning this, Money?"

"I thought about taking you out when you first came back to town and was acting all brand-new. But I really started thinking about it when you brought that girl around and took up for her." The smile was gone and the full menace was on display.

Something in Khalil's earlier words had tipped me off. He acted like Mexico hadn't threatened him, just like Prophet, which made me think it was a hoax. I hadn't wanted to think that of Money. We should have been beyond that.

Looking at Mexico, I guessed it wasn't like that at all.

"Get up, Trice. No man deserves to die down on his knees," Money ordered as he pulled a gun on me.

A chill ran down my spine as I got to my feet. I'd suspected Money was playing me, but to pull on a gun on me? Would he kill me?

This cut deeper than my father.

I'd expected Tyson to be evil, but Money, my friend?

"This is how you wanna do this?" I asked as I raised my hands.

"What, you think you was just gon' ride off into the sunset and live happily-ever-after down there?" Money snorted. "They change the name of the town to Tyson's Hill or some shit? Roll out the welcome carpet?"

"It's not like that!" I snapped.

"Fuck it ain't. You come through here each trip actin' all holier-than-thou. Fuck you, Trice. I wanted to pop you so bad after that first visit. Everybody thinks Trice is so special. He's the one. He's gonna make it. Nobody speaks that shit about me, Pretty, Read, or Khalil. Why you so special?"

"I'm not." I hadn't asked to be "the One" for my town or my friends; they just picked me to be.

"Damn right you not. You just like everyone else. A stupid fool destined to live and die here. I knew you'd try to be all loyal and come back here. Shit, I almost expected you to call Prophet and the jig be up, but of course not. You wanted to save everybody and be Mr. Hero."

I couldn't lie and say that things were going to be okay. He had killed Mexico, and shit would only hit the fan from there.

"We were brothers," I said.

Money came closer, nearly right up on me, aiming at my chest. "We grew up together. You remember all that? All those times we would sneak into strip clubs, steal from the gas station, and stay up watching movies? You remember all that, T?"

Sweat was beading on my neck with the uncertainty of how this would play out. The last time I'd been in front of a gun, it hadn't ended well. "We thought we owned the streets."

"We had a favorite movie we would watch every time we got together. We saw ourselves in the characters, even though we knew how it ended for them." He aimed at my head. "And this is just like that. You know how it ends for you, Trice."

"You think you O-Dog?"

Money nodded. "Hell yeah, I do."

O-Dog's character fit Money to a T. Money was reckless and cruel, just like O-Dog. I knew who Money pictured me as, and at times, growing up, watching the movie, I saw myself in Caine's character, too. But now things were different. Now I had something to live for. I had someone waiting on me at home. I had something to fight for.

"O-Dog wouldn't do this."

"In my movie, he would," Money said through gritted

teeth. "Everybody's gotta die someday, and today just happens to be your day. I changed my mind. Get down on your knees."

I refused to do such a thing. "I'm not going to beg you for my life, Money. So just shoot me and get it over with, because it's not going down like that."

"I'll tell you *exactly* how it's going to go down. I'ma put a bullet through ya head and send you to Tyson and your mom. I'ma mourn you just like everyone else around here, and wonder where it all went wrong. And then, I'ma go to Pacific Hills and fuck yo' bitch."

He'd had me when he mentioned my mother, but I lost it when he addressed Nandy.

In seconds, I'd knocked the gun out of his hand and taken him down to the ground. Blow after blow, I fed my fist into his face, releasing all of the pent-up anger I'd stored for months.

Money struggled to get me off him and to swing back, but he was no match for the rage inside of me. His blood was hot on my fists and it soon caked his face.

I knew if I didn't stop, I'd kill him, and as much as the situation called for it, I couldn't.

I fell back, scooting away from him and breathing hard. "It didn't have to be like this."

Money groaned, coughing up blood and touching at his face.

I stood, unsure what to do. The right thing and the wrong thing weren't clear. Leaving him felt wrong, but so did taking him to a doctor. Either way, we were in a world of shit with Mexico's body lying in the room.

Peering over at Mexico, innocent and dead, I knew that leaving this town was for the best.

Right or wrong, Money needed a doctor and the law.

I turned to step over to him and stopped immediately.

He had another gun.

"Fuck you," he snarled harshly at me as he could barely hold the gun in his hand.

There was no speech this time, he just pulled the trigger, once, twice, and fell back.

There was no pain, just numbness, but assessing the wounds, I knew I was a goner.

I could hear my heartbeat fading in my ears as I sank to my knees, already beginning to die.

Blinking, feeling the heaviness coming on, I wondered if I was going anywhere. Mostly, I wondered if she'd be there, waiting for me, with open arms.

40 | *Nandy*

Tyson was an incredible writer, I discovered as I lay in his bed in the pool house. Page after page, his story pulled me in.

The dark picture he painted when it came to his character Tyrin's youth and his city was both haunting and welcoming. This fictional world of violence, alliances, and hopelessness was enough to make me gasp and fear for the outcome. But then, there was his friendship with the girl from the suburbs of Pacific Heights. It gave me hope. Queen was her name, and when he was with her, a ray of light would shine so bright, eliminating all the darkness of his hometown, Oakwood, that had seeped into him.

There was a lot I didn't know about Tyson, and while this was a work of fiction, it was easy to read between the lines.

I sat up in bed, clutching the composition book in my hands, envious of Tyson's talent.

His voice was so strong, detached, yet rich with the pain of his upbringing and losses.

Deep down, even though I knew he loved me, I wondered if I could ever reach him, if I could ever touch his soul enough to ease all the bad and give him true hope. If I could—

"Nandy!"

A crazed cry shot through the air and I dropped Tyson's book.

I recognized the voice as belonging to my mother, but it was the urgency and desperation in her tone that alerted me that something was amiss.

Under my kimono I was completely naked, but I had no time to be ashamed or guilty as my mother rushed into the pool house. The tears running from her eyes and the worry etched on her face startled me, and somehow, I just knew.

"Trice has been shot!"

My heart swelled in my chest, and a fierce pain sent my hand clutching at my collarbone.

No.

My eyes drowned in a sea of sadness and I had to blink it away to see my mother. "I–is…is he dead?"

"I don't know," she let out as she hung in the doorway, seeming too overcome with shock to move any closer.

They got him.

He'd gone back to that awful place, and they got him.

I hung my head. "No."

There was no time to fully break down as my father entered the pool house next. "We gotta go."

Jordy was behind him, looking worried as he studied our mother and then me. "What's going on? Where's Trice?"

My father took charge as my mother began to weep. Just like me, my mom was as tough as they came, and she wasn't one for tears or weakness. But this broke her, just like it was breaking me.

"Nandy Alyssa," my father said, his tone clipped of any emotion. "Go inside and put some clothes on. We have to go, now."

I did as told, finding myself in my bedroom pulling on a T-shirt and jeans combo along with a pair of sneakers. I yanked my hair into a ponytail and covered my head with a Cross High baseball cap to conceal myself even more.

As I reached out to close my bedroom door behind me, I could see that my hand was shaking.

Oh God, he's been shot.

I struggled to keep it together as I quickly made my way down to the first floor, where my family was waiting.

The whole way to the hospital in Lindenwood, I didn't speak. All I could do was sit and remember our summer together. I'd been so wrong about Tyson, misjudging him due to his rough roots. In the beginning, I'd been so consumed with my image and vapid world. I wasn't sure where I was headed in life, or what my future held. Tyson, he'd been sure of only one thing: that he'd die before he was twenty-one.

Somehow, we'd fallen in love. But before we could keep it, Lindenwood rang to collect the boy who'd come to mean so much to me.

It had all been so fleeting.

Tyson Trice wasn't a thug from Lindenwood. He was a knight. *My* knight. My summer knight. And I loved him.

At the Lindenwood General Hospital, we had barely parked before we all rushed out of the car. My father took the lead, storming across the parking garage to the nearest entrance.

It was like a maze, finding our way to the emergency room. My mother was silent, shaking, and somehow I had the sense to hold Jordy's hand, squeezing extra tight to keep him close and safe.

In the emergency room, we came to a stop, momentarily surprised at the sight of Travis Catalano arguing with some doctor carrying a clipboard.

"Sir, for the last time, only family is allowed to know what's going on with patients," the tired doctor explained.

Travis, a bit delirious and frazzled, got in the doctor's face. "Are you fuckin' blind? I'm his brother, now tell me how he is!"

"Travis." My father stepped forth to deal with the situation.

Travis moved to where my mother, Jordy, and I were standing. He looked unlike I'd ever seen him before. His shirt was stained with blood, and the sight of it sent my hand to my mouth to keep the sobs from escaping.

"What happened?" my mother managed to get out.

Travis hung his head, his face contorting in pain. "I don't know, Max, I don't know." He gestured toward my father and the doctor. "They rushed him into surgery, and they won't let me know what's going on."

Travis was strong, and yet before us, I could see him breaking. His eyes were wet, but he didn't cry. Instead he punched the nearest wall, fuming as his face burst red. "They won't let me see him!"

I threw my arms around him, knowing we could lean on each other, two halves of a whole.

"He's going to be okay, Nandy," Travis swore as he held me tight.

An alarm went off, and collectively we lifted our heads.

"Code blue. Code blue in the ICU, all units report to the ICU," a monotone voice announced over the PA system.

A set of doctors rushed by.

My knees gave out as I screamed. "No!"

Travis kept a strong hold on me, saying something encouraging in my ear, but it didn't reach me.

Tyson.

They took Tyson.

He wasn't coming back.

No.

41 | *TRICE*

My house wasn't boarded up anymore. It looked brand-new. The grass was green, healthy, and freshly cut. Flowers bordered the front porch. I could hear birds chirping, but I couldn't see any. The rush of the wind was the only other sound that I could hear.

It felt like I'd been standing in front of my house for years, just waiting for something to happen.

As I watched, the front door opened and a boy ran down the steps with a big toy truck in his little hands. He was grinning wide and happy, racing to the front lawn to play.

The next person to come out the front door was my mother.

She walked down the steps and looked after the little boy before facing me, her expression solemn.

I couldn't breathe. She was here and alive. I stared at her, watching her look at me.

Mom.

"Well, I do believe you've been standing out here long enough," she said as she came over to me. She stood in front of me, admiring all that I was, it seemed.*

"You knew I was out here this whole time?" I asked.

She lifted a brow at my tone. "Yes, I did. Figured it'd do you right to suffer awhile for coming to see me so early."

I bowed my head, feeling ashamed. "I've done some things, Mom. Terrible things, illegal things, things you taught me better than."

She nodded. "I know. Here, I know everything. I'm not happy with you, Tyson. You knew better to get into that mess. To do those things with those boys. Even if it served a greater purpose, I wouldn't have been happy with you. You know better."

"I just wanted to get us a better life."

"I never had a chance, but you did."

Her defeated tone soured my mood. "Everything happens for a reason, huh?"

"Who knows, maybe I died so you can live."

"Bullshit, Mom."

She reached out and smacked me hard across the back of the head. "Who do you think you're talking to? And another thing, who raised you to speak to your elders the way you have? If you could feel pain, I'd knock you out of your shoes."

She was both mad and right. I didn't feel pain and, looking down at my chest, I wasn't even bleeding anymore. Wherever we were, pain didn't exist. Or maybe it did, because even standing with my mother, the woman I'd missed so greatly over the past eight months of my life, I wanted and needed someone else.

"I've been angry with you, with myself, for what happened," I said.

"You're not the only person angry right now, Tyson."

I could only imagine how Nandy felt in the aftermath of my death. "I was just trying to fix things for the boys, as a means to say good-bye."

My mother shook her head. "Prophet was right, you know. You should've left this place good and alone."

I sighed. "It's a good thing I'm dead, because I would never hear the end of it from him."

My mother narrowed her eyes. "Is that what you want? To be dead and here, like me? You're only seventeen, you haven't even lived your life yet—you haven't completed your education, you've barely fallen in love, and I want that for you. I want to see you happy more than anything."

It was hard to answer, so I didn't.

In the yard, the little boy went at it with his toy truck. There were no other kids, and yet he seemed as happy as could be. From his dark skin and familiar face, I got a sense of nostalgia.

"That's me?" I asked.

My mother softened. "My little boy."

No one else was in sight. "Is he here, too?"

My mother barely blinked. "Sometimes, when I want him to be. Mostly it's just you and me."

"How could you want him here?"

"Here, things are different. He's different—he's the man I fell in love with. We're a family. We have a chance. At one time, he was the love of my life. He gave me you."

I wanted to understand, but I couldn't. "He took you from me. He separated us."

"And now here we are, huh? Together again. Are you happy?"

It was like she was digging to get the words out of me, and I didn't have the heart to utter them. I stalled, once more examining wherever it was that we were. It was our old street, full of our neighboring houses, and they were all well-kept like ours. No one was outside, and there was no sign of another person. Not even a car driving by or parked in a driveway. It was just the three of us in this little world of Lindenwood before.

"Where are we?" I asked.

"Where I'm happy. Where it's just you and me, and things are good." She observed the younger me. "This is where I get to see you as a normal boy who has a chance to be happy."

"So, this what we're doing from now on?" I wanted to know.

My mother frowned and shook her head. "No, this is what I'm doing. You're going back, where you belong."

"Mom."

She reached out and touched me, feeling more real than ever. "It's okay. I'm not hurt or upset. I know that this isn't what you want anymore."

Her words were true and omniscient. Still, I felt a flinch of guilt. "I'm sorry."

"It's okay to move on. It's okay to want more."

"How do you know how I feel?"

"You feel guilty for wanting to be with her more than me. You feel awful, because you want to live and to love her, and not be dead and gone like me. You feel bad, because you've healed and are moving forward and found a reason to live. You feel sorry, because you're choosing her over me. It's okay, Tyson. I want you to be happy, and if it's with Nandy, so be it."

She knew me and what I wanted more than anything, and it hurt, because it still felt like I was betraying her. "I didn't want to be happy. I didn't want a life without you."

"I know, baby. But you were meant for more than this. You've got quite a life ahead of you. Don't lose it now."

"You think I could've been happy here?"

She looked at the little boy playing with his truck in the grass. "You are."

This was the goodbye I'd never gotten before. It was rewarding as much as it hurt. "I love you."

"And I'll always love you." She wrapped her arms around my middle and hugged me close.

Holding her back, I felt peaceful. "Goodbye, Mom."

"No." She leaned back and peered up at me, smiling softly. "I'll see you later. Much later."

Blinking my eyes open, I came back to reality. I'd had that dream every night since being shot. Each time, I would stand there and watch the house and wonder where I was and what was going on. This was the first time I'd seen and spoken to my mother. Something deep down told me it was going to be the last. That it was the goodbye that I had never gotten, and now that I'd gotten it, I had to do as she wanted and move on.

Surveying my surroundings, I found that I was still in the hospital. The left side of my chest throbbed slightly.

For as long as I lived, I was going to make an effort to never get shot again.

"Shit," I let out as I sat up in bed, then winced at the dull pain in my shoulder.

Movement to my right caused me to look over and discover Parker. He had the newspaper in his hands and immediately set it aside at the sound of me waking up.

In the doorway, I caught sight of my doctor stepping into the room.

"Trice, hey, how you feeling today, buddy?" He greeted me with a big smile as he came to the foot of my bed. He was the same doctor I'd had the first time I'd been here.

"Slightly shot," I told him.

Parker sighed, and the doctor—Dr. Lehman—chuckled.

He gazed at his clipboard. "Don't worry, Mr. Smith, it's all right here—recovering from a gunshot wound comes with a side effect of sarcasm. Perfectly normal."

He was joking, but Parker wasn't laughing.

In the past week, as I'd drifted in and out of consciousness, it had become clear that Parker's patience had been tested. He was tired and upset, and each interaction with him showed me that more and more. He'd stayed by my side, however, and carried out my wishes for no visitors outside of family.

The first time I'd woken up, I'd noticed a poster with an inspirational writing quote hanging on the wall, a toy type-writer on the nightstand beside my bed, and that the blinds had been pulled back to let in sunlight. All of it was a sign that Nandy had been in my room, decorating to make me comfortable.

But I hadn't seen her.

According to Parker, the first time I was awake and speaking, Nandy wasn't at the hospital long after my surgery. He wasn't sure if she'd come back, either.

I didn't want to see anyone then.

I'd almost died, according to Dr. Lehman. I remembered sirens and loud voices all bombarding me. In my blurred vision, I'd managed to make out Travis's face beside me as we were moving. Later, I realized we'd been taken to the hospital and his words of my being all right were the last I'd heard before I'd been taken to surgery.

They hadn't been sure I was going to make it. I'd had an open chest wound. There were lots of tubes and a ventilation machine, I saw during one of my many bouts of conscious-ness. Dr. Lehman and his team had had to operate to close my chest. I wasn't too sure of the details; I just knew that I had Travis to thank for my survival. Had he not been there, or if he'd come later, I would've died.

Now, I sat up in my hospital bed, my arm in a sling and my chest sore from the stitches. I was alive, but barely breathing.

Where was she?

Dr. Lehman went over my paperwork with me, discussing how I was recovering and my vitals. I wasn't listening. I was just waiting for him to finish and go so I could ask Parker what I really wanted to know.

"You're going to be fine, Trice. You're very lucky to be alive, do you know that?" he said as he stood staring at me. "I expect you to make a full recovery, just like last time, although it'll be a little longer before you can participate in any sports."

It wasn't like I was an athlete anyway, but I knew school was going to be a bitch. Not just from the wound, but from the stares alone. If anyone had been afraid of me before, they were going to be terrified now.

If Parker let me back into his home.

"Just do me and everyone else a favor and try not to get shot again, okay?" Dr. Lehman said after discussing rehab and my healing with Parker and me.

I managed to smirk. "I'm not sure I know anyone else who wants to shoot me, so I'll try to be on my best behavior, Doc."

Wednesday, I'd spoken to the police about what happened. I barely knew the clean version, and there was no way in hell I was going to incriminate myself with the truth. I tried to play forgetful, mentioning only remembering leaving home and seeing my friends, and then stopping by Khalil's.

I feigned cluelessness as I brought up needing to see Mexico about a car issue, and told the officers that it was fuzzy from there. They said my story matched Travis's, which was a surprise, because I'd yet to hear Travis's story and what he'd been doing at the garage.

I told the cops that Mexico had been lying there dead, and

before I could call for help, Money attacked me. He had been in the hospital for a few stitches and was now in lockup for Mexico's murder. Who knew if Money would come out and bring us all down with him for our whole operation?

I was still holding my breath on that.

Dr. Lehman smiled at my sarcasm once more before leaving me to Parker.

I faced him. "Is she here?"

He shook his head. "No, Trice. This hasn't been easy for her."

I looked elsewhere. It wasn't easy for Nandy? I knew there was truth to what Parker was saying, but still, her absence hurt.

"I pray you never see a day where you have children and you have to watch them break down like I had to watch mine," Parker went on. "Jordy and Nandy, they didn't take this too well, Trice. I want you to think about that and carry it with you. I'm not buying Travis's story, and despite the fact that the police do, I'm willing to bet something else was going on. You're grounded."

His words turned me back around. He was joking, right? "Where am I going to go?"

Parker stood from the chair and walked around my bed to the window. "For starters, you're coming home, to Pacific Hills. I was going to give you a choice between my banning you from coming to Lindenwood and being grounded, but then, I'm sure you wouldn't like the idea of not seeing your friends."

"My *friend* shot me," I said.

Nothing had changed. My goodbye with Khalil was the final goodbye. If anything, Money had made it even easier to choose to remain away. To take Prophet's and Nandy's advice.

"What were you doing at an auto garage in the middle of the night?" Parker glanced back at me. "Tell me the truth."

I wanted to, but what did it matter?

What did any of it matter?

All I wanted to do was get back to her and she wasn't even here.

"I'm sorry," I said. "It was reckless and stupid, and I'm sorry I wasted your time in trying to fix and save me. I'm sorry for the pain I've caused you."

"So that's it? You came here to see a friend, and then you went to the garage?"

Without blinking, I nodded. "Yes. Money came out of nowhere."

Parker regarded me with suspicion. He eyed me like the father he was, one who was serious and compassionate. Willing to punish me and help me at the same time.

He wasn't like my father.

I could've left it there, with him in the dark. But I wasn't ungrateful for the time I'd spent with him and the Smiths. Parker was every bit a part of my second chance, and lying felt unfair.

"Say that there was more, that I was doing something that wouldn't fare well with the police, what would you say? Where would that leave things between Nandy and me?" I asked.

Parker became solemn as he shoved his hands into his pockets. "First, I would like to know if this is the end of the unspeakable activity. Next, I would like to know if my daughter was involved in any way. And last, I would like to know the extent of what you were doing before I can make a judgment call. Are you going to need a lawyer?"

"Right now, I don't think so. I went to the garage clean.

There's nothing they can put on me that's out of the ordinary. On paper, it looks like attempted murder," I said. "I don't know about motive for Mexico, but Money was jealous of me. He was angry I got out and that people expected more for me. He set me up."

Parker began to pace. Everything about Parker was white-collar and by the book. He worked in an office all day designing commercial aircraft, and was a loving husband and father by night. I felt guilty for bringing him in on my troubles. If this was my third chance, I wanted to go all in and not lie.

"Start there," Parker said. "You and I will discuss the not-so-legal bits of what you were doing there, but as far as the police are concerned, you were there for the mechanic and your jealous friend assaulted you."

"He called me last Thursday," I said. "The phone number was different. I realized it at the last moment. I didn't want to think that he could go there."

Parker took in this information. "He probably bought a prepaid phone. Either way, we can work on the setup angle to tell the police. The police are saying the mechanic had been dead for a while, so if you can get the kid you visited to give your whereabouts before the murder, you can swing this. You just have to say Money got you to the garage that night, that he set up the appointment. It looks like he beat you there, and why would he do that unless something else was going on? Do you understand what I'm saying?"

"Yes," I said. With Mexico already dead, we were in a hole. Money wasn't psychic, he had reason to want me dead, but he wouldn't know where I would be that night unless we had spoken.

"The bigger problem is, what does Money know that can put you away?"

"He'd put us all away and further incriminate himself, but with this murder, he has nothing to lose," I said.

"Was it a chop shop?" Parker was able to come out and guess.

"Yes."

He rubbed at his jaw. "You better hope that garage is spotless and nothing can tie back to you. I think we can get out of this. You just have to hope Money doesn't talk."

Parker seemed on board and willing to help. The extent of his willingness to take care of me made me envy Nandy for how good of a father she had.

"I'm sorry," I said. "For all of this. Nandy and I were just hanging out and he called me out of the blue. I just thought something was wrong and my friends were in trouble. He was my friend, we grew up together. I never saw him turning on me."

"The thing about growing up in a rough environment and getting out, it's hard to go back, because there's always going to be someone mad that you made it and they didn't. We'll see that you get out of this unscathed."

"And Nandy?"

Parker sighed. "I'm sorry, Trice, she just hasn't taken this well. Max is trying to get her to come up here. She came here the first night, and it looked bad. I don't want to see her go through that ever again, you hear me? If you say this is it, let it be it, because I do *not* ever again want to see my daughter break down the way that she did over you."

"I just need to see her, to tell her I'm okay and that I love her," I told him.

"Max is doing her best," said Parker.

Getting shot wasn't the worst part. That was easy. *This* was hell.

Footsteps sounded into the hall, and Parker and I faced the door, where Travis was sneaking in.

He gave an awkward wave to Parker, who shook his head, still upset over it all. "I probably got a few minutes before they kick me out."

Parker began to leave. "I'll make sure you're cleared." He faced me as he headed for the door, raising his finger. "You're still grounded."

For some reason the gesture made me smile. "I'll be here."

Travis came to my side and sat down. He examined me and seemed spirited that was I okay. "Two in the chest, and you lived. Just don't go actin' like you 'Pac or some shit," he joked.

"I never wanna get shot again," I told him.

"I'll bet." He leaned over. "You okay? Parker seemed a little tense."

"I'm going to tell him the whole story," I confessed. "It could come in handy. For now, I need the story you told the cops. What were you doing there? You could've gotten killed."

Travis almost seemed to shrug. "Every Batman needs his Robin." He stared down at his hands. "I didn't feel right about you not taking my car. I thought it was all fishy that you had another idea. So I followed you to your friend's house, and then to the garage. I waited outside, and when I heard the shots, I panicked and dialed the cops before rushing in to see what happened.

"That other guy was passed out, and you were lying in a pool of blood. The scariest thing I've ever seen." He faced me, appearing serious. "I just kept thinking we should've gone together, that we should've had a plan. Maybe you wouldn't have gotten shot if I'd asked more questions. Maybe we would've figured out the setup sooner."

"You saved my life," I said.

He nodded as he scratched his jaw. "Don't go thinking I did it out of love or something. I did it for the street cred, you know? Imagine all the girls come time for school."

He was joking, but I was serious. "Thank you, Travis. I mean it. It's a crazy way to find out who your real friends are, but for what it's worth, it means a lot."

He reached out and pressed his fist to my good hand. "Just don't make this shit a habit, okay?"

I lay back. "I'm done dragging you and me into messes. I'm sure your parents are freaking out."

"Oh yeah. I'm in Lindenwood dodging bullets, trust me, my mom's a little on edge."

The clock on the wall read early afternoon. "How long have you been here?"

"I never left."

I sat back up. "Huh?"

"I told my dad I wasn't leaving Lindenwood until I was sure you were okay, which definitely pissed him off. But being that I detect that they like you more than me, I'm willing to bet that's why they even agreed to put me up here."

He'd stayed in Lindenwood for me?

It was sobering to find out that I had more support in the Hills than Nandy and the Smiths. I had Travis.

"I appreciate the gesture," I said. "How were the police?"

"I think they bought my story. I said you were stopping by a friend's and I followed behind in my car because you mentioned a mechanic you used to know who customized cars. I told the cops we were at the garage to see if I could drop off my car to get my rims done, and by the time we got there, it was too late, but you saw a light on and went to see if the mechanic was there. From there, it escalated to gunshots, and I called the cops."

Giving money to Khalil was the perfect alibi for going to see Mexico so randomly from Pacific Hills.

Maybe it would all work out.

"I just wish I knew where things are with Nandy." I sighed as I lay back and stared at the ceiling. How poorly could she be taking it that she didn't want to see me?

Travis frowned. "I only saw her that first night. It wasn't pretty. Smith's a tough girl, but this was a lot for her, man. You better be done with this place, because I don't think she can take any more."

"He is done." A third voice filled the room.

Prophet was standing in the doorway. His expression mirrored Parker's, tired and concerned, but also pissed off.

"Travis, this is Prophet. Prophet, this is—"

"We've met," Prophet said as he came over.

Travis gestured toward Prophet. "When they found out I saved you, they sorta demanded to put me up. My dad found a hotel, but Alma's pretty scary."

I faced Prophet. "That was nice of you."

"He saved one of our own," said Prophet. "It was nothing. You and I need to talk." He glanced at Travis. "Alone if you don't mind."

Travis agreed, standing and pounding his fist against mine once more before exiting the room.

Prophet took his seat and fixed me with a look that let me know I had a lecture coming. Between him and Parker, they both needed lessons on sympathy. Didn't a couple of bullet wounds warrant some ease?

"I told you to stay away," he said.

"I heard you, Prophet." I sighed.

"Yes, you *heard* me, but you didn't listen. Hearing and listening are two different things, my friend." He examined my sling. "I'm making this place a no-fly zone for you. If anyone catches you in town, they'll send you straight back to the Hills. There is nothing for you here but tragedy, Trice."

"Money set me up. He told me Mexico was blackmailing us."

"Khalil and I figured something was up. He called me as soon as you left, and it wasn't too hard to gather that something was going on."

"Do you think he'll talk?"

"About the operation?" Prophet sat back in his seat and picked at the loose threading on the arm. "You don't worry about Money. I've got that taken care of. He killed Mexico, and that's that, he's done. He can't put that on us."

"He can still take us down."

Prophet rolled his eyes as he sat up. "Here we go with the not listening thing again. I said leave it alone. I've got family where Money's going. He won't talk, or he won't live, it's that simple. Eye for an eye, Trice. He tried to kill you, and for what? Because he didn't take advantage of the same opportunities that you did? He didn't get shot and his family's not much, either. He could've easily bettered himself on his own.

"But he didn't. Instead he got mad and took it out on you. You have more to lose than him, and he wanted you to lose." Prophet shook his head. "I wish you had come to me."

"What if he would've come after you?"

"Better me than you. Besides, I have a gun, you don't. This is your third shot, do you really wanna mess it up?"

"I just want to stand up and walk to her." It was all that I could think about. Seeing Nandy, holding her, and telling her how I felt. Our last moment together wasn't enough. I needed more time and more memories.

I wanted to go to Cross High and let Lydia read the rest of my story, to see if I really had a shot at this writing thing. To see where the future lay for me. I couldn't do that in Lindenwood, and I'd known it before Money pulled the trigger.

"But she's not here," I said softly.

Prophet touched my hand. "Feisty's got strength, Trice. Don't count her out just yet."

It was hard to count on someone who wasn't there.

And then, she was.

Movement in the doorway caught my attention.

She looked as if she hadn't slept in days, but that wasn't what got me; it was her choice of attire: black. From the jacket she was wearing, to her dress, to her shoes, she was dressed in all black, as if she were attending a funeral.

Prophet noticed her as well and stood. "I have your number and we will talk weekly. Someone's gotta keep you in line." He patted my hand before meeting Nandy at the door. "He's not dead yet, Feisty."

Nandy took her bottom lip into her mouth, her eyes beginning to water as she looked at Prophet.

I should've been happy that we were alone once Prophet stepped out of the room, but I wasn't.

Why the hell was she wearing black?

Slowly and tentatively, Nandy approached the chair. She shrugged out of her jacket and revealed the dress she was wearing. A low-cut number that gave a nice look at her cleavage. It definitely wasn't funeral-appropriate. I wasn't sure if she were testing me or tempting me.

She sat in the chair, fiddling with her hands.

As happy as I was to finally see her, my temper flared at the signs before me.

Time ticked by, and I wasn't sure who would speak first. She sure as hell wasn't looking at me.

"Hey, Nandy." It came out fake and cheery, but at least I spoke.

Her eyes flickered to me. She definitely hadn't had a good night's sleep in days. "Are...are you going to grow your hair out again?"

Squeezing my eyes shut, I almost laughed. This was how it was. No other girl could get my blood boiling like Nandy Smith. She walked a fine line of turning me on, humoring me, consoling me, and making me want to strangle her so easily.

Were we really going to beat around the bush about my fucking hair?

Finally, I came out and said it. "Are we done?"

Her gaze fell to her lap. "I've prepared for that."

"Is this what you want? Is that why you're dressed for a funeral?"

She sniffled and wiped at her eyes. "I... I think it'd be easier to pretend, than to face what happens next with you and your retaliation."

I lifted a brow. *"Retaliation?"*

"You wrote a story about a boy who gives up his hardness and ties to his past for the girl he loves, but you couldn't even do that for me. I never asked you to choose, but you chose this town over me. You let them drag you back in, and you almost died, Tyson. So I would rather sit here and pretend that it's the end, than to go on and let you put me through this. This town will not stop until it kills you, but you're too loyal to see it. This person *shot* you, and what, now you're going to band up with your friends and hunt him down? I won't watch you do that. I can't."

She had to be fucking kidding me.

Despite it all, I managed to laugh. "You know why I got a lot of love for you and your father, Nandy? Instead of making me choose between being grounded and staying away from this city, Parker just grounds me. And you decide to see me as dead as long as I'm attached to this place. Your timing and belief in tough love are just funny to me. Meanwhile I'm lying here all shot and shit, which is not a fucking cakewalk, and these are the things I'm dealing with. By the way, I'm fine, thanks for asking."

"Fuck you, Tyson!" she snapped at me. "You have *no idea* what it was like to wait for you. What it was like for my family to get that phone call, and come here and see you lying in a bed with machines hooked to your body. I wanted you to stay with me. You chose your friends! You wound up in the hospital, and they didn't know if you were going to make it!"

"So instead of sticking by me, you bounce and write me off as dead?"

Nandy shook her head. "I can't watch you do this."

Parker was one thing, Prophet as well, but Nandy? I couldn't hack it.

"I woke up, and all I wanted to see was you, but you weren't here, and you haven't been here. I don't want your tough love right now, I just want you," I told her.

Tears spilled down her cheeks. "I can't be your ride or die. I don't know how, and I don't want to support this lifestyle."

I felt like an asshole for laughing at her, but she sounded so wrong with her slang. "I never asked you to join me in this lifestyle. I don't need you holding me down in that way. I don't want you in this place any longer than you have to be. I fucked up, okay? I see that now."

Her sobs caused a misty sensation to sting my eyes.

Nandy reached up and wiped at her face. "I waited for you. And they called my mom and told her what happened. I didn't know what to think. If you were mad at me for not saying how I felt, or if you were too caught up in this life that you won't leave to care. You think I always get what I want? Since I was seven years old, I've only wanted you, and you keep leaving me!" She laid her head on the bed, shoulders shaking with her sobs.

As fucked up as it was, I understood. It was easy for her to pretend that I was dead this time than to let me walk away a third time to potentially really die. Prophet had told me to stay away, and I'd gone against his word to save them, risking everything selfishly. For so long, my loyalties had lain with Prophet and the boys, but it was here in my hospital bed that I finally understood that they didn't need me. That they would fare well on their own.

My mother wanted me to be happy, and I was—with Nandy, with the Smiths, and with my friends in Pacific Hills. It was all that I really needed.

I reached out and stroked Nandy's hair, getting her attention. "Money shot me. He didn't like that I was going to do better. He didn't like that people saw more for me than for him. He was my friend since I was nine years old, and he shot me. I felt myself dying, Nandy. I don't know about God or anything, but I thought that maybe I was going somewhere, and maybe she'd be there.

"I had a dream that I saw my mom. She was alive and happy and *right there*." For the first time since Tyson had tried to kill me, I felt myself cry. "All I wanted since I got to Pacific Hills was to be with my mother, but when I found her, it wasn't enough. She knew it, and so did I. All I could think about was, if I had another chance, that if God was real and he could just give me another shot, that if he could give me the strength to live and to get up and make it back to you, that I'd do better. I don't want to die before I can spend my life with you."

Nandy's lips trembled. "You mean it?"

"I don't want Lindenwood. There is nothing for me here."

"And if something happens and they need you again?"

As much as it hurt to know the fact, I said it out loud. "They can take care of themselves. They don't need me. You do. And I need you."

Nandy buried her face into my bed, crying some more. "Please don't leave me, Tyson. I'll accept whatever you want, if it's this place, if it's Pacific Hills, just don't go."

I hated that I was making her cry. "You once told me that maybe while I was in Pacific Hills I'd find something to believe in. Well, I did. I believe in home, I believe in this family, and I believe in us," I told her. "I love you, Nandy."

When she didn't respond, I said it again, and again, until I was sure she heard me.

Nandy sat up and grabbed a tissue from the box on my nightstand, going and wiping up her face.

"Come here," I said as I patted the bed.

She eyed me skeptically. "I don't want to hurt you."

"Your not being here hurt me more than this did," I said. "I realize what's important now. I wanna grow and explore, I wanna see Thailand with your family, and maybe someday, you and I can go and see some of Africa together."

Nandy got up from the chair and carefully lay with me on the bed. She rested her head into the crook of my neck, and

I wrapped my good arm around her. She was still crying as she clung to my good side.

"What do you want?"

"Two things," she said softly.

"I'm listening."

"To be here for you."

I rested my head on hers. "That's all I want, too."

She looked up at me. "One more thing."

"Yeah?"

She took a fistful of my hospital gown into her hand. "I think I want to break your ankles like in *Misery*, and to tie you to a bed so that you never leave my sight again."

It was morbid and uncalled for, but it was just enough to make me laugh.

"Let's just go home, okay?" I said.

Nandy managed to nod. "Okay."

A couple of weeks later I sat in my bedroom, struggling to type with my good hand. I was supposed to be going easy on my left arm, but the desire to get the story out, the new and improved version, pushed through the pain. Shayne had gone back home to give the Smiths and me space, but she often came by to help out. She even offered to type for me, but the stubborn part of me wanted to do it all myself.

I winced as a deep burn shot through my left shoulder. "Shit."

"You better not be in here typing again." Nandy's voice preceded her into my room, and in seconds she was by my side, hands on her hips.

When no one else was around, sometimes she'd wear this little nurse's uniform she'd got at a costume store. It was another incentive to get well soon.

Things were different, in a way. Per my condition, Parker had me back in the main house so that the others could help me, and I was working with a private physical therapist the Smiths had hired to see me through recovery. This time around, I was more optimistic and ambitious about recovering and going forward than the first time, an attitude my doctor thought helped.

The shooting was open and closed, as far as the police were concerned. I'd told them all about seeing Khalil and showing Travis the way to Mexico's. I'd confessed that Money and I'd had tension since my move to Pacific Hills, and that he'd called me to see how I was doing out of the blue a few times, and how I'd thought we'd made up. I let it slip that I might have mentioned coming back to town to see Khalil and show Travis the shop that night. Everything fell together as Khalil and the others backed up the story of the tension Money and I'd had, and the murder was what sealed Money's fate.

According to Prophet, Money had an "accident" in prison and was too shaken up to speak about our past runs for Mexico. As much as I wanted to keep tabs on that, for my sake, and my future's, I made it a goal to keep in contact with Prophet only for positive things, like Rain's growth, how Khalil and Read were doing, and Prophet's seeking higher education.

It was tricky, but I had faith that maybe more than one Lindenwood boy could see a brighter day out of the city limits.

Travis was dubbed a hero, and because I owed him in more ways than one, I hung out with him at the Crab Shack a few times to heighten each time he told the story of how we survived a shoot-out. I might have had a knack for penning a good tale, but no one told a story like Travis Catalano.

"School starts in four weeks," Nandy observed as she peered at the calendar above my desk. "Nervous?"

"After this summer, I think I can tackle anything, even school in Pacific Hills."

Nandy tossed me a smile and slid onto my lap. Too bad she wasn't wearing her little uniform. "How much are you changing to the story?"

"I think the lesson and moral can use some work. I think Tyrin needs to experience betrayal and the possibility of losing Queen to see what he has in front of him."

Nandy leaned over and kissed me, wrapping her arms around my neck gently. "Sounds good. Figured out a title yet?"

I thought about it for a moment, going over the name that had come to me the first time I'd sat at my laptop. It brought me back to the moment in Lydia's office the first time we spoke. "I'm thinking *Summer Knights*—with a *K*."

Nandy ruminated on the name. "I like it. Very transitional for Tyrin's character crossing over to new territory. Plus, I've always had a thing for knights in shining armor. Reading about them in stories and seeing movies, I couldn't help but want one of my own."

I held her as close as I could with my right arm and stared at the beautiful girl before me. "You know what your problem is, Nandy?"

★ ★ ★ ★ ★

PLAYLIST

Suicide | Pusha T + Ab-Liva.
I Care 4 You | Aaliyah.
Dear Mama | 2Pac.
All the Above | Maino + T-Pain.
Bitch, Don't Kill My Vibe | Kendrick Lamar.
Non-Believer | La Rocca.
Make it Home | August Alsina + Jeezy.
What You Want | Mase + Total.
Through the Wire | Kanye West.
When We Were Young | Adele.
LoveHate Thing | Wale + Sam Dew.
West Coast | Lana Del Rey.
Something to Believe In | Aqualung.
Made You Look | Nas.
West Coast | Coconut Records.
Shouldn't Come Back | Demi Lovato.
Why I Love You | B2K.
Don't Forget about Us | Mariah Carey.

Ask of You | Raphael Saadiq.
Come Back in One Piece | DMX + Aaliyah.
m.A.A.d city | Kendrick Lamar + MC Eiht.
Summertime Sadness | Lana Del Rey.
Like You'll Never See Me Again | Alicia Keys.
Close to You | Rihanna.

ACKNOWLEDGMENTS

First, I have to thank Jeremy, the first of the two boys who inspired Trice. Without Jeremy, there'd be no *A Love Hate Thing*. We met when we were either eight or nine—a friendship that definitely left its mark on me. He used to come around during the summer with his grandfather who would do lawn work, and he'd hang out with me and my older brother. When my brother was away, I got to boss Jeremy around and get him to do whatever I wanted. He was mine. Until he wasn't. One day he just stopped coming. I saw him briefly again years later in school, but then he was gone again. The very idea of this book is based off a "what-if." Like, what if he ever came back, what if our puppy love blossomed into more? So, for always, this book is for Jeremy, and that what-if. PS: I'll always remember square dancing in the street with you. ;)

Second, I'd like to thank the real Trice, the boy whose toughness and mystique inspired the older version of Tyson Trice. We met senior year of high school, and his hardness left an imprint on me. I always wanted to write about the idea of cracking the code of the tough guy. So thank you, Trice. If you're out there, I hope you're doing well.

To Josh Schwartz, because *The O.C.*!!! It's my number one favorite show of all time, and I'm not even going to pretend that a lot of the elements of this story weren't inspired by the wonderful blueprint of *The O.C.* I mean, Kyle and Shayne are a humble ode to the great Seth and Summer because you can't not root for them. Thank you for creating a masterpiece and a classic teen drama that's inspired me in more ways than one!

Kendrick Lamar, because Trice too, is a good kid from a mad city. Your pen game is never wrong, and someday I will meet you and shake your hand to get some of your writer magic.

Wale, ugh, thanks so much for penning "LoveHate Thing." Beyond being an amazing song, it definitely came in handy for my title.

To my parents, especially my mom. I never wanted to go to college. I always in my heart just wanted to be a writer, and she never judged me for that. PS: Hey, Mom, a *Grandison* is in print. :) And to my dad, for always encouraging me and believing—and all those random ideas you shoot me. Ha!

To Brittney Coon, for all the late-night texts, emails, PMs, and packages of support.

And last, they say it takes a village to raise a child, and through this experience I realized it takes a village to produce a book! I'd like to thank my agent, Uwe Stender, for championing me and believing in my art (we got one!). I'd like to thank Natashya Wilson, my editor, for helping me shift and tone the novel. Mostly, thank you for believing in it and giving it a chance and making my dream come true. This story's always been special to me, and hopefully now it can be special to the world.

To the team at Inkyard Press, thank you sooo much for the effort you put into this project. A special thank-you to Gigi Lau, for the amazing cover design, and Bee Johnson, the artist responsible for the cover. It's such a beaut and captures the true love/hate essence of Trandy!